A
Marine
To
Remember

Book 1: Semper Fi in Love

Danette Fogarty

Dear Readers:

This is the very first book I wrote so it holds untold sentimental value in my heart. I've updated it and reworked it until I felt it was a better story for you to read.

It is my greatest wish that you enjoy the wild ride Eryn and Chase take you on during their journey and hope you'll continue to read the series to see what their friends, Mitch, Abi, and Emma end up doing in their own quests for love.

I dedicate this book to my husband, Ben. He has shown unwavering support and devotion to my writing and he will always be my "leading man."

Every time I write a book, I realize how many people contributed to it, whether it was a phrase, a gesture, a recommendation, or just their support. Thank you to all of my friends and family.

Bless our men and women in uniform!

Thank you,

Danette

Chapter 1

Chase Johnson walked along the beach; sand between his toes and a light breeze blowing from the ocean before him. He counted himself as one lucky man at the moment.

He was a Master Sergeant in the Marine Corps and was pleased that his last tour in the Corps was here in Hawaii. It was beautiful on the island of Oahu and especially in Kaneohe Bay, where Marine Corps Base Hawaii was located. The atmosphere here was laid back and allowed him to take some time to enjoy his surroundings.

As he walked down the long stretch of beach, he watched his dog, Ed, chase whatever it was that dogs found so fascinating.

When he was alone like this, his mind began wandering back to a time in his life that was the most unsettling in his memory. He tried to tamp down on the thoughts as he walked, trying, instead, to focus on the blue water of the Pacific, the breeze blowing the palm fronds on the nearby trees, other people who wandered the beach like he did.

None of it really helped keep the memories at bay but he tried to push them back. That was the only time in his life and his career that he could truly say he regretted. Unfortunately, the memories haunted him incessantly.

Growing frustrated with his train of thought, he whistled to Ed and started back toward his house near the beach. There was really only one thing that mattered and that was his career.

He now held one of the top jobs in the field of Crash, Fire, Rescue. And there wasn't anything he could really do to change the past. Now was the time to focus on his future because he'd earned that if nothing else.

Looking up, he watched a plane flying over, probably headed for the airport in Honolulu. The trail of vapor that followed it in the blue sky made him think of the direction he was going in.

Warrant Officer Eryn Smith, was buckling her seatbelt as the flight attendant passed her aisle. The flight from Japan was uneventful so Eryn used the time to get her mind focused on being back on U.S. soil. Japan was a great place to be stationed. It was exciting and exotic up until last year. This was a chance to put all the hurt that followed her in that time behind her and make a fresh start.

She looked out the window, wondering what this change would mean for her. She hoped it helped her reconcile the regrets she had in her mind. Regrets were funny things in that way; they tended to pop into your mind and heart when you least expected them to. They took over and wouldn't let reason intercede until you evicted them and Eryn was surely not successful in doing that quite yet.

This opportunity in Hawaii meant she could start a new life. No way was she going to let her past dictate her future. It was time to take control of her life again and she was pretty sure this new duty station was the key to making that happen.

Of course, you could never predict what hand fate would deal you during your life. Was it really fate "dealing" you a hand or other factors that influenced your fate? Only time would make it all clear. She was sure this was the first step in finding her way again. All she needed was to catch a break.

Putting her things away, she prepared for landing on the island of Oahu, smiling at the thought of her new adventure.

May, 2002: Marine Corps Air Station, Cherry Point, North Carolina

Staff Sgt. Chase Johnson headed down the stairs of the Crash Barn, thinking about his recent promotion in Crash, Fire, Rescue. Finally, he was a Section Leader. It was the chance for him to show his leadership skills and he wasn't going to screw it up like his predecessor did.

He loved firefighting, the action and training it required drew him in. That, combined with the ability to work with a variety of aircraft used by the Marine Corps pilots was a great fit for him. He knew it the first day he attended CFR training in Texas. He was cross-trained for structural firefighting but didn't like it nearly as much as working with the jets and helicopters along with their crews.

The challenges in this job were great but the reward was him being promoted. He counted himself lucky in the fact that he found what most people sought in their chosen career fields. And the fact that he was a Marine through and through certainly helped.

The Marine Corps' stringent guidelines were easy for him to adhere to and there was no need to deviate from them in his eyes. After his last re-enlistment, he made the decision to continue on until retirement since he already completed over half the time needed anyway.

This promotion was just the first step up into the higher echelons of his field. Although he was still a junior Staff Sgt., he was now entrusted with training and leading twenty-five junior enlisted men. This was certainly a turning point in his career and he wanted to make it count.

"Staff Sgt.," Gunnery Sgt. Mitch Frinnel called out of his office door.

Chase heard his name and was jolted from his thoughts. Following his Crash Chief into the office, he took a seat across from his supervisor.

"How is it going, Staff Sgt.?" Gunny Frinnel asked, making notes about a meeting on his calendar.

Chase nodded, "Fine, Gunnery Sgt.," He replied. "The section seems to be okay with the changes I've made to the training roster and rotations."

Mitch Frinnel nodded again, making some notes. He'd known Staff Sgt. Johnson for four years now and was really starting to like the direction the Staff Sgt. was going. He was confident that Johnson would do well and move up the ranks without too much difficulty. He just needed some experience and that's what Mitch meant to give him. It was rewarding to provide Marines with positive attributes with their first chance at responsibility. So far, he felt Chase's performance was excellent but he couldn't just say that outright.

A Marine to Remember

"Good to go, Staff Sgt.," He smirked, "Keep me posted."

Chase was practically beaming, "Aye, Gunnery Sgt."

He left the Crash Chief's office. That was the best praise he could receive since taking his new position.

Anyone looking at the two men would never guess that they were friends outside of work. Rank mattered while on duty and since Mitch was the Crash Chief and Chase was one of the Section Leaders who reported to him, they tried to keep their work interaction as professional as possible.

Sgt. Eryn Fredricks was sitting at her desk, typing up a letter for the Crash Chief when Staff Sgt. Johnson passed by her. She looked up briefly and only enough to nod an acknowledgement of his presence as a senior member of staff. She'd been working at Cherry Point for several weeks and immediately realized her work was cut out for her.

Crash, Fire, Rescue was considered a man's job and the men never seemed to tire of letting her know this in not-so-subtle ways. They weren't so bad that she was offended and certainly didn't violate any Marine Corps regulations but women were a fairly new concept in the field even after being allowed to enter into the field for decades.

It was certainly a change but she really did love her work and knew it was a good fit for her. Even if others didn't agree with her decisions, she was sure it was right.

Typing her letter, she let her mind wander. Her father, a pilot in the Marine Corps who achieved the rank of Colonel, most certainly didn't approve of her career choices. In his eyes, this meant that his daughter should be in the officer ranks, and preferably, a pilot.

Mumbling under her breath, she remembered the repeated arguments she had with her parents over the subject. Her parents' home was a battleground between father and daughter since she announced her decision to join the Corps in the enlisted ranks. Colonel Fredricks didn't look down on the enlisted ranks, he only felt that his daughter wasn't reaching for her potential.

The thought still stung after almost two years but she was ready to face that fact that it may never be.

Eryn thought about the fitness reports she received since joining the Corps. She was sure her father saw them as well. They reflected her success and she hoped he would see that fact and reconcile it for himself as she was doing. She was also very sure not to let anyone know her father's rank or even that he was in the Corps. It was important to her to gain rank based on her own merits, not who her father was.

She loved being a Marine. The travel required and the exposure to different people and cultures always seemed a bonus to her. Even as a child, she never minded when it was time to move to a new duty station. She took on the challenge of change with vigor while her sister, Sarah, cried and fussed and was a complete nuisance.

There was never a time in her life when Eryn didn't feel like a part of the Marine Corps family. The lifestyle suited her and she intended to remain with it as long as the Corps would have her.

Now she was here at Cherry Point, a newly promoted Sergeant, and eager to prove herself on the job. She was now assigned to Administration, which consisted mainly of paperwork.

It wasn't what she preferred to do but she was qualified and a woman so it wasn't unusual for her to be assigned here. Her typing and organizational skills proved to be a plus so she bided her time until she could be placed on a section and use her training.

Finishing the letter, she printed it out and laid it on a pile of paperwork that needed to be reviewed. Her Officer in Charge (OIC) and Non-Commissioned

Officer in Charge (NCOIC) were generous with praise here and made her feel like a part of the team at Cherry Point.

The only person Eryn couldn't seem to get along with here was Staff Sergeant Johnson. He never seemed very impressed with Eryn's capabilities and took every opportunity to let her know of her shortcomings as he saw them.

It wasn't as if she needed constant reassurance or praise but he was openly hostile towards her and she couldn't figure out why. The man seriously grated on her nerves and she was afraid she would say or do something not becoming of a Marine if he didn't ease up a bit.

He intimidated her, which blew her mind. Her father was the master at that so she shouldn't be easily rattled and yet, Staff Sgt. Johnson put her on edge all of the time. So far, she managed to hold her own with him but she felt like it might be a losing battle. Defeat, or the possibility of it, left a very bitter taste in Eryn's mouth.

"Sgt. Fredricks," Chase called from the doorway of the Admin office, "do you have the daily rosters for this week?" He needed to get upstairs to address his section and was impatient.

And there he was, Eryn thought. The one man who made her sit up taller and tense her shoulders.

She watched him walk toward her desk and couldn't help but notice his maleness.

He filled the room, not only with his physical appearance, but with the energy he exuded as he moved. She studied his movements as he crossed the room.

Standing a few inches over six feet gave him an imposing posture. He was firmly built; the flight suit couldn't hide that. What the heck! She scolded herself for her thoughts. How embarrassing to be focusing on a superior's body build. With a flush, she looked down and started looking for the papers he requested.

"Any day now, Sergeant," Chase said tersely as he reached her desk.

Eryn found the papers and handed them to him, "Yes, Staff Sgt.," she said quickly, internally moaning at the lack of confidence in her voice. "I also have the monthly reports you requested this morning." There, now he could leave her alone with her embarrassing thoughts.

Chase took the papers from her and scanned them with a frown planted firmly on his face. He looked over each report thoroughly before putting them back into the folder she handed him.

Eryn knew that look and it wasn't a good one. The dread of another verbal encounter with him formed a brick of dread in her stomach.

"Well," Chase looked up from the papers to Eryn. "It looks as though everything is here, Sergeant." Seeing how uncomfortable she looked, he added, "Did you miss your manicure to get these done?" The comment was one he regretted as soon as the words left his mouth but he just said it anyway.

Eryn was appalled at his nerve. Why did he need to say the most pompous, rude, and obnoxious things to her? Nothing she ever did was good enough for THE Staff Sgt. Johnson.

"No, Staff Sergeant," She said, each word clipped. "I don't get manicures." Oh he was ticking her off big time.

Chase looked at Sgt. Fredricks' clenched jaw, knowing she was royally pissed, but he couldn't help but bait her.

He looked down at her hands and snorted, "I guess not."

The comment was said over his shoulder as he turned to walk toward the door.

Once he reached the door, he turned around and looked at her again, "Did I offend your female sensibilities, Sgt.?"

She was steaming. The man was the king of audacity. Why did he find it so necessary to ruffle her feathers every time they spoke?

She held up her hands and said, "No, Staff Sgt., I don't have female sensibilities." There, she would show him she wasn't a doormat for him to walk all over.

Chase laughed sarcastically, "I guess you don't then." He said and turned to head back upstairs.

"Ahh," She grunted and immediately looked over to see the other two Sergeants in Admin looking at her.

She could've kicked herself for walking right into his little verbal spider web. Why did she always rise to the bait he laid out for her? It was apparent he harbored some personal aversion toward her but she couldn't figure out one thing she ever did that would've provoked the open hostility he exhibited. She could take his crap but even a saint had her limits.

The rest of the day was managed, but only because she was able to slam a few doors to relieve her frustration. She was able to think up some very colorful adjectives for him as well and laughed to herself when she thought of them.

During her lunch hour she was able to plot out some ways in which to torture him and that helped a lot. Nothing like a little revenge planning to make a girl feel better.

Eryn was getting ready to lock up the Admin office at the end of the day when she saw Gunny Frinnel poke his head into the room.

"Sergeant Fredricks, a moment please?" He said and returned to his office.

Oh great, now she was in trouble with the Crash Chief! Ugh, this day was not going her way. Gunny Frinnel was third in charge at Crash Crew and oversaw the crews. He earned Eryn's respect almost immediately with his fair but firm attitude.

Eryn believed a good leader and a true Marine possessed those particular attributes. She herself hoped to possess them one day. She trudged toward his office, prepared to account for whatever action he took issue with.

She entered the office and noticed Staff Sgt. Johnson sitting on the sofa across from Gunnery Sgt. Frinnel's desk. Here was the exact opposite of Gunny Frinnel in Eryn's opinion.

He sat there looking so smug and Eryn wanted nothing more than to walk over and slap the look off of his handsome face. She was frustrated with him and her reaction to him and knew she just wasn't up to another go-round with him. One lesson in humiliation was more than enough in her view. Only because of her mother's relentless teaching of manners, she was able to nod to the arrogant Staff Sgt. and sit in a chair across from Gunny Frinnel. She hoped the meeting was quick for all of their sakes.

"Sgt. Fredricks," Gunny Frinnel began, "we've noticed that you have done an excellent job in Admin since you came aboard." He was all business, no reason to beat around the bush. "I also know you've requested Section duty repeatedly since you've arrived and we've decided to honor your request."

Chase watched the Sergeant as she sat down in Gunny Frinnel's office. He couldn't miss the look of surprise followed by repugnance when she noticed he was here.

So, he thought, she was tougher than she acted. He got a kick out of her looking uncomfortable and couldn't, for the life of him, understand why. He leaned back and watched them talk.

Eryn was nodding as Gunny Frinnel spoke, a smile taking the place of the frown she had when she noticed Staff Sgt. Johnson.

"Master Sgt. Jenkins agrees with the decision so we'll put it into place immediately." He was glad to grant anyone under his command a chance to develop their skills.

Eryn was trying so hard to keep her enthusiasm to a minimum on the outside but on the inside, she was doing cartwheels. This was what she wanted since training to be an aircraft firefighter. Just then she noticed the smug Staff Sgt. out of the corner of her eye.

She looked over at Chase pointedly, "Am I going to be working for you?" She couldn't help the venom that dripped from her words.

Gunny Frinnel cleared his throat before Chase could answer, "You'll be on Staff Sgt. Greene's section."

The look of relief on Sgt. Fredricks' face was so obvious that Chase felt offended. He knew he gave her a hard time but that was no reason to be so pleased that she didn't have to work with him.

Gunny Frinnel continued talking with Eryn while Chase was lost in his thoughts. He noticed a few things between the two of them during the few minutes in his office. That was something he'd deal with in a bit.

"You'll have the weekend off and then begin Section on Monday." Mitch said quickly and stood, which said the meeting was over.

"Aye, Gunny," Eryn said and shook his hand. "You won't regret this decision and thank you for the opportunity." She nodded to Chase and went to the door but said to Mitch, "I won't disappoint you."

Once Eryn left, Chase let out a breath. What just happened?

Gunny Frinnel walked back behind his desk and started organizing paperwork.

He looked up at Chase, "Geez, what did you do to her?"

He grinned at the snap of Chase's head while looking from the door Sgt. Fredricks vacated to him.

Chase stood quickly, "What?" He started pacing, "I didn't do anything to her and if she said I did well then she's lying!" His volume was increasing with every word.

"Whoa, Chase," Mitch laughed, "I can see what's going on here."

Chase stared at his boss and friend. Work hours were over so the previous formality was long gone. "I said nothing was going on." He practically spat out the words.

Mitch put up his hands in an effort to calm Chase down. "I didn't accuse you of anything, Chase, and I was just making an observation." He looked Chase in the eyes, "What I saw was an attraction, especially on your part."

Chase snorted and looked away.

Mitch knew he was pissing off his friend but what the hell, "I know you don't like it one bit either."

Mitch sat down behind his desk and looked at Chase. It didn't take a rocket scientist to see how this little bombshell would play out in Chase's mind. There were rules in the Marine Corps and in Chase's mind and this didn't exactly fall in line with those. It was funny that he never noticed the tension between them before today. He'd bet his last dollar that Chase had no clue about it either.

Shocked was the only thing Chase could be. How could anyone even consider that he and Sergeant Fredricks shared an attraction?

He looked at Mitch, his eyes slits of anger, and said, "You are full of crap!"

Chase sat down then stood up again because he couldn't still his mind or body.

"How could I possibly be attracted to that debutante?" Chase demanded, not sure if he was more pissed about the statement or the fact that Mitch seemed to be enjoying his discomfort a little too much.

Mitch stood as well and crossed to the front of his desk, "Listen, business hours are over so I'll be your friend instead of your boss here." He waited for Chase to sit down and started to talk, "If you are attracted to her," he put up his hands when Chase attempted to reply, "you are both adults and can act on it." He put his hands down when Chase's head dropped, "The only thing I ask is that you keep it away from work."

This was bullshit in Chase's mind. It was one thing for Mitch to suggest a supposed attraction between him and someone but an altogether different matter if it was a lecture on what was appropriate for work. He stood and walked to the door.

Mitch felt sorry for Chase but some things needed to be said.

"First of all," Chase stopped at the door and looked at Mitch, "I'm not attracted to her." He was getting madder at Mitch's smile, "And, even if I was, I sure as hell wouldn't let it affect my career!" He opened and closed the door forcefully behind him.

Mitch popped his head out of the office door as Chase was stomping down the hall and shouted, "I'll see you Monday!"

He was sure that Chase was responding under his breath in a not-so-nice way but Mitch couldn't make it out. He closed the office door with a chuckle.

Chapter 2

A week later, Chase was still turning the conversation with Mitch over in his mind. No one discussed the supposed attraction between Sgt. Fredricks and him and that was a blessing as far as Chase was concerned

It shocked him as to how Mitch even came up with the idea. Really, Chase only saw Sgt. Fredricks in passing so how could such a thing even develop.

So he was picky about his paperwork and maybe he was a little hard on her about it. It never occurred to him that it was too much for her to handle but remembering her look of repulsion in Gunny Frinnel's office, he was re-thinking his behavior.

The more he thought about it, the more he admitted that maybe there was something there.

Chase called the other Section Leader, Staff Sgt. Greene, and after some subtle inquiries, learned that Sgt. Fredricks was doing well.

She was a model Marine and Crash Crewman, according to the Staff Sgt., and Chase could respect her for that. Thinking about her responses to his behavior over the past weeks, he found he respected a lot about her. And now that Mitch brought it up, he was hard pressed to think of anything else. Dammit!

He walked outside the crash barn and stood looking at the flight line. No planes were flying now so it was very quiet. Too quiet to think of anything but the woman who now occupied his thoughts.

She just wormed her way in there and now she wouldn't get out. Could he really be attracted to her? The thought exhilarated him but also scared the living crap out of him.

Each day, when the Sections relieved each other, he would seek her out with his eyes. He was to the point now that he had to do something or else he'd go mad.

Resignation in his mind, Chase went back into the Crash Barn to finish up his work for the day.

Eryn drove into Crash Crew and parked in the designated area. She grabbed her bag and got out of her vehicle. Being on Section was great, mostly because she didn't have to deal with Staff Sgt. Johnson as much. That wasn't the only reason, but it was definitely in the top two or three.

Entering the building, she headed for the locker room where everybody stored their items. Preparing for the Section relief, she went into the office to speak to Staff Sgt. Greene.

The Sections relieved one another every other day during the week and rotated schedules on the weekends. Eryn thought it was great because of the hours it provided while not on duty.

It was similar to a regular fire department but, since the airfield had pretty set hours, they were able to make plans for the off time. Not to mention she could avoid the irritating Staff Sgt. Johnson.

What was it about the man that put her on edge? Staff Sgt. Greene came out the office and Eryn was forced to stow her thoughts. There was work to do.

Two weeks later, Chase reached his limit. He entered Mitch's office, closed the door, and plopped down in the closest chair.

"Fine," He spat out. "I'll give in and admit that I'm attracted to her." The words were hissed. It didn't help that Mitch seemed puzzled by the statement.

"Oh," Mitch said, "Okay."

Chase was pissed that Mitch could sit at his desk looking so cocky while Chase was tormented.

He glared at Mitch, "You with your meddling and putting ideas in my head."

Desperately trying not to laugh, Mitch just nodded. He figured out what Chase was talking about and was amused by the look on his face.

"You are a jerk!" Chase said. "But you're right," he through his hands up in a gesture of helplessness.

Mitch couldn't hold back and started to laugh.

Chase threw a pen at Mitch, "Stop laughing, you jerk!" He was not amused, "It's not funny."

Mitch ducked and the pen flew past him into the wall. "I'm sorry, Chase," He said trying to stop his laughing. "I know this isn't exactly easy for you to admit but it's just being attracted to a woman here. You're not solving world peace."

Chase glared at him.

Mitch sighed, stood up, and walked around his desk. He didn't like speaking to someone from behind his desk unless it was work-related.

"You know, most guys wouldn't do this much thinking about it." He smiled reassuringly and playfully slugged Chase in the shoulder, "Why don't you just ask her out?"

The suggestion surprised him. Was the man nuts? He might as well have suggested Chase take a nun to a bar for drinks.

"She hates me." Chase mumbled as he ran his fingers through his hair.

Mitch shook his head to deny it but didn't respond.

Sighing, Chase leaned forward in the chair. "I've gone over our conversations and realize now how rude I was to her."

The admission left a bitter taste in his mouth and a pit of guilt in his gut. He always tried to be fair with the Marines and knew he failed in this instance.

Mitch nodded, "Okay, so just ask her out." He wouldn't let Chase say anything, "Just do it, don't think about it." He ushered Chase out of his office before he could come up with an argument.

Chase went to the door, "Okay."

After leaving Gunny Frinnel's office he thought he'd have a better chance of getting hit by lightning than asking Sgt. Fredricks out on a date.

He walked out of the building and rounded the corner facing the parking lot when he spotted her near her vehicle. Maybe lightning was close by? He started toward her and winced when he noticed her make a sharp left turn to give him a wide berth. Well, it was now or never, he thought and made a beeline for her.

"Sgt. Fredricks!" He called out.

He honestly didn't think she would stop but she was trained to respect and acknowledge superiors.

Oh crap, Eryn thought. What does he want?

She turned to face him and answered, "Yes, Staff Sgt."

They hadn't spoken in weeks and she was truly relieved to not have to endure the verbal sparring.

It was somewhat humbling to see a look of apprehension cross her face when she was looking at him. He mentally kicked himself for putting it there. This was going to be tougher than he thought and he looked around to make sure no one was within ear shot.

He was a foot away and stopped, "Um, Sgt. Fredricks," he started. "It's been brought to my attention that I may have been a little too hard on you since you arrived here." Her look of surprise made him hopeful, "It seems I owe you an apology."

A slight breeze would have blown her over. She was pretty sure her jaw was so slack it was touching the pavement beneath her feet. The almighty powerful Staff Sergeant Johnson was issuing an apology? There really was a God! He was looking at her expectantly and she had to shake herself mentally so she could respond.

"I accept your apology, Staff Sergeant," She muttered. Wow, she thought, Eryn you are witty.....not!

He took the acceptance as a good sign and asked, "Would you like to have dinner with me to make up for my behavior?"

Just asking the question made him feel like he was in grade school. His palms were actually sweaty and his breathing labored.

Eryn noticed that he looked like he was being tortured. Good! Why on earth was he asking her out? This was crazy and she couldn't even think of anything to say in response to his question so she did what any confused woman would do......she laughed.

Chase expected anger, maybe some negative words but not laughing. His face grew tight and he was getting more upset the more she laughed. She didn't need to humiliate him.

Eryn finally got herself under control and wiped the tears from her eyes.

"I'm sorry," She said while trying to compose herself but failing miserably. "I'm just shocked by your question."

It was too late now, he was downright pissed. The embarrassment of her reaction combined with his pride was deadly. Not wanting to subject himself to her ridicule, he turned to walk away.

"Forget it," He called over his shoulder.

The only thing that surprised Eryn more than his asking her out was his retreat. Now she felt awful about her reaction and seeing him walk away felt wrong so she ran after him.

"Staff Sgt?" She called as she caught up to him.

He was at his car and preparing to get in and she didn't want him to leave until they talked about this.

"I'm sorry about laughing but I hope you'll look at this from my point of view," Eryn stated.

The right words were escaping her but she had to say something to him. He was looking at her with a rather nasty look on his face.

"Okay, you give me a ration of crap every single time we speak and now you want to have dinner to make up for it?" She felt a slight sense of pity for him now, but only a slight bit. "And then you act like I should be grateful for the offer."

Chase opened his mouth to respond but thought better of it because the words that would be spoken would be rude. His hands were on the steering wheel and he was just staring out the windshield. His gut was on fire and yet he couldn't leave.

"I really just don't appreciate you laughing at me," He said tersely.

He wasn't the only one here with ruffled feathers.

Her retort was not exactly nice, "Well I don't appreciate you playing these humiliating little games with me."

Now she couldn't just stand there so she turned and started walking back towards the crash barn. She heard a car door slam and boots hitting the pavement but didn't stop walking.

Chase grabbed her arm and whirled her around to face him. He could tell he'd made a mistake as soon as he saw her eyes. They were on fire and he was pretty sure she would deck him if given the opportunity.

It took every ounce of control Eryn possessed to not punch him square in the face when he grabbed her arm.

"Please remove your hand," she said in a deadly calm voice.

She was too calm in Chase's estimation; he dropped his hand from her arm and cursed himself inwardly. This was not how he treated any woman and especially not one he wanted to see socially.

"I'm sorry, Sergeant," He whispered. "Would you consider having dinner with this ass?"

How could he possibly make her smile after his behavior? And yet, she was so tempted to smile. This whole thing was nuts! It was like playing with fire and nothing good possibly could come of it. She was sure of that but yet she was tempted. How did they erase the animosity between them and go out?

It was easy for Chase to see Eryn's indecision.

"I did this all wrong. I was nervous and embarrassed and knew Mitch was a jackass for telling me all of this and I don't grab women and I certainly don't treat them poorly," He rambled.

She felt sorry for him again. His nervousness made him seem so boyish and cute.

"Sgt. Fredricks," He smiled, "it's just dinner." He held his breath waiting for her response.

Eryn took a deep breath, "Okay," she checked her watch. "I guess I have to eat. I'm off tonight so I'll be out of here in about fifteen minutes. How about we meet at Denny's in Havelock?"

Eryn smiled when he nodded and turned back toward his car.

As Chase got back into his vehicle, he watched Eryn disappear around the side of the building and let out a sigh. It occurred to him that absolutely nothing about her was predictable. His eyes moved over and noticed the blinds of the Crash Chief's office closing.

On her way to dinner, refusing to use the word "date," Eryn took the time to admire the area. Cherry Point was located at the edge of the small city of Havelock, North Carolina. They were only twenty minutes from the coast and the area was heavily wooded. There weren't that many restaurants so everyone knew where Denny's was.

She pulled into the parking lot and saw that Chase's jeep was already there so she parked next to it.

Chase arrived fifteen minutes earlier, driving straight from the base to the restaurant so he could secure them a table. The reasons for this seemed plausible earlier but now he was unsure. What would they talk about? He didn't know much about Sgt. Fredricks except what he saw at work.

That was the purpose of this, he said to himself. But now, he was sitting here like a lovesick teenager and getting irritated by that. He had to think of this rationally, they were just two co-workers having dinner. Yeah right! As soon as he saw her walk into the restaurant all rational thought left his brain.

Eryn looked around and finally found Staff Sgt. Johnson sitting in the back corner. He was standing and waved her over.

Wishing she'd at least checked her mirror in the car, she ran her hands down her sides to make sure her clothes were okay and made her way toward the table.

Chase never saw Sgt. Fredricks in civilian clothes before. If he thought she was attractive in the flight suit, her regular clothes made her gorgeous and his blood pressure skyrocketed in response.

She had on a short-sleeved, light blue sweater, and jeans. Her hair was loose, something else he never saw before. As a woman marine, she was required to wear it up in a bun during duty hours.

Now he could see that it was almost halfway down her back and was an exotic mix of gold and light brown.

She smiled shyly as she neared the table, not really sure what to say or do.

Chase smiled, "Hi," he gestured for her to sit first then sat down in the booth across from her.

Her hair mesmerized him. It drew his attention and he couldn't stop staring at it. The sun was setting behind her and the rays captured the colors through the window, making it look like a halo around her head.

What was wrong with him? Here he was, a grown man, and considered himself pretty reasonable on a good day. So what was he doing obsessing about this woman's hair? Perhaps if he could touch it then he'd stop thinking about it? His thoughts were interrupted by Eryn's voice. Her tone was serious.

"Staff Sgt. Johnson," She began, "why am I here with you?"

Before he could answer, the waitress came over to take their drink orders. They each ordered lemonade with strawberry flavoring. Eryn took it as a good sign but still wanted him to clarify it for her.

Once the waitress left their table, Chase started, "Well, Sgt. Fredricks," he stopped abruptly when she placed her hand over his.

The heat from her skin touching his shot up his arm and jump-started his pulse into overdrive.

"Eryn," she whispered since she was feeling shy, "please call me Eryn since we're in a social setting." The heat crept up into her cheeks.

Chase was excited to be with her but her touching his hand had a strangely calming effect on him. The paradox of that made him smile.

"Okay," he answered and found he liked her first name. "Eryn it is, but then you need to call me Chase." Her responding smile brought a warmth into his chest. "Since we're in a social setting."

Eryn chuckled, she appreciated his attempt at humor to put them both at ease. They were both more than a little uncertain about this. She decided it was only right to at least attempt to be a decent dinner companion so she jumped into conversation topics she knew would be safe.

Work was what they had in common so they discussed that first. The talk revolved around to their respective careers.

"What made you join the Corps?" Chase asked, thinking that he was sincerely interested in her answer.

Eryn wasn't at all sure she wanted to talk about it but she also didn't feel comfortable lying about her circumstances.

"My father," she hesitated but only a moment, "He's a Marine."

He understood completely and nodded, "My dad, uncle, and older brother are all Marines." There never was a "former" Marine as far as he was concerned. "It's pretty much a rite of passage in our family."

Relieved that he didn't dwell on her father, she smiled. "I think it becomes genetic."

"Another thing we have in common," Chase smiled.

Their food arrived so conversation was intermittent while they ate their food. When they did talk, it was easy, and about nothing too complicated.

After the meal, they each ordered a cup of coffee. Chase hoped she was as reluctant to end their evening as he was. He remembered that he never really answered her original question as to why she was here with him.

"Why are you here with me, Eryn?" he asked.

He looked into her eyes, liking the way they danced when she was animated.

Eryn waited, contemplating her answer.

"Well," she paused, "at first I really thought you were just jerking my chain." He opened his mouth to respond but she put up a hand letting him know she wasn't finished. "But I realized that my wit and beauty were just too much for you to resist so you simply had no choice but to ask me out." She smiled mischievously.

Her brazen statement made him laugh, "Yes, that's it, I'm sure."

She was a complete surprise. It would be an adventure to try and figure out what made her tick and it would be most pleasurable to do, he was sure of it.

"If you want me to be honest," she hesitated long enough to let Chase nod before she continued on, "I thought you were the most arrogant man ever." She smiled, to let him know she didn't really believe that now. "The dinner invitation really threw me off."

Chase smiled, she was adorable.

"But," she emphasized the word. "All of a sudden I realized that I would like to find out why you wanted to see me away from work." She shook her head because she was still unclear about it. "Maybe it's my weird sense of curiosity."

He considered her statement carefully before he answered. "You surprise me, Eryn. You're straightforward, smart, pretty, and a damn fine Marine."

"Well," she was a little flustered by the compliments, "that's the nicest thing you've ever said to me, Chase."

Dinner finally ended and they debated for a few minutes about who would pay. It was decided they would go Dutch which only reinforced Chase's thoughts on how strong and independent Eryn was.

With the sun's warmth gone, the temperature dropped and Eryn was shivering as soon as they came out of the restaurant. She rubbed her arms absently.

Chase removed his jacket and placed it around Eryn's shoulders when they came out. His father always told him to be a gentleman and he certainly wanted to show Eryn he was capable of being one. He placed his hand on her lower back and guided her to where their cars were parked. She didn't object to his touching her, which he was thankful for.

Each discovery about who she was made him more attracted to her. Reaching their vehicles, he was saddened by the fact they would part ways now.

"Eryn," he whispered because he was nervous, "I don't want to say goodnight yet; do you want to see a movie or something?"

Eryn stopped and turned to face him. His blue eyes lit up even in the limited light provided by the building.

"I'm on recall status unfortunately," she said sadly.

It was a letdown for her, knowing they should be sensible. Spending more time with him was so tempting but she needed to be ready to return to work quickly.

It was ridiculous but Chase actually forgot that she was on recall. The thought made him upset because he never forgot how work was. He resigned himself to being very distracted by this woman and the thought didn't exactly settle well in his gut.

"Sorry I forgot," He muttered.

Eryn smiled warmly, she almost forgot herself when she was around him.

The need to kiss her came up so quickly, he was unable to resist it. His lips were aching to touch hers.

Eryn recognized the look in Chase's eyes because it so closely reflected her own. For some inexplicable reason, it didn't matter that he was a superior to her and they were standing in a public place.

She sensed his intentions and whispered, "Yes," as his head dipped lower. The touch was feather light but the impact of it was like an atomic bomb to her system.

As soon as their lips met, Chase lifted his hands to touch her hair. As soon as his hands made contact with the silkiness, he was lost. He couldn't help but bury his hands in her beautiful tresses and moved closer so he could kiss her more deeply.

Eryn moved her hands up to touch his face. The kiss was so tender and yet so arousing that she couldn't keep it up without exploding. She pulled away after a moment, her breathing ragged.

"Well," Chase spoke first, "that was interesting." It was all he could think of to say and was relieved when the comment prompted a chuckle from Eryn.

Eryn shook her head, "I'm not sure that is exactly the term I would use," she smiled, "I'd probably describe it as wildly intense."

Her words caused a reaction in his body he was embarrassed to reveal. "And I would have to agree," he smiled, like an idiot. "There's a problem though, Sgt. Fredricks," He looked into the beautiful green depths of her eyes, "that's something I know I want to do more of."

Eryn stopped and just stared at him. Having a man express those feelings to her was like putting gasoline on a fire. She was burning up with need but couldn't admit that to Chase. This was not good.

"We're in trouble here," She stated.

She spoke what she knew they were both thinking. Without waiting for him to answer, she walked over to her car and got in. She pulled out right away and waved to Chase as she drove away.

Chase stood there in the parking lot and watched her go.

The next morning Chase didn't get a chance to see Eryn, but not for lack of trying.

While the sections were doing their turnover, he had to attend a last minute meeting with the Crash Chief. He slept in bits and pieces the night before; dreaming of green eyes and honey-gold hair. The meeting was uneventful and he only heard about one half of what was being said.

Mitch was well into the meeting and wasn't sure if Chase was listening to any of the information. Mitch wondered what happened the night before after he closed his office blinds but wasn't going to ask Chase about it outright.

Chase caught the questioning look Gunny Frinnel shot at him but wasn't sure he could provide any useful answers. So much for not letting Eryn affect his work. One dinner and a kiss and he was blown away.

But it wasn't just a simple kiss was it? It was an explosive kiss that drove him nuts!

But that was beside the point, he yelled at himself. He should be able to get through the day right? He managed, somehow, to get through the meeting and make his way back to his office.

Time alone sounded good before facing the duties of the day. He poured a cup of coffee and sat down behind his desk.

Swiveling his chair around to look out the window, he noticed Eryn going to her car. Damn it, he didn't know she was still here! Maybe they could've talked? Not, there was no way he could talk to her without everyone else figuring out how he felt. Figuring out what? That they'd gone out to dinner and shared a kiss?

What would he say? "Hey, Eryn, thanks for the meal and the kiss, you've worked your way into my brain." Not exactly the smoothest way to start a conversation.

He watched her while she was putting the top down on her convertible, noting that her movements were very graceful. Why hadn't he noticed that about her before?

He stood up, inexplicably drawn to her, and moved closer to the window so he could see her better. She tossed her bag into the back of her car and walked around to the driver's side. She backed out of the parking space and suddenly stopped, turned her head up, and looked directly at him. Their eyes met and his heart stopped. She smiled a slow and sexy smile, put the car in gear, and drove off. Chase was sure he'd remember that look for a long time.

Chapter 3

Eryn drove back to the barracks after leaving Crash Crew. She parked her convertible in its designated spot and sat there for a while, lost in her thoughts.

The last twenty-four hours were so strange that she wasn't sure what to make of it all. She was always level-headed when it came to men; inexperienced, yes, but always very level-headed.

Her relationships were always very casual since she never wanted any distractions with her education, and now, her career. Heck, she hadn't even had sex yet because there was never anyone she thought would be worth it before now.

But now, here was this man that made her mad one minute and curled her toes with amazing kisses the next. She did not have a clue about Chase Johnson. It was also completely stupid for her to just sit here in her car thinking about him. She grabbed her bag and headed up toward her room.

The parting look she gave him at Crash Crew played back in her mind, making her smile. She "felt" him watching her when she was leaving and couldn't help but look up. The feeling started when she walked out to her car and she couldn't shake it. It was just this connection that existed between them and she was confused because she wasn't sure when or where it happened.

She was pretty sure that Chase was as clueless as she was by the shocked look on his face when she pealed out of the parking lot at Crash Crew. So now she was stuck here, alone with thoughts of a man she thought she despised. Great!

She was opening the door to her barracks room when she thought about her sister, Sarah. She acted like this when she was falling in love. The thought made her stop just inside the door. What nonsense!

She was a grown woman and, unlike her sister, a Marine for crying out loud. She just needed to pull herself together and clear her head. She dropped her bag down on the floor and threw herself onto her bed. Sleep was what she needed, yes definitely.

The next morning, Eryn got up and put on her running clothes. She always found solace in running. The simple act of it made her think clearer so she ran when she had something difficult to work through.

Sleep eluded her the day and night before because of Chase. He took up residence in her mind and she prayed that running would evict him, even if for only a little while.

When she got home yesterday, she thought being physically tired would help her sleep and get a reprieve from him. Unfortunately he was as embedded in her subconscious as he was in her conscious.

She thought dreamily about the dinner they shared; he still refused to call it a date. Then, for a while, she focused on all the times he made her feel small and inconsequential and that riled her up to thinking he was not good enough for her.

Finally she drifted off, only to be overcome by some pretty erotic dreams involving her and Chase. Her subconscious was at war with her common sense. How did it all happen within such a short space of time?

She woke up early and came to the conclusion that they were headed nowhere fast. It was one dinner! She kept yelling at herself.

Walking to the track, since it was close to her barracks, she thought about the dreams.

They were pretty nice, she had to admit. If the man could do half as much in person as he did in her dreams, she would be in big trouble. Cursing herself for still fixating on Chase, she shook her head and started stretching out.

The morning was still cool with low humidity. It was a rarity in North Carolina this time of year and she was thankful to get the run in before work. The sun was just coming over the horizon when she stepped on the track. Starting out a casual pace, she thought about how the dawn held a peace and beauty that was lost on the rest of the day. She was thankful she was on section now and no longer tied to her desk so she could do this more often.

Breathe, run, breathe, run Eryn chanted in her mind. She was just finding her rhythm when she heard footsteps behind her.

It wasn't unusual for her fellow Marines to take advantage of the break in weather to run so she moved to the side if someone needed to pass her. After a lap though, she was surprised that the steps were in perfect sync with hers.

She turned her head slightly to catch a glimpse of the other runner only to stop abruptly when she saw that it was Staff Sgt. Johnson.

Chase decided to run this morning before Section made relief. He noticed Eryn was at the track when he arrived and counted himself lucky to see her. She obviously hadn't noticed him so he decided to run with her pace. It was a good pace and he had to admit and the view was pretty fantastic.

She had a runner's body, long and lean. Even though she was shorter than the women he usually chose to date; only a little over five feet, she was curvy in all the right places.

He was silently thanking the Marine Corps for making the running shorts so form fitting when he saw her stop abruptly. His brain was preoccupied with watching her body so he wasn't prepared for her sudden stop and plowed into her.

The impact made Eryn land on her butt a few feet away from where she stopped. She noticed Chase on the ground as well so she was happy she wasn't the only one caught not paying attention. Each of them sat where they landed and looked at one another.

Time stopped, chests pounded, breathing was ragged, and neither of them could speak.

Eryn was the first to crack; trying to stifle a laugh. Chase was right behind her and soon they were both laughing. Other runners slowed but continued on when they saw no one was hurt.

Chase managed to catch his breath and spurted, "Imagine running into you here," between gasps.

"Funny, real funny," Eryn replied as she got up.

After checking to make sure all her limbs were still intact and functional, she turned to look at Chase.

He had the oddest look on his face and she was frozen to the spot wondering what he was thinking.

Chase watched her and when their eyes met, the intensity of his gaze multiplied. She was looking at him looking at her. He couldn't remember feeling so awkward and captivated at the same time. He didn't say anything, instead, he allowed her to look at him and hoped she liked what she saw. A smile of male satisfaction surfaced and he was helpless to repress his physical reaction to her.

When Eryn noticed he was enjoying her open inspection of him, she had to look away. Awareness and confusion warred in her head. A blush found its way up into her cheeks and she looked at the ground. Embarrassment was something she rarely felt except when in close proximity to Chase. The whole thing seemed impossible to digest. As suddenly as she stopped, she turned, and, without a word to Chase, started running again.

Chase noticed the flush in her cheeks but was surprised when she just started running away from him. He watched her run and saw that she was really moving now, not at the regimented pace she was running earlier. He was curious about what she saw and thought while she was looking at him. It was important that he know so he took off after her.

Eryn was across the running track and knew he was running after her. There was a connection between them, an energy she couldn't sufficiently categorize. An overwhelming sense of panic engulfed her and she picked up the pace of her running. She knew he was a stronger and faster runner but it didn't matter. She couldn't face him and the confusion in her mind and body he caused; she had to get away from him. Even if it was a temporary reprieve, she craved the space to think.

Chase caught up to her fairly quickly and he could feel the uneasiness permeate off of her. He didn't know what to say or do so he didn't stop her; only ran slightly behind her. He wanted her to think she had the distance without letting her get away completely. It was a perverse thought but he couldn't stop it.

Eryn didn't even remember leaving the running track and heading for the barracks until she could see the building in sight. She hoped she could keep running at this pace until she reached the security of her room. Probably not, as her lungs were burning and she was having trouble regulating her breathing. It didn't matter; she couldn't, or wouldn't, stop. She was overcome by desire for self-preservation.

Eryn stopped just before she reached her barracks. She could hear Chase's steps stop as well and she didn't know what to say to him. He probably thought the whole thing was really weird. Her feelings about him were too intense and extreme that she had trouble dealing with them. She only wanted time and distance to sort them out, if that was even possible.

Eryn was just about to the steps leading to the second floor of her barracks when Chase called after her, "Eryn, stop please."

He didn't yell or say it forcefully; it was more soft and pleading. He cursed himself for sounding so desperate.

She stopped. Something in his voice made her pause. She turned around to look at him, her breathing jagged.

"What did I do?" Chase asked quietly as he walked slowly toward her.

It was like he was approaching a skittish animal; he wanted to show her that she could trust him.

Eryn looked at him, his intense, blue eyes boring into hers. She stood there for what seemed like an eternity, not really knowing what to say.

"No," she finally managed to say breathlessly. "I'm not sure what to say or do around you now!" She blurted out loudly, surprising them both.

She watched him just staring at her.

"I mean," she paused, "just a couple of days ago you were picking on me and patronizing me and I despised you and now...." She let the sentence fade away, not sure what would need to be said. Her face flushed again.

Chase didn't know what to say to it either but he just didn't want to let it go, "Now what?" he asked as her moved closer to her. His eyes never left hers.

Chase shared her confusion; he sure didn't know what the hell they were doing here. He only wanted to keep talking to her.

"Now," Eryn said when he stopped mere inches in front of her, "I don't know."

She heard the defeat in her own voice and despised it. She never backed down from an obstacle; it just wasn't in her nature. Yet, here she was, walking away from this. She looked into his eyes, the deepest pools of blue she could ever remember seeing and shook her head in resignation. Without saying anything else, she turned and went the rest of the way up the stairs and into her room.

Okay, Chase thought, she needed some time to sort it out. It wouldn't hurt him to do the same. Fighting the need to follow her up to her room, he turned and walked back to the track to get his vehicle.

Eryn showered, dressed, drove to work, did a shift change, completed the truck check lists, and didn't remember a second of doing any of it. This was now turning into a serious problem. She worked a critical job and knew that if she didn't do it right and take it seriously, someone could get hurt or even killed.

So why was she allowing this man to distract her so much? He was in her head and absorbing all of the brain cells and she was helpless to stop him.

The day was spent holed up in the office of the Section Leaders. If someone was brave enough to stop in or ask a question, the answer was short and terse. Luckily the Section was behind on paperwork so it gave her an excuse to stay there. She was pretty sure that Staff Sgt. Greene knew she was out of sorts and supplied the opportunity for her to deal with it privately.

At about five o'clock she emerged from the paperwork and the office, tired and hungry. She entered the outer office and noticed Staff Sgt. Greene at another desk watching her. She enjoyed working for him because he was a good Section Leader.

He enjoyed helping the Marines on his watch but he expected them to earn their paychecks and use their training. He took the job seriously but not at the expense of morale. Eryn thought herself lucky to be assigned to his Section and learned a lot in a short period of time.

Staff Sgt. Greene looked up when Sgt. Fredricks exited the office and rose from the chair he was using. "Sgt., He said, and nodded in acknowledgement.

"Staff Sgt.," Eryn replied. "The paperwork you requested is completed and on your desk." She felt some satisfaction at being able to help the Section.

He nodded again and motioned for her to go back to the office she just left, "A word with you." He said with a no-nonsense tone.

Eryn thought she was in for a reprimand over her earlier behavior with the other members of her Section. She hadn't yelled but certainly wasn't very nice to anyone either. She followed him into the office and took the seat across from his desk and waited for him to speak.

"Okay, Sgt.," he began, "what's up?" He folded his hands in front of him on the desk.

She was confused, "Staff Sgt.?" She asked, having a pretty good idea of what he was asking but choosing to play dumb because it seemed like the safer option.

Staff Sgt. Greene was impatient, he knew she was smart enough to know what he was asking. "Come on," he replied with a look of ambivalence, "I think I've got a pretty good handle on how you work and your personality while here and today wasn't it."

Darn it! She knew he had a point and took a moment to consider her reply. She couldn't act like a girl and complain about "boy problems." She was an adult and should be able to act like one. The fact that she had to remind herself of that was really irritating. She had to respond.

"Well, Staff Sgt.," she started, "I'm just having an off day I guess. We all do that once in a while." She babbled on before he could interject. "I'll buckle down."

Her excuse was a flimsy one and she wouldn't blame him for calling her on it but it was all she could think of.

"Okay," Staff Sgt. Greene nodded, "if that's it, fine, but try not to let your "off" days torture the rest of us and make me question my decision to allow you on this Section."

Eryn knew he meant what he said, the man didn't make idle threats. She sat up straighter and looked him directly in the eye, "Staff Sgt., I will not let you down."

He was satisfied...for now, with her answer. "I hope not." He said and looked at his watch. "Now, go home."

She was confused, it was her turn in the rotation to pull duty at the Crash Barn with the skeleton crew. It didn't seem right that she should get the night off. "I'm sorry?" She asked him.

"You heard me," Staff Sgt. Greene flipped through the paperwork she just completed. "Staff Sgt. Johnson called earlier and said he saw you have a collision with another runner this morning." He looked up at her, "I thought you may need some time to go home and get some rest. Do you need to go see someone at Medical?"

Eryn could barely restrain the rage running through her veins. She gritted her teeth, "Staff Sgt. Johnson called you?" She didn't even think she could answer his previous question.

"Yes," He returned, "Now get out of here."

Eryn stood, "Aye, Staff Sgt.," she turned and left the room.

It was definitely a test but she passed at keeping her anger in check long enough to get her things and head out to her car. Once in the safety of her vehicle, her frustration fell away. She slammed her hands on her steering wheel.

That man! She screamed inside her head. He thinks he has the right to just say and do whatever he pleases? First, he tortures me, then he flatters me, then he kisses me, and now he interferes with my job! There was only one acceptable form of punishment in Eryn's mind......DEATH! With a morbid sense of exhilaration, Eryn tore out of the Crash Crew parking lot in search of her target.

Chase lived off base; he liked having his own place away from work and his coworkers. Some of his fellow Marines lived in base housing with their families or in the barracks but had very little, if any, privacy.

He was lucky to find a comfortable two bedroom bungalow with a partial view of the Atlantic Ocean. The place was only fifteen minutes from work and had a nice little porch out front.   It was only a rental but he made some minor improvements and considered the place his.

He sat on the porch with this dog, Ed. He liked to do that on warm evenings, listening to the ocean in the distance and enjoy the solitude. A beer in his hand, he rocked back and forth absently on the porch swing. He requested tomorrow off to help a friend move but that fell through so he thought he'd drink a little tonight and enjoy the lack of anything to do tomorrow. He'd get drunk, sleep in, and do some repairs around the house.

But now, his mind wandered to the day's events which led his brain straight to Eryn. After speaking to

Staff Sgt. Greene this morning, he felt a moment of regret in revealing information about her mishap. But she was emotionally compromised, in his mind, and he was worried about her.

Women tended to handle this emotional stuff poorly and he didn't want her screwing up at work. He was only thinking of her career and Crash Crew. The alcohol was starting to work on his thoughts and so he'd keep rationalizing his actions.

The night sounds were interrupted by the noise of a car spitting up gravel down his driveway. Who the hell was driving like a maniac? He set down his beer and prepared to get ready to kick some ass when he recognized the car as Eryn's. As she got closer, he could make out her features and she did not look happy. A feeling of dread dropped like a rock into his gut.

Eryn screeched her car to a halt and sent gravel flying. She was upset; no, she was downright mad and he could feel the daggers shooting from her eyes into his head. She slammed the door and stomped toward him, her rage making her reckless.

Chase walked down the steps of the porch and made his way toward her. A rigid stream of excitement started in his stomach and spread through his body when she was in the vicinity. He was so aroused by the time he was near enough to speak to her that he was in pain and hoping she didn't notice his condition.

Eryn was trying to figure out where to hide the body. Anger was pumping full stream through her body and she was allowing it to take her over.

After she left Crash Crew she went back to her barracks room and found the recall roster from work. She looked up his address, guilt only giving her a momentary pause, and took off to give him a piece of her mind. She knew this was highly inappropriate to use the work roster for this but she didn't care. He needed to pay for his pompous attitude and actions.

She was close enough to make out his features clearly and she noted that he looked like he was in pain for some reason. If he wasn't now, he would be in a few minutes. She was sure of that. Hopefully he would plead and beg for her not to end his life. A wry smile crossed her face at the thought.

"What the hell were you thinking?" Eryn shouted when she was within striking range.

She followed up the demand with a hard shove to his chest. The action made him take a step back.

Chase wasn't expecting the yelling or the push so he stepped back to gain his balance. He would allow her one but that was it.

He wasn't sure why she was pissed off, "What?" He yelled back.

Eryn's face contorted, her jaw tightening. "You called my boss," she ground out between her teeth. She pushed him again with no results. "You told him that I'd taken a little tumble and I should go home early." Her voice was up an octave and she was screaming at him. "How demeaning!" She poked her finger into his chest, "The little girl got hurt!" She wanted to slap him but held back, "You are a chauvinistic ass and I despise you!"

He stood there and listened to her tirade, torn between being amused and contrite.

He was done giving her the upper hand, "Excuse me!" he shouted back finally startling her into silence.

She crossed her arms across her chest and waited for him to say something.

Chase took a deep breath, trying to calm himself down, "I'm sorry," he said.

"Sorry," she repeated quietly. "Sorry," she echoed more loudly. "SORRY!" Was yelled more loudly and with great sarcasm. "Well that just makes it all okay." She was on a roll and wouldn't back down. "I'm humiliated and my boss thinks I'm weak but that's okay because you said you're sorry." She pushed him once more and sneered when he had to step back to compensate.

Chase was fully pissed now. If she wanted a war, she'd get one now.

Eryn saw the change in his eyes; they went from clear blue to a deep smoky color. But now she was charging with anger and couldn't stop from getting in his face.

"You are the most egotistical man I have ever met!" She said with disdain. She saw Chase flinch in response as though she'd just slapped him. "You are a pig and I wish I'd NEVER gone to dinner with you and NEVER kissed you!"

Just as suddenly as the anger came, it dissipated. She felt drained and tired and just stood there breathing. She saw his fists were clenched and wondered if, for only a moment, if he would hit her. There was still enough rational thought left in her brain to figure out that if they continued on this tirade, someone was going to get hurt. It was time to go.

Chase was livid. And now she was leaving? After the crap she said? This was ridiculous, he wanted to give a snappy comeback, "No you don't!" He yelled after her.

Eryn turned around very slowly. She was trying to get some semblance of control over her feelings and was failing. "What?" She asked incredulously.

"You," he pointed as he started walking toward her. "Don't regret any of it and the only reason you are yelling at me is because you want to be with me." There, he thought, hah!

Eryn's jaw was tight, she was so mad she couldn't think of how she would get un-mad. "Okay," she sighed, "you've gone off the deep end." The words were clipped as she turned to get back into her car.

Chase closed the distance between them and reached her as she was trying to get in. He grabbed her arm, swung her around, and kissed her.

This kiss was not like the first one. This kiss was pure heat. At first, Eryn resisted but she only intensified the friction being generated between their fused lips. She felt the magnetism between them and finally gave in to it. She couldn't stop after that.

His tongue found hers and tangled it into a wild dance she'd never done before. The kiss was so bruising and lasted so long that they both had to stop just to get a reasonable amount of air into their lungs.

Panting, they looked at one another and felt a shift. Without coherent thought, Eryn grabbed the back of Chase's head and brought it down to meet hers again.

Chase was sure she was going to kiss him again but she put her forehead against his and stood there, her shoulders heaving with every breath. His senses were reeling!

"That's one way to shut me up I guess," Eryn whispered.

Chase chuckled, "Maybe we could continue this inside?" He turned and took her hand to lead her toward the house.

Eryn's smile was sad because she was torn between what she desperately wanted to do what was the right thing to do.

"No," she said softly.

When he stopped and looked at her, the decision was even shakier. She leaned forward and kissed his cheek.

"I need to go," she whispered and turned to walk the few feet to her car, got in, and backed out of the driveway.

Chase watched her go and thought that she had to stop walking away from whatever was between them. When he couldn't see the car anymore, he walked back up to the porch, sat down, and continued drinking his beer.

Chapter 4

The next couple of weeks were primarily about Eryn and Chase avoiding one another as much as possible.

Crash Crew was small and rumors could start with little or no help. They didn't speak directly and hadn't since the evening in Chase's driveway. There was an unspoken decision to maintain a strictly professional relationship with no outside contact. They were able to communicate by email or written note if something had to be relayed at work. No one seemed to notice, or so they thought, until one Friday evening.

Eryn was sitting in Staff Sgt. Greene's office and finishing up paperwork when she heard a page for her to report to Gunny Frinnel's office.

She was surprised because it was after hours and the Crash Chief was usually gone by now. Looking at the clock, she figured she would be relieved for the night in about ten minutes so hoped the meeting would be short. She wasn't exactly sure what this was about but it was best to keep an open mind. Walking downstairs, she racked her brain trying to think of anything she could've done wrong. Other than kissing a certain person, nothing sprang to mind. Plus, nobody knew about that.

She walked down the hallway toward the Crash Chief's office. She knocked and listened for the Gunny to say "enter" before going in. Once she opened the door and went in, she stood at attention in front of Gunny Frinnel's desk.

"Have a seat," Gunny Frinnel said and pointed to a chair. He was scanning some papers on his desk. Finally, he closed the folder and looked at Sgt. Fredricks.

Eryn wasn't sure what this was about but she had a feeling it wasn't going to be good.

"Sgt. Fredricks," Gunny paused for a moment. "I've been keeping an eye on you since you started on Staff Sgt. Greene's Section and noticed that you've been doing a great job." He smiled briefly and then leaned back. "But," he stood abruptly, "What the hell is going on between you and Staff Sgt. Johnson?"

Eryn sat in the chair and stared at him. How could she or Chase think they fooled anybody? How humiliating! She was horrified to think that Chase blabbed or she was so transparent about her feelings.

Seeing the look of horror on Sgt. Fredrick's face, Gunny Frinnel put up his hands.

"I realize that this may be somewhat inappropriate, my asking about your personal time, but I have noticed a few things here and there between the two of you," he stopped and waited to see if Eryn was going to have any comment.

He noticed she didn't seem to know what to say.

"If I've noticed," he sighed, "someone else has or soon will so I'm going to give you the same bit of advice I gave Staff Sgt. Johnson." He wanted to smile when her head snapped up in shock. "Accept it, act on it, but keep it away from work." He was done saying his peace and, when she still didn't say anything, he sat back down behind his desk and started reading papers again.

Eryn felt like a fool. She stood up, exited the office, and walked down the hall as if she were in a fog. Once the relief of not being officially reprimanded sunk in, she was able to make Section relief and leave the building with very few words to anyone. These last couple of weeks were so weird. Now she was acting strangely and seemed to have forgotten what was important.

Once in her car, she sat there thinking. She was a Marine for crying out loud! In the last month she managed to despise, fall for, and despise again one individual male. She was acting like, like, like……a nincompoop! She was not some empty-headed teenage girl seeing boys for the first time, although that's what she was acting like.

Putting the car in gear, she slowly backed up and started out of the parking lot. Not to mention, she was thinking that she had participated in quite a few very odd and disturbing conversations with several men. Was she losing her mind or simply recognizing that the men she worked with all lost theirs?

Feeling wiped out and defeated, Eryn decided to head down to the beach for some heavy thinking. She needed some alone time and common sense and she'd be back in control.

The beach was only about fifteen minutes away from work and the drive was a welcome distraction for Eryn's crazed thoughts. She was grateful because she sincerely needed the peace right now. Feeling the sand between her toes and the ocean breeze on her face would be just what she needed.

After parking, Eryn took off her shoes and walked a ways down the beach to a spot where she could be alone.

There weren't that many people now, which was nice. Not that she worried, she was fully capable of taking care of herself. The beach was practically deserted so it was easy to find a patch of sand all to herself. She decided on an area near the tree line that bordered the beach to sit and contemplate the last couple of weeks.

Danette Fogarty

The sun was beginning its decent over the horizon and it spread a rainbow of colors across the sky. Thoughts whirled around her and Eryn just let them come. The only problem was that they were all about Chase. He always seemed to find his way into her mind at the most inopportune times.

At work, she saw something that reminded her of him. She sat in the same chair he did most days. They touched the same pens and papers. She could even smell the lingering scent of his cologne every now and then.

Her room wasn't safe either. She would wake up dreaming of the kisses they shared and an ache would work its way up into her gut. She longed to touch and be touched by him. This whole train of thought was gibberish and far too emotional for Eryn to stomach right now. But what was she going to do? She jumped to her feet and swung her fists into the air in frustration.

Chase was walking down the beach and noticed Eryn right away. He could not forget that beautiful mane of golden hair that beckoned his fingers. He also couldn't forget the beautiful silhouette of the woman who was haunting his thoughts and dreams. There was no way he could forget those kisses either. He hoped they would be able to share some more of those.

As he watched, she jumped up and swung her arms out like a child throwing a temper tantrum. He chuckled as he watched her being so out of control. She always managed to surprise him.

Eryn was startled out of her self-pity party by a feeling of being watched. She turned and saw Chase walking in her direction.

Damn, she thought, not now! Not when she wanted to be unglued and crazy. She plopped back down in the sand, wrapped her arms around her legs again, and watched him approach with a decided amount of dread.

Chase was close enough now that he could see a look of apprehension cross Eryn's face. He didn't like that he was the one who kept putting that look on her face.

When he was a foot away, he stopped, his hands clenched at his sides. He wasn't sure what he should do. After standing there for a minute, he tossed his pride out the window and knelt down in front of her.

"I've been thinking of you every moment of every day since we first kissed." He looked directly into Eryn's eyes and tried to gauge the response his words had on her.

Eryn believe him because he looked as tortured as she was feeling at the moment. The words were a surprise to her though; she wasn't sure what she expected but the words weren't it. She stared at him as intensely as he was staring at her. It was like they were each trying to figure the other out. There was an overpowering attraction that just wouldn't go away and they couldn't ignore it any longer.

Chase took a deep breath, "I know we work together. I know I'm a pain in the ass, and I know this is probably not the best idea, but I need to see you and be around you and I don't know what the hell to do about it!" The words came out in a rush of quiet desperation but he had to get them out before he lost his nerve.

Eryn listened carefully to what Chase was saying. The man was kneeling in front of her and saying all the things she was thinking and feeling. She wanted nothing more than to touch him and show him how she felt but she was scared.

It was easy for Chase to see the battle going on in Eryn's head. He only hoped she would choose to explore the attraction he knew they were both feeling. There wasn't anyone else in the world right now except for Eryn.

The setting sun created spectacular shades of light in her hair and illuminated her beautiful green eyes. She was the most beautiful woman he'd ever seen in his life. He knew as sure as his next breath that he could wait for forever for her to decide.

Lucky for him, waiting forever was not necessary since she silently reached out her hand to take his. Thank goodness because he was impatient as hell.

Eryn linked her fingers with Chase's and got up on her knees in front of him so they were face to face.

Chase was watching their hands come together and didn't notice her moving right away until he looked up and they were eye to eye.

The wind picked that moment to come up off the water and swirl her hair around them. It created a soft cocoon for just the two of them.

Eryn took his other hand and fingers became one as they leaned in closer for a kiss. Their lips met and retreated over and over again, producing an almost painful ache of desire. Time flew by and yet if felt like only a moment passed between them.

They came out of their intimate haze and found the sun gone below the horizon and the stars twinkling in the sky. There were lights along the beach that provided limited illumination.

Chase couldn't make out Eryn's features clearly but he could hear her labored breathing. Or maybe it was his; he wasn't sure. In an effort to calm his raging libido, he brought her hand to his lips.

"Wow," he whispered.

Eryn didn't make any effort to move, only smiled. He said exactly what she was thinking. She sighed when Chase started to run his hands up her arms to her shoulders. He started massaging the muscles and looked at her.

His hands had a mind of their own and moved up her neck, gently guiding her head back toward his. Even though only their lips were touching, the connection was complete. Chase moved his lips against Eryn's in the softest way he knew. He wanted to keep that connection but was worried she would pull away.

Eryn could feel the heat searing through her body. It caused a sensation of wonder. This was pure magic they created. Once his hands were back on her shoulders, she had to touch him back. Bringing up her hands, she placed them flat against his chest and wanted to smile when she felt the hitch in his breath at her touch.

The moment she touched him, sparks flew between them like the Fourth of July. The temperature between them jumped up a thousand degrees and they could feel nothing except the burning need to keep touching.

Opening her mouth slightly, Eryn tentatively touched her tongue to Chase's lips. Someone moaned and she wasn't sure if it was him or her who did it. Not that it mattered, the pressure inside her was increasing to the point that she couldn't form a rational thought. She only felt that intense heat and need created by Chase as he did the most delicious things to her.

The kiss went on and on and was so wonderful that Eryn forgot where they were. She didn't notice the other people on the beach until a couple of teenagers shouted, "Get a room!"

Eryn blushed and quickly pulled away from Chase.

There was no way Chase was going to be embarrassed by what they just shared no matter who saw them.

"Hey," he whispered as he cupped her chin and brought her face up to meet his, "don't be like that." He smiled and tried to coax one out of Eryn.

Eryn thought that he looked so devilishly handsome when he smiled. However, even his smile couldn't completely erase the embarrassment of her actions. She was raised better than this. Frustration moved in and replaced the heat of attraction and she threw her hands up into the air again.

She shook her head and muttered, "I don't normally do this."

Eryn made a circle with her fingers to encompass them.

"And," she got into her feet, "I certainly don't do this with a man I'm twisted up about."

Chase felt cold without the contact between them. He only regretted that they were interrupted. Listening to Eryn reveal her feelings, even partially, was surprisingly nice. He could relate because he wasn't a pro at this either.

Standing up and holding out his hand, Chase said, "Let's get out of here." He helped her up and they started back up the beach to where Eryn was parked.

As they walked, Chase could feel the hesitation in Eryn. He knew they were moving fast but he didn't want to admit it. When he looked at her, he could see something akin to fear but it passed so quickly across her face, he wasn't sure. She had no reason to fear him, he'd never hurt her. He just wanted to have her to himself so they could talk and, hopefully, a little or a lot more. They needed privacy and they sure wouldn't get it here. The building need made him increase his stride and he didn't realize he was practically dragging Eryn up the beach.

Eryn was almost tripping in the sand because Chase was moving so fast. What was the hurry?

It took her a minute or two before she figured it out; he wanted to have sex. It was only a natural progression and, if she was honest with herself, she wanted it too. He was a healthy male who would expect that she was ready for the next step. Heck, if they weren't interrupted on the beach, they may have made love right there.

Thinking of that made Eryn feel a fresh wave of embarrassment. It wasn't as if she didn't want to make love with Chase, it was just that there were a few problems she could see with it.

First, she was totally inexperienced. She knew it would end up being a mess with her feeling like some horny teenager. Second, she wasn't sure she was emotionally ready to take such a big step. She always thought of her first time as something that would be magical. And third, how did she approach the subject if she decided she wasn't ready? What did one say? Heck, she didn't even have on her "sexy" underwear so how was she supposed to do this? Her uncertainty sank in and she started slowing her pace. After a couple of steps, she stopped altogether.

Just as they reached the parking lot, Chase felt Eryn drop his hand. He stopped walking and turned to look at her. The fear he thought he saw earlier was back in her eyes. He was definitely not imagining it now.

What was she afraid of? They were both consenting adults. There was a chemistry between them unlike anything he ever felt before. Maybe he was too rough earlier in his urgency to get her alone and he scared her. Women were sensitive about that sort of thing. Without speaking, he took her hand in his and noticed it was cold.

"It's okay, Eryn," Chase whispered. "I just want us to talk about this alone to explore what's between us." Her eyes were getting wider as he spoke. "What's wrong?" He asked, surprised by her reaction.

Eryn was mortified. She couldn't tell him that she was afraid of having sex or that she'd never done it before, could she? Was that what perspective lovers did? Having never had one, how did she know? There wasn't a book on this sort of thing, was there?

She wanted him to touch her the way he did before to reassure her that this was right. She knew he wanted her just as badly but she was at a loss. Could she wing it and pretend she was sophisticated and had no problem going home with him?

Chase was getting really nervous because Eryn looked completely confused. She wasn't' even looking at him; she was looking through him. "Eryn?" He asked with concern laced in his voice.

His question snapped out of her own internal debate and she looked up, "Chase," she finally said, "I don't know how I feel or exactly what I feel but I know we can't do this." Her words were shaky but at least she got them out.

Surprised, Chase looked at her with questioning eyes. He told her how he felt; he practically spelled it out for her. She admitted she was twisted up over him. They were all over each other on the beach but now she had cold feet. Not exactly what he wanted to hear.

"Why?" Chase asked. It was all he could think to say since his brain was still controlled by his libido.

Eryn looked away for a bit but then looked at him directly, "Well," she said softly, "I think it's just too fast and we need time."

Chase watched her and could see that she was sure of her answer but he wondered why she was unsure of how she felt. After all, they circled each other for weeks and they both admitted there were feelings between them plus they just demonstrated that blatant attraction fully down at the beach. It was logical to him that they should at least consider the next logical step. Once his mind was made up, Chase really did not want to change it. He wanted Eryn with him both physically and emotionally. What could he say to change her mind?

Seeing that Chase was giving her an incredulous look, Eryn decided that now was the time to leave before they ended up in an argument. The embarrassment was too much. She just wanted to go home and cry and figure it out herself. Pulling her hand out of his, she started to make a beeline for her car.

Chase watched her and could only think about the fact that she was walking away....again.

Eryn was almost to her vehicle when she heard Chase behind her.

"You know," Chase yelled to her back, "I really hate it when you do that!" Not the greatest zinger in history but he needed to get it out.

Turning around slowly, Eryn tried to keep her temper in check. "What?" She returned loudly.

"You," Chase pointed at her as he walked toward her, "always walking away."

That did it, Eryn thought. There was no way they'd get out without a fight. "I most certainly do not!" she shouted as she walked toward him.

Still moving, Chase countered, "Do too!"

"Do not!" Eryn said through gritted teeth.

They were only a foot apart now and Eryn's temper was boiling over. She looked at Chase like she didn't know him.   How could he be so wonderful to her one minute and so horrible to her in the next? He pushed her buttons and she was determined to push back.

With a sweet smile, that was anything but sweet, "I only walk away when there is nothing left to say," she sneered in his face.

The gloves were off!

"Well, I," Chase's jaw was clenched so tight, it was starting to ache, "have a helluva lot to say." He took a breath, "I admit I have feelings for you, I look out for you, I bare my soul," another breath, "which is what you women seem to want," he started pointing at her, "and you just walk away."

Eryn was so pissed she couldn't speak.

Chase thought he had his say until he saw how red Eryn's cheeks and neck were. He was actually glad she did not have a weapon in her possession because he was pretty sure she would use it on him. They were doing so well, and now, disaster was happening.

"You," Eryn drew out the word, trying to gain some semblance of composure, "You admit only that you can't stop thinking about me. That is, my friend, a far cry from admitting actual feelings." She took a deep breath, "You look out for me by calling my boss at work and reveal something completely irrelevant that it makes me look incompetent!" She got right up into his face and stared him down, "And finally," she wanted to hit him so badly right now, "I...AM NOT....YOU WOMEN, so don't treat me like I am!" Eryn was a derailed train, there was no stopping her now, "All I wanted to do was get home so that you didn't know I never slept with a man and that I was embarrassed!"

She started crying, not sure if she was madder at Chase or at herself for admitting what she clearly did not want to admit.

Chase stopped dead. He was so angry when she got in his face that he almost didn't hear her admission. She never slept with a man? Okay that stopped everything to a screeching halt.

"You slept with women?" Chase asked before he could think about it.

Eryn's jaw dropped open and she let loose, "Oh my God!" She pulled back and punched Chase right in the gut.

Not expecting her to hit him, Chase wasn't prepared and doubled over at the pain filling his abdomen. Obviously he said the wrong thing.

Eryn started walking around him in a circle, "Are you stupid?" She asked in a high pitched voice.

82

All of the feelings bubbling up inside Eryn were too much to handle so she sat down on the sidewalk and started crying. Not the whimper kind of crying but the gut-wrenching, let-it-all-out crying.

Chase was ashamed of his own insensitivity. He wasn't normally such an ass; or if he was, he never realized it before now. Here she was, trying to explain something personal to him and he blew it big time. The fact that she was actually considering him to be her first lover was very humbling. Of course, that possibility was gone considering how insensitive he was being.

Chase couldn't help thinking that this could have all been avoided if she would've just come out and been honest with him. Then again, he didn't really have the best track record with responses. But, he would have taken it slow and reassured her and made it special. Why was he just sitting here thinking this and not saying any of it to Eryn?

Eryn watched him as he came over and sat beside her. He gently guided her head so it rested on his shoulder. She was too tired to resist.

"Eryn," He whispered into her hair, "I'm sorry I was an ass."

Eryn chuckled through her tears, "You were an ass."

Smiling, Chase looked down at her sad face. At least she kept her sense of humor. "Don't be embarrassed."

The simple fact was that Eryn was embarrassed about this and certainly didn't want to talk about it with Chase. She tried to get up but Chase held her to him.

Not wanting things to be unsettled between them, he looked at her, "I wasn't expecting you to go to bed with me."

Eryn looked up into his eyes. They were illuminated by the street lights that bordered the parking lot.

She smiled tentatively, and asked, "You weren't?"

Chase smiled, "I was definitely hoping for that to happen, but not expecting it." She was silent so he continued, "I just wanted to talk and be alone with you. I'm sure if things would have progressed, I wouldn't have been opposed but, I swear, I wouldn't have pressured you." He swiped a tear off her cheek with his finger, "I'm not very comfortable with this relationship thing."

Eryn responded with a snort, "You think so, huh?"

Her sarcasm aside, he wouldn't be deterred, "We have a few issues with being co-workers." He wanted to compose his thoughts, "I don't know what will happen; I only know that I want to explore what could happen." His hand rubbed her arm, trying to comfort and reassure her.

Eryn felt horrible. First, she was ashamed for fighting with him, second, for not knowing how to talk to him rationally, and third, for admitting something way too personal in a public place and yelling about it so the whole world knew.

This was not turning out to be a bright, shining moment in her life. Chase really was trying to make her feel better about it and she was deeply touched by the gesture. She knew it wasn't easy for either of them and they proved they weren't good at it either. Even if she was confused, she owed it to Chase to be open and honest with him and him with her.

"I'm just very inexperienced," she was looking at him but feeling the heat of embarrassment work up her neck and into his cheeks. "I didn't want you to think I was less of a woman."

It was tough for Chase to digest that statement, "Sweetheart," he kissed her cheek, "that is the problem here," he kissed the other cheek, "I think of you as all woman."

Eryn laughed, feeling a little better. He was paying her a compliment and she appreciated it.

Chase stood and pulled Eryn up and into his waiting arms.

"Now," Chase set her a step back from him so he could look into her eyes, "I think I'll walk you to your car like the gentleman I need to be, kiss you goodnight as chastely as I can, and follow you back to the base." He turned her away from him and led her toward her car.

When they got to the car, he opened the door, kissed her very sweetly, let her get in, and shut the door for her.

She started up her vehicle and waited for him to get into his jeep and pull up behind her. She drove out of the parking lot and back to the base, glancing at his headlights behind her and feeling cherished for the very first time in her life.

Later, once she was back in her room, she put her things away and got ready for bed. As soon as her head laid down on the pillow, she passed out from exhaustion. It was the first time in a while that she slept so well.

Chapter 5

The next morning, Eryn woke up refreshed. She was tidying up her barracks room when she noticed the blinking light on her answering machine. She wasn't sure how she missed it the night before. It wasn't work; she had a pager for that when she was on recall. Hitting the play button, she sat down and listened. The message was from her father.

She listened to the whole message and frowned. He tried to call her every other week or so to check in because he seemed to think she couldn't get along without him. She was a fully capable adult so they continued this parent-child battle.

Eryn usually just dealt with his interfering but now things were different. If Chase thought that them working together was a complication, he had no idea about how much of a hiccup her father was. Chase didn't know about him and Eryn was in no hurry to throw that particular log into the fire. Deciding it was best to just get the return call over with, she picked up the phone and dialed her parents' home in Beaufort, South Carolina.

"Hello," her mother answered in a bright voice.

Eryn was relieved it was her mother instead of her father.

Eryn smiled, "Hi, Mom," she responded.

Danette Fogarty

Beverly Fredricks was happy her youngest daughter called. They didn't talk to her nearly enough.

"Oh, Eryn," she said, "We were hoping you would have called back last night so you and your dad could've talked." She pulled out a pie from the oven. "He'll be in North Carolina in three weeks for some inspection and he wanted to see you."

Eryn listened quietly as her mother went on to tell her what was going on with her sister, Sarah, and her new home but Eryn tuned out as soon as she heard that her father was coming to North Carolina. This was not good news.

Promising to call back soon, Eryn ended the call as soon as she could. After that, she needed to get out of her room so she did some errands. When she was walking up the stairs to her room, she could hear the phone ringing. She raced to unlock the door and lunged for the phone.

"Hello," she said breathlessly.

Chase smiled, "I don't think you should answer the phone like that anymore." He cleared his throat, "I get mental images of how I could make you sound like that." He couldn't help but smile.

Eryn shook her head, "I was hurrying to get into my room and answer the phone." She blushed and tried to sound censuring but his innuendo was sweet.

Hearing her embarrassment, Chase decided to let it go, "We just finished out morning paperwork and everyone is out doing something," he sat back in his desk chair, the phone cradled in his neck, "I thought I'd call and see how you were doing."

His concern made her feel warm, "I'm actually pretty good," she answered as she was putting away the items she bought. He sounded so good, she wanted to reach out and touch him. "I'm glad you called." She closed the door to her room and sat down. "I've been thinking about you." Saying intimate things felt right but weird at the same time.

His body responded to her words immediately; she only had to talk and he was lost. "I've been thinking of you too," he replied.

"What exactly were you thinking?" Eryn asked him, not realizing how loaded the question was.

Chase was getting harder by the second and if this kept up, he'd have to cut the call short and scramble to find some composure before someone from work came into his office.

"A lot of things," he said softly. He could hear her blushing through the phone. "But," he paused for effect, "mostly I was thinking that I haven't taken you out on a real date yet." Just saying it made him nervous because he wasn't one hundred percent sure she would say yes.

"Oh yes," Eryn answered quickly, "when and where?" she asked excitedly.

After discussing it for a few minutes, they decided to have dinner at a nearby seafood restaurant they both heard great things about. Chase mentioned that it also had a fantastic view of the Atlantic from every window. They discussed dates and finally came up with one that would work for both of them, barring any work complications.

It was easier for Chase to get off of night duty so they agreed on one of his duty days. Eryn was off and would had ample time to get ready for their date.

Once they hung up, Eryn jumped on her bed like a school girl. There were definite perks to this relationship thing. Not even the thought of her father's impending visit could bring her down right now. She loved how the feelings lifted her up into a sort of haze. Sometimes she was unsure if she would laugh or cry. Of course, no one could know about the date but that made it even better somehow.

In South Carolina, Eryn's mother was having a conversation with her father that wasn't going very well.

"Eryn called," Beverly said to her husband when they were in the kitchen.

He just arrived home from a golf outing and she was excited about her conversation with her daughter.

Tom Fredricks looked up from the refrigerator where he was getting a cool drink, "Oh," he took a quick sip and gained a nasty look from his wife, "Is she upset that I'm coming up there?"

He knew his daughter was stubborn; something she inherited from him, and that she wouldn't be thrilled with his interfering.

Eryn seemed to view his visits as orchestrated attempts to keep her under his control. It wasn't exactly true but there was enough truth in it to make him feel slightly guilty. She was his baby and that would never change.

"No" Beverly answered, "I think she's in love."

She took the juice carton out of her husband's hand and poured some into a glass.

The comment brought Tom's head around so fast, he felt light-headed for a moment. He looked at his wife, clearly not believing her.

"I don't think that's possible," he said in a clipped tone. Making a mental note, he would call his contacts at Cherry Point and do some digging.

Beverly put her arms around her husband's waist, "I think it's possible," she paused to see how mad he was, "only I don't think she even realizes it yet."

She wasn't sure if mentioning her suspicions to Tom was the smartest thing, given how over protective he was. She knew there was something distracting Eryn so it stood to reason but she also knew her husband would never believe any man was good enough for his daughters. Lord knew how awful Tom was with Sarah's husband, Rick, before they were married.

Tom kissed his wife, "I'll be sure to speak with her about this when I get there," he said reassuringly.

Making the decision to do a bit more than that, he figured his wife didn't need to know about that. She certainly wouldn't approve.

"You'll do nothing of the sort, Tom," Beverly said in her most stern wife voice.

Surprised by her tone, Tom looked at her, "What?" Tom asked.

"You heard me, Tom," Beverly said, "you let her figure out what being in love is all about and don't interfere."

Nodding, Tom kissed her again, and said, "Okay."

It was a shame since both of them knew he would do no such thing.

The day of their first official date was a long one for Eryn. She could hardly contain her nerves and she wasn't exactly sure why. She woke up early that morning and did all of her errands quickly so she had plenty of time to get ready.

Once she was done, she went back to her room and took a long, relaxing bath, shaved her legs, and actually bought some very sexy underwear....just in case.

If she had any say so, something would definitely happen between them. Since their night at the beach, they talked almost daily and the fears she had before about intimacy were beginning to dissipate. She knew any lovemaking with Chase would be great.

Eryn covered all her bases at work as well. She was scheduled for duty the next day but asked permission to go in late. Staff Sgt. Greene agreed to the request with no questions asked, which made her wonder if something was said. She brushed off the paranoia. They were both extremely careful about that since Gunny Frinnel's little meeting. Even since setting up their date, they almost completely avoided each other at work.

Looking at the clock, Eryn realized Chase would be there any minute. Her pulse started speeding up and she smiled. There was a pretty lengthy debate about him picking her up at the barracks because if the wrong person saw, they might be in for a few more meetings like the one Gunny Frinnel called.

Chase didn't care about the risk and wanted to pick her up. He wanted it to be a "real" date he said and Eryn was impressed with his attitude. She went back and forth about their situation daily in her mind.

Walking over to the mirror, Eryn took another look at herself. She spent a lot of time on her appearance today since she wanted to look different than Chase usually saw her. She worked in a male-dominated field but she knew how to look all woman when the situation called for it.

She wore a simple black cocktail dress that was her monthly splurge. The matching black pumps gave her a few inches in height but really made her legs look long and sexy. She did her hair in long cascades of curls that ran halfway down her back and used combs to strategically pull back the sides. Makeup was somewhat of a challenge since she wanted a darker, sexier look but she felt she pulled it off. Her eyes were a smoky mix of gray and silver that gave them a mysterious look. She also went darker on her cheeks and lips for drama. Her ensemble was completed with some simple diamond studded earrings and matching necklace that was a boot camp graduation gift from her parents. With one last look, she smiled, hoping that Chase liked the look.

Nerves ran around her stomach and mixed with the pings of arousal Chase created. If this was how she felt before he even showed up then what would happen when they were together? She thought it would be a lot like when they start the training fires at work; once you add the flame to the fuel, it would increase to an insane temperature.

Eryn ran her hands down the sides of her dress in an effort to quell her nerves and calm her thoughts. She worried constantly about her nervousness and inexperience being a turn off to Chase.

"Stop," she said aloud. They would just have to play this by ear.

Eryn took a deep breath and walked over to the window in time to see Chase's jeep pull up.

Chase pulled in the parking spot in front of Eryn's barracks and took a deep breath. He was never this nervous before a date. He wasn't exactly Don Juan but he wasn't a slouch in the dating department either. Checking his watch, he was glad he wasn't late.

He just got off an hour earlier, raced home, changed about five times, and, finally, was satisfied with his choices. He hopped in the jeep and came over to Eryn's barracks wondering the whole time how they would be. His palms were actually sweaty which made him smile to himself. Shaking off his nerves, he got out of the jeep just in time to see Eryn coming down the stairs toward him.

Chase stood there and looked up. Her eyes met his and he wondered where all the oxygen went because it sure wasn't in his lungs. He couldn't breathe, couldn't think, and definitely couldn't speak.

She was absolutely stunning! Was she the same woman he worked with? Here was a beautiful, sexy, sophisticated creature, walking toward him and he couldn't come up with a single thing to say.

Eryn came down the stairs slowly. She was feeling really self-conscious and was afraid she'd fall down the stairs or something equally as embarrassing. Plus, her heart practically jumped out of her chest when she got her first look at Chase.

He was gorgeous! She was so used to his flight suit that it took a minute for his new look to sink in. He wore a grey suit perfectly fitted to emphasize his broad shoulders and trim waist. His regulation haircut was styled a little bit to give him a more polished look.

Once she was close enough, she could smell his cologne which was distinctly male and smelled heavenly. She really looked into his eyes and stopped. His gaze was so intense that she was sure she had a smudge on her face or something. But he wasn't saying anything, just looking at her with a penetrating stare.

"Hello, Chase," Eryn finally said, thinking her voice sounded weird.

Chase snapped out of his trance, "You are beautiful," he said in barely a whisper.

A tingle of awareness shot through Eryn's body at the tone of his voice. She'd never heard a man speak to her like that before.

"Thank you," she answered with a little more confidence. "You look pretty great yourself."

Chase felt the heat creep up into his cheeks. It wasn't every day that he received a compliment from a woman that made him feel a little embarrassed. He realized he was just standing there and looking at Eryn and felt like an idiot. Finally, he crossed to her and led her around to the passenger side of the jeep.

Eryn smiled at Chase's nervousness because she felt it just as much. Looking at the jeep's height, she realized the trickiness of trying to get into it with her dress and heels. Well, she would adapt and overcome. She hiked up the hem of her dress to make it easier but didn't realize the view she was now giving Chase with her efforts.

Chase was trying to be a gentleman and help Eryn but he noticed the top edge of thigh-high stockings and almost doubled over with the shot of desire to his gut.

Was it possible to feel this strong of an attraction after only a few kisses? He sure as hell hoped to test that particular thought. Shaking his head in frustration, he reigned in his animal impulses, took Eryn's hand and helped her into the jeep. Once she was in, he walked around to the driver's side and mentally chastised himself for his lecherous thoughts. But, hell, the woman turned him inside out! Then again, this was their first official date; maybe he needed to slow down. If the last three minutes were any indication of the way the evening would go, he was in some serious trouble.

The ride to the restaurant took about twenty minutes and was spent in relative silence. Neither Chase nor Eryn really knew what to say.

Eryn was trying to study him discreetly while trying to hold her hair back. The top was off the jeep so the wind was blowing. Chase didn't mind and it gave him a carefree and reckless presence.

The approaching evening was balmy with only a hint of natural breeze so the wind moving through the jeep was very refreshing. She kept stealing glances at him and noticed his jaw was set as if he were deep in thought. Did his thoughts mirror hers? Was this a good idea? Probably not. Their careers could be really affected if anyone found out but there was nowhere else she'd rather be.

Still lost in her inner turmoil, Eryn didn't realize they arrived at the restaurant until Chase parked the jeep. She shook herself back to the present and found Chase looking at her with the oddest expression on his face. He looked like he was starving and she was the only available food source. The look was so unnerving that she wasn't sure she'd be able to get through the evening without having a complete meltdown.

"I'm sorry," Eryn said softly, twisting her hands in her lap, "I was daydreaming." Another flush moved into her cheeks.

Smiling, Chase gently lifted her chin up with his fingers so she would look at him, "Don't ever apologize for that, Eryn," he smiled, "I was just enjoying the view."

She wasn't sure it could, but her flush just increased tenfold.

Chase dropped his hand, "Are you ready?" he asked and was pretty sure he wasn't just talking about dinner.

"I'm ready," Eryn answered calmly. She definitely knew she wasn't referring to dinner.

Chase jumped out and came around the jeep to her side. He helped her out and held his hand to the small of her back as they walked into the restaurant.

Once inside, they were behind a group so Eryn let her eyes wander around the room.

The atmosphere was very romantic with a nautical theme. The tables were strategically placed just far enough apart to afford privacy to those who desired it but still maximized the space to seat as many patrons as it could.

Candles were logistically placed to allow a glow throughout the room. Having never been there, Eryn took it all in and wanted to see everything. She heard some great things about it and wasn't disappointed at this point. Before she could stop it, the thought that her dad would love this place popped into her head. Just the thought of him tonight brought a frown to her face.

Chase felt the shift in Eryn, she tensed and her expression turned serious. "Is something wrong?" he asked, concern in his voice.

Eryn was upset that he saw the look on her face; she replaced it with a reassuring smile. "No," she tried to sound cheerful, "I was just thinking that my father would love this place."

A Marine to Remember

"Okay," he gave her a puzzled look, "and that upsets you?"

Waiving her hand in dismissal, she sighed, "No." She noticed the group in front of them moving and the hostess motioning them to move forward, "I just don't always get along with my father and don't want to think of him tonight." She wanted to be honest with Chase, even at the expense of her pride.

He could understand family dynamics and how complicated they could be, "Well," he stopped just long enough to give the hostess his name then turned back to Eryn, "we won't think about him tonight."

He was completely fine with not thinking about Eryn's father tonight himself. The man would probably have some things to say if he could read Chase's thoughts about his daughter.

Eryn smiled, and started watching the interplay between Chase and their hostess. As soon as Chase spoke to her, she started smiling and gave him a look that Eryn could only describe as purely female.

Since their table wasn't ready just yet, she recommended, in a sweet, southern drawl, that Chase and Eryn get a drink in the adjoining bar area and someone would get them when their table was ready. Chase nodded to her and started toward the bar area with Eryn and didn't give the woman another look. Eryn felt a little charge of pride knowing she had the most handsome man in the room with her for the evening.

They ordered drinks, a white wine for Eryn and a beer for Chase.

Chase paid for their drinks with a nod to the bartender and turned to Eryn, "I'm only having one beer since I'm driving."

Eryn was again, surprised at his manners and found them almost as arousing as his physical appearance.

"Thank you," she said softly and leaned in to kiss him on the cheek.

A few minutes later, the admiring hostess came in and showed them to their table.

Once she sat down, she wanted to laugh at the woman's obvious interest in Chase was going unnoticed. She was practically mooning over him and the fact that he didn't see it was surprising to Eryn but cute. He gave the girl a short smile of dismissal and turned his attention to Eryn.

"You amaze me," Eryn said with a chuckle.

Chase looked up from his menu, "I amaze you?" He asked back, "Why?"

She almost felt sorry for the hostess' disappointment; almost. "You just crushed the hopes of our hostess, who all but threw herself at you, by the way." She said with a teasing smile.

Not knowing what she meant, Chase glanced over at the entrance where the girl stood and then back to Eryn with a questioning look.

Eryn shook her head in amusement, "Never mind," she said and picked up her own menu. "I do have to say though, you are not nearly the monster I originally pegged you to be." She looked at the menu but didn't see any of it as she was trying to get her thoughts in order, "And you are just about the most conscientious gentleman I know." His look of shyness only made him seem more endearing, "You are very thoughtful and I'm very impressed."

He smiled and laughed, in his own discomfort, "Well I try," he responded and turned his attention back to his menu.

The waiter came over to their table and talked about the specials for the evening and take their drink and appetizer order. Eryn appreciated the distraction, even if it was just for a few minutes. It gave her some time to catch her breath, the one that she couldn't catch since he picked her up at the barracks.

When the waiter returned with glasses of water and their appetizer, they placed their orders. Chase ordered steak and lobster while Eryn decided on a seafood medley dish that sounded great.

Once they were alone again, Eryn smiled at Chase, "You look like a steak guy," she said with a gleam in her eye.

Chase picked up on her teasing tone, "I love meat," he said in a deep voice.

They started to relax and moved on to talk about the view of the ocean the restaurant provided, the weather, the interesting hostess, another couple they saw in the bar. It was all silly, small talk but it was safe.

The rest of the meal passed in a blur and was wonderful. Not only was the food as delicious as they both heard, but the conversation was fantastic. Eryn knew they had a lot in common from their impromptu dinner at Denny's but was surprised by how much they shared. This was an intimate setting so maybe that was the reason they each started to open up about things they didn't normally share. The fact that their interests were so closely paralleled amazed her. They were so engrossed in their conversation that they barely noticed the waiter when he brought the courses of food.

At some point, Chase reached across the table and took Eryn's fingers into his palm. He caressed the back of her hand with his thumb, causing a delectable sensation to move up her arm. Eryn moved her chair closer to his so they could speak more intimately. It was like they were each finally able to open up a little more and take in the feelings between them.

Chase finally surfaced from his dreamlike state when the waiter asked if they would like coffee and dessert. He could barely remember eating the food; he was so captivated by Eryn and their conversation that nothing else was really that important. He was relieved that the waiter was describing the dessert dishes to Eryn so he could catch his breath. What was happening? She had him so completely wrapped up in her and it was new and scary. He looked up to find both Eryn and their waiter looking at him, waiting.

"Oh," he cleared his throat, "I'll have some coffee." He was embarrassed for being caught off guard.

Eryn looked at him and wondered what was going on in his mind, he looked so serious. She thought they were having a great time and then when the waiter came over, he pulled his hand from hers and she was lost. How odd, she thought, that a simple break in contact could make her feel that way. Maybe he was thinking the same things?

Chase smiled, "What did you order?" he asked, hoping that they could get back to their earlier connection.

He sounded okay so she relaxed, "Well," she looked around as if she was going to share a secret, "I am a certified chocoholic so I had no choice but to order the chocolate sin."

Her teasing was contagious so he leaned in, 'Would you mind if I had some of your chocolate sin then?"

Without thinking, Eryn whispered, "You can have as much as you like."

She recognized the awareness her words created. Although she was nervous again, she liked the feeling.

"It's okay, Eryn," Chase smiled, "I know you meant the dessert."

He was so sweet to put her at ease. It touched her.

"That's the problem," she said as she looked across the table into his eyes, "I'm not sure that's what I meant at all."

All the air was just sucked out of the room. Chase's groin responded so quickly he couldn't even hide it if he had to stand up. Trying to shift positions so as to not completely embarrass himself, he looked down at his water, finding it very interesting.

How was he supposed to react to her comments? They were so honest due to her inexperience but that made it so erotic. He took a

A Marine to Remember

drink of his water to cool down his libido when he noticed someone approaching their table. He didn't know the man but figured out pretty quickly that Eryn knew him. Her face paled as soon as she saw him, giving her a ghostly appearance.

"Eryn?" Chase took her elbow trying to make sure she was okay.

She looked down, then up at Chase, mustering a smile, "I'm fine," she said in a rushed breath.

Oh Lord, what just happened? They were having a great dinner and then she saw her Uncle Ben, her father's oldest and dearest friend coming over to their table. This was not going to be fun. Manners forced her to paste a smile on her face.

"Uncle Ben," She stood and tried to sound enthusiastic but failed. She kissed him on the cheek, "I didn't know you were here."

Ben laughed and looked from her, to her companion, then back to her again. "I'm not surprised," He squeezed her hand reassuringly, "I could have set off a grenade right next to your table and I don't think either of you would have moved."

Eryn turned crimson red. She could see that Ben was really interested in checking out Chase.

"I'm sorry," she said and looked at Chase with a sympathetic smile, "Ben, this is my....." she didn't know what to say, "friend Chase Johnson. Chase, this is my Uncle Ben."

Chase stood up and shook hands with Eryn's uncle. He could tell from the man's appearance and demeanor that he was a Marine and, Chase suspected, an officer. You didn't spend your whole life around the Corps and not recognize the signs. The man was smiling but Chase suspected he was wondering who Chase was and what he was doing with Eryn.

"I'm not really Eryn's uncle," Ben said to Chase. He could see the young man was curious and he didn't want to cause problems, "I'm a close, family friend." Looking at the young man, he was impressed. "You are a Marine." It was a statement.

Chase nodded, "Yes, sir." He felt obligated for some reason, to explain his own connection to Eryn. "Eryn and I work together at Crash Crew."

Eryn wanted to crawl under a rock. Uncle Ben looked back and forth between Chase and her and she had a bad feeling about the look on his face. She jumped when Uncle Ben let out a whoop, attracting attention from the other diners.

Ben was floored, "Oh, this is good," he drawled.

As if the situation couldn't get worse, it just did. Eryn cringed inwardly. How could an evening that was probably one of the best ones of her adult life turn into a humiliating lesson? If she could've, she would've crawled under the table and hid but that was just not going to happen. She managed to gather what little whit she had about her and touched Ben's arm.

"I'm sure you're dining with Aunt Colleen and I know you don't like to keep her waiting," Eryn said lowly.

It was a blatant dismissal and completely rude but she was desperate.

Chase could hear the tone in Eryn's voice and was confused. Her "uncle" was finding a lot of things she was saying and doing funny and Chase couldn't figure out why.

Ben winked at Eryn and turned to face Chase, "I hope to see you around again Chase." He meant it and hoped it came across in his voice.

Leaning over, Ben kissed Eryn's cheek, then started to walk away but curiosity nipped at his heels and he turned around.

"By the way," he looked pointedly at Chase and asked, "what rank are you, son?"

Odd question, Chase thought but wasn't ashamed of his rank and he wasn't going to lie so he looked into Ben's eyes, "A Staff Sergeant, sir," he said proudly.

Ben nodded and turned around to walk back to his wife and dinner companions. A chuckle built up in his chest and he wondered how long it would take for all hell to break loose.

Chase had a lot of questions but he couldn't bring himself to ask them with Eryn looking as upset as she was. Her whole demeanor changed as soon as that Ben character showed up. Even after they sat back down, she barely touched her dessert and couldn't seem to wait to leave.

Chase paid the bill, left a hefty tip, and walked out of the restaurant behind Eryn. As soon as they were back in the jeep, Eryn started chatting about nothing. It didn't take a rocket scientist to figure out she was trying to distract him and keep the conversation light. Well, the fact that the closeness they shared earlier was now all but gone, he was upset. The plan was that he would suggest they go back to his place but now he wasn't sure. Looking up, he turned to ask her if she wanted to go home and found her staring at him very intensely.

"Kiss me," Eryn practically demanded.

Chase's body reacted much quicker than his mind. He was worried about her but there was no way he'd deny her. Wanting to be gently, he brushed her lips with his in a feather-light kiss.

A Marine to Remember

Eryn knew he was letting her decide. Well, she decided she didn't want to be gentle right now. Her emotions were in a jumbled mess and she was scared. Too bad, her body said, it wanted more.

She reached up and pulled his head toward hers. His quick intake of breath told her she surprised him with her move and that made her smile. It was amazing how his reaction drove her desire. Once his lips were on hers, they fit so perfectly. She wanted to drown in the onslaught of sensations that poured through her body.

Their lips were melding with so much heat that Chase couldn't tell where he ended and Eryn began. Her tongue probed his lips, anxiously looking to gain access. Once he opened up to her, she was absorbed into him.

Eryn felt the heat pouring off of them and knew she was melting into a puddle of want and need. She was feeling greedy and welcomed the explosion of emotions and desperation that seeped into her pores. She wanted to kiss him forever and do so much more that she couldn't even think straight. She almost clawed at his jacket trying closer and moaned when he set her away from him. She didn't like how cold she felt without his touch.

There was only so much temptation Chase could take before he reached the point of no return. They were quickly racing to that point when he realized where they were and what they were doing. He wanted Eryn in his bed so badly but he had to be the voice of reason here. Not to mention the uncomfortable and unspoken exchange between her and her Uncle Ben in the restaurant. Chase never took advantage of a woman's emotional state before and wasn't going to start now.

He sat in the driver's seat, watching both him and Eryn breathing raggedly because of their kissing and he wanted to kick himself. This nobility thing didn't sit well with him given the disposition of his crotch right now but some things couldn't be helped. He was watching emotions skitter across Eryn's face and he was worried. He could see hurt, embarrassment, and finally anger but he wasn't sure exactly who she was mad at.

Wanting to say the right thing, Chase smiled and looked at Eryn, "Well that was awesome but I'm not sure what it was all about." He didn't want to upset her but he to know where this was coming from and going to.

"I don't know," Eryn muttered. She was so confused but realized he had the right to ask the question.

Chase sighed, "Well," he took a deep breath, "who is Ben exactly and what was left unsaid?"

A Marine to Remember

Although Chase knew he needed to ask to clear the air, he wasn't sure if he wanted the answers. She looked so upset, he wanted to gather her up in his arms and hold her until the hurt look in her eyes went away.

"The kiss we just shared," Eryn started to say then stopped because she didn't know what to say.

Chase nodded and finished for her, "Was one the most passionate kisses of my life and I want to make sure it was because of us." He expected Eryn to agree or say something but she just sat there in stilted silence. After a few minutes, he got frustrated, "Fine," he spat out. He started the jeep and tore out of the parking lot.

They were almost halfway back to the base when Eryn gently reached over and touched Chase's arm. He finally looked over and she was mad at herself for the hurt look in his eyes, "Let's go to the beach so we can talk," she said loudly to be heard over the wind rushing by the jeep.

Chase nodded, if she wanted to talk, then they'd talk. He turned down the beach access road a few minutes later. He was glad the evening wasn't ending but was afraid of what they'd talk about.

Chapter 6

Chase barely turned off the key to the jeep when she jumped out. Fear of what Chase would think when he found out about her dad made her nervous. She pulled off her shoes and hosiery and threw them in the backseat.

Chase saw Eryn pulling her hosiery off and wanted to give her some privacy but he'd seen the slip of skin on her upper thighs and the awareness pummeled into his body with a vengeance. Her pulled off his suit jacket and tie and followed suit, throwing them in the vehicle before starting toward the beach.

They walked down the sandy incline in silence. Once they reached the more packed sand by the water, Eryn took Chase's hand into her own. He didn't resist the gesture, which eased her nerves a little bit. Neither of them spoke, they just walked down the stretch of beach, letting the water play over their feet as it came onto shore.

Eryn was trying to shore up any reserves of emotional strength she could. What she had to say was tough and she was mad at herself for not thinking this through. Well, probably because it wasn't an issue before now. After a few more minutes, she stopped and faced Chase. She looked up into his eyes as the last remaining light of the day reflecting in their deep blue hue.

"I'm sorry about spoiling the evening," Eryn said while trying to hold back tears.

Chase could see how horrible she felt and didn't think she should, "Hey," he smiled, "you didn't spoil anything, Eryn." He wanted to reassure her, "It's not exactly how either of us pictured it would be but that's okay." She was sort of smiling so he felt like his words helped.

"Yes," She answered, and appreciated his efforts in trying to comfort her. "Let's sit down."

She started up the beach, away from the water's edge and found a place to sit.

They sat down in the still warm sand and held hands.

Eryn cleared her throat, "I'm not sure where to begin." She was stalling because she wanted to say the right thing. There was no use in trying, she just had to spit it out. "Ben is a very good friend of my father's because they attended OCS together years ago."

"I know your dad is a Marine," Chase answered quickly.

He didn't understand the issue since his dad was a Marine too.

"Yep," she said solemnly and waited for her words to sink in.

Finally, Chase's brain caught up and he looked at Eryn intently, "What rank is your father?" he asked in a demanding tone.

Eryn whispered, "Colonel."

Chase shook his head, "Holy shit!" he yelled and jumped up.

Now her reluctance to talk about her father made sense. Not only would her dad be the most possessive SOB, but if he found out they worked together, Chase's career could be cut very short indeed.

He started pacing. He wanted to kick himself for telling that Ben guy his rank and that he and Eryn worked together. Just fantastic! He finally sat down and put his arms on his knees and his hands on his face.

Eryn was almost reassured when Chase sat back down. She knew he had the right to tell her to hit the road now. She wouldn't blame him one bit. Her father was always there, looming over her life. Why shouldn't he spoil this too?

"Thank you for not leaving," she said to Chase.

Chase was surprised by her statement, "Eryn," he looked into her gorgeous green eyes, "I'm just floored because this is a pretty big complication for both of us." Wanting to lighten the tension he asked, "Why can't your dad be a CPA?"

Eryn huffed, "I wish," and she was being honest. Unfortunately, she had to tell him the rest of it. "There's more," she watched him take a deep breath and nod before she went on, "Ben is a Colonel here at Cherry Point so he's pretty much the eyes and ears of my father."

His stomach was now in his feet. This just kept getting better, Chase thought sarcastically.

"I suspect," Eryn said while putting her hand on Chase's arm and resting her chin on his forearm, "he's going to call me and ask about you, Uncle Ben that is, but I don't think he'll say anything to my father right away." She kissed his skin, wanting to reassure him she hadn't meant for any of this to happen. "I didn't know he'd be at the restaurant."

Did she think he was dense? Chase's feathers were ruffled.

"I know you didn't," he said a little louder than he wanted to. Seeing her look, he kissed her hand, "You can't fake this."

Eryn smiled, she felt so happy and so sad at the same time. She knew he was talking about their feelings.

"What are you going to tell him?" Chase asked. He wanted and needed to know.

She had a decision to make. Not being completely sure of Chase's intentions and not wanting to sound like an idiot, she said, "I guess I'll tell him that I met someone who I think is great." He smiled and she went on, "I do think he'll ask about our work situation," she was worried and knew he knew it, "and I won't lie."

Admiring her courage, and wishing she wasn't in this situation, he kissed her forehead. He knew his own family could be difficult, being Marines. Her situation was way more complicated. She deserved a lot more credit than he gave her up to now because she knew full well about her father and what his rank entailed.

"I wouldn't want you to lie, Eryn," he cupped her cheek with his palm, "as long as you know what the consequences could be."

Eryn nodded slowly. Her mind was muddled by all the thoughts running through it. "I know the consequences." She stood up and started walking down the beach to where the jeep was parked.

A Marine to Remember

Chase watched her walk a few yards then got up to follow. He caught up quickly and took her hand in his.

"I don't like this and I'm worried about what you're thinking," he said softly.

She shook her head, "No," she almost yelled, "I'm worried about what you're thinking."

It was simple; they had two choices. They could stop now and go their separate ways or they could stay together and fight the proverbial wolves.

Chase sure as hell didn't want to stop. Eryn brought out feelings in him he didn't even know he possessed. It was exciting to be around her; they had a lot in common, and he was pretty sure he was falling in love. If her feelings even remotely echoed his they would both be stupid for giving up. Of course, he could only speak for himself here. He needed to know what she intended to do.

"Do you want to stop now?" He tipped her chin up and searched her face. The vulnerability in her eyes shook him to the core.

The setting sun cast a warm blanket over them.

Under different circumstances it would be a dreamlike setting that Eryn might retell in a diary or to her girlfriends. They'd be kissing and touching and planning on where to take their relationship. But no, now they were debating on whether or not her father's position would influence them. The situation sucked!

The decision made, she kissed him, "No!" Everyone else could just go to hell as far as she was concerned.

Chase saw the second she made up her mind. A gleam streamed through her eyes even before she said the word. He didn't expect the tears that followed and wasn't sure what he should say or do. Instinctively, he wrapped her into his arms.

Eryn was grateful for his support, physically and emotionally. "I understand though if you don't want to see me anymore." She was talking into his shoulder and wasn't sure she could face what he might say. "I won't play games and pretend it wouldn't hurt if you said you wanted to stop."

Anger shot through Chase and he backed up a step so he could look at her, "Hell no!" he said.

Relief washed over Eryn like a soft caress. She threw her arms around Chase's neck and started kissing him.

It would be so easy, Chase thought, to lose himself in her kisses but they had to clear everything up. Reluctantly, he put his hands on either side of her face and pulled back just far enough to look into her eyes.

"I don't know what we're going to do about this but we'll work it out," he said assuredly.

Once Eryn nodded in agreement, he took her hands and led her the rest of the way back up to the parking lot. He figured a cold shower was in order for the evening but he had to get her back to her barracks room and himself home first.

He helped her back into the jeep and drove back to the base. Once in the parking lot, Eryn got out quietly and smiled. They didn't kiss goodnight; they just didn't want to push their luck any further. Chase sat in his jeep and watched Eryn go up the stairs and into her room. He didn't pull out of the parking spot until the light went on in her room.

Eryn slept in fits that night. The uneasy feeling stayed with her and she figured it was an omen of things to come. This could all blow up. Of course, if her father was anyone else, it wouldn't even matter.

Perhaps it was that simple fact that had her so upset. You can't control who your parents were or what they did but it sure did stink if they have the power to interfere with your life.

She lay there in bed, tossing and turning in her mind. She knew that she could wish all she wanted that things were different but they just weren't. Life wasn't always fair. She tried not to think about how this might overflow onto Chase as well. He'd become as ingrained in her head as he was in her heart. It was thoughts of Chase that finally gave her enough peace to fall into a deep sleep.

When the alarm went off at five o'clock, Eryn thought she'd slept with sandpaper under her eyelids. Running always helped clear the cobwebs so she headed over to the running track first thing.

She'd just started he second lap when she heard steps behind her. She knew he'd come. Their thoughts were paralleled in so many ways. The surprising part was that it happened so quickly. Her heart started picking up pace and she was pretty sure it wasn't just from running. After the third lap, he moved up so he was running beside her.

They didn't need to speak while running. It was an unspoken understanding that they needed to be reserved to be seen in public together.

Chase glanced over and noticed sweat trickling down Eryn's neck and running down the soft skin of her chest. How could something so minor turn him on so much?

They finished twelve laps and nodded to one another as they left the track in opposite directions. Eryn smiled and waved as she saw his jeep pass her barracks. This whole thing with her dad was just a small hurdle they'd jumped over.

Back at work, everything seemed normal. Staff Sgt. Greene was surprised when she didn't come in late as she requested. He didn't ask why and Eryn didn't answer.

She'd been working a couple of hours when she heard an announcement that she had a phone call come over the loud speaker. She went into the Section Leader's office and picked up the extension.

"Sgt. Fredricks," she said confidently.

Ben smiled, "Hey, sweet pea," he greeted her with her childhood nickname.

Well, Eryn thought, he sure wasn't wasting any time was he? She knew the call would come, she forewarned Chase, but she didn't expect it at work. The fact that Uncle Ben sounded so chipper and used an endearment took the edge off of Eryn's nervousness.

"I was wondering if you were free for lunch," Ben asked.

Well, she could do that. "I have off from eleven-thirty to thirteen hundred." She didn't want to ask for more time off since she already asked yesterday.

Ben shuffled papers, "I know," he signed one and set it aside, "I'll see you at thirteen hundred." Before she could answer, he said, "I'll call your Section Leader and request the meeting formally so you can get the time off." Someone entered his office and he needed to hang up, "I'll let you go, the usual place."

Eryn heard the dial tone before she could even get her thoughts in order. She didn't know what to think; he didn't seem upset but he cut the call short.

She hoped Staff Sgt. Greene wouldn't be too pissed when he heard about the meeting. Yeah right, like a Colonel just comes along every day and requests a meeting with one of his Sergeants? This had disaster written all over it.

She left the Section Leader's office and went back to the desk she was working at. Maybe one of the jets would call an emergency, just a little one that required her to stay here. Okay that was just wrong, wishing for an emergency.

But she was desperate. She had no idea how to explain to Ben, a man who was practically her second father and someone she'd respected her whole life, on why she decided to break the rules where Chase was concerned. Not to mention what would happen if he decided to say anything to her father about it.

An hour later, she was still contemplating the situation when Staff Sgt. Greene came out of the office and walked over to where she was sitting. He didn't look thrilled and Eryn's hopes fell.

"I just got off the phone with a Colonel over at the base General's office," he looked pointedly at her, "and he wants a meeting with you." He sighed, "Should I be asking what this is about?"

Eryn tried to look innocent, "I don't know exactly," she wasn't really lying.

He nodded and turned to go back into his office.

At thirteen hundred, Eryn walked into a local café a couple of miles from the base. She met Uncle Ben, and sometimes Aunt Colleen, here a couple of times to catch up. She wished Aunt Colleen was here today to be a buffer.

She saw Ben right away and wove her way around the other diners to where he was sitting. He stood when she got to the table, and waited for her to sit before he sat back down. She always thought he was so dashing.

Studying Ben, she smiled. He changed into civilian clothes, like she had, since they were off the base. And, even though he and her father were the same age, she thought he was very handsome. She smiled tightly, waiting for the inevitable.

"Relax," Ben said as he motioned the waitress over, "this isn't the inquisition, you know."

Eryn nodded, and gave her drink order to the waitress. Once they placed their food orders and the waitress left, she leaned forward, "I know. I was just trying to put this off a little while longer." She took a deep breath, "Like, never."

Ben laughed. "You are a feisty one. That's probably why I love you like you were my own daughter."

She felt the emotions welling up and wanted to keep them tamped down. Ben noticed too and gave her a bit of time to compose herself. She appreciated his consideration.

Ben didn't want to torture Eryn so he sat forward and took Eryn's hand into his and patted it. "I know who this guy is." There was no reason to tip toe around it.

Eryn's shackles were up. She knew it, he knew it. The anger skittered across her face as plain as could be.

Nodding, Ben grew serious, "He's a good Marine with a flawless record, and I already know how you feel about your career." She was going to say something but he put up his hand to hold her off, "All I want to know is, how serious this is?"

That was the question wasn't it? How could she answer something she didn't know?

"I can honestly say I don't know," she answered. He sat back and waited for her. She looked into his eyes, "I think I love him but I'm not sure."

He was proud of Eryn, it took a lot of character to answer a question that he really had no right to ask. None of this was fair to her.

Ben nodded, "I just don't want either of you to deal with any repercussions from this in your records books."

Her temper flared, "No," she pointed at Ben, "You don't want my father to butt in and do something."

Ben was shocked by her statement. His sweet pea really had grown up. Not only that, but she sure had her father pegged.

His best friend, Tom, was one of the best Marines he knew. He was also one of the hardest fathers to love and wanted his family to obey him like his troops. It didn't work that way but, even after all of these years, Tom just didn't get it.

Ben was proud of Eryn for forging her own way. It showed how much she was like her father but neither of them would admit that. One thing he knew, Tom would never think a Staff Sergeant was good enough for his daughter. A shame too, since this man, Chase, seemed like a good one.

He looked at Eryn apologetically and said, "You're right."

Eryn tried to calm down. This was Uncle Ben. She'd known and loved him her whole life and he wasn't like her dad. He always supported her but he knew the score and, with her father, it wasn't going to go in her favor.

They finished their meals in silence and left a half hour later with Eryn promising to call him soon.

The drive back to Crash Crew was good. Eryn felt a little better with the first hurdle being cleared. The day was nice and she wanted to feel more positive. She knew that Ben might say something to her dad about Chase but she thought he would, at least, downplay the situation to give her some time.

She wasn't necessarily afraid of her father, she just wanted to make sure the relationship was worth the fallout her father would most likely cause. It was kind of a relief to have someone else know. The big question was, were she and Chase up to dealing with it. She was willing to fight but she also knew they needed to keep it quiet for a little longer.

It was almost fifteen hundred by the time she got back to the Crash Barn. She made her way up to Staff Sgt. Greene's office and knocked. When she entered she saw him sitting at his desk. She was about to walk over to the adjoining desk to start some paperwork when he looked up.

"Gunny Frinnel wants to see you in his office right away," Staff Sgt. Greene said matter-of-factly.

Eryn's shoulders sank. She was used to the tone but didn't always care for it.

She nodded, "Aye, Staff Sgt." She turned and left the office.

Her stomach was churning, trying to eject the lunch she just ate, as she made her way downstairs to the Crash Chief's office. It wasn't a big stretch for her to figure out what this might be about although she hoped she was wrong. She knocked and waited.

Once she heard the gruff, "Enter." Eryn opened the door.

"You wanted to see me, Gunny," she asked and stood at attention in front of his desk.

Gunny Frinnel looked at Eryn then at the door, "Close the door and take a seat, Sgt."

She was still wondering what this meeting was about and his tone didn't give anything away. She did as she was asked quickly. As soon as she sat down, he stood up.

"Why is one of my Marines getting a call from the Commanding General's office?" He asked, his stone and stance saying he was clearly not happy.

Logically, she should have known, but she was still surprised. News traveled fast and she shouldn't be surprised. Staff Sgt. Greene was by-the-book and he wouldn't been required to notify the Crash Chief if there were any problems. A call from a high ranking officer could definitely be considered a problem.

She wasn't sure how she'd get through this but there was no use in lying now. Why did this have to come up now? She was practically squirming in the chair while he watched her intently.

"Well, Gunny," she took a breath to game some composure, 'I happen to know Colonel Chapman." His look of censure made her realize the words did not some good.

Gunny Frinnel's scrunched up brow made her worried.

"I don't mean *I know him*," she inflected the words, "I meant I know him through my father. They are friends."

Gunny Frinnel was surprised. Not that her father couldn't be friends with anybody, it was just that he didn't know what that had to do with her missing time at work.

He nodded and asked, "Why did he request a meeting with you?"

If Eryn thought she was uncomfortable before, she was mistaken. Her palms were soaking wet now and she felt like a five-year-old in a principal's office.

"He was concerned," she mumbled.

Did he hear her right? "Concerned about what?" Gunny asked.

Looking up at the ceiling, Eryn prayed for some divine intervention. She so did not want to be having this conversation. She fell in love, so what! Why did everyone seem to have a vested interest in her life? This was evolving into a more complicated situation by the minute.

"Gunny," she was beginning to get defensive, "am I in trouble?"

She hadn't done anything wrong and she resented the fact that everyone made her feel like she had. Oh but you did, her inner voice shouted, you fell in love with one of your bosses.

Gunny Frinnel picked up on the tone quickly, "Is there something you've done, Sgt. Fredricks?" He couldn't put her through this any longer. "Sit tight," he said and walked back around his desk. He picked up the phone and said, "I need you in my office...NOW."

Eryn didn't know if she was more confused or scared. There was a churning in her gut that told her she was missing something here. Gunny Frinnel dismissed her right after he hung up the phone but told her to stay in the building. She went back upstairs to the crew deck without responding.

She was walking into the Section Leader's office to let Staff Sgt. Greene know she was done when she heard him on the phone.

"Aye, Gunny," He said and hung up the phone. He looked up at Eryn and shook his head, "I don't even want to know," he said, effectively cutting her off. "I'll rearrange the hot spot schedule so you can stay here at the Crash Barn." He nodded in dismissal.

Eryn took the hint, "Aye, Staff Sgt." She was just outside the door when she heard him call her back into the office, "Yes, Staff Sgt?" She asked.

Staff Sgt. took a minute and said reluctantly, "I don't know what's going on but I'm assuming it's not good." He looked at Sgt. Fredricks with sympathy, "Let me give you some advice here, Sgt." He saw her nod,

"Think about your career and whether the Marine Corps is your top priority."

Eryn was pissed. Of course she couldn't very well tell her Section Leader to bite it but she wanted to. Just because some crazy stuff was going on and she missed some work, they all think that she didn't make the Corps a priority. She was here, wasn't she? Just because she was a woman, there were always double standards. What could she say?

"Yes, Staff Sgt.," was her response.

Eryn left the room and was proud of herself for not slamming the door.

Eryn spoke with her crew and explained the change in the schedule. They didn't seem to mind and she was glad about that. At least somebody wasn't pissed off at her. She sat with them in the TV room until she was needed back down to Gunny Frinnel's office.

It was a comfortable room even though she didn't spend a lot of time in here. There was a big screen, a dozen or so recliners, stereo system, and even video games. It was a great place for the crews and their guests to relax. It was geared more toward the guys but that never bothered her before today. She was zoning and didn't hear the page for her.

Lance Corporal Selton nudged her arm, "Sgt., you were just paged to the Crash Chief's office."

He looked a little worried since Sgt. Fredricks was a good crew chief and was always on top of things.

Eryn wanted to kick herself. She never wanted her crew to think she wasn't on her game; it undermined their trust in her leadership skills.

"Oh, sorry," was all she could muster before getting up. She smiled and walked downstairs.

As before, Gunny Frinnel's door was closed and she knocked. This time there was a very curt "In." Great. She walked into the office not sure what she'd find. She saw Gunny first but then looked over and saw Chase sitting on the couch. Now she was confused. Looking at him, she remembered that's where he was sitting when she was assigned to section. Did that mean she was being removed?

Pushing aside her assumptions, she sat down in a chair near the Gunny's desk. She looked from one man to the other, hoping somebody would clear this all up. Whatever happened, happened.

Gunny Frinnel watched Eryn and felt kind of bad that she was in the dark. This situation was way out of control now and he felt responsible for some of it. She wasn't looking all that well so she wanted to clarify and get them out of his office so he could go home.

"I don't think that anyone can do anything here at Crash Crew that I don't know about, Sgt. Fredricks." He looked from Eryn to Chase, and back again. "I've spoken with Staff Sgt. Johnson."

Eryn's head snapped around as she looked at Chase. What did he say?

Gunny Frinnel knew she was wondering what Chase told him. "He didn't tell me anything I didn't already know, Sergeant." There was a hint of a smile on his face.

It was too late. Eryn's blood was at its boiling point. She looked at Chase and saw that he didn't look any happier than she was at the moment. It didn't matter, he shouldn't have said anything!

"I am," Gunny Frinnel interrupted the glare she directed at Chase, "believe it or not, supportive of your relationship." He stopped to let the words sink in. She didn't look any happier. "However," This was the tough part, "I warned Staff Sgt. Johnson about keeping this quiet and it seems we've come to a point here where perhaps that isn't possible."

Eryn didn't get where he was coming from. How did he know they were seeing one another? Why did he think the situation was at an impasse?

"Gunny," she said, "I guess I don't understand, which may make me look stupid, but I don't care." She looked back at Chase, hurt clearly in her eyes.

Chase sat in the office and watched the exchange between Eryn and Mitch and couldn't think of anything to say. He was frustrated and, frankly, scared out of his mind. He thought that Eryn probably felt the same way but he didn't dare say anything. He couldn't.

The discovery of their relationship by a family friend wasn't a big deal except that this "family friend" was a high ranking officer, who, with one phone call, could ruin his career or, worse, Eryn's. So, as cowardice as it was, he just sat there. He saw the questions in Eryn's eyes but couldn't answer them.

Finally, Gunny Frinnel got down to business.

"No one here at Crash Crew knows what the situation is between you two and I'd really like to keep it that way." He wasn't smiling anymore. "Sgt. Fredricks," he sorted through some papers, picked one up, and handed it to her. "I've assigned you to attend an administration class with Sgt. Jeffries for the next week. I've given you the weekend off."

He turned to Chase, "Staff Sgt. Johnson," he handed Chase a piece of paper, "I've assigned you to Rifle Range duty next week." He sat down at his desk and said, "Dismissed."

A Marine to Remember

When Eryn and Chase both stood to leave, he looked up, "I hope the both of you will take the weekend to think this matter over." He nodded and looked back down at the papers on his desk.

They left the Crash Chief's office and Eryn stopped, waiting for Chase to say something. Instead, she watched him walk down the hall toward the door. His posture definitely said "back off." Eryn turned, tears in her eyes, and walked back toward the stairs that led to the crew deck.

Mitch stood in the doorway of his office and didn't know if he was more pissed at the guy who was holding this over their heads or Chase for not being the man Mitch thought he was.

Chase got into his jeep and sat there for a few minutes staring off into space. Dammit!

He hit his steering wheel in frustration. Why didn't he say anything? Because, dammit, he didn't want anyone to see how he felt about her. He started up the jeep and shook his head. There was a nice cold beer waiting for him at home, along with his dog. After this, he deserved it.

Eryn took the orders up to Staff Sgt. Green's office and gave them to him. He took them without comment and went back to work on the schedule. She spent the rest of the day on pins and needles. She wondered what Ben would tell her father, if he would say anything at all.

She wondered what Chase was thinking and was mad that he didn't bother to mention that Gunny Frinnel knew anything. Was he feeling what she was feeling? Her gut told her to fight, that's what Marines did!

Isn't that was boot camp and her Aircraft Firefighting training taught her? Isn't that what her father taught her since she was a little girl? After being told over and over throughout your life that you should fight for what you wanted, how could she suddenly back down now?

Chapter 7

Later that evening, Eryn laid on her bunk and ran over the situation in her head for about the zillionth time. Unfortunately she was assigned to stay over at the Crash Barn so couldn't even call Chase to find out what was going on. She wasn't going to stop seeing Chase but she knew she had to be even more careful about it now. No one here needed to overhear a conversation.

Luckily all the guys were in the TV room watching a movie. Since she was the only female on duty she had the female bunkroom to herself. Too bad there wasn't a phone line in here. She managed to fall asleep but dreamed about Chase. They were actually happy and nobody cared what their jobs were.

Eryn got through the morning relief without incident. If Staff Sgt. Greene suspected anything, he wasn't talking, and that was fine with her. Any bit of relief was welcomed. He was walking with her across the truck bay when he turned to her.

"Well," he smiled and said, "Let's get this turned over so we can go home."

Eryn blew out a breath, his disappointment from yesterday seemed to have dissipated, "Aye, Staff Sgt." she said with a smile.

She really had to stop with the paranoia. It was aggravating and would give her an ulcer. She went to her locker and grabbed her bag. The Section Leaders did the actual turnover so she didn't have to be up in the office and that meant that she didn't have to see Chase.

It was Friday so she had the next three days off before her class. Just thinking about that made her smile. She headed out of the Crash Barn to her car. She may be confused about a lot in her life, but right now, she was just going to put it away.

Surprisingly, the drive back to her barracks room was pleasant. It was still early and the heat was mild. Not to mention, just getting physically away from Crash Crew was a relief.

Now it was Chase's turn to sit there and wonder. She had a mean streak and right now, was happy about him having to suffer a little bit. After what he said, or didn't say actually, yesterday, she felt he deserved it.

Once in her room, Eryn saw the light on her answering machine blinking. Maybe it was Chase? Her heartbeat sped up at the thought. Once she pushed the play button and heard the sound of her father's voice, her spirits plummeted. She wanted to panic. Why were her thoughts and feelings so scattered these days? They changed like the wind and it was really tiresome. Did Ben tell him anything? What would he do? The message was direct.

"Eryn, it's your father," he announced, "I wanted to let you know my trip has been delayed." He paused for a moment, "I will call and let you know when I've rescheduled. I love you."

Eryn sat there and thought that, even though he said the words, his tone didn't really make her believe them. It was a shame really, they were so close all the while Eryn was growing up. It was only when she decided to go the enlisted route in the Corps that their relationship seemed to crumble.

There was good news too. This was a reprieve of sorts and it bought her time to search out her feelings for Chase. Maybe they could even see where this was actually going. At least her dad didn't sound upset so she was pretty sure he wasn't aware of what was going on.

After going in the bathroom and splashing water on her face, Eryn came back out and sat at the desk in her room. She had the whole weekend and she wondered if she'd hear from Chase. Should she make the first move and call him? He was at work now so that wouldn't be too good. She didn't know if he was assigned to after-hours duty at the Crash Barn so it might be weird if she called to find out. Now she regretted not seeing him during relief; she could've found out what the plan was.

There was no use freaking out about it now, Eryn, it was done, she said to herself. This love stuff was tough! Did she even know for sure that she was in love? Her sister, Sarah, always acted so stupid when she was "in love."

Sitting there, Eryn figured she was in love the minute she decided to ignore her Crash Chief and her Uncle Ben and pursue a relationship with Chase. She was willing to take on anyone and anything just to be with him.

Eryn got up, went for a run, came back to her room, and showered. She checked her machine, and not seeing any messages from Chase, started to worry again if they were doing the right thing. Dammit! Why did this have to be such a big mess? She was starting to get a headache from all of this so she decided to lay down and take a nap. She could worry about it later. She didn't know if it was the physical toll all of this took on her or the fact that she wasn't willing to just give in to it right now, but she drifted off to sleep quickly.

Eryn woke to the phone ringing and prayed someone would answer the darn thing. She was in her barracks room so it was just her. She grappled around and found the receiver. The cobwebs were clearing as she sat up.

"Hello," she said groggily. She looked over and saw it was almost three in the afternoon. Holy cow, she slept the day away!

"Hey, did I just wake you?" A woman's voice asked on the other end of the line.

Smiling, Eryn recognized the voice immediately. It was her friend, Emma. They met a few years earlier at boot camp and happened to both get stationed at Cherry Point. Emma was in communications and loved her job with the Corps as much as Eryn did.

Eryn stretched, "Sorry, I didn't realize I was sleeping that long." She yawned.

Emma giggled, "Well, I'm calling because a group of us are going out to some clubs in New Bern tonight and I wanted you to come along." She waved to another friend who was passing by her barracks room. "We haven't gotten together in a while."

Her friend's good mood was contagious. Eryn hesitated though, thinking that maybe Chase would call and they could talk about what happened at Crash Crew. But the little independent voice in her head asked, 'are you supposed to sit around and wait for him?'

"I don't know," Eryn said in an unsure voice.

Emma wouldn't take no for an answer, "Come on, it'll be fun. Just us girls." There were people yelling in the room next to hers so Emma laughed.

Weighing her options, Eryn was ashamed of herself. She was acting like a lovesick puppy when she should really get out there and have a good time with her friends.

Eryn smiled, "What the heck," she said to Emma, "what time should I be ready?"

She spoke a few more minutes with Emma and hung up laughing. Emma was one of those people that just made you feel good by being around her. She was energetic and vivacious and looked at the world like her personal party. When Eryn asked Emma what she should wear, Emma said, "something wild and sexy." Eryn wasn't even sure she could pull it off but it was funny that another person liked her to dress that way too.

They decided that the group would pick Eryn up at six-thirty so she started to get up and get ready for her girls' night.

Miraculously, Eryn was actually ready by six-fifteen. She washed her hair and blow dried it, which she rarely did because of the length. She put it up in curlers and concentrated on applying her makeup very heavily compared to how she usually wore it. She wasn't an expert at the look but she paid attention to some demonstrations at the mall and thought she did a decent job.

Her eyes were done in very dark colors that gave them a mysterious look. Her outfit consisted of a very short and very tight black leather skirt she borrowed from a friend and a silver tank top. She topped the look off with a borrowed pair of over-the-knee boots. She looked in the mirror at the final look and was pleasantly surprised. She looked like a woman who was young and ready to take some chances. If only her insides reflected that as well....

Putting a determined look on her face, she turned from the mirror and decided she would have fun tonight. She deserved it after the fiasco she encountered at work and with Ben and Chase. Tonight was about having fun and hanging with the girls.

When she looked out the window, she saw a black Durango pull up and knew it must be them. The window were down, the music blaring, and Emma jumped out of the passenger side.

When Eryn came out of her room, she saw some of the guys from her barracks whistling and smiling like men do. Shaking her head and smiling, Eryn went downstairs.

Emma looked from the guys to where Eryn was coming down the stairs and her jaw dropped. "Whew, look at you!" She said to her friend.

Trying not to blush, Eryn hugged Emma, "You told me to dress sexy," she said with a lot more confidence than she felt. She spun around as if she were a model, making Emma clap.

"It will definitely do," Emma said as she moved toward the vehicle.

Eryn got into the SUV and smiled. Emma introduced their group and everyone was very nice and welcoming. Eryn met two of the girls before so she didn't feel uncomfortable.

The drive to New Bern was about thirty minutes and the girls laughed and sang to songs on the radio during the drive. The mood was light, which Eryn was thankful for. She definitely needed a distraction.

New Bern was a larger city than Havelock, where the base was, and had a few good clubs. Eryn didn't know what the plan was, but she was open to anything at this point.

Once their designated driver, Laura, found a spot, everyone got out and checked their appearance. Eryn smiled at the other girls; she didn't bother to primp because she wasn't in the market for a man tonight. The one she was currently dealing with was enough. Like a reminder, Chase's face popped into her head......again. Why did he have to show up? She turned to the others, who were deciding which club they should go to first, and put Chase out of her mind.

The group settled on a more upscale club to start out with. One of the other girls, Kim, said she'd been there before and it was great.

After walking a few blocks, the girls entered a place called, The Club. Eryn shook her head, what a witty name. Not wanting to be sarcastic, she pasted a smile on her face and followed the other girls. They group paid the cover charge and went inside.

Surprisingly, it was a nice place. There was a massive bar made of beautiful, carved wood down at the far end. The dance floor was between the bar and the main seating area. Most of the seating was circular booths covered in red leather fabric and had large round tables. It was kind of elegant with the low lit atmosphere. There were a few people there already so the ladies made their way to a large booth. As she walked, Eryn thought maybe Chase would like this place.

"Stop it!" She said to herself. She turned red when the group stared at her. Obviously she said the statement out loud.

Emma looked at Eryn, "Stop what?" she asked.

Eryn was mortified that she voiced her thoughts. "Nothing," she mumbled while waving her hand.

Oh, this was bad. She was talking to herself and thinking about Chase way too much already. She was relieved when the group shrugged off her little outburst and started sitting around the table in the booth. There was a great view of the room from their book and everyone looked around, commenting here and there on the other people in the club.

After an hour, the conversation wrapped around to include work. Two of the girls in their group were in the Navy while the other four were Marines. Eryn listened for a while, then got distracted with the music the band was playing.

"Are you bored?" Emma asked while nudging Eryn's arm.

Eryn smiled, "Not at all, just relaxing." It felt so good to not have to worry about anything. It was the most at ease she'd been in days. "I'm listening to everyone."

Emma nodded, "I can relate, being surrounded by men at work can be draining. It's nice to hang out with the girls for a change."

"Exactly," Eryn agreed.

Of course, Emma didn't know the men in her life were more about her love life than her work life.

Emma recently transferred from Communications to Air Traffic Control so she knew what it was like to be in a male-dominated work environment.

The waitress came up to the table and asked if the women were ready for another round of drinks. Eryn looked at her and thought she was cute but had a total look of boredom on her face. It was obvious she didn't appreciate the female customers as much as the male ones. They ordered their drinks and went back to talking. A few minutes later, a couple of guys walked in and stopped the conversation.

Emma's friend, Kim, stopped mid-sentence when she spotted the two men at the bar. "Yum," She said loudly.

Everyone's eyes followed the direction of Kim's. They were Marines for sure. You could tell by the way they carried themselves and, of course, their haircuts. Eryn had to admit, there was something about a Marine that made the ladies take notice. Even the women Marines seem to prefer them.

Another mental picture of Chase popped into her head and stopped Eryn's thoughts mid-stream. That was like the eighty-third time this evening and she was tired of him invading her mind. Mentally, she swept him aside and concentrated on the two men who grabbed the table's attention. After a few seconds, she thought they looked familiar. When she concentrated, she recognized them.

Oh crap! They worked at Crash Crew with her. Why couldn't she just get away from the men she worked with?

Frustration built up inside her and she couldn't take it. She knew the towns were small here but this was just getting depressing. When she scanned the faces of her group, she noticed the women were practically drooling over the two guys.

A few minutes later, Nina, one of girls in their group, got up and sauntered over to where the pair was sitting at the bar. Eryn watched her swagger toward the men with the traditional female "I'm available and interested" way. Could Nina possibly be any more blatant? Eryn doubted it.

They guys realized it too because Nina had their total and undivided attention once she walked up to them. Eryn could definitely see why; she was a tall, lanky blond with gorgeous features. She was the type of women men looked for in the magazines and commercials.

Looking around the booth, Eryn started to feel a little inadequate. Before, she never thought it did any good to compare yourself to other women; it was a waste of time hoping you looked different than how God made you. But, here she was, doing it anyway and feeling like she came up a little short. She couldn't flirt like Nina. She watched her new friend with the guys and was in awe. Nina was actually flipping her hair! Eryn thought that only happened in the movies and always thought it was fake before tonight. Of course, the guys didn't seem to mind one bit.

Emma nudged her again, "She's a pro."

Eryn nodded, "Yep," and took a drink of her wine. She hoped the alcohol would help her feel a little less.......less.

The group watched as Nina did her magic and started making noises when it was clear she invited the guys over to join their group. Eryn hunched over her drink in an effort to look disinterested.

Nina smiled as they came up to the table, "Ladies," she winked, "this is Lance Corporal Edwards and Corporal Gracen."

Eryn thought these two guys were pretty nice and she started hoping they didn't recognize her.

"Or," Nina purred, "Bryan and Joe." She giggled and touched the men's arms.

The ladies gave a collective, "Hi."

The guys sat down at the booth between Nina and Kim so Eryn hoped they wouldn't recognize her.

Kim made the introductions, "Gentlemen, this is Emma, Eryn, Jessie, Laura," she smiled sweetly, "you've met Nina and I'm Kim."

Oh Lord, Eryn thought. Nina's voice was too sweet. Eryn ducked her head lower when she noticed Lance Corporal Edwards look at her like he knew her but couldn't place her face.

The men ordered another round of drinks for the ladies then asked Kim and Nina to dance. Once they were out on the dance floor, Eryn let out a sigh.

"Hey," Emma said, "what's up?"

Eryn felt foolish for being so paranoid, "I work with those guys at Crash Crew."

Emma nodded and smiled, "Afraid of the teasing, eh?" She looked at Eryn sympathetically.

Smiling back, Eryn answered, "Yep."

Eryn excused herself and went to the restroom. She was in there twenty minutes later when Emma came in.

"I thought maybe you'd drowned in the toilet or were trying to escape out the window in here," Emma said sarcastically.

Even though Eryn knew Emma was teasing her, they both knew there was some bit of truth to the trying to escape part. Eryn was grateful that her friend wasn't criticizing her for her cowardice reaction.

A Marine to Remember

"I'm sorry," Eryn said. "There is so much going on with work right now and I just didn't need the added pressure of this."

Eryn tried to freshen up her makeup, obviously trying to delay going back out to the table. The alcohol and her turbulent feelings regarding Chase were making it near impossible to think straight.

Emma came up beside her and looked at Eryn's eyes in the mirror's reflection.

"What's really wrong?" she asked Eryn. There was something more than a little ribbing at work bothering her friend.

Pasting a smile on her face, she looked into her friend's eyes in the mirror, "Nothing I can't handle."

The women both knew Eryn was lying but they were good enough friends to let it slide....for now.

Needing to say something Eryn cleared her throat, "I have some stuff to square away at work and my father is planning one of his visits in a couple of weeks." She hoped Emma wouldn't pry any more than that. Emma was one of the few people who knew who her father was.

"I get it," Emma said and placed her hand on Eryn's shoulder. She squeezed it quickly.

Eryn went back to pretending to check her makeup, "I just have to toughen up a little."

Emma laughed and said, "Stand tall, Marine." She winked and walked out of the restroom, leaving Eryn alone.

A few minutes later, Eryn went back out to their table. Unfortunately the guys were back at the booth and seemed to be having a good time with the female attention they were getting. Having four good looking women hang on your every word was probably pretty good, and she had to admit that they were cute.

Bryan and Joe stood when Eryn came up to the table. The Marine Corps drilled the manners into the young men and women who joined their ranks and Eryn appreciated it. She smiled her thanks and looked away as much as possible in an effort to avoid the guys recognizing her.

Another hour passed and everyone was laughing. They had a couple more rounds of drinks by then and nobody was feeling any pain. Eryn felt just this side of drunk and was relaxing. She liked this, not caring. Everything felt funny and she was tingling all over. She managed to tell a joke that made everyone laugh when Bryan stopped and stared at her very closely.

"Do I know you, Eryn?" Bryan asked.

Eryn's stomach knotted. Everyone was looking at her so she couldn't very well lie. "Yes, LCpl. Edwards," she smiled sweetly, "you do know me." She was being very brave or very stupid right now.

Bryan looked at Joe then back at Eryn. "Sgt. Fredricks?" He asked with a totally blown away look on his face.

Cpl. Gracen did a double-take too and looked at Eryn wide-eyed.

Eryn felt sorry for their discomfort but she was also a little mad that they seemed so shocked by her dressed-up appearance. Did she look that bad at work?

"It's okay, guys," Eryn said brightly, "you guys are out having some fun and the ladies here sure do appreciate it."

She was the highest ranking non-commissioned officer so she would be the one to set the tone in the social setting. She didn't have any interest in teasing them or ruining their good time. She grabbed Emma's hand.

"I'm going out to the dance floor to dance with my friend here and give you guys some time with the other ladies," she jerked her head toward Emma letting her know they had to move.

She and Emma walked out to the dance floor and started dancing to an eighties song they couldn't remember the words to. A few minutes later, Laura and Jessie came out to join them. Everyone admitted that the guys were really only interested in Nina and Kim so the rest of them would just be scarce.

After dancing for a while, the women decided they wanted to go to another club with a bigger crowd. The two couples were still at the booth when they went back to get their things.

Laura asked Nina and Kim, "Are you guys coming?"

Being the designated driver, Laura quit drinking alcohol after the first round and stuck with soda. She was the one who needed to make sure everyone was accounted for and had a ride home.

Kim and Nina looked at each other and then the guys, "I think we'll stay," Nina said.

Eryn laughed because she looked like she was going to pounce on poor Joe like a cat.

Joe spoke up, "We'll make sure they get back home okay if they don't catch up with you." He smiled at Bryan and then looked over at Eryn and said, "I haven't been drinking so they'll be fine."

Eryn was proud of her fellow Crash Crewmen. She nodded to Joe to let him know she appreciated his being responsible.

"Have fun," Eryn said and left with the other ladies.

The foursome walked a couple of blocks and found a club called Blaine's. It was definitely full and looked a little wild compared to where they just were.

Once they went in, Eryn could see why it was popular. This was the place to go if you were young and single. The music was a mix of techno dance with the base so loud, it reverberated through your body. There were neon lights in a variety of colors blinking and moving around the place. Everyone here was here to have fun.

After a few minutes, they found a table that a couple were vacating. Jessie went up to the bar and came back with a tray of shots. Eryn eyed the glass and wondered if she should try it. She never tried hard liquor before, instead she always stuck to wine. Well, the wine she drank at the other club loosened her up so she smiled at the group and lifted up the shot glass with the three other ladies.

"What shall we drink to ladies?" Eryn asked the group.

Laura, the only one who didn't have a shot, raised up her glass of soda, "How about men, music, and good friends?"

Everyone nodded, smiled, and drank. The fluid was sweet and went down very easily. They made another quick toast and downed the second shot right away. Within minutes they were out on the dance floor and acting wild.

There was no shortage of guys around when they were dancing. Every few songs, the group would go back to the table for another round. Dancing helped them sweat out some of the alcohol but not nearly enough.

With the shots in her system, Eryn was a wild woman on the dance floor. She didn't feel anything so let her body move how it wanted to the music. Her dance partners came and went and she didn't notice them.

The group stayed close so there wasn't much of a chance for everyone to dance to intimately. She noticed a few guys wearing interested looks and that reinforced her good mood. It was nice to know she was attractive to more than one person.

Why would she tie herself down to one man when there were plenty of them around to look at her like this? She didn't have to have a man dictate to her.

On the way back to the table for another round, she was trying to figure out who she was talking about; her father, her Crash Chief, or Chase? Her thoughts were not easy ones and she easily cast them out thanks to the alcohol. She just wanted to enjoy her time with her friends.

Emma came over to the table with another round of shots and looked at Eryn, a silly grin on her face.

"Are you okay?" she asked Eryn, who was having trouble sitting up straight.

"Yep," Eryn said a little too quickly. "Does drinking always make you think such crazy thoughts?"

The question made Emma laugh some more, "Oh yeah."

Eryn was relieved she wasn't the only one who felt so funny from the drinks. Laura and Jessie met them at the table and Eryn could see that Jessie was having trouble walking straight. They were laughing and teasing one another when Laura announced that they had to get going. Jessie, Eryn, and Emma started grumbling and whining and saying they didn't need to go yet.

It took a lot longer to get back to the SUV then it did to get to the clubs. Eryn was laughing at everything. The fact that she and Emma were stumbling every couple of steps didn't help. It was so funny that they all needed to lean on one another to get down the street.

Laura was leading the way and turned to the other three, "At least two of us were able to find some guys."

With her mind so fuzzy, Eryn couldn't think straight and blurted out, "Oh, I'm not looking for a guy cuz I found one already."

The group stopped at the exclamation.

Emma stared at her friend, "I knew it!" She laughed and pointed a finger at Eryn, "You are way too screwed up for this to be anything but a man."

Nodding, Laura piped up, "Why didn't you say anything?"

Concentrating on walking straight took Eryn's mind away from answering. Finally she was steady enough to respond, "Nothin to say," her tongue tripped over the words. "We work together so that's off limits and he's enlisted so my father will NEVER approve."

She found it odd that she needed to get drunk in order to say what was really bugging her.

The three women stopped again, "Oh geez," Emma said loudly, "you are screwed!"

Laura and Jessie laughed and Eryn peered at her friend through slitted eyes.

"I am not," she finally slurred, "I just have to tell them all to go to hell!"

The group rallied, "Yeah," they yelled, "tell them to go to hell!"

Emma leaned against her friend, "It's not that bad, just tell the guy how you feel and your dad to just deal with it!"

Eryn smiled at her friends. She knew Emma was the one who never flinched at bucking the system and told it like it was so she felt better.

Snorting, Eryn turned to Emma and said, "You're right."

"Of curse I am," Emma slurred her words slightly and poured herself into the vehicle.

It took about ten minutes for Laura to get the drunk women into the SUV, buckled in, and on the road back to the base. They giggled during the ride, trying to one-up each other with exaggerated stories. Laura laughed and reminded them that she would remember this when they were sober.

Once the group dropped Eryn off at the barracks, she stood outside and waved to them until they got around the block. She made it upstairs and into her room without too much difficulty and was surprised that she wasn't the least bit tired. She sat on the edge of her bed and thought about Chase. Without realizing it, she picked up the phone and dialed a local number.

Chapter 8

Chase was lying in his bed, wide awake, and listening to the sound of the breeze blow through the trees outside his bedroom window. He could hear the ocean in the distance and wondered why the sounds didn't calm him tonight as they usually did.

Of course, that was before Eryn. Now that she was in his mind, he couldn't get her to leave.

After the disastrous meeting with Gunny Frinnel yesterday, he came home fuming.

He was mad at Eryn for knowing that Ben guy. He was mad at Eryn's father for making her question herself. He was really mad at himself for not saying anything and being so crazy about her that he couldn't think straight.

When he got home earlier, he ate dinner, took Ed for a walk, and did some stuff around the house in an attempt to keep her out of his brain.

Nothing helped so at about seven he called her room. When he got no answer, he hung up. He didn't want to leave a message, what would he say anyway? He tried to call her every hour until eleven then he decided to go to bed and try to get some sleep. Now, he was tossing and turning, and punching his pillow.

Ed looked up from his designated spot on the floor and made a little whining noise.

"It's okay," Chase said to the dog, "we're going to sleep."

He reached down and scratched Ed's ears a few times then laid back down. It was going to be a long night.

The cab pulled up to the end of Chase's driveway and Eryn sat there looking out the window. She was wringing her hands in her lap and feeling really unsure about this.

What was she thinking, coming out here at this hour? It was crazy! Of course it sounded perfectly logical when she was sitting in her barracks room a half hour ago. She wanted to see Chase and find out just where they stood. The situation was only going to get worse if her father found out or if another co-worker found out so they had to come up with a plan. Calling him just didn't seem right; she needed to see his face.

The cab driver cleared his throat, "Is this the right place, ma'am?" he asked his passenger. She was a pretty girl who'd obviously been drinking.

Eryn smiled at his face in the rearview mirror, "Um, yes," she handed him some bills and started to climb out of the cab. She was only a little steadier than when the girls dropped her off at the barracks earlier.

A Marine to Remember

The cab driver rolled down his window when she was out of the car, "Did you want me to wait, miss?"

Eryn smiled and shook her head no. He was sweet. She turned as the cab started down the road.

This sure did seem easier when she was coming up with the idea. She tried to walk straight down the driveway and it was very rough going. She needed to ask him about possibly paving it. The gravel was a killer with heels and under the influence of alcohol. She laughed at her own thoughts.

"Shhh," Eryn said aloud to herself.

When she was about ten feet from the front door she tried to judge the best point of entry into the house. Ringing the doorbell or knocking didn't seem like a good option. She was going to surprise Chase so she needed to be very stealth-like.

Apparently, Eryn didn't take into account the effect that eight shots and four glasses of wine would have on her stealth-like abilities.

It didn't help that she kept laughing at her sad attempts to be quiet. She rounded the house and saw an open window that looked easy to get into.

Rolling her shoulders, Eryn went up to the window and tried to put her head in, only stopping when her face came into full contact with the metal, mesh screen. Her face burned from pushing against the rough material.

Okay, she said to herself, think.

Stepping back, Eryn eyed up the screen. It seemed easy enough to pull out. After a few minutes of not being able to figure out the stupid thing, she just put her hand through the screen and pulled. Grabbing the frame, she tossed it aside into the yard. There, that was easy. She looked inside and thought this was probably the living room. Good.

The plan was to get into the house without Chase hearing her, sneak into his bedroom, and seduce him while he slept.

Well, she hoped he wouldn't sleep through the whole thing, just long enough for her to get into his room. She stopped when she heard a noise inside. She ducked down in case it was Chase.

She listened and thought it didn't sound like Chase, she heard a clicking noise then she heard some heavy breathing above her head.

When Eryn peeked back into the window, she came face to face with a dog. Chase's dog, she supposed.

"Hello there," she whispered loudly.

A Marine to Remember

The dog just stood there and stared at her. His tail was wagging so Eryn took that as a good sign. He apparently didn't see her as a threat which was good.

She figured he wasn't going to maul her so she proceeded to find something to put her foot on to help her get into the house. She got her footing and watched the dog, who just watched her. For a moment, she wondered if he was just luring her inside and then he would try to bite her. When he started licking the hand she had inside the window sill, Eryn took that as an invite.

"Don't mind if I do," she mumbled and smiled at her new furry friend.

Her foot slipped so she figured she'd have to just jump in. She hiked up her skirt and did a hop to get some leverage with her upper body. She was shimmying in through the window when the dog decided he would start licking her face. It tickled so she started giggling.

Trying to shoo him away, Eryn whispered, "We have to be quiet."

She had one foot through the window when she felt something grab her by the arms and pull her the rest of the way through the window. She landed on her butt with a thud, the room spinning around her head.

Chase was in bed dreaming of Eryn. They were walking down the beach, hand-in-hand. He could feel her hair brush against his skin as it blew in the ocean breeze. She was everywhere. He was so happy; a kid without a care in the world. The sand was warm and inviting as they walked along. The sun was bright and cast a warm glow onto everything around them.

He didn't want to wake up from the dream but something jolted him awake. His training put him into immediate full alert. How long was he sleeping? He looked at the clock and saw it was only a little past one in the morning. Ed was gone from the room so Chase figured he'd bumped into something. The dog was not very graceful.

He was about to lay back down when he thought he heard giggling. Who the hell would be in his house giggling in the middle of the night? He got up and quickly pulled on a pair of gym shorts, all the while listening.

He walked into the living room and saw Ed sitting in front of the window. The dog seemed to be waiting. It took a second for Chase's eyes to adjust to the room's darkness and, when he did, he noticed two hands and a boot coming through the window.

His brow furrowed, Chase moved toward Ed and the person trying to get in. Either this was a very snazzy burglar or it was someone who wasn't very bright. He glared at his dog, saying, I'll talk to you later about your guard dog skills. This was ridiculous! He grabbed the person and pulled.

A bundle of leather and long hair fell onto the floor in a heap. Chase reached over and turned on the nearest light. By the time he turned around, the intruder was standing up and pushing hair out of her face. It was Eryn.....what the hell?

"Eryn?" Chase asked, feeling silly.

Eryn stood in his living room and stared at Chase. Once she got a good look at him, all coherent thought flew out of her head.

He was standing there with nothing on but workout shorts. The short kind that showed off how long and lean his legs were. They also hung low enough that she could see his belly button and the hair that trailed down beneath it. He wasn't wearing a shirt so she saw his exposed abs. She looked him up and down and noticed he actually had a six pack!

Her eyes started traveling upward and noticed his broad chest with just a dusting of hair. His bare arms were perfectly formed. She wished those arms would wrap around her right now and kiss her. She was full of need and want and he just looked really pissed off.

Ed sensed that this wasn't going well and walked over to Eryn. He nudged her hand with his head, prompting her to pet him. Eryn obliged and smiled. At least the dog wasn't upset about her being here.

"Hey," she muttered to Chase.

Chase looked at Eryn with an equal amount of irritation and confusion. Did the woman not use front doors? She was studying him and he was looking at her and nobody was saying anything. Well, her eyes were saying something and they were making his body take notice. Okay, he had to think of something else besides the look of wanting in her eyes or he'd drag her to his bed and try to find out what all of her secrets were.

Eryn couldn't speak; she didn't know what to say. She just kept petting his dog.

"Eryn," Chase was trying to remain calm, "what are you doing sneaking into my house in the middle of the night?" He thought it was a logical question. She didn't answer and he was getting more annoyed, "Why are you here?" he asked again. Her not replying was making him mad. She started to weave a little and he looked closer, "Are you drunk?"

Eryn knew it was no good to lie, "Yep." She answered and smiled brightly. "I came over here to try to surprise you and sneak into your bedroom and seduce you."

A Marine to Remember

Okay, now he was in trouble.

Her admission did nothing to help quell his lusty thoughts. She was vulnerable and drunk and he wanted her so badly that he was in pain.

This was one of those times when he kind of resented being raised to be a gentleman. A beautiful woman admits she wanted to seduce him….a saint would be tested and Chase was most definitely no saint. He had no choice but to take her back to the barracks and hope the hang-over she was going to have tomorrow would be enough of a lesson.

"Well," Chase shook his head, "let me change and I'll get you back to your room."

He turned to go to his room when he felt her hand on his arm. Her touch sent a shock wave up his arm and landed right in his groin.

When her touch stopped Chase, Eryn took it as a sign he didn't really want to take her back to her barracks room. She circled him and wound her arms around his neck. Stepping closer, she rubbed her body against his and loved the way his eyes darkened.

The blood was draining from his extremities and Chase didn't care. Her leather skirt brushed up against his thighs and her perfume smelled intoxicating.

Eryn wasn't going to let this time with him pass her by. She wanted him so much and didn't really care about the consequences. He was pulling away and she wouldn't let him. Her desire controlled her actions and, combined with the alcohol, gave her the boost of confidence she needed to continue her seduction.

"Chase," Eryn murmured into his ear, "I want you so much."

She pulled back enough to see the reaction of her words on him.

"I've wanted you since we first went to dinner, the first time you kissed me." She spoke up before she lost her nerve, "I think about us naked and making love in your bed." She almost purred, "It will be soooo good, Chase."

Chase was fighting his desire and thought maybe he shouldn't. To her way of thinking, this was the best time to let go. He looked at her, wanted her, but knew he shouldn't.

"Listen," Eryn said, "I don't want to play games here because I'm no good at them and I'm too drunk to care." She smiled when he smiled. "I just want to be with you in every sense of the word." That was the plain and simple truth for Eryn.

Hearing Eryn say the words was like throwing gasoline onto an already raging fire. He couldn't remember a woman ever speaking so openly about wanting him. It made him feel sexy but he also wanted to keep Eryn safe. He couldn't take advantage of her like this. The thoughts warred inside his head. She wanted him and he sure wanted her so what was the problem? The problem was, he cared about Eryn.

His internal struggle ended his thoughts. He wouldn't stop wanting her but making love tonight would be a bad idea with her being so drunk. He wouldn't have either of them living with regrets.

When they finally made love, and they would, it would be with their minds and bodies. He agreed with Eryn, it would be so good. He took a breath and reluctantly pulled Eryn's hands from around his neck.

"Baby," he whispered, "I'm going to take you home now."

He talked to her like she was a child. The look of rejection crossed her face and he hated that he put it there but she would thank him later.

Eryn was devastated. He was turning her down. She broke into his house and wanted him so badly and he was saying no. He wanted to take her home....NO WAY!

Chase could see her thoughts and knew she was up to something. Before he could step back, she lifted her lips and kissed him. This was not like other kisses, this one was demanding. She was demanding he keep up with her. Her tongue ran across his lower lip, enticing him to open up and kiss her fully.

They stood in his living room, Chase holding her so close, his hands running up and down her back. Her hands on his head, holding him to her so she could get closer. The only sounds were of their ragged breath.

His lungs burning from lack of oxygen, Chase finally stepped back. Whoa, she could pack a punch. He couldn't say anything and watched Eryn stand there, the look of want filling her features.

Finally, Chase turned and walked back to his room quickly. He wanted to get his urges under control. Ed followed him with his tail wagging. He gave the dog a nasty look and Ed just tipped his head as if he were asking, "What did I do?" Chase shook his head in exasperation.

"You know what you did," he said in hushed tones to the dog, "I'd like to be mad at you but this whole thing has just been too weird."

Ed gave him a look and yawned. Obviously not wanting to be around Chase, the dog sauntered out of the room. Now Chase laughed. Maybe the mutt knew something he didn't. He pulled on a t-shirt, jogging pants, and shoes. When he came back out to the living room, Eryn was sprawled out on his couch. She looked very determined and Chase's mouth went dry.

"Chase," Eryn said softly and crooked her finger toward him, "come here."

She was tenacious and Chase was feeling a little unsure about his decision right now. He had every intention of helping her up but when he went to take her hand to help her up, she threw him off balance.

He ended up practically on top of her. Rolling his eyes, he tried not to think about how good it felt and how right it felt to be here with her like this. Somebody sure had a funny sense of humor to keep putting him in these situations with Eryn. Her arms were wrapped around his neck again and she was kissing his neck. Their bodies were tangled and he wondered how it happened.

Eryn was smiling wickedly, "I've got you right where I want you now." Her words slurred a little bit but she looked smug.

Chase couldn't help but smile. "I guess you do," he said.

He looked down at her and was having trouble breathing. Their bodies were pressed together, his leg between hers. It was too much, he had to kiss her one more time and then he would take her home.

Once their lips were melded, he realized he was in way over his head. One kiss would not be enough; it only made him ache more for her. He tried to gentle the kiss and ease away but Eryn wasn't having any of it.

Eryn assaulted his lips and he could only go along for the ride. It was a wild ride too. She ran her hands down his sides, wishing his clothes were gone so she could feel his body. Her tongue would be gentle then would be wild inside his mouth, begging him to make her feel more. She knew she gave him no choice but to oblige her insistent kisses. That's just what she wanted.

Their tongues met and Chase was knocked back with another wave of desire. It was like having an explosion in your gut. There was something else there too that he couldn't define. It was like a calmness deep in his chest. The contradiction threw his mind into a whirlwind of confusion.

Eryn wanted more, more of Chase, more of them together. She maneuvered her body so she turned them over with her on top of him. She pulled up her skirt and straddled him on the couch.

How the hell did she get them turned around? He lay on the sofa, looking up into her beautiful eyes. Her palms were resting on his chest, her fingers moving over his t-shirt. Was there any woman as beautiful as Eryn? The woman was drunk and broke into his house and here she was, trying to seduce him. And here he was, letting her.

A Marine to Remember

Her eyes were so sure. He looked up at her again and was about to change his mind about taking her home when she collapsed on top of him.

"Eryn?" Chase asked, shaking her lightly.

He got worried when she didn't respond. He could feel her breathing so she was okay.

"Eryn?" he asked again and rubbed her arms to try and wake her.

When he heard Eryn start to snore, he laughed. This was about par for the course in their relationship. She actually passed out on him!

A while later, Chase stood in his living room and watched Eryn. He loved her. He knew it before now and he just didn't want to admit it.   He watched her sleeping and knew he had two choices here. He could let her sleep it off on the couch or he could take her back to the barracks.

If she stayed, they ran the risk of doing something they both wanted to but didn't need right now to complicate an already explosive situation. Plus, she'd be feeling pretty bad in the morning and she didn't need him around her then. Although it was funny to think about, he decided he wouldn't be a cad.

Chase looked over to see Ed lying next to the couch, and Eryn.

"Coward," Chase hissed at the dog and went out pull the jeep up in front of the house.

The ride back to the barracks gave Chase some time to think. He could honestly say he never met anyone like her. Plus, the sheer oddness of what they shared up to now astounded him. But all the craziness and being unsure didn't seem to matter to his heart. Despite the complications, he wanted to be with her.

He looked over to see Eryn slumped against the door of the jeep. There was a little trickle of drool coming out of the side of her mouth and he was pretty sure the position she was sitting in was not a comfortable one. He laughed outright, knowing that she would be totally pissed if she remembered this evening.

They got through the gate and to the barracks with no problems. She was still out when he pulled up to her barracks and he didn't think she would come to. So, he did what was necessary and threw her over his shoulder.

It was slow going, but he managed to get her upstairs and into her room without making too much noise. He didn't see anybody so he hoped no one saw them. Once inside, Chase carried her over and gently laid her down onto her bed. She didn't even budge.

Not knowing if he should help her change or leave her as she was, Chase looked around the room.

It was like any other barracks room; except it was Eryn's.

There were a few personal items but not a lot. A trinket box was on the dresser and a couple of pictures. Her room definitely wasn't cluttered. Not that he thought it would be, Eryn was always neat at work so he figured she would be here too. Once he saw the picture on the nightstand next to her bed, he picked it up.

Eryn was standing there with an almost identical version of herself, her sister he assumed, and they were flanked by who he thought were her parents. Her mother was very pretty; he could see that Eryn and her sister inherited her looks. His eyes fell onto the man who he assumed was Eryn's father. So this was the infamous Colonel? He looked imposing.

He looked at the picture a few more minutes and thought that the man seemed to be staking his claim on the women even in a photograph. Maybe he was being paranoid but he knew Eryn's father wasn't going to like him.

Chase looked at his watch and figured he better get going before someone saw him or recognized his jeep. He ran his fingers along Eryn's jaw, loving the softness of her skin. She moved into his touch and that made him smile. She looked so peaceful. He kissed her forehead and left.

Chapter 9

Eryn woke up to loud ringing in her ears that wouldn't stop.

"STOP!" She yelled and was rewarded with a pounding in her head.

She cracked one eye open and could see it was daylight and way too bright in her room. How did she get home and in her own bed? Trying to sit up, she felt dizzy and laid back down. She put a hand to her forehead and tried to remember the night before.

Emma and her friends picked her up, they went out, got drunk, and she came back to her room. Then……she had to think hard and that hurt her head. The memories came back slowly, the cobwebs of a hangover hanging heavy in her brain. Once she did remember though, she turned bright red.

She remembered Chase's house, breaking in, his dog, seducing Chase. What else happened? Oh no, oh no, she kept saying in her head. What did she do exactly? Her whole body was red with embarrassment. How was she going to face Chase now? What did they do? What kind of woman got so drunk she couldn't remember? The questions came fast but she couldn't answer them because the phone started ringing.

She grabbed the phone and mumbled a raspy, "Hello," into the receiver.

"Eryn?" Tom Fredricks asked. It didn't sound like his daughter.

Eryn bolted upright which made her head spin and her stomach pitch. She didn't need to talk to her dad in her current state.

Tom repeated the question, "Eryn?"

She knew she had to answer, "Yes, Dad, I'm sorry; I'm not feeling that well this morning." She tried to sound convincing and it was the truth to some extent.

Without acknowledging her explanation, he started in. "I've been trying to reach you all morning."

Eryn's feathers were getting pretty ruffled, "As I said, I'm not feeling very well."

Tom said, "Oh," as if he just heard her for the first time, "I was hoping to have lunch with you."

Why was he saying that? "Yes, we'll have lunch when you get here in a few weeks."

Clearing his throat, Tom frowned, "I'm here now and I'd like you to meet me for lunch today."

The adrenaline sped through Eryn's body. He was here? Oh crap! What happened to him being delayed?

Desperately trying not to sound as petrified as she was, she said, "I thought you weren't coming for another couple of weeks." Really smooth, Eryn. She admonished herself.

"The command straightened out the snags and I was able to come up now." He was becoming impatient. "These things happen, Eryn." He looked at his watch, "Do you want to have lunch with me?" He shouldn't have to ask the question twice.

Eryn was afraid of upsetting him but she couldn't lie, "Not really, Dad, I don't feel good at all." It wasn't a lie, she wanted to throw up so badly. "Could we make it dinner?"

He didn't answer right away so Eryn started feeling really self-conscious. She could literally hear the gears in his mind turning over the phone line.

"I am supposed to be having dinner with Ben and Colleen so you may join us if you like," Tom said sharply.

He was sure his friends wouldn't mind; they loved Eryn, but he hoped to have some time alone with his daughter.

The finality in his tone put Eryn squarely in her place. She tried to sound upbeat, "I'd love to."

Tom thought something wasn't right with his daughter, "Eryn, is everything alright?" he asked.

A Marine to Remember

The correct answer to the question would have been "Hell No," but Eryn was pretty sure she didn't want to dive into that particular conversation with her father. There were so many things unresolved between her and Chase and last night's events only made it all worse.

She had to lie, for now, so she murmured, "Yes, I'm just tired."

Tom gave Eryn the name of the restaurant they were to meet at and asked if she wanted him to pick her up. She declined and he wasn't surprised. She didn't want her officer father picking her up at her enlisted barracks. He may not agree with it, but he understood her point.

Eryn hung up the phone and could breathe normally again. It took her a few minutes to get the energy together to get out of bed. She was pretty sure there were little men hammering something inside her head and she must've swallowed a bag of cotton balls at some point. She got her stomach to calm down enough to get up and cross the room.

Grabbing a towel, she went into the bathroom at a snail's pace. Two barracks room shared one bathroom so it could be tricky to get in but, thankfully, no one was around this morning.

After a nice, long shower, Eryn felt semi-normal. A few aspirin and a glass of water later, she thought she was climbing toward almost okay.

The rest of the afternoon was spent getting ready for dinner and trying to get her head on straight. She knew her father had certain expectations when it came to appearances and being prompt.

When she was ready for dinner, she looked at herself in the mirror and sighed. The difference between the reflection last night and tonight was phenomenal. Tonight she piled her hair up on her head in a sophisticated twist. Her make-up was light and her outfit, which consisted of a simple skirt and white blouse, gave her a much more conservative look. Sighing, she grabbed her bag and left.

Eryn pulled up in front of the restaurant in New Bern a while later and sat in her car. It was an upscale place; not surprising given her father's preference. He always liked to eat here when he was at Cherry Point. She got out of the car and was glad the restaurant offered a variety of dishes since she didn't think she could stomach seafood right now.

When she walked in, she thought of how much the place reminded her of the restaurant Chase took her to.

Enough! She chastised herself. There was no way she could get through this dinner with her dad if she was thinking about Chase. Her stomach growled as if to say, you're here to eat.

She found her dad sitting at the bar that was off to the right of the entrance. He was nursing a drink. Eryn walked over and gave him a kiss on the cheek.

"Hi, Dad," She said as she slid onto the seat next to his.

Tom smiled and replied, "Hi yourself." His daughter looked like his wife, whom he adored, "You look lovely."

Eryn looked around, "Are Aunt Colleen and Uncle Ben here yet?" she asked, hoping that they would be a buffer between her father and her.

"Actually," Tom smiled but it didn't quite reach his eyes, "they decided to cancel. I guess Colleen isn't feeling to well." He looked thoughtful for a moment and said, "Although she sounded just fine when I spoke to her this morning."

Eryn wasn't sure if she was upset with Ben and Colleen for begging off or relieved. They would be a cushion but, then again, if the conversation somehow steered toward her personal life, she knew Ben wouldn't lie. She wouldn't expect him to either.

Eryn looked around, trying to get her mind off of it, "Is our table ready?" she asked. Her stomach was really growling now.

Tom put a tip down on the bar for the bartender and grabbed his glass, "Yes," he responded and motioned to the hostess.

They were seated right away and given menus.

Once they were settled at the table, Tom turned to his daughter, "Are you having a cocktail this evening?" he asked.

The thought of drinking alcohol made Eryn's stomach roll. "No," she said quickly.

Tom laughed, which made his daughter look at him with a surprised expression. "Hangovers will do that to you, you know." He laughed again when her eyes went wide and her mouth dropped open. "I was young once," he said.

He wanted her to know he could relate but he wanted her to know it was serious.

"I just don't want you to make a habit out of it." His fatherly tone was severe as he spoke.

There it was, Eryn thought, the lecture. Why did their conversations always have to take this turn? She would feel like they were so close to regaining their balance and he'd turn on her. It made him seem so perfect and her so imperfect. The disappointment felt like a brick in her stomach.

A Marine to Remember

Eryn took a breath, "I know." She tried to mask the defensive tone but it was too late.

Nodding, Tom tried to smile, "I'm only trying to help, Eryn."

Eryn couldn't stand what she felt like was a patronizing tone. "Dad," she couldn't hide the resentment from her voice, "why can't we just go ten minutes without you lecturing me or making me feel like you're lecturing me?" The question surprised her and, apparently, her dad too.

Tom looked down at his menu, not seeing anything on it, and looked back up to his daughter, "I apologize, Eryn," he put his hand on hers, "it's just that I've seen Marines abuse alcohol and ruin their chances for advancement."

She sat there in astonishment. The man didn't even realize he was lecturing her while he was apologizing for lecturing her! Setting her shoulders, Eryn looked directly at her father.

"I know about that, Dad," she snapped and took a deep breath, "I just don't understand, for the life of me, how YOU, my father, don't think I know that." She tried not to cry when he only stared at her. "I'm an adult."

His temper rising, Tom shook his head. Couldn't his daughter understand that no matter how old she was, she was still his daughter? It was a parent's natural tendency to protect. Why did children never acknowledge that?

"I know that, Eryn," He didn't want them to argue. "I am just trying to help you avoid making mistakes."

Eryn looked up at the ceiling, then back at her dad.

She tried to gain her composure before answering, "That's the funny thing, Dad, no matter what you say or do, I'm going to make some mistakes." He opened his mouth to respond but she put her hand up to stop him, "Learning from my mistakes is what I need to do."

The server came over just then and they stopped talking. They placed their orders and gave their menus to the young woman, who smiled and left.

Watching her father's set jaw, Eryn knew the conversation was over.

After a tense dinner, Eryn was relieved when she got back to her barracks room. She threw her purse on the desk and plopped down in a chair. Kicking off her shoes, she absently rubbed her feet while she stared into space.

The dinner replayed in her mind and she was disappointed. After her outburst, her dad refused to speak of anything except neutral subjects and, by the end of the meal, Eryn was ready to scream.

Her father's inability to see her as an adult continued to frustrate her. Letting out a breath, she told herself there were some people who could not change, no matter what you did.

She stood up to change out of her outfit when she noticed the answering machine light blinking. She pressed the play button and started unzipping her skirt. The first message was from Emma. She was asking if Eryn survived the previous night's antics. The fact that Emma sounded pretty hung over made Eryn smile. It was good to know that others suffered as well. The second message was from Uncle Ben.

"Eryn," He said, "I wanted to speak to before you went to dinner. I don't think he knows about your young man but he suspects something."

Eryn couldn't deny that Uncle Ben sounded a little bit worried. That brought a little clarification to the conversation at dinner. A couple of times her father asked her about dating.

The last message was from Chase.

"Eryn," He said slowly. "I just called to see if you were okay today since you were pretty out of it last night."

She could hear the smile in his face and shook her head.

"I was a perfect gentleman although it was pretty tough, given your insistence on throwing yourself at me." He laughed, "I hope you'll give me a call tonight."

Eryn finished changing, preferring to give herself a few minutes to figure out how not to be embarrassed by her behavior with him last night. She still wasn't sure exactly what did happen and that made her a little afraid to talk to him. Did she ask or did she just shut up and hope he explained? Face the music, Eryn, she told herself and dialed his number.

Chase was sitting on the porch when he heard the phone ring. He made it inside and picked up on the second ring.

"Hello," he said expectantly.

The only person he wanted to talk to was Eryn.

What did she say? She closed her eyes, "Hi, it's Eryn." Oh that was slick.

Relieved it was her, Chase smiled like a kid on Christmas morning. "How are you feeling tonight?" He wasn't sure what she would remember, if anything.

A Marine to Remember

"I'm okay," Eryn said breathlessly. She loved the sound of his voice.

Even through the phone, the woman tied him up in knots. His body responded to her so easily. "I didn't know how you felt and I wanted to check up on you."

He wanted to talk to her about other things but didn't know how to start. He ended up tripping up and sounding stupid.

"What were you doing tonight?" He asked, thinking he really did sound stupid.

Eryn sighed, "I was having dinner with my father." She said it quickly.

Chase felt the tone of the conversation change as soon as she said "father." Her tone was pretty revealing too. Obviously it didn't go very well.

"And?" he asked, just wanting to get it done with.

She took a deep breath, "Well, we didn't have a heart-to-heart talk but he didn't pry so that was pretty good." She wouldn't give Chase the details until she knew them herself.

He was relieved, "That's great," he smiled, "one less thing for us to worry about right now."

She didn't want to take it personally but she couldn't help it, "Listen, my father is not a "thing" to be worried about." Her tone was definitely saying she wasn't happy.

"I'm sorry," Chase said, "I only meant that if he isn't on to the situation then we don't have to worry about him right now." He wasn't trying to sound as thoughtless as his words were. Not to mention, he suspected Eryn was upset and spoiling for a fight.

Hating the turn in the conversation, Eryn didn't say anything for a minute. She was so excited when she called him and now they were both uptight and leery of how to talk about her dad.

She knew she was to blame for being out of sorts from drinking and the stressed relationship with her dad. That was certainly not Chase's fault. But, her father was not going to go away and, if Chase thought differently, he was clearly mistaken.

Eryn knew what the repercussions were and would take them on if necessary. The thing she wasn't sure about was if Chase knew. She wanted to smooth things over with him.

"Ben called and said that Dad knew something was going on with me," she tried to sound less freaked out than she felt; "I know Ben didn't say anything to him."

Chase listened to what Eryn said and didn't know this Ben guy well enough to make a judgment on what he did or did not say.

She still wasn't sure if he believed her but she didn't care about that right now. "Chase, I'm coming over to your place to talk to you," she blurted out. She must be crazy or maybe a little drunk still because she never just invited herself to a man's house.

"I'm not sure that's a good idea." Chase said. He knew her silence meant she felt hurt and rejected, "Now, be careful how you take that," he rushed on, "I only meant that it's tough for me to keep my hands off of you and I think us, here alone, would be too great a temptation for me."

Well, Eryn thought, she didn't expect him to say that. Did he say she was irresistible? The admission aroused Eryn. "Really?" she asked, knowing it was a loaded question.

"Eryn," Chase's voice cracked, "don't do that."

It was fun to tease him. It was nice to know that she wasn't the only one going crazy. "Sorry," she said softly.

Yeah right, Chase thought. "I doubt that," he said laughing.

His laughter was contagious. "What do we do now?" she asked. She wanted to see him.

Chase looked at his watch, "How about the beach in fifteen minutes?"

Brilliant idea as far as Eryn was concerned, "Okay," she hung up the phone and ran around her room getting changed.

Eryn pulled into the parking lot and looked around. She didn't see Chase's jeep so she sat in her car and waited. Her heart was pounding and she thought it would jump right out of her chest when she saw him pull into the parking spot beside her car.

As soon as Eryn opened her car door, Chase was there to help her out. He swept her up into his arms and gave her a kiss on the lips. She felt so different as soon as his lips touched hers. It was like everything would be okay.

Chase lowered Eryn to the ground, trying not to embarrass himself with how much he wanted her.

Eryn was smiling up at Chase when she felt a nudge on her leg.

"Ed," she squealed, "my partner in crime." She laughed as he licked her hand.

Chase smiled, "So you remember that part I see."

"Yes," her eyes narrowed, "I remember trying to seduce you and then nothing. How did I get home?"

She was humiliated just asking the question. She wanted to know but was kind of afraid of what she did.

Chase didn't want her to feel bad, "Well," he paused for dramatic effect, "I drove you home after you practically attacked me." He laughed when she cringed, "I had to carry you up to your room."

Eryn's mouth was hanging open. Just the mental picture of that scenario made her want to curl up into a hole and hide.

"It wasn't easy either," he sighed, "have you put on some weight?"

She punched him in the arm. Even if it was teasing, it still made her feel ridiculous.

"That's not a very romantic thing to say you know," she snarled, but wasn't mad about his teasing.

Chase kissed her hand and murmured, "Well," He put his arms around her and held her, "I'm not exactly the wine and roses kind of guy."

She didn't agree, "I think you may be exactly that," she said and leaned up to kiss him again. "I would adore you any way you are."

Eryn locked her car and they turned to walk down to the beach. Ed was trailing happily behind them.

They were quiet while they walked down toward the water.

Eryn stopped and plopped down in the sand, pulling Chase down beside her.

The woman could definitely be assertive, Chase thought. He smiled at the look of frustration on her face because it aroused him.

"You don't want to walk down to the water?" he asked.

She was trying to get a handle on feelings here, she couldn't walk and do that at the same time. "Not now," she answered absently.

Ed was in front of them, sniffing around looking for who knew what. They watched him for a few minutes until the silence made the tension too much to bear.

Desperately trying to get a handle on her feelings, Eryn turned to Chase, "I know I used that word "adore" before and I don't want you to think I'm implying anything or expecting to put a label on our relationship or anything like that."

She didn't want Chase to see how embarrassed she was so she looked at their feet in the sand.

Even though he didn't exactly know what she was asking or expecting him to say, he smiled. "I was actually flattered."

Eryn's eyes lifted to meet his, "Really?" she asked.

It was so easy to please her, he thought. Another thing he found irresistible about her.

"Really," he answered softly. Would it always be so easy to get her to smile?

Eryn was happy he made it okay for her to be this restless and unglued.

Chase turned so his body was facing her, "I think we should have a talk," his tone serious as he spoke.

"Okay," Eryn said in a deadpan voice.

Smiling, Chase tipped her chin up with his hand, "It's not a bad thing, you don't have to be worried."

Well, Eryn thought, he could say that but it didn't stop her. "I'm not worried," she said defensively and they both knew she was lying.

Lifting her hand to his lips, Chase kissed the back of it softly, "Yes you are," he whispered against her skin.

Eryn pulled her hand from his and almost whined, "I don't really want to talk, Chase."

She was fidgeting with the hem of her shirt in an effort to keep herself from jumping him or screaming like a lunatic in frustration.

Chase couldn't let her avoid this so he ducked his head so his face was in her line of sight, "It's not bad; I just think we need to make some decisions."

Her feelings plummeting, Eryn was getting scared. He was letting her down easy....oh great. This was the crap that happened when you opened up your heart! She couldn't hear it, wouldn't hear it, so she stood up and started running down the beach.

Sitting there, Chase was thrown by her reaction. He watched her run and wondered why she felt she needed to. Ed thought she was playing so took off after her.

He got up and started walking in the direction she'd run. What did he say to make her do that? He didn't know why, but Eryn was very confusing. Most women liked it when you "talked" but not Eryn; she took off running.

Figuring she had enough of a head start, Chase started running after her. She wasn't going to get very far because he had her car keys in his pocket.

Eryn's chest was on fire! She didn't know if it was from running or fear or both. Ed kept up with her and that upset her even more. She stopped and looked at the dog.

"Ed," she shouted, "Shoo!" It was hard to form the words when she was out of breath.

The dog didn't seem to care and definitely didn't listen. He just sat in front of her staring at her.

They were about a mile down the beach when Chase caught up to her. She was about to take off again when he yelled, "Eryn, stop!"

Eryn did as he demanded. She turned around to face him, tears streaming down her face. She didn't even know when they started.

"What's going on, Eryn?" Chase asked when he was closer. He was really confused.

He looked beautiful, standing there, looking at her. Why did life have to be so complicated? Why couldn't she keep a man?

She looked up in dismay, "I know you want me to leave you alone and you're trying to let me down easy."

Whoa, Chase thought, "What?" he asked, not knowing where that came from.

She hated having to explain. "You don't want to see me because of my father." She put her hands on her hips, "Or maybe because I was drunk and broke into your house, or tried to seduce you and then passed out," her chest heaved with emotion, "or that I went out to your house and yelled at you." She absently wiped the tears from her cheeks, "I am sorry about that, by the way." Now she was rambling and couldn't stop. "Or because I insulted you; take your pick."

She was going on and on and Chase didn't know how to make her stop, so he grabbed her and pulled her to him.

His lips came down slowly, his eyes looking into her tear-drenched ones. Their lips met and fit perfectly together. It felt like the only thing in the world that was absolutely right.

One minute Eryn was raving, the next, she was wrapped in the most delectable kiss ever created. There were so many sensations running through her, she could only hold on to Chase's arms and let them wash over her. She knew now what the beach went through as the waves crashed over it, assaulting it with their power.

Chase smelled all male, like a drug to her senses. His lips were soft but were also demanding. They begged her to surrender to them just by the way they moved over her own. She was aware of every inch of him that was touching her body. His hand was on her back, rubbing it in small circles and making her skin tingle.

It was impossible to contain her reaction to the physical awareness between them. She opened her lips and welcomed him fully. Her grip tightened when their tongues touched and danced in the way of lovers. She couldn't tell where her body ended and his began.

Chase wasn't sure how long they stood there kissing and really didn't care. He didn't want to stop. Their breaths mingled and the want they generated in his body was pretty intense. She was like a drug to him; one that he didn't have any problem with being addicted to. The only reason he stopped kissing her was because Ed was nudging his thigh, wanting attention. Reluctantly, he pulled his lips away from Eryn but he kept his arms around her.

"I love you, Eryn," he whispered.

Danette Fogarty

Chapter 10

They stood there in silence, the words hanging in the air between them.

Chase couldn't believe he said it out loud. Saying the words would make her even more afraid. Maybe this was too fast for her?

Eryn was shocked. She did not expect Chase to say that. He looked as shocked about saying them as she was about hearing them. She didn't want to torture him by staying silent.

"Well that's good," Eryn whispered, "because I love you too." She looked up into his eyes and hoped she never would wake up from this wonderful dream.

Chase smiled and lifted her up into his arms. He spun around in a circle, making them both laugh. It was corny and silly but he didn't care.

Eryn was a little dizzy when Chase placed her back on her feet.

"I was really afraid that you didn't want to go on seeing me." She looked out at the darkening water, "Especially with the possibility that my father could make trouble for us." Even with all that looming over them, it was okay when he was with her.

All that mattered to Chase was that she was with him. The rest would work itself out.

"I'm not really that worried about your dad," he said as they started walking back toward where the cars were parked. "I'm more worried about someone at work giving us trouble and him finding out about that." Her dad was definitely a hard ass from what she said. "We'll just have to wear your dad down." He smiled and kissed her forehead.

Oh, he was saying all the words Eryn wanted to hear. She could believe, right now, that it was going to be okay. Her father would eventually understand and work would go on for both of them.

Once they were nearer to the parking lot, they sat down in the sand and starting talking.

They discussed silly things like which movies they wanted to see or embarrassing moments from their childhood. The subjects skipped around without rhyme or reason and were only interrupted with kisses.

Soft touches exchanged in between thoughts. Their skin burned with wanting to learn each other's secrets. Plans about their wishes for the future were whispered in the night air. When they looked over a while later, they saw Ed passed out in the sand at their feet.

Eryn looked at her watch and yawned, "I don't want to leave," she leaned over and kissed Chase.

Not wanting to leave her, he sighed. But he knew she had to get home and get some sleep.

"You're tired, baby," he tapped her nose with is finger.

They stood up, Chase whistling for Ed, and started up the short distance to their cars. There was a grassy area just before the asphalt and Eryn stopped when they reached it. She reached up and put her hands on either side of Chase's face and gently guided his lips to hers for one more kiss. This kiss, was one for the books. It made her toes curl and her belly ache to get closer to him. Maybe it was so much more because she was desperate to stay with him.

Chase pulled away but he sure didn't want to. "Okay," He smiled down at her, "we'll never leave if you keep kissing me that way."

Eryn giggled, "That's the point," she said with a mischievous look.

"Don't do that," he barked, but it had no bite behind it. "It's hard enough to leave you." His body was screaming at him to take her home right now.

Seeing Chase so riled up made Eryn feel powerful. She couldn't help but bait him. "We could always make out in the back of your jeep."

Chase looked around and groaned. The woman was torturing him.

A Marine to Remember

Feeling more turned on, Eryn ran her fingers down his neck, "Or we could go back to your place and discuss things we started on the beach."

He needed strength, "Don't, Eryn," he said roughly. He wasn't mad but it was taking a lot out of him.

Eryn's eyes were serious, "I've never been in love and I've never made love and I want to now," she kissed him, "with you."

They stood there staring into each other's eyes.

Finally Chase spoke, "Eryn," he looked at her with all the love inside him, "I want you more than anything." Hopefully she knew how difficult this was for him. "But I want this to be special," he ran his hands down her arms and took her hands in his, "I want this to be the most beautiful thing you've experienced."

If Eryn wasn't already head over heels in love with him, she would have fallen right then and there. He was magnificent, wanting to give as much as he took. She couldn't believe the depth of his understanding. It was crazy that she ever thought he was cruel.

After another twenty minutes of saying goodbye and stealing kisses from one another, they managed to get into their cars. Chase waited for Eryn to back up her car, then he followed her in his jeep.

He wanted to follow her back to her room or, better yet, have her follow him to his house and make love but he settled for the end of the gravel drive. She turned to go to the base. He waited for her tail lights to disappear before pulling the jeep out in the opposite direction and heading home.

Neither of them noticed the other car parked at the far end of the parking lot or the man sitting behind the wheel watching them both very intently.

"So that's what you've been up to," Tom Fredricks said aloud.

He pulled out and drove his rental car back to the base.

Eryn promised to call Chase as soon as she got to her room and let him know she made it okay. She was surprised that the machine picked up since she had a longer drive than he did. Maybe he was outside with Ed or stopped to pick something up on his way.

She talked when the machine beeped, "Chase," she whispered, "I just wanted to let you know I made it back to my room okay but I wish I was with you instead." She sighed, "Thank you for tonight, it was wonderful." She felt warm and cozy in the thought of their feelings. "I love you," she said and hung up the phone slowly.

Chase was at his house; sitting on the couch and listening to Eryn as she left a message. He wanted to pick up the phone and talk to her but he didn't. The feelings for Eryn overwhelmed him and that, combined with this physical ache, made him hesitate. He just needed a little time to let it all sink in.

Ed was on his own pillow across the room. Chase thought the dog was looking at him with pity in his eyes. Chase figured Ed knew what he was going through, having had a summer fling with a poodle down the street last year. Okay, Chase thought as he stood and walked toward his bedroom. He must have it bad if he was comparing his feelings with his dog's.

Walking into his bedroom, Chase pulled his shirt off and threw it into the laundry hamper. He loved her. He wanted her. And, for some reason, he wanted them to wait a little while longer. It wasn't like him to make the "grand gesture" but, here he was, being a gentleman. Again.

He got stripped down to his underwear and got into bed. Tonight he would dream about Eryn.

Eryn woke up refreshed. She slept great, her sleep filled with dreams of Chase and a house full of children. Ed was running around and they were all laughing. It was such a wonderful dream that she didn't want to wake up.

Unfortunately, she forgot to close the curtains all the way so when the sun was high in the sky, it shone through and right into her eyes. Looking at the clock, she was surprised that it was only a little past seven. She got up, closed the curtains, and tried to go back to sleep but, after an hour of tossing and turning, she decided it was no use.

She put on her running clothes thinking that maybe running would help her get rld of some of this pent up energy. She pulled her hair back in a ponytail and started walking over to the track.

After sitting down and stretching for a few minutes, Eryn noticed a shadow fall over her. She looked up with a smile on her face, thinking it was Chase, but stopped when she saw it was her dad instead. Her happiness deflated like a popped balloon.

"Good morning, Eryn," Tom said with a smile.

Eryn smiled again so he wouldn't think she was expecting someone else, "Dad," she returned, "I'm surprised to see you here."

Tom looked puzzled, "I don't know why, I run pretty regularly."

A Marine to Remember

Feeling stupid for saying it, Eryn blushed. He did have a point.

Holding out his hand, Tom helped Eryn up to her feet, "Since we're both here, why don't we run together?"

The fact that her dad asked her surprised her again. He normally didn't even associate with her when they were on the base. He made the distinction between them since he was an officer and she was enlisted. The two didn't normally associate socially. Not that is was a black and white rule where they were concerned because they were family, but he still followed it up until now.

Knowing there wasn't really an option, Eryn answered, "Sure."

They walked over to the edge of the track together and started out.

Chase drove to the track this morning hoping to see Eryn. She mentioned last night that she might run so he practically jumped out of bed this morning, anxious to see her. He arrived to the track and smiled when he saw her warming up.

He was about to walk over when he noticed another man walking up to her. He looked familiar to Chase and it took a minute for him to figure out where he'd seen the guy before. His stomach dropped to his feet and he stayed where he was. This was the guy in the picture on Eryn's nightstand; it was her dad.

Not wanting to approach them, Chase decided to grab a seat in the bleachers for a while. He could've walked up to her here; it was an open track and he worked with her, but he thought it would be too much of a risk. Instead, Chase sat there and watched.

It didn't take long to for him to see Eryn was not happy. Her body was stiff while running; the tension permeated off of her. Seeing her like that pissed Chase off. No one should make her feel that way. Every protective instinct inside him was firing; he wanted to go down to the track and save her from the obvious stress that being with her father created.

He didn't understand their issues since his relationship with his own father was a warm one. They didn't show a lot of physical affection but Chase knew his father loved him and would be there for him if Chase ever needed him.

Watching the pair run, Chase was impressed that Eryn was able to keep up with her father since the man's stride was twice that of his daughter's. He watched her father closely as he moved around the track. In his observation, he saw that the Colonel exuded aloofness.

It would definitely be an uphill battle if her father didn't approve of their relationship. Chase didn't necessarily want that to happen but it might just be unavoidable. Watching him further, Chase decided that no one would be worthy of this man's approval right away but Eryn was worth any obstacle.

Eryn felt Chase long before she saw him. She felt that inexplicable connection between them. She wanted to look around for him but didn't dare with her father right next to her. After a lap, she figured he was in the bleachers since she didn't see him beside the track.

She wanted to relax into the run but her father being next to her was making it very difficult. He kept up a brisk pace but didn't make it too grueling for her. That was weird too; usually he just ran at his own pace. Why was he acting so strangely?

After four miles, Eryn decided she was done. She hoped she could just say goodbye to her dad and get a chance to talk to Chase. Her father followed her over to cool down, which made her think he had different plans.

"How about having breakfast with me?" Tom asked while they were stretching.

What could she say? "Uh, sure," she answered and felt stupid for being so off guard around her father.

Tom nodded, "Okay, I'll meet you at the café in about thirty minutes." Without saying anything else, he walked off toward his rental car.

"Okay," she said after him. What just happened? She did not know what he was up to.

Her father was pulling out of the parking lot when she felt Chase behind her. She couldn't help but smile when she turned to face him.

Chase searched Eryn's face, "Are you okay?" he asked, hoping her father didn't make her too miserable.

Even her father's crazy behavior couldn't keep her from being happy to see Chase.

"Yes," She answered and wished she could kiss him. "I'm supposed to meet him in about," she looked at her watch, "twenty-eight minutes for breakfast."

"I want to touch you so much," Chase whispered.

Whoa, Eryn wanted to do the exact same thing. It was funny that their thoughts were so closely related.

"I know, I was just thinking that myself." She grinned, "I was hoping you would be here this morning and we could run together."

Chase understood her disappointment, he felt it too. He didn't want her to leave and he knew she didn't want to but she couldn't upset her dad right now.

"You need to get going," he said sadly, "I'll run for a little while then head on home."

Eryn nodded, "Okay, I'll call you later," she said as she started walking back to her barracks.

"You better," he said.

Her face lit up, she could see the want in his eyes and knew it was just a matter of time. She waved and turned to go back to her barracks. She heard steps right behind her and turned back to see him coming up to her.

"Hey," Chase said when he got close enough to her, "I love you." He said it loud enough so only she could hear it.

Eryn touched her own lips, wishing they were his and whispered, "Hey," then she laughed, "I love you too."

She turned back around and jogged toward her room, the smile staying firmly on her face.

Tom Fredricks sat in his rental car a block down the road from the running track. He saw the young man come up to Eryn right after he got into his car and decided to stick around and see if this was the same man from last night. He frowned when he saw it was.

For a second, Tom felt bad for spying on his daughter. He just couldn't stand the thought of her not telling him about this man. He wanted some answers. Seeing Eryn was on her way to her room, he pulled out and went back to his room to call Ben.

Eryn was on time at the café but it was close. Her father actually pulled in behind her, which surprised her yet again, and she saw him smile at her as he got out. Good, he seems relaxed, she thought as they met up by the door.

After going in, they found the closest empty table. Her father held her chair for her as she sat, then took the seat across from her. It was weird having him do something he normally only did for her mother.

"Thank you," Eryn said to him.

Tom nodded and sat down. He picked up a menu and studied it for a minute then laid it down on the table.

They made short work of ordering their breakfasts and smiled at the waitress.

"Thanks for running with your old dad," Tom said when they were alone.

Eryn chuckled, "I don't think I would classify you as 'old', Dad." It was nice, them joking a little. "I still don't know why you slowed to my pace." She was curious to see what he would say.

Tom was thoughtful for a moment, "It wasn't difficult since you're pretty fast." He winked, "But my old bones needed a break too."

Teasing from her dad was so weird and it made her think about how much they'd grown apart since her decision to join the Corps. They used to do it all the time.

"I'm glad to oblige," she said.

Their breakfasts arrived so they both stopped talking and dug in.

After they finished their meals, they were sitting there with a cup of coffee.

Tom looked over at his daughter, "You know," he said and waited for her to look at him, "I wanted to say I'm sorry for the conversation we had at dinner last night."

Eryn was silent because she wasn't sure where he was going with this.

"I do know that you'll make your own mistakes and you'll have to learn from them," he covered Eryn's hand with his own, "but I need you to remember that

I'm your dad and will always be protective of you and your sister."

Squeezing her dad's hand, Eryn smiled. She missed seeing this side of her dad. He was always like this when she was a little girl.

"Thanks, Dad," she said softly.

Sometimes it was hard to be a woman when you were your father's little girl.

Tom sighed, "Just bear with me here; I'm trying." He wanted Eryn to know he wanted to try to be close to her again.

Eryn was torn, "I'll try," she said, but knew giving in on one level would mean possibly giving in on more and she just wasn't going to do that.

Of course, this was the best conversation they shared as adults so maybe he was changing. It gave her hope that he would be supportive of her and Chase.

Tom paid the bill and walked out behind his daughter.

"I know you have a class this next week but I was hoping to have dinner some time before I leave on Friday," he said as he opened her car door.

It shouldn't have surprised Eryn that he knew she was scheduled to be in a class, but it did. How could they move on when she would always be upset about him butting into her life? She was trying to be open but he made it difficult. Then again, their breakfast was nice so she let it pass for now. She stood on her toes and kissed her dad lightly on the cheek.

"I'll see you soon," she said and got into her car. He was definitely a handful.

Eryn drove back to her barracks, her mood much lighter. She was relieved that she and her dad were actually getting along. That, combined with her feelings of love for Chase, made her feel like the world was beautiful.

Her father surprised her so much today with his change in attitude. She thought maybe he was actually accepting her being an adult and having her own career. Now it felt like it did when she was little.

Eryn tried to focus on reconnecting with her dad and how they might find a way back to what they shared before. She looked at the clock in the car and thought about calling Chase to tell him the good news but she had a ton of errands to do before her class started. Maybe if she hurried up and did her errands, they could get together tonight? The possibility made her tingle.

Once she got back to her room, Eryn collected her laundry and made out her to-do list.

At the running track, Chase was well into his third mile when Mitch Frinnel caught up to him.

"Hey," Mitch said as he set his pace to match Chase's.

Chase smiled at his friend, "Hey," he responded with a smile.

They didn't normally talk while they ran. It was kind of an unspoken rule so Chase was surprised when Mitch started up a conversation.

"I saw Sgt. Fredricks running earlier." He glanced over to see what Chase's reaction would be.

Chase didn't answer, just kept running. He wasn't mad at Mitch for pointing out his attraction to Eryn anymore; the man did him the biggest favor ever. For some reason though, Mitch was set on stating things Chase already knew.

Mitch decided to go a bit further, "It's obvious you know," he said to his friend.

Okay, now Chase was getting a little tired of the word games. What did Mitch want him to do? He didn't want to run anymore so he stopped and stepped off the track.

"What?" he demanded when Mitch walked over to where he stood. "What is so obvious?"

Mitch smiled, "You're in love, Chase." He just blurted it out because it was fact.

Chase started laughing and patted Mitch on the back as they walked toward their cars, "I told her last night, smart ass."

"Well I'll be," Mitch responded. Wonders never ceased!

Chase drove home to clean up before he met up with Eryn. They never set up a specific time but he figured it would be later in the day. He drove by her barracks and didn't see her car so either she was still with her dad or she was doing something else.

He half expected a message on his machine when he walked in the door and was a little disappointed that there wasn't one when he checked. At least Ed was glad to see him.

Not wanting to sit around and wait for Eryn's call, Chase decided to clean the house. As he moved from room to room, he could imagine Eryn there with him.

Sharing his life was a new concept. Sure, he dated before but he never considered a woman in his house. He just never opened himself up to the possibility before now.

Danette Fogarty

After cleaning, Chase showered and changed into shorts. He didn't bother with a shirt since it was so warm outside. He grabbed a beer from the refrigerator and went out onto the porch. He settled into the chair and fell asleep with Ed lying lazily beside him.

When Chase woke up, the sun was high in the sky. He was surprised that he fell asleep like that. Maybe it was being so content with Eryn that he was more relaxed.

His stomach growling told him it was time to eat so he went inside to make lunch. Ed was mysteriously absent so Chase poured some food in his bowl for whenever he decided to show up. Eventually he would come home and be starving.

After lunch he finished picking up a few things around the house. When Eryn called he would invite her to his place for dinner. Having her here would be a huge temptation for them both but it was okay. Maybe it was time they took the step they were carefully avoiding.

Thinking of her and him and what they might do, he couldn't resist talking to her. He picked up the phone and dialed her number. He already had it memorized, which surprised him too. The machine picked up and his smile slipped a little. He left a message for her asking her to call him.

A Marine to Remember

With nothing to do, he decided to figure out what he would make them for dinner. It had to be great. After checking the cupboards, he couldn't find anything he thought would be okay so he got his keys and went down to the grocery store.

After shopping carefully, Chase got home to find that he still didn't have any messages from Eryn. He tried not to fixate on it; she probably had stuff to do before her class. It was probably a good thing that he was going to cook dinner, then she wouldn't have to worry about that.

At five o'clock he called her and left a message saying that she should call him and that he was going to make them a mouth-watering meal at his place. At six he started the steaks and potatoes, wanting to show her how great of a cook he was. When the food was done and on the table at six forty-five, he called her again. He didn't leave a message, just figured she was out. At eight o'clock, when the food was barely touched, and put in containers in the refrigerator, he was finally pissed. He called her a third time and tried to be nice, but failed.

"Eryn, I guess you didn't want to come over," he took a breath, trying to calm down; "I think the polite thing would have been to call and let me know that." His temper was barely hanging on by a thread. "Don't bother to call, I've made other plans." Satisfied that he said his peace, he hung up.

Eryn finished her laundry about one in the afternoon. She was at the Commissary picking up groceries when she ran into her friend, Emma. They chatted about the Friday they went out while standing in line to check out.

When they were walking out to their cars, Eryn told Emma about what was going on with her father. She left out any mention of Chase and she wasn't sure why. Maybe it was time she told someone.

"Em, why don't you come over to my room in a little bit and we'll watch a movie and talk about boys." Eryn wiggled her eyebrows.

Emma laughed, "Oh you will tell me about this guy you blabbed about."

Eryn laughed and looked around to make sure no one was nearby. "You'll have to be sworn to secrecy."

Leaning in, Emma whispered, "I'll meet you in fifteen minutes."

They got into their cars and Eryn pulled out of the Commissary parking lot first. She could see Emma was still parked and figured her friend forgot something.

About two blocks from her barracks, Eryn was looking into her rearview mirror and missed seeing a bicyclist dart out in front of her car. Once she saw him, she swerved into the other lane to avoid him and didn't see the other car coming until it was too late.

Metal crunched, wheels skidded, and smoke filled the air. Eryn felt an intense pain in her chest and tried to stay awake when she heard someone at her car window, but the hurt was too much so she let the darkness engulf her.

Chapter 11

Emma was on her way to the barracks when she saw the traffic was stopped. Crap, she would be late getting to Eryn's. The cars were directed around what appeared to be an accident.

Oh, it didn't look good, Emma thought as she saw the ambulance and fire trucks. When she was finally beside where the accident took place, all the blood drained from her face. It was Eryn's car! Or, more accurately, what was left of Eryn's car.

Pulling over as soon as she could, Emma ran back toward the accident. She stopped the first MP she found.

"Can you tell me what happened?" she asked the young Marine.

The Marine shook his head, "I'm not sure," he thought this woman looked like she was going to faint.

Emma was impatient, "I think the driver of that car is my friend, can I get through?"

He pointed to the ambulance, "They're loading her now to take her to the base hospital."

Nodding her thanks, Emma ran over to the ambulance and started to get in when the paramedic tried to stop her.

"I'm her friend!" Emma yelled.

She was just this side of hysterical at this point. No one was going to keep her from being with Eryn.

The paramedic nodded and let her get in.

When Emma was seated near Eryn's head, she looked over and gasped. She barely recognized her friend with all the blood on her face.

The paramedic talked as they started to move. He told Emma that Eryn had sustained some cuts on her face from flying glass and they thought she had some broken ribs. They would know more once she was at the hospital and the doctors looked her over.

The five minute ride to the hospital was the longest in Emma's life. They pulled up and the trauma team was waiting to take Eryn inside. A nurse came up to Emma and asked her to have a seat in the lobby; they would let her know something when they assessed Eryn's injuries.

Emma sat down and cried. When she calmed down, she decided to get a drink of water. She got up and went to the water fountain at the far end of the lobby. After getting a drink to ease her parched throat, she looked up and saw a bank of telephones.

Eryn's father! Emma walked to the phones and looked up the base directory. Eryn mentioned he was staying at the Temporary Officer's Lodging. Finding the main number, Emma dialed it with trembling fingers.

Emma sighed when a voice picked up and said, "Colonel Fredricks." Good, he was there, Emma thought.

"Mr. Fredricks," Emma got out, trying desperately not to cry.

Tom didn't recognize the voice, "Yes, who is this?"

Swallowing hard, Emma blew out a breath, "Sir, this is Emma Cantrell, Eryn's friend from boot camp." She was trying to stay calm for both their sakes.

"I remember you, Ms. Cantrell, how can I help you?" he said stiffly.

Tom wondered why the young woman was calling him. He was impatient because he was about to walk out the door to join some friends for golf.

The tears fell down Emma's cheeks and she choked out, "I'm calling to let you know that Eryn has been in a car accident. I don't know the extent of her injuries; she's at the base hospital."

Tom's heart stopped, not Eryn! "I'll be right there," he said and hung up the phone.

Sitting down so he wouldn't pass out, Tom picked the phone receiver up and tried to call the hospital to get information from the doctor. The Emergency Room nurse wouldn't budge so he hung up in frustration. Knowing he needed to call his wife, he pressed his fingers to his eyes. He wouldn't cry.

Tom called the house first and, not reaching Beverly, called her cell phone. Thank goodness she answered.

"Honey," Tom said softly.

Beverly stopped walking, "What's wrong?" she asked, sensing the change in his tone.

Tom tried to keep his fear in check, "It's Eryn, honey."

Telling his wife what little information he knew, Tom's heart was breaking. He knew Beverly could see right through him. They decided she would fly up and he would go to the hospital to find out what he could. Hanging up the phone, Tom was thankful that his wife was the rock of their family. He walked out of the room and jumped into his rental car.

Emma was sitting in the lobby when she saw Eryn's father come in. She waived him over.

"Thank you for calling me, Emma," Tom said.

He didn't say anything else since there was nothing more important than his daughter right now.

Emma sat with him in the waiting room, each of them lost in their own worries. It took almost another hour before a nurse came out. They stood up, prepared for whatever the woman said.

The nurse smiled when she walked up to Ms. Fredricks' family. "The doctor will be out shortly to give you an update." She walked back toward the triage area.

Tom Fredricks stayed standing when Emma sat back down. He couldn't just sit here and do nothing. He started pacing around the room and sneaking glances at Eryn's friend, Emma, who sat there crying silently.

Finally, the doctor came out, "Fredricks," he said loudly.

Tom raised his hand and walked over to the doctor, Emma right behind him.

"I'm sorry for the wait," the doctor said directly, "she's got a couple of broken ribs and a severe concussion." He was no-nonsense, "We were doing some tests to make sure there were no brain bleeds or a collapsed lung." He sighed, "Other than that, she's got some nasty cuts and bruises."

Tom nodded, not sure what he should be asking.

The doctor smiled, "A couple of the facial cuts were deep and required stitches so she'll have to have those removed in about a week or so. She's pretty banged up but she really was lucky," he nodded to the young woman next to the man.

"Thank you," Tom said.

He patted Emma on the shoulder and walked back over to the phones to call his wife and Ben to let them know what was going on.

Tom smiled into the phone, "Honey, she's going to be okay."

Tears of happiness ran down Beverly's cheeks as she hung up the phone with her husband. They arranged to have their friends, Ben and Colleen pick her up at the airport and take her right to the base hospital.

Tom called Ben and Colleen and gave them his wife's flight information. Then he walked over to get himself a cup of coffee and one for Eryn's friend, Emma.

He was relieved Emma knew he was here. He and Eryn didn't normally let any information about their relationship become public knowledge. It was mostly his decision and he made it mostly to punish his daughter for her career choice. Not wanting to go down that road, he walked over and handed the coffee to Emma.

"Thank you again, Emma, for calling me." He was still a little emotional but he was coping a lot better.

Emma smiled warmly, "Well, sir, I knew you'd want to know as soon as possible and be here for Eryn."

Truth be told, Emma was also glad to have someone else here to help keep her from crumbling into an emotional mess.

They both knew that if Emma hadn't called him, there could have been a pretty big delay in notifying Eryn's family. It depended on the flow of information. He was thankful to Eryn's friend for sparing their family that.

A few minutes later, a nurse came out to take them back to where Eryn was. She was still in an ER treatment room, waiting to be transferred upstairs to her regular room. They walked into the room and Emma gasped when she saw Eryn. Tom went over and gently held Eryn's hand in his.

Eryn was very still in the bed, the medication helping her sleep.

They stood there for a few minutes and Eryn's eyelids fluttered open.

It was hard to focus, Eryn thought. She could see movement but everything was cloudy. Her head wouldn't clear enough to focus on anything. She heard someone whisper her name; it sounded like her father. When she tried to say something, nothing came out. Her chest hurt so badly every time she took a breath and her head was throbbing so badly, she wanted to cry.

Tom Fredricks looked at his daughter and wanted to cry. He couldn't believe this was Eryn laying in front of him. She was so white, she almost blended in with the sheets she was covered with. The swelling in her face made her practically unrecognizable.

"Eryn," Tom whispered.

She moved at the sound of his voice but flinched. He knew she was in pain and left to see if he could find a nurse.

Emma moved over and sat beside her friend, "Eryn," she murmured through tears, "it's Emma."

Eryn was trying to turn her head toward the sound of Emma's voice but it wouldn't cooperate.

"Emma," She finally managed to get out. She wondered if anyone heard her.

Emma smiled and leaned in, "Yes, sweetie," she said through tears because she was so happy Eryn was going to be okay.

Once Eryn could make out Emma's features she asked, "Where's Chase?" It hurt her throat to talk, it was so dry.

Emma pulled away from Eryn and looked around nervously.

She leaned back in toward her friend, "Eryn, who's Chase?" she asked.

Tom Fredricks came back into the room with the nurse. She put a needle into Eryn's IV and Eryn drifted off within a minute or so.

Looking around, Emma didn't know what to do. She didn't know who this Chase guy was and she sure wasn't going to ask Eryn's dad about him. If Eryn was secretive with her, it was a pretty fair assumption that her father didn't know anything. He was probably the guy Eryn mentioned on Friday when they went out and the one she was going to talk about today. Damn!

The nurse was shuttling them out of the room so Eryn could be taken up to her room. Emma went out, feeling bad that she couldn't call Chase and let him know what was going on.

Once they were back in the waiting room, Mr. Fredricks went to get some more coffee. Emma didn't know if the MP's notified anyone at Crash Crew about Eryn so she took the time to give them a call. She spoke to the dispatcher and gave her contact number in case they had any questions. A few minutes later, the phone rang.

"Sgt. Cantrell?" The man asked.

Emma answered, "Yes."

"This is Gunny Frinnel, Sgt. Fredricks' Crash Chief," he said briskly, "what's going on with Sgt. Fredricks?"

Emma relayed what information she had to the Gunnery Sgt. and hung up. She was beat and needed to go get her car back to her barracks. Plus, Eryn's parents needed some time with her. She walked back to the waiting room and found Mr. Fredricks slumped in a chair. She smiled.

"Mr. Fredricks, I'm going to go home now. Please tell Eryn I'll be here tomorrow." She started to walk away and stopped when he said her name.

Tom stood and walked over to Eryn's friend. He gave her a hug that took her by surprise.

"Thank you, Emma," he said softly.

Not wanting to cry again, Emma nodded and clenched her jaw. She turned and left the waiting room. At least her friend would be okay.

Beverly made it to the hospital around eight that evening. Her plane ended up being delayed, which only made her crazier with worry. Ben and Colleen picked her up, giving her the most recent information they could, and they all three drove straight to the hospital. Ben drove as fast as he legally could to get them there and Beverly was thankful.

After arriving, and not seeing Tom, Beverly went to the information desk and asked about Eryn's room number. The three of them rushed off to the elevator and made it down the corridor to where Eryn's room was in record time.

Seeing her daughter, the dam of emotion she was holding onto fell apart. She started crying quietly as she saw her baby lying there. Tom was next to her, holding her hand, and Beverly could never remember seeing him look so helpless. She thanked God that he was here and was able to wait with their little girl.

"Tom," Beverly whispered as she came up behind him. She was afraid to disturb Eryn.

Turning around, Tom stood and grabbed his wife into a fierce hug. He was relieved she was here.

When Tom released her, Beverly was able to move closer and get a good look at their little girl. Eryn looked so little and weak, it was unbelievable that this was their daughter. Beverly leaned over and brushed a strand of Eryn's hair off of her forehead. Her other hand was holding onto her daughter's.

Looking at her husband, Beverly asked, "How is she?" She worried they found something else wrong with her baby.

"She's been sleeping because of the medication they gave her." He looked at his friends and smiled weakly. He pulled his wife into his arms when she started crying again, "Shhh," he whispered, "she's going to be alright."

Even hearing her husband say the words didn't quiet alleviate all of Beverly's fears.

Eryn could not open her eyes, they were just too heavy. Her chest felt like five elephants were standing on it and everything hurt. She was trying to wake up but it was hard to do. She could hear voices, her father, her mother, and Uncle Ben. She couldn't make out what they were saying and she wanted to wake up so she could talk to them.

She felt a hand cover hers. It was soft and warm and made her feel better. She heard a voice say, "Sleep, my love, we're right here," and knew it was her mother's. The voice soothed her enough to let her slip back into a sweet oblivion.

Chase walked around like a caged animal in his house. After he called and left Eryn that angry message, he couldn't sit still. He even took Ed down to the beach in an effort to calm down. When he got back, he was sure that she would've left a message and they would make up. But after checking the machine, and seeing no messages, he got angrier. Ed sensed his master's mood and hid out under the bed. Even his dog's avoidance upset him.

He was so sure that when they spoke this morning that she was as anxious to see him as he was to see her. Well, for some reason, she didn't want to see him and didn't even want to tell him why. It was after nine and he needed to be up early for the rifle range this week. There was no use dealing with this anymore tonight.

He was getting ready for bed when the phone rang. His heart beating fast, he picked up only to find it was a wrong number. Finally, he crawled into bed and thought that four thirty would come really early and he needed to get some rest. But now he felt rejected and only wanted to talk to Eryn.

Eryn felt warmth on her skin. It was bright, so bright. She opened her eyes to see the curtains were open and sunlight poured in. Looking around, she figured out that she was in a hospital room. What happened? Thinking hurt but she tried to remember, there was a bicyclist and another car. Her heart started racing in fear.

"Eryn, sweetie," A soft voice spoke.

Eryn was able to turn her head and saw her mother sitting next to her. She started to cry because she was relieved her mom was there.

Beverly stood and tried to soothe her daughter, "Shhh, it's alright darling," she murmured. It broke her heart to see her baby crying.

Eryn opened her mouth, "Mom," came out in a croak. Her mouth and throat were bone dry.

Beverly tried to get her daughter to relax, "You hit another car and broke some ribs. You have a nasty bump on your head and some cuts and bruises." She smiled at her daughter, hoping she was reassuring, "The doctor wants you to stay here today but, if you feel up to it, you can go home tomorrow." It was agony seeing Eryn like this but she tried to keep her tone calm.

Not feeling like she could possibly "feel up to anything," Eryn nodded.

"How's the other driver?" she asked her mother, hoping no one else was hurt.

"He's fine," Beverly said. She rubbed Eryn's hand softly. "He got a cut on his knee from hitting it on the steering column." She brushed Eryn's hair with her fingers, "His truck was a lot sturdier than your little car." She knew Eryn would be relieved knowing no one else was seriously hurt.

Eryn nodded again. She tried to relax and remember what happened. She could remember the sound of metal crunching and tensed at the memory. She tried to brace herself for the impact and yelled out in pain when something hit her chest. Then everything went black. There were sounds; voices around her, doors swooshing, but it all seemed like some crazy disjointed dream. The pain brought the reality of the situation to her every time she tried to move. Getting anxious, she tried to sit up. She needed to get out of here.

Arms came around her to help her sit up and, when she looked up, she saw her father. He looked almost frail to Eryn, his eyes were creased in concern and Eryn was afraid for him.

"Daddy," she said softly; tears washing down her cheeks.

Tom sat on the edge of the bed and held his daughter as well as he could while trying not to cause her any more pain.

Eryn felt better knowing her parents were there.

After a few minutes, she had to lay back down; she was drained. When her dad helped her get settled back against the pillows, she smiled up at him, "I'm so tired," she said. She was asleep before she heard her father answer her.

Chase arrived home after his first day at Rifle Range tired and cranky. It was an easy assignment but he was thinking about Eryn. Sleep eluded him, making him think of her and her alone. There was no one else he wanted to see or talk to. She snuck into his thoughts throughout the day and haunted him. He was still royally pissed that she didn't call him the night before but he had to think there was a good reason for it.

Walking in the door, he patted Ed's head and smiled at the reassuring tail thumping against the floor in greeting. At least Ed was glad he was home.

After giving Ed some food and more water, he walked over to the phone and saw the answering machine light was blinking. He felt kind of smug thinking it was Eryn calling and apologizing for standing him up. Good, he thought. He wouldn't let her off the hook easy but he would let her off. Smiling, he pushed play.

Mitch's voice came on, "Chase, call me at Crash Crew as soon as you walk through the door."

Something about Mitch's tone made Chase's insides freeze.

After hearing his name paged, Mitch walked back to his office quickly. He knew how Chase felt about Eryn and didn't want to be the one to tell Chase she was hurt. He was glad Chase was assigned to Rifle Range because he'd probably be a basket case if he were at Crash Crew. Things were escalating and Mitch wasn't sure he liked it a whole lot. His heart was heavy when he reached his office and picked up the phone.

"What's up?" Chase asked.

Mitch sighed, "It's Sgt. Fredricks," he started, "she was in a car accident yesterday afternoon and is at the base hospital."

Hearing Mitch's words, Chase felt all of the air being sucked out of his lungs. His heart was beating way too fast and he didn't know what to think or say.

Not liking the silence on the phone, Mitch shouted, "Chase!"

Chase shook his head as if to clear out the confusion. It didn't help.

"Yeah, I'm here," he answered.

After a few seconds, Mitch started to give him what information Crash Crew had.

A Marine to Remember

"Do you understand?" he asked Chase when he was done. "She's okay, nothing life threatening." He paused again. "I'm going up there after work, do you want to go with me?"

"Hell yes, I'm going," Chase said sharply.

Knowing there was nothing left to say, Mitch said, "I'll see you later then."

He hung up the phone and let out a breath. He was sure glad it wasn't him going through this right now.

Eryn woke up and saw shadows in the room. She wasn't sure how long she slept but figured it was for at least a couple of hours. Testing her muscles out, a little at a time, she found she felt slightly better. The emphasis was on slightly though and she cringed when she tried to take a deep breath. Looking over to her right, she saw a huge arrangement of flowers on the table next to her.

"We didn't know what you liked so we told the florist to just go crazy," a familiar male voice said.

Eryn scanned the room and saw Gunny Frinnel sitting in the corner. She watched as he got up and crossed to her left side.

"How are you doing?" Mitch asked in a light tone.

"Like I've been hit by a car," Eryn answered.

She tried to sit up but the pain shot through her. Arms came around her sides to help her sit up. When she looked up, she saw Chase standing just behind her.

"Hey," she said and sucked in a breath with the pain.

Chase whispered into her ear, "Hi, baby."

He was so damn worried about her. She looked pretty helpless in the bed. He almost broke down when he walked into the hospital room and saw her for the first time.

Eryn looked over to Gunny Frinnel then back to Chase, "Are you guys checking up on me?" she asked, trying to sound better than she felt.

Gunny Frinnel tilted his head. "It's my job," he said dryly.

Chase leaned closer, "It's my pleasure," he said into her ear.

Eryn smiled. Chase's breath tickled her ear and made her feel shivers down her neck. She smiled sweetly at him. Once she looked back at Gunny Frinnel, she could see her was uncomfortable with the intimacy between her and Chase.

"We're sorry you're in the middle of everything here," Eryn said to Gunny Frinnel.

Mitch put up his hand, "Yeah, yeah," he answered. "We've got to get going. I think your parents will be back here soon."

Chase knew that was his cue to leave but he didn't want to. He was definitely grateful for the chance to see Eryn, even if it was only for a little while. He was especially grateful that she was going to be okay. Kissing her gently on the forehead, he moved around so he was at her side.

"I'll call you soon, okay?" Chase said with a smile.

Eryn nodded and smiled back. The men were leaving as her parents came in with Ben and Colleen.

Col. Fredricks nodded to the men and smiled at his daughter. Good, she was awake.

"Who was that?" he asked as came in.

Eryn smiled, she was glad to see her parents. "That was my Crash Chief and a Section Leader from work." She yawned.

Tom took his daughter's hand in his, "You scared us, honey."

He had tears in his eyes and couldn't remember the last time that had happened.

"It's okay, Dad," Eryn squeezed his hand in reassurance.

She wanted to comfort her parents but she was so tired.

Beverly Fredricks rubbed her daughter's other hand, "You rest now, sweetheart."

Eryn yawned again and drifted off to the sound of her parents' voices. It was comforting.

The next morning, Eryn woke up and felt a lot better. She was able to stay awake and was thankful for that. About ten in the morning, the doctor came in and told her she could leave the hospital. She would need to be on sick leave for at least four weeks to let her ribs heal but then she could go back to work. Eryn listened closely, wanting to do everything she could to get back to work, and Chase, as soon as possible.

She was surprised when she heard her father tell the doctor that she would be going to South Carolina to recuperate. The doctor nodded and told them that she could follow up with a doctor down there if she had any problems.

Eryn was changing into some clothes Emma brought over from her room after the doctor left. She was excited to get out of the hospital.

"I need to pick up some more of my things from my room before we leave," Eryn said to her mother. She wanted to take a few minutes to call Chase too.

Nodding, her mother smiled. "I thought you might," she answered. "We'll stop there before we head out to the airport."

A few minutes later, they were outside waiting for Uncle Ben and her father to pull up the cars. Their flight was this afternoon so they had to get going soon.

Tom pulled up first, "Why don't I get the things from your room and meet you at the airport?" he asked as he kissed his daughter's cheek.

Eryn would've preferred to do it herself and call Chase but she could always call him when she got down to her parents' place. She smiled and gave her dad her room key.

Tom Fredricks drove over to his daughter's barracks room and got out of his car. He had to keep reminding himself that Eryn would be okay. He didn't like the feeling of almost losing his baby and would do everything in his power to avoid that at all costs. He would do anything to make it easier on her from now on.

Walking up the stairs, Tom was filled with shame. He never told her how proud he was of her accomplishments in the Marine Corps. He would do that first thing.

After opening up the door to her room, Tom spotted the bag Colleen and Emma packed for Eryn the day before. He grabbed the bag and turned toward the door when his eye caught the blinking light on the answering machine. He pushed play, wanting to make sure he passed on any well wishes she might have.

"It's Chase," the first message started, "I guess you don't care that you told me we'd meet later today?"

Tom could hear the coldness in the man's voice and disliked it immediately. Who did this guy think he was? Didn't he know Eryn was in an accident? He pushed delete and wanted to punch the guy in the face. Eryn didn't need to be around someone who was so insensitive.

The second message was from a young lady named Laura asking Eryn to call her. Tom would definitely pass that on to Eryn.

The third message made him mad as soon as it started. "Eryn," the man sounded gruff, "I haven't been able to eat or sleep; I want to see you." Tom listened closely, "Thank God you're alright."

After the message ended, Tom did the only thing he could and he pressed delete and walked out the door with Eryn's bag.

The ride to the airport had Eryn on edge. She wanted to stop by her room and call Chase but there wasn't time before their flight left. Of course, that didn't stop her from thinking about him. She was so sure he would've called but her Dad told her that she only had a call from her friend, Laura. She shouldn't be surprised since Chase told her he wasn't good with emotional stuff but it still hurt.

Eryn called Gunny Frinnel when they were at the airport waiting to board. She wanted to let him know where she'd be during her sick leave. She filled out the appropriate paperwork at the hospital and knew he'd get a copy but she wanted to make sure. She also knew he'd pass it on to Chase and that was what she was counting on.

She and her mother were flying down today and her father would be joining them in a few days. Since her accident postponed some of the meetings he had scheduled, he needed to attend them now.

Maybe his delay would give her some time to call Chase. It would be a lot harder to talk to him with her dad around. It was bad enough she wouldn't be able to see him for the next few weeks at least.

"Okay," Tom Fredricks clapped his hands when his daughter hung up with her Crash Chief, "I'll see you in a few days."

He leaned over and kissed his wife and then his daughter.

Eryn nodded, "Thanks, Dad."

Smiling, Tom hugged her gently and turned to leave the airport. He'd been chomping at the bit since he heard the messages on her machine. He wanted an explanation of this Chase character's tone. He wanted some answers now and he was going to get them.

Tom drove straight to Ben and Colleen's house. He smiled when Colleen opened the door and told him Ben was out back on the patio. Tom walked through the house and out onto the patio expecting an argument from his friend. Ben was sitting there with a drink in his hand and motioned to the seat next to him before Tom could say anything.

"I know why you're here," Ben started. As soon as he saw his friend, he knew that Tom knew about Eryn's young man. "You found out about this guy and you're hopping mad."

Tom was even more frustrated that his friend wasn't surprised he was here. He threw his hands into the air.

A Marine to Remember

"Does everybody know except for me?" he asked incredulously.

Since his friend hadn't sat, Ben motioned for him to sit again. "C'mon, sit, we'll talk."

They sat there for a while, not saying anything. Colleen came out and brought a drink for Tom and a refill for Ben and they still didn't talk.

When Tom couldn't stand it any longer, he erupted. "What's going on Ben?" he demanded. "Who is this guy and why the hell didn't you tell me about him?"

Ben took some time to answer, "Well," he propped his feet up on a stool in front of him. "I found out accidentally and, I have to say, it was pretty damn funny." He chuckled.

Tom didn't think this was funny at all. "I," he started and stopped when Ben interrupted him.

"She knew I wouldn't lie to you if you asked me about it and she asked if I would just keep from saying anything until you found out." He put up a hand when his friend wanted to say something, "I think you realize that she's a grown woman, right?" he asked, knowing the question was rhetorical.

Thinking about what his friend was telling him, Tom seethed with anger.

Ben put his feet on the floor and turned to face his oldest friend, "She's smart, pretty, and a damn fine Marine, Tom," he said while looking him in the eye and hoping he would see reason.

Being the last person to know any of this, Tom was still pissed off. When did they all decide to turn against him? He wasn't going to put up with being the odd man out in all of this.

"She's my youngest, Ben." He looked over at his friend and said in a strained voice, "I expect more from her than I should, I know that."

Ben snorted.

Sighing, Tom looked down into his drink, "We almost lost her and I don't want some dumbass jerk coming in and hurting her." He slammed his hand down on the table. "I'll be damned if I'm going to sit back and watch that happen."

Ben knew Tom well enough to know he would follow through on his words. He didn't agree with Tom when it came to the girls but he could understand where the feelings were coming from. Of course, knowing that didn't necessarily make it right. He especially didn't want his friend to do something stupid.

"If it's any consolation," Ben said, "I've met him and he's a good guy."

Tom waited a minute and shook his head, "Not from what I've heard."

Ben knew the conversation was over and felt sorry for Eryn and her young man.

Chapter 12

Chase made it through the week of Rifle Range but it wasn't easy. He didn't remember most of what happened since his brain was so preoccupied with Eryn.

He went to the range, worked, then came home and sat on the porch wondering what she was doing. Now that Friday was here, he was on his last nerve. Even Ed seemed restless now. Did the dog actually miss her too?

Sitting down on the chair, he looked out over the yard. Thank God he told her he loved her before the accident. This would change their careers and someone would probably need to transfer but he was sure he and Eryn would make it through.

Of course, it would be helpful if he knew how Eryn felt. How did he talk with her? Mitch said she was staying at her parents' place in South Carolina during her sick leave so at least Chase knew she was okay but she hadn't called him. He sure wasn't going to call her there and run the risk of causing problems between her and her father. She would need to call him.

After about an hour of sitting on the porch, he was just drifting off to sleep when the phone rang. He ran inside and tripped over his shoes trying to get to the damn thing. He didn't recognize the number except for the prefix which meant it was from the base. He answered quickly.

"Hello," he said quickly, sounding different; not himself.

Tom Fredricks sneered, "Hello," he said coldly. "I'm looking for Staff Sgt. Chase Johnson."

Oh, there was no mistaking the tone. Chase knew this was an officer. "Yes, sir," he said quickly.

"Staff Sgt.," Tom said, "this is Col. Tom Fredricks."

Oh crap, Chase thought to himself. Not now. Not when he hadn't talked to Eryn and he was going nuts.

"Yes sir," he finally answered.

Tom was no nonsense, "I'd like to meet with you tomorrow morning." He didn't even give the boy a chance to reply. "Do you know the small café just outside the west gate of the base?"

Chase answered quickly, "Yes, sir," and felt like an idiot. He didn't want to be intimidated but he was. He straightened his shoulders, "I know where it is," he said with a stronger tone.

Nodding, Tom gave him the time and promptly hung up the phone.

The next morning, Chase pulled up in front of the café a few minutes early. His stomach was in knots and he was cranky from lack of sleep. Since he hadn't spoken with Eryn, he didn't know what, if anything, she told her father. This could go very badly and he was mad that Eryn hadn't called him since she started leave to tell him what he should or shouldn't say.

With a deep breath, he got out of his jeep and went inside the café. Looking around, he tried to figure out which of the customers was Eryn's dad. He'd seen the picture in her room but couldn't get his mind straight. With everyone in civilian clothes, it was hard to pick someone out.

Scanning the room, his eyes fell on a tall man walking toward him dressed in khaki pants and a polo shirt. That was him, Chase knew it. If the menacing stare wasn't enough, his resemblance to Eryn confirmed it. He hoped this would go well but wasn't sure at all since he was basically walking into a situation unprepared.

Thinking of all of his conversations with Eryn, he tried to remember what she said about her dad. She mentioned that she was inexperienced because of his tendency to be overprotective of her with men. That combined with his chosen profession meant he would be a force to be reckoned with.

A Marine to Remember

Chase also wasn't comfortable commenting on anything to do with their careers without having talked to Eryn. He spent the night before going over all the scenarios but he really wasn't sure what he would say.

Tom stuck his hand out when he was close to Chase, "Staff Sgt.," he said.

Chase took the offered hand and shook it firmly.

Well, Tom thought, the boy had a good grip and carried himself well. He watched the boy enter the restaurant and was somewhat satisfied with the boy's behavior this far. Of course he would need to do a lot of fast talking to reverse Tom's opinion of him from the voice mail he heard in Eryn's room.

They walked back to the table Tom secured earlier. Tom observed Chase as he moved. He noted that the Marine dressed nicely with freshly pressed pants and a collared shirt. He didn't want to scare the boy before he got some answers but it was tough for him to reserve his judgment.

The men sat down and gave their drink order to the waitress.

Tom spoke first, "I suppose you want to know what this meeting is about." He saw Chase nod and started, "I didn't know about you which, at first, tells me that my daughter didn't want me to know about you." He watched Chase closely. "I cannot tell you how much that bothers me." He sighed. "My daughters mean the world to me and I will do anything to protect them."

Chase couldn't mistake the tone of the last comment. So….this wouldn't be good.

"I wasn't happy when Eryn decided to join the Marines and was even more upset about her going into the enlisted ranks." Tom stated.

Finally, Chase had to speak up, "She's a fine Marine, sir."

Tom smiled with pride, "I know, but thank you for agreeing with me on that."

It gave him some relief that this Chase kid seemed to respect his daughter but it wasn't enough for him to change his mind about their relationship.

Tom smiled at the waitress as she poured coffee into their mugs. He waited for her to leave and looked back at Chase.

"I have done some checking up on you," he said and almost smiled at the temper he saw flare up in the boy's eyes. "You come from a family of Marines and you have an excellent record."

Chase was pissed off. This guy was really taking liberties. He nodded and waited.

"Unfortunately," Tom paused and looked straight into Chase's eyes, "that doesn't mean you're what my daughter needs right now."

Letting the words sink in, Chase wanted to remain calm, but it was tough when someone was telling you that you weren't good enough.

"With all due respect, sir," he said to Eryn's father, "that's for Eryn to decide."

Tom shook his head, "No," he clenched his jaw, "it's not."

All Chase could think was how he now understood why Eryn didn't tell her dad anything. He was used to issuing orders and having everyone do his bidding. Well, Chase wasn't a pushover.

"Sir," he said calmly, wanting to tread cautiously, "Eryn is an intelligent woman. I believe she cares deeply for me and, to be honest, I love her."

Chase watched Eryn's father and knew he didn't choose his words carefully enough. The man's eyes were brewing and Chase knew he was probably losing ground.

"I respect Eryn as a fellow Marine and as a woman," Chase said directly. "We are both very conscientious about our careers and will not do anything to jeopardize them."

Sitting forward, Tom nodded. "On that," he said, "we agree." He half smiled at Chase, "My daughter is on the fast track to Warrant Officer." He noticed Chase's look of surprise and shook his head. "She hasn't told you, has she?" he asked smugly.

Chase was shocked. He didn't know what to say.

"She's slated for some big things in her field and starting a relationship with you won't help her." Tom looked at his watch then back to Chase. "This is nothing against you, son, it's just that Eryn will give up all she has to gain for you and your career."

Chase's head snapped up. He thought about it for a second and realized that Eryn's dad was right. She would sacrifice for him. She would put his career first because that's how she was.

"Yes, sir," he said sadly, "I believe you're right."

The waitress came over and offered refills but both men refused. They were getting to the point of this meeting now.

Chase leaned back, "What exactly do you want from me, sir?" Chase asked knowing he wouldn't like the answer.

It occurred to Tom that maybe this Chase kid would be more level-headed than his daughter was and that could be a good thing for them all. He folded his hands together on the table.

Sternly, he stated, "I can arrange for a transfer for you."

That was not what Chase was expecting Eryn's father to say. His eyes widened for only a second then he looked down at his coffee. Obviously this guy was serious about getting rid of him. It didn't seem real to Chase, more like a bad dream.

Tom knew the boy was thinking about it, he could literally hear the wheels turning in his head.

"Staff Sgt.," he used the kid's rank to drive the point home, "I only want what's best for my daughter. If you love her, you'll agree."

Chase's pride was hurt, his feathers ruffled, his whole world was being turned upside down. This man wanted him to step aside and let Eryn continue on a career path that she hadn't even told Chase about. Why hadn't she told him about it? She never said much to him about her career goals but she let him talk about his with her.

It was tough to think straight. How well did he really know Eryn? Why didn't she share his goals with him? If she wasn't honest with him about that, did she really even care about him? He looked up into Col. Fredricks' eyes and set his jaw.

"I can't make this decision without speaking to Eryn," Chase said to her father.

He didn't want to talk anymore so he threw some bills on the table and got up to leave.

He was getting into his jeep when Eryn's father came up to the door.

"Staff Sgt.," Tom said, "it won't matter. My daughter will agree with my decision." He handed Chase a piece of paper, "Here's the number for my room at the base. Call me when you've made your decision."

Chase sat there and watched Eryn's dad walk away and get into his own vehicle. He pulled out of the parking lot and Chase was still sitting there. Chase's heart was breaking into a million pieces and he just wanted to get out of there so he put the jeep in drive and tore out of the parking lot.

Not knowing what he should do, Chase drove to an apartment complex off base where Mitch lived. That SOB is the one who got him into this mess and now he was going to help Chase figure this out. Unfortunately, Mitch was gone for the weekend. Great, Chase thought sarcastically.

Chase drove home but didn't remember getting there. He wasn't supposed to go into work until Monday and didn't know what the hell he should do. That left a day and a half for him to think about what happened between him and Eryn's father. The man clearly wanted Chase as far away from Eryn as possible but Chase wasn't going to agree to anything without speaking to her first.

Without thinking about it, he called her barracks room. He felt stupid once he remembered she wasn't back yet from South Carolina and wouldn't be for weeks.

Pacing around the house wasn't getting him anywhere so he decided that he might as well take Ed for a walk. Maybe it would help both of them figure this out. Grabbing Ed's leash, he walked toward the door with Ed dutifully following him.

They walked down to the beach. Chase wondered how his life got so complicated over the last weeks. Looking at it now, it felt like his time with Eryn was some kind of dream. He was angry about her dad sticking his nose into their business. He was also upset and hurt that Eryn hadn't even called him.

If she knew her dad knew about them then why didn't she stand up to him about their relationship? And why did he feel like he was the only one willing to sacrifice for their relationship?

Once the niggling of doubt started in his gut, Chase couldn't shake it. By the time he got back to the house from his walk with Ed, his mind was whipping itself into a blur of doubt and fear and anger. When he saw that there was no message from Eryn on his answering machine, he knew what he needed to do.

The pain of rejection had him by the throat and didn't have any intention of letting up. He went to bed without eating and spent the whole night tossing and turning.

Sunday morning he woke up to a throbbing headache and still no word from Eryn. It was clear that she wasn't willing to go up against her father so he really had no choice. He picked up the piece of paper Mr. Fredricks gave him the day before and dialed the number.

Tom just got into his room from having a heated breakfast/debate with Ben and Colleen and he wasn't happy. They didn't agree with his tactics and told him so in no uncertain terms. He didn't care though, this was Eryn's future and Tom wouldn't have it go into the toilet. He heard the phone ring and walked over to the desk.

"Col. Fredricks," he said sharply into the receiver.

Chase cleared his throat, the man on the other end of the line did not sound happy.

"Yes, sir, this is Chase Johnson," the words tasted bitter coming out of his mouth. "Make it happen," Was all he could say before he hung up the phone.

A Marine to Remember

After Chase put the phone down, he went into his room and sat on the bed. Ed sat on the floor in front of him, looking sad.

In South Carolina, Eryn was going stir crazy. After almost two weeks, she was still having trouble getting around. She prayed for some time alone so she could call Chase but her mother and sister were always hovering. They were worried, which Eryn could understand, but they were smothering her too.

She would try to stay up late but ended up falling asleep from exhaustion or the stupid pain medication. In her dreams, Chase would come to her and take her away to his house. They would make love and talk about their future. Her parents would be happy that she found someone. The fact that she and Chase worked together wouldn't matter to anyone. The dreams were the only thing that kept her from freaking out completely.

Her father arrived home a week ago and he didn't seem like himself. He was really serious and wouldn't look Eryn in the eye for some reason.

She knew something was up but didn't really know how to approach him with her concerns. It wasn't surprising that her accident shook her parents up and Eryn thought maybe her dad was having difficulty in dealing with that.

Uncle Ben called earlier in the week and asked to speak to her father. She was surprised that he didn't take the time to chat with her. Her father took the call in his den and didn't come out for a long time. When he did finally come out, he looked tired. When Eryn asked if he was okay, he brushed her off saying, "It's just work."

The day before, Eryn heard her parents talking in hushed tones and her father sounded angry. Something was up with him but she didn't want to upset the tenuous bond they were reforming.

This was the first time she'd spent any real time with her parents since joining the Marine Corps. On one level, she liked being babied so the urge to keep calm and not make waves won out.

The third week of her sick leave was much better. She finally found the time to call Chase. She tried his house dozens of times but the recording kept saying the number was disconnected. That was so odd since they were required to keep good contact numbers for work. Maybe he went to a cell phone since most people were getting into that these days. It was odd that he wouldn't tell her about it or pass a message through Gunny Frinnel.

She checked her answering machine remotely and there were no messages from him there either. A heaviness settled into her chest and it had nothing to do with her broken ribs.

The fourth week, she was able to take brisk walks and get out of the house. Her ribs were still really sore and rebelled against the movement but walking made her feel better and gave her time to think. She kept trying to call Chase's house but had no luck.

The urge to call Crash Crew and ask Gunny Frinnel about it nagged at her mind and she finally gave in and called him. She was even more frustrated when she found out he was on leave himself. She was finally at her wits end.

A couple of days before she was due to return to Cherry Point, she came home from one of her walks excited to tell her parents about her progress.

When she walked in the front door, she heard her parents right away. For the first time she could remember, her mother was raising her voice to her father.

The anger Eryn heard in her mother's voice rocked her to the core. She went into the hallway and called their names. Both of her parents came out from the kitchen and stood there looking at her. Eryn could plainly see how upset her mother was. She looked at her dad and suspected, by the contrite look on his face, that he was the source.

"Is everything alright?" Eryn asked as she looked from her mother to her father and back again.

Beverly walked over to her daughter and embraced her. After a minute she pulled back far enough to look into Eryn's eyes and smiled.

"It's okay," Beverly said sweetly, "I'm just upset with your father." She looked at her husband then back to her daughter, "I'll get over it."

Tom walked around his wife and daughter and to the front door.

"I have to get back to work," he mumbled and left quickly.

Beverly watched her husband leave and went into the kitchen to fix some lunch.

Eryn stood in the hallway of her parents' house and wondered what just happened.

About two weeks after his conversation with Eryn's father, Chase was called into the Crash Chief's office at work. Chase knocked and knew it was all business when he heard the stern, "Enter," shouted from inside. After walking in, he looked at Mitch's unhappy expression and sat down across from his friend.

"What the hell is going on around here?" Mitch asked with a seething anger pulsating through his body.

Chase didn't know what to say so he played dumb, "What did you hear?" he asked.

Mitch stood up, walked around his desk, and leaned against the front of it with his arms crossed over his chest.

"Imagine my surprise," he started, "this morning when I get a message saying that one of my Staff Sergeants is getting orders out of here." He was so mad he clenched his fists, "And imagine my greater surprise when I see the Staff Sgt. getting transferred is you."

Not wanting to answer, Chase shrugged. What could he say? He tried to play it off.

"Orders come down all the time," he said, trying to sound calm.

Fire was shooting through Mitch's veins and he shouted, "Bullshit, Chase! Not when you've only been here two years!" He picked up some papers and dropped them in Chase's lap. "You haven't been here long enough!"

It was clear that Chase couldn't lie to Mitch. After all, he was a friend, not just his boss.

"I couldn't say anything," he answered and looked away, not wanting to upset his friend any more than he already had.

"Yes," Mitch shouted at Chase, "you could have!" He grabbed the papers from Chase's hands and threw them back on the desk. "You could have said something to me and we would've worked something out." Chase's silence only made him more frustrated. "What's going on here?" he asked.

Mitch walked back around his desk and sat down. It was hard enough losing good Marines to orders but this was a lot more than just a simple set of orders. Mitch had suspicions but if Chase was tight-lipped about it, his hands were tied.

Chase looked over at Mitch and knew he was busted. He was embarrassed for letting someone bully him into this decision to begin with. He was hurt by Eryn and her refusal to be honest about their relationship with her father. He wouldn't admit that the orders were from the obnoxious Col. Fredricks. That would have far-reaching repercussions for all of them.

"Mitch," Chase finally said, "I love her and I'm doing what's best. That's all I can say." His voice was littered with resignation that bore a hole into his gut.

The explanation wasn't even close to adequate but it confirmed some of his suspicions. Her father got to Chase. Dammit! Why did people feel they had the right to interfere with others? He should've asked himself that months earlier when he brought it up to Chase.

Shaking his head, Mitch said, "I understand." He looked back down at the papers.

Chase got up and left the office without a word.

At the end of the day, Chase went home and finished up packing his house. He'd been doing a little bit every day since he agreed to the transfer. There wasn't much left so he got the boxes out and finished it up.

He received his official orders and was going to Camp Pendleton in southern California. A few of the guys he served with previously were there so he'd have no trouble getting there and fitting in. He already called his parents and asked if he could drop Ed off with them until he was settled. The house here was rented with the furniture so he only had to take his personal effects with him.

There was a good week for him to get to California so he was driving. He'd get a chance to drop Ed off at his folks' place and spend a couple of days with them which was nice.

The last few days here at Cherry Point were busy ones for Chase so he didn't have time to think about

Eryn. He was doing this because he loved her and he wanted her to be happy. At least that's what he kept telling himself during the day.

At night, however, the doubts would wiggle their way into his mind when he was trying to sleep. The meeting with her father replayed in his mind every night and he couldn't think of a better alternative. If he fought this, it could cost them both their careers. He loved Eryn and would give up his career for her but he'd never expect the same from her. It wasn't fair and he wouldn't put that on her. He would just do what had to be done. It was that simple.

Chapter 13

The first couple of days back in North Carolina were tough on Eryn. She got back on a Wednesday and had to have a series of doctor's appointments at the base clinic before she could be cleared to go back to duty.

After two days, she was released to go back to work. The clinic gave her several copies of her release so she went and dropped off a set at Crash Crew. She wanted to see Gunny Frinnel but he was out to lunch. She ran a few errands and got back to her room a little later than she expected.

There was a message from Gunny Frinnel on the machine, "Sgt. Fredricks, welcome back, we'll see you in the morning."

Eryn smiled at the message. He was a man of many words, like usual.

After she was unpacked and got her room reorganized, Eryn tried to call Chase again. It was almost midnight but she didn't care. Why was his phone disconnected? Well, she would see him at Section change tomorrow so she needed some good sleep so she looked great.

Not seeing Chase for a month only reinforced Eryn's feelings for him. She was so in love with him she was crazy. Not just that, but she was ready to revamp her stand on intimacy now.

They would get married eventually, she was sure about that. There were couples who worked in the same field and they made it work so why couldn't she and Chase do that?

When she fell asleep, she dreamed about them playing with their children. A cute little boy who looked like Chase ran around them and an adorable little girl with long curls smiled sweetly at them. Everything seemed so right that she drifted off to a peaceful sleep.

The first day back at work was very rough for Eryn. She tried to say it was because of being off the routine for so long but it was really because she hadn't seen Chase.

A stack of papers was waiting for her on Staff Sgt. Greene's desk that needed her attention. She eagerly jumped into the task and was going through them throughout the morning. A few emergencies happened in the last week which generated a ton of paperwork. A necessary evil for their profession.

At shift change Eryn looked for Chase and was dumbfounded that he wasn't there. He should've known she was coming back today. She was sure

Gunny Frinnel would've told him. She couldn't ask because she was afraid of starting up some rumors.

After spending the morning holed up in the Section Leaders' office doing paperwork, Eryn's stomach started grumbling. Looking at her watch, she was surprised that it was already lunchtime.

She went downstairs to the Mess and grabbed her lunch out of one of the refrigerators they kept at Crash Crew. A lot of the Section members brought their own food because of the long hours.

Everyone welcomed her back and asked how she was. There was some playful teasing about her "just trying to get off work," but she took it on the chin. A few guys accused her of "driving like a girl," and that made her laugh. News of the accident traveled fast so she didn't have to retell it, for which she was thankful. Their concern made Eryn feel good.

Biting into her ham sandwich, Eryn sat back and listened to the guys talk around her. She was wondering about Chase and not paying much attention to them until she heard the words, "send off party."

She laughed, "Private Logan," she said to her section worker, "did you guys have a party and forget to invite me?" she joked with her crew and they seemed to like it.

"No, ma'am," Pvt. Logan answered, "Gunny Frinnel said you were still on sick leave with your parents or else we would've called you," he answered and poked Pvt. Pritchard in the side. "Besides, there were no women allowed! We wanted to send Staff Sgt. Johnson off right."

They guys were laughing and teasing and Eryn was stunned. She was sure all the blood drained from her face and the bottom dropped out of her stomach. It was hard to see, hear, think, or react.

"I'm sorry?" Eryn squeaked out.

Pvt. Logan answered, "Staff Sgt. Johnson, from the other Section. He got orders a couple of weeks ago and we had his send-off party last Friday." He laughed at some comment one of the other guys made, "I think he left a couple of days ago."

The poor guy didn't realize he just delivered the worst news of Eryn's life to her.

"Oh," she mumbled, "I didn't know."

She stood up and threw the rest of her lunch in the trash can. She couldn't eat now even if she wanted to.

Walking out of the room in a stupor, she managed to make her way out to the parking lot and got into her car. She needed some time to compose herself and figure out what was going on.

A Marine to Remember

What the hell happened? Why didn't anyone tell her Chase got orders? Why hadn't Chase called her himself?

Possible scenarios ran through her mind. Maybe he did call and her parents didn't tell her. She hoped that wasn't the case. She got out of her car and stood next to it, letting her thoughts run through her mind.

The airfield was noisy with the F-18s practicing their carrier landings. They were touching down briefly on the runway then taking off again, otherwise known as touch and go's. Normally she would be inside where the noise wasn't as bad but her thoughts were so loud that they easily drowned out any sound the planes made.

After a while, she went back inside but her mind wouldn't stop. The anger inside her rose as the minutes passed. By four o'clock she couldn't take it anymore; she needed answers.

Gunny Frinnel was packing up for the day when he heard the knock on his office door. He said, "Enter," and waited.

Eryn walked into the Crash Chief's office and just stood there. She had no idea what to say.

As soon as Mitch saw it was Sgt. Fredricks, he put his bag down and sat down behind his desk. He motioned for her to take a seat and waited for her to sit down. Judging from her expression, he didn't think this was work-related. God, he was glad he wasn't in a relationship!

Taking a breath, Gunny Frinnel asked, "Yes, Sgt.?"

Eryn wanted to answer but didn't have a clue about how to say something.

Mitch could see that she was mad and he respected her for keeping a lid on her anger. He'd seen that look before though, usually on his sister's face. It meant he would be receiving the brunt of the anger that some other jerk was responsible for. The realization hit him hard and fast. Dammit, Chase!

"Gunny," Eryn said in a whisper.

Her voice cracked, which ticked her off. She was sitting in front of his desk, her head down and twisting her hands as if she could wring water out of them or something.

"Why?" she asked.

It was the only thing she could say without falling apart.

Sitting back then forward again, Mitch couldn't believe this crap. That ass hadn't called her and told her was leaving! That was low, especially for Chase. What the hell was going on around here? Looking at

Eryn, he could see she wanted answers. The shit of it was; he didn't really have any to give her.

"I don't know," Mitch said, "he wouldn't tell me."

Eryn's head shot up, confusion running through her mind. Why wouldn't Gunny Frinnel know about the orders ahead of Chase? Why wouldn't he tell his friend and boss that he put in for a transfer? Was he trying to protect her? There was no reason since Gunny already knew how they felt about one another.

Mitch interrupted her thoughts, "I was just about as mad as you are right now." he said softly and wondered what else he could say to help her.

Eryn listened to what he was saying and then, as soon as she took it in, the situation cleared.

Her voice flat, she said, "The only reason he wouldn't tell you was if it was arranged in a hurry."

Nodding, Mitch realized that she was a very smart lady.

"Where did the orders come from?" Eryn asked harshly.

It was almost a demand but she didn't care right now. She knew the answer, she just needed to hear it from someone else.

Mitch reached into a drawer on his desk and pulled out a folder. He handed it to her and let her look through it.

"They came from Headquarters," he answered.

Eryn nodded, scanning the documents. If they came from Headquarters then this could be a coincidence. Once her eyes found the signature though, she knew it was no coincidence. She looked up and, if Gunny's expression was any indication, he didn't think it was either.

She closed the folder and handed it back to Gunny Frinnel. They both knew that if none of the parties involved stepped up, they had no proof of anything. Even if someone blabbed, what did it matter? The fact was that Chase left. He gave up on them. He didn't fight like he said he would. If he lied, then he really didn't love her.

"Gunny," she looked at her Crash Chief with tears in her eyes, "would you mind if I went home? I'm not feeling very well."

Mitch was torn between feeling pity for Sgt. Fredricks and anger at the jackass he called his friend. He didn't know who was worse in all of this, a parent who interfered, or Chase, who gave up on a good woman. All he could do was nod at Sgt. Fredricks. Once she left his office, he slammed his hand down on his desk and swore at Chase Johnson for a long while afterward.

Eryn felt sick to her stomach. She used up every ounce of constraint she had to make it out to her care and out of the parking lot without shedding one single tear. She was going to go to her room but chose to drive to the beach instead. She could always think there.

Ten minutes later she pulled into the first public access area and parked her car. She got out and started walking. This was where they met up that night after work. It's where they talked about their future.

Eryn stumbled and landed on her knees in the sand. Sobs wracked her body, the pain streaming through her. What future? They had no future since Chase just packed up and left at the first sign of trouble. That wasn't love!

She couldn't believe that someone who said they loved her so much would hurt her so deeply. Eryn couldn't figure out if she was talking about Chase or her father. It didn't matter now, did it? They both thought they could control her life. Well, now it was her turn to control her own life.

Sitting there in the sand, Eryn waited for her mind to calm down and her body to settle. What was that saying; living well was the best revenge. If there was one thing Eryn wanted at the moment, it was revenge. She would show them alright! It was time to grow up. She'd beat through this and get on with her life.

Standing up, Eryn took off running down the beach. It didn't matter that her ribs hurt like hell; her heart was broken and that pain was far worse.

August, 2012

Marine Corps Base

Kaneohe Bay, Hawaii

"Master Sgt?" Cpl. Billingsley asked when he walked into the Admin area of MCAS Kaneohe Bay Crash Crew.

Chase looked up, "What did you need, Corporal?" He asked as he looked back down at the paper he was reviewing.

Cpl. Billingsley came over and placed a set of papers on the Master Sgt.'s desk.

"Well, the Sgt. Major's office just called to say we've been assigned our new OIC (Officer in Charge)," he said and waited for the obligatory nod from the Master Sgt. before leaving the office.

Breathing a sigh of relief, Chase picked up the papers and scanned them. Being the acting OIC for the last couple of weeks was tiring and he was glad to be able to hand it over to the person slated for the job.

His last OIC had to retire unexpectedly due to medical reasons so the squadron wasn't prepared to have anyone else come in. Chase was expected to keep things running smoothly and he'd done a good job so far but he would be glad to be done with it.

Chase walked out into the hallway toward the Admin office and poked his head in the doorway.

"Cpl.," he said, "Who is it?"

The position of OIC in Crash, Fire, Rescue didn't necessarily get filled by someone in the field since it was primarily administrative. Although that would be fine, it was better if the OIC was trained in the field and understood it.

"Uh," the Corporal said as he shuffled papers.

Chase rolled his eyes and demanded, "Sometime today, Cpl." The kid was good but really unorganized.

Cpl. Billingsley smiled, "Aha," he said. "It's a Warrant Officer 2 Smith."

Nodding, Chase stepped back into the hall. He remembered someone named Smith being mentioned in the Crash Crew newsletter a few months back. He was supposed to have really turned the airfield in Japan around. Stopping, he turned back around toward the Admin Office.

"Do we have an arrival date?" Chase asked loudly.

More papers shuffled, "I believe it's 1 September, Master Sgt." the Corporal replied.

Great, Chase thought to himself, only a couple of weeks left. He could handle that.

Going back to his office, Chase finished up the paperwork he was working on earlier then went down to his Crash Chief's office. He'd never worked with a female Crash Chief before he was stationed here at Kaneohe Bay. Not sure what to expect, he was definitely happy with the job Gunnery Sgt. Abigale Rochelle was doing. She was well acquainted with the equipment and the crews respected her.

Chase liked that she was easy going, unless you ticked her off. A respectable trait that he himself had, so they got along easily enough.

He knocked on the Crash Chief's door and waited about a second before pushing the door open fully. Gunny Rochelle only closed the door completely if she didn't want to be disturbed.

"Hey," Chase said as he leaned against the door frame.

Abi answered, "Hey yourself, Master Sgt.," but didn't look up from the papers she was looking at. "I'm working on schedules so is it okay if I multi-task while you're in here?"

Another thing Chase appreciated about the Gunny, she didn't waste time. "Not a problem," he stated while crossing his arms.

After a minute of no talking, Abi finally looked up, "What did you need, Master Sgt.?"

Chase shook himself mentally, "Oh, sorry," he mumbled and stood up straighter, "we got our new OIC."

Intrigued, Abi gave him her full attention and put the pen she was holding down. Good news.

"Smith from Japan, I think," he said with a smile.

Sitting there, Abi thought he was joking. When it was clear he was serious, she started laughing.

Chase wasn't sure what was so funny. He didn't say anything as a joke.

Trying to stop her laughing, Abi stood up, "This is going to be good," she mumbled under her breath.

Still confused, Chase looked closely at her, "Okay, what did I miss?" he asked in a suspicious tone.

Figuring this wasn't funny to anyone else but her, Abi put on a serious face.

"Nothing," she said and cleared her throat, "Warrant Officer Smith is very good and really did wonders over in Japan in the last couple of years."

He couldn't shake the feeling of suspiciousness stuck in his jaw.

"Yeah, that's what I heard too." he commented.

Looking at his watch, he realized he was due at a meeting.

"I'm headed over for a meeting with the CO, I'll catch you later." He said and walked out of the Crash Chief's office. He heard Gunny Rochelle say, "Aye, Master Sgt," and giggle.

A few days later, Chase was sitting in his office and thinking about the conversation with Gunny Rochelle. He'd had an uneasy feeling since then and couldn't figure out why. Maybe he should say something to her about it? This feeling of something was at the base of his neck.

Shaking it off, he figured it was just because he was overworked and stressed out with covering the

OIC duties. When the new OIC showed up, his problems would be solved and he could concentrate on his own duties.

Besides, he thought as he looked out the window of his office, his dog, Ed, was getting really ticked off with the lack of activity lately. That was saying a lot since Ed was getting pretty lazy in his old age.

"That dog is worse than a wife," he mumbled to himself and settled into the never-ending mound of paperwork on his desk.

Eryn spent her first full day in Hawaii unpacking her stuff and settling in. Since she wasn't married, she decided to stay at the Bachelor's Officers Quarters.

It wasn't the best situation because the room was small and impersonal, but it was only temporary until she figured out what to do. She would probably get an apartment in a few months once she got her bearings.

Finishing up with the last suitcase, Eryn jumped when her room phone rang. She didn't think anybody had her new number yet. Maybe it was her dad since he apparently knew where she was at all times.

"Hello," she said tentatively into the receiver.

Abi Rochelle smiled, "Eryn?" she asked.

The voice was familiar, but Eryn couldn't quite place it, "Yes?"

"It's Abi Rochelle," Abi said laughing.

No way, Eryn thought, "Oh Abi!" she shouted into the phone, then felt silly. "I haven't heard from you in ages."

It was nice to hear from her old friends. She and Abi met years ago at Cherry Point after she and Chase broke up. Why did he pop into her head now?

"How are you doing?" Eryn asked as a fresh slice of pain pierced her chest. No, she demanded to herself, you will not think about that.

Abi smiled, Eryn sounded the same, "Well, I guess you're my new OIC."

Relief washed over Eryn. Thank goodness she'd know someone. "That's great!" she said enthusiastically.

They spoke for a few minutes more and then made plans to meet the next day for lunch.

Eryn went back to unpacking and was smiling. Having Abi here with her was a lucky break. It also meant that two of the higher ranking positions at Crash Crew would be filled by women.

Getting out her carry-on bag, Eryn pulled out a picture of Paul. She brushed her fingers over the glass and set the frame on her nightstand. Now wasn't the time to deal with all the ghosts; that would happen soon enough.

The next day, Eryn pulled into the parking lot of a little restaurant not far from the base. It was nothing more than a shack but the smell was heavenly. She walked in and looked for Abi. A smile split her face when she saw her old friend waving excitedly in the back. Yep, that was Abi.

"Abi," Eryn hugged her friend tight when she got to the table. "You haven't changed."

Abi snorted and replied, "I think I've aged about a hundred years but you look fantastic."

Eryn blushed and muttered a thanks as she sat down. They placed their orders with the waitress and chatted about what was good to eat.

"Damn it's good to see you," Abi said with a big, goofy grin on her face.

Folding her hands on the table, Eryn leaned closer, "So, what's new?"

Occupying her hands with the straw wrapper, Abi wasn't sure where to begin.

"Funny you should ask that," she sighed and said, "I'm sure glad you're sitting."

Abi's tone put Eryn on edge immediately.

"What?" she asked, "Did I come to a hell hole that needs to be completely turned around?" Smiling, she took a sip of water, "Cause, let me tell you, that was a pain in the butt."

Shaking her head, Abi smiled. It didn't reach her eyes though.

It was easy to see that Abi was reluctant to tell her whatever the problem was. That wasn't a good thing since Eryn always remembered Abi to be straightforward.

"What is it?" Eryn asked in a serious tone.

Not sure how to say it, Abi took a deep breath. "Well," She delivered the good news first, "you've got me to work with and the Section Leaders are great."

Eryn nodded, "Yes, and what's the bad news?"

The pit in Eryn's stomach grew, making her nauseous.

"Just spit it out," Eryn said quietly.

Wanting to just get it over with, Abi blurted out, "Chase Johnson is your NCOIC."

A Marine to Remember

Eryn sat there and stared at her friend. The information was sinking in and suddenly the air in the room was non-existent. This couldn't be happening! Not now! Not after ten years ago and then last year! Was she being punished? Pain, hot and fresh, made its way through her chest.

Abi grabbed her friend's hand. She wondered if Eryn was going to faint or something, she looked so pale. On the positive side, at least she was able to warn Eryn before she went to work and came face-to-face with the Master Sgt himself.

"It's not the worst news," Abi said trying to lighten the mood.

Eryn smiled, "It's not," she sighed and picked up her fork, only to put it right back down. She couldn't eat yet. "It's just not what I needed right now."

Abi's brow furrowed, she looked at Eryn with a question, 'tell me everything.'

Sitting back, Eryn started to catch Abi up on what happened in her life over the past ten years. Abi knew that Eryn was accepted into the Warrant Officer program but then they parted ways.

Eryn started telling her friend about going to Quantico, Virginia for training. Her parents were so happy she was an officer and Eryn herself was proud of her own accomplishments. After graduating, Eryn was sent to Okinawa, Japan.

Once she was in Japan, she ended up meeting a man named Paul Smith. He was charming and sweet and didn't care that she was a Marine. Eryn explained that Paul knew about the relationship with Chase and understood her fears. Even though Paul knew she wasn't completely over Chase, he wanted to marry her anyway, so they got married.

They were married three years ago and everything was fine. They even started to talk about kids. Then, Paul was killed in a mid-air collision during a training exercise. He died instantly.

Abi sat there and listened to her friend, her heart aching. Some of the stuff Eryn told her she knew already. Crash Crew was a relatively small MOS and you heard things. It was what Abi didn't already know that made her worried.

Even if Eryn herself didn't know it, Abi could see she wasn't over the failed relationship with Chase. That wasn't good for any of them but they would deal with it. Of course, nobody would come through it unscathed and that was a shame as far as Abi was concerned. Squeezing Eryn's hand again, Abi showed her support.

290

A Marine to Remember

After Eryn spilled her guts, she felt better but kind of embarrassed. Would Abi think she was being overly dramatic? Better that it was out now.

"Okay," Eryn said, "your turn." She looked at Abi and smiled.

It was easy to listen to Abi. Eryn smiled and nodded in all the right places. Abi's life was a good one and Eryn was relieved that her friend seemed happy.

They started talking about old times back in Cherry Point and laughed at all the crazy things they did. The years slipped away it was like they just talked days before. Now that they were thrown together, it would be fun.

An hour later, Abi checked her watch. "Oh, I gotta get back to work," she said reluctantly.

Eryn was torn. Curiosity about her new workplace and fear about running into Chase played tug-o-war inside her. She paid the bill, waving her hand at Abi's objections.

They walked outside to their cars and hugged one last time before parting ways.

Abi opened her car door to get in and stopped, "You know," she smiled, "he doesn't know it's you coming in as the new OIC."

Looking puzzled, Eryn thought about it and smiled slowly, "Oh, the name change right?" she asked.

Nodding, Abi winked and got into her car. She pulled out and shook her head. The glint in Eryn's eyes meant that Chase Johnson was about to be pretty uncomfortable.

Getting into her own car, Eryn laughed at Abi's mischievousness. Eryn wished she had as much of it as her friend. Compared to Abi, she was almost boring. She started up the car and decided a drive was in order to clear her mind and keep her from driving over to Crash Crew.

Chapter 14

Hours later, Eryn was windblown but happy. Hawaii was extraordinarily beautiful. The landscapes constantly changed from sandy beaches to rugged mountains with rolling hills in between. It was green and lush.

Luckily, there were only three main freeways so it was easy to figure out how to get around. Honolulu was forty minutes from the base on the leeward side of the island.

Kaneohe Bay was on the windward side of the island which meant it got more rain but was no less breathtaking. The Koolau Mountains basically cut the island in half and made a spectacular backdrop as Eryn drove. There were gorges worn in the side of the mountains from the rain that created waterfalls when the rains started. It was almost hypnotic just exploring.

Eryn got back to her room in the early evening with a cleared head and renewed determination. She sat down and took the time to dissect her situation.

She currently had the upper hand in that she knew about him but he, apparently, didn't know about her. Normally Eryn didn't consider herself a vindictive person but the hurt still ran deep and it would be tough to contain it. Everyone had a mean streak and hers was directly related to Chase Johnson.

Feeling restless, Eryn decided she had to talk to someone about all of this. She called her parents' house, hoping her mom would answer.

"Fredrick's residence," Beverly Fredricks answered with a light tone.

Eryn smiled, her mother was always so upbeat. "Hi, Mom," she said hurriedly.

Beverly smiled, "Hi yourself, are you settled?" she asked.

Not wanting to chicken out, Eryn blurted out, "Yes, Chase Johnson is here, he's my NCOIC."

Reserving judgment, Beverly nodded, "Okay, tell me what's happening."

Eryn launched into the explanation of how Abi called her and they met for lunch. Her mother listened quietly as Eryn talked about what this meant career-wise and on a personal level.

They talked for a long time and hung up after Eryn promised to call her mother after she met up with Chase in person.

Beverly hung up the phone and smiled. The animation in her daughter's voice was unmistakable. Even if fear and anger with the driving forces, it was enough to make Beverly believe that Eryn might get back into her life. Ten years was a long time to live in limbo and Beverly prayed her daughter could learn from the past and move on.

Even though it was mid-week, Chase felt like it was a Monday. Murphy's Law was in full force today, making everything go wrong.

Ed was screwing around this morning so Chase was late getting to work; something he NEVER did.

A meeting he forgot about started at 0830 and he made it there just in time. The squadron CO was complaining about all the things going wrong so everyone was in a bad mood by time the meeting ended.

At least Crash Crew wasn't singled out but there were still a few comments that ruffled his feathers.

After returning to Crash Crew, some of the equipment was malfunctioning so he had to deal with that fiasco. A couple of the guys on one of the Sections were written up for poor behavior over the weekend so he needed to deal with that.

By mid-morning, he was ready for a break but the paperwork on his desk was growing and he needed to get a handle on it.

The next time Chase looked up, it was lunchtime. His neck was stiff and his stomach growled with hunger. He stood up and rotated his neck. After a bit, he went out into the hall to grab a drink from the water fountain and passed Gunny Rochelle on her way out. She smiled at him and Chase nodded.

After he got a drink, he stood there for a while looking at absolutely nothing. An uneasy feeling was settling inside his chest again. The one that said something was going to happen but he didn't know what it was. When he turned to walk back to his office he happened to glance out the window that looked out onto the parking lot.

Chase's heart stopped dead in his chest for a moment. He took a gulp of air to fill up his suddenly, empty lungs and stared with wide eyes, out the window. Was he hallucinating? There was Eryn Fredricks, standing in the parking lot talking to Gunny Rochelle. They were hugging and laughing.

Maybe he was dreaming. Walking closer to the window, Chase figured the mirage would disappear any second now.

He blinked a couple of times and looked again. Holy shit, it was her! He stared in fascination. It was her, only better. She was drop-dead gorgeous. The hair that haunted his dreams for ten years blew in the gentle breeze. It was thick and hung down halfway down her back now. It looked a little darker than he remembered. Looking down, he felt his hands itching to feel it.

When he looked out again, he felt like the ground under his feet shift. She was here! As he stood there staring, he noticed there was something different about her now but he just couldn't place it.

Eryn pulled into the Crash Crew parking lot at lunch time. It was a last minute decision she wondered about while driving over. Abi was just coming out of the building when Eryn got out of her car so Eryn thought maybe everyone was already gone for lunch and she could poke around a bit.

"Hey there," Abi said smiling. Oh crap, she thought to herself. She just passed Master Sgt. Johnson in the hallway on her way out.

Eryn smiled back, "Hey, I thought you'd all be gone for lunch and I could sneak in."

Shaking her head, Abi leaned up against the car, "No such luck," she answered. "Besides, you think the new OIC coming in for an impromptu visit isn't going to start the tongues wagging?"

Laughing at Abi's comment, Eryn shook her head. Before she could answer, a wave of awareness

Danette Fogarty

came over her. The hair on the back of her neck stood up and she knew he was watching her. Turning slowly, Eryn's eyes scanned the area and building until they landed on Chase standing in a window staring at her.

"Crap!" Abi said, "I should have told you first thing." She didn't want Eryn to be pissed at her.

Staring at Chase, Eryn said calmly, "It's okay, Abi, better to get it over with now."

Nobody moved. Eryn stood where she was and Chase stood in the window.

It reminded Eryn of one of those National Geographic shows on lions, how they sized up their prey. She was pretty sure they were both sizing one another up right now. Her heart was beating so loudly; she thought it might beat right out of her chest.

She jumped when Abi touched her shoulder, breaking eye contact with him.

Abi wasn't sure what to do, "Are you up to this?" she asked Eryn.

Eryn knew it was about time she stood her ground. She looked at Abi with a confidence she wasn't sure she could back up.

"Yes," Eryn answered calmly.

Eryn turned back to see the window vacant.

Thinking of the show on lions, she figured if they didn't back down, then she wouldn't either. There may be yelling and bloodshed but she wasn't going to be the one who flinched. The only question in Eryn's mind was who was going to hurt more, her or Chase?

For a second, when he first saw Eryn, Chase thought maybe he died and this was his last vision. When she didn't move, he wondered if she was daring him. He wasn't sure what but it didn't matter. She was here and he couldn't stop looking at her.

Cpl. Billingsley came up behind the NCOIC as he was looking out the window, "Master Sgt.?" He asked.

Chase tore his eyes away from the parking lot, "Yes," he said impatiently. He wanted to focus on Eryn and what she was doing.

"I'm going to chow now if that's okay," the Corporal said.

Turning back to the window, Chase nodded, "No, go ahead." He shouted after the Cpl., "Take an extra half hour since you're getting out of here late."

"Thanks," Cpl. Billingsley said as he left the building.

Chase would've liked to say he was being charitable but, the fact was, he was trying to get rid of as many witnesses as possible. Once he was sure the Corporal and everyone else from the office was gone, he went out to where the women were standing.

Eryn knew the moment Chase was coming toward them. She didn't just see him, she felt him.

He looked like some knight coming out to slay a dragon or something the way his shoulders were set. She would have laughed if she wasn't so on edge about seeing him again. She wasn't the monster here, he was. He should be afraid of her. A mental image of a lioness on the hunt sprang to mind so she made a mental note to avoid watching animal shows for a while.

He was walking toward her and she was forcing herself to forget how good he looked and focus on what he did. He was the one who left without as much as a goodbye!

Pulling herself together and going on with her life was the only option at the time. She would not let him hurt her again; she was going to protect herself at all costs. But even repeating that to herself, she wasn't sure she believed it.

As Chase got closer, Eryn felt more of the physical responses she tried to forget. Heat crept into her chest, her hands were clammy, and her breathing became ragged. All of her senses were on full alert. She was trying desperately to shore up her defenses and not let him know how he made her feel.

The fifty feet that separated them was the longest distance Chase ever crossed; at least in his mind. He kept his eyes glued to hers as he walked, the questions running through his mind were fast.

What was she doing here? Was she here with her father? How did she and Gunny Rochelle know one another? Was this a trick?

Chase's face contorted into a grim line of annoyance. He didn't need to deal with this right now. They were getting a new OIC at work and he should be focused on that and not these teenager-like feelings.

Eryn squared her shoulders as Chase crossed the last few feet that separated them. She couldn't help but notice the look in his eyes; apprehension, curiosity, annoyance, but definitely not welcome. Great.

Stopping just out of arms reach from Eryn, Chase took a breath. If he got any closer to her, he would reach out to touch her. What the hell did he say now? He looked over at Gunny Rochelle, his jaw set.

"Gunny," he chose his words carefully, "do we have a visitor?"

Always a gentleman, Eryn thought sarcastically.

Abi smiled, "Master Sgt. Johnson, I'd like you to meet our new OIC, Eryn Smith."

Nobody moved and nobody spoke.

Eryn watched as the information hit home. Chase's face paled and he looked back and forth between her and Abi. It was almost comical. Almost.

"What the hell," Chase said under his breath and looked away.

A thousand thoughts ran through his mind, none of them appropriate. This had to be some kind of a joke. He just could not deal with this right now.

Looking back at Gunny Rochelle, Chase said, "I'm going to lunch," and walked over to his vehicle.

The woman stared after him as he got into his jeep and tore out of the parking lot.

Once Chase's vehicle was out of sight, Eryn turned to face Abi. "Well," she huffed, "that was a fine how do you do!"

Abi looked at her friend and couldn't hold back, "I'll say."

They both started laughing.

Now that the official confrontation was over, Eryn felt better. This would definitely be interesting.

"You want a tour?" Abi asked.

Eryn nodded and the women walked into the Crash Barn.

An hour later, Chase pulled into the parking lot at Crash Crew. He made it back from lunch, but just barely. It took every semblance of self-control he had to drive back to work. This was crazy! He was trained to handle highly stressful situations, save lives, and, if necessary, take lives. How come he couldn't come up with the right words to say to the woman?

Because, he argued to himself, she wasn't just any woman. She was the woman who haunted his dreams for ten years,; who made it impossible to commit to anyone else.

Sure, he'd managed his share of relationships over the years; he was no monk. He just wasn't able to give more than his physical self. Every time he tried, he thought about Eryn.

Finally, he had to give up on that train of thought or he would go crazy. There was no use going down that road. But now, she was his boss? Oh, he was pretty sure that the Great Almighty was having a big laugh at his expense right now. He got out of his jeep and walked to the building.

Danette Fogarty

Gunny Rochelle was in her office when the Master Sgt. returned from lunch. She heard him enter the building and thought a herd of elephants would have been quieter. He was barking out orders as he came down the hall.

Turning to face him when he entered her office, Abi was thankful she and Eryn did the tour quickly so Eryn could get out before he returned. She figured this wouldn't be pretty but she'd been up against bigger and badder before now.

What Abi didn't count on though, was seeing a man who was so obviously hurt. His appearance threw Abi as he stood there in the doorway to her office. He was still in love with Eryn!

She suspected as much when she saw him stalk out to the parking lot earlier but wasn't sure. Did either of them know they never really got over one another? She sure wasn't going to be the one to bring up that little bit of information. It was easier to sit back and see what happened. After all, somebody needed to keep a clear head around here.

Chase paused at the doorway to the Gunny's office for a minute. When he came in he closed the door behind him and plopped down on a chair in front of her desk, sighing. He expected her to give him some kind of lecture but she just sat there looking at him.

Abi knew he was waiting on her, "Yes, Master Sgt.?" she finally asked.

Snorting, Chase looked around the office and shook his head, "How long did you know about this?" he demanded.

She was trying so hard to not smile, but it was tough. "Since the day you came in and told me who our new OIC was."

Abi watched the emotions play across the Master Sgt.'s face and she felt sorry for him.

After another minute of silence, Chase spoke up. "We have a history," he said quietly.

Nodding, Abi leaned forward, "I know."

She kind of figured Chase would think she'd judge him and take Eryn's side but she really wasn't in a position to do so. Eryn was a friend of hers but Abi was smart enough to know there were always two sides to every story.

"Listen, Chase," she said and felt a little funny using his first name, "it's your history so it's really none of my business."

Chase nodded but didn't say anything.

Abi smiled, "She told me some of it but that has nothing to do with the working relationship between us."

This conversation was not sitting well with Chase; he couldn't even comment because he didn't know what to say. He was slightly relieved that Abi seemed to be neutral in all of this.

Sighing, Abi looked serious, "Look, Eryn and I are professionals so we won't bring anything personal to work." She waited for a comment and got nothing. "We won't be ganging up on you."

Standing up, Chase nodded again, and left her office without a word.

Eryn returned to her room and practically fell against the door when she was inside. She could finally breathe!

Seeing Chase took an emotional toll on her and she still couldn't believe it. It wasn't so much about what happened but what didn't happen that upset her. They didn't talk, not one word. At the time she was relieved but now she was ticked off about it.

Pushing away from the door, Eryn walked over and sat at the desk. Was their time together so inconsequential to him?

Now, fate turned the tables and she was in charge, at least at work. She wouldn't use her power to torture him but it did allow her a sense of distance. After all, officers and enlisted personnel weren't supposed to fraternize. Of course, she berated herself, those kind of rules didn't stop you ten years ago!

Crossing her room, Eryn fell onto the bed and stared at the ceiling.

An hour later she was still in the same spot. She wanted to yell and pound her fists but it was really pointless. Ten years ago, he squashed her like a bug emotionally and that couldn't be changed.

Eryn turned her head and looked at the picture on the nightstand next to the bed. The picture of Paul was there and always brought up a mixture of emotions.

Sometimes she honestly thought that Chase hadn't done such a number on her because she found Paul. He provided the safety she desperately needed. Sure, they didn't have the fireworks but they had a mutual respect that lead to a comfortable love. A safe love. He saved her. Memories came flooding into her mind before she could stop them....

They met through a mutual friend. With Japan being her first duty station as a Warrant Officer, she was really trying to find her way. She and another Warrant Officer were sitting in the Officer's Club one night when a group of guys walked in. She and her friend joked because they knew instantly the group was made up of pilots. You could always tell. As they were talking, her friend recognized one and called him over.

His name was Paul. He was a pilot assigned to an aircraft carrier in Japan. When Paul found out what she did, they jumped into an excited debate about whose job was more important. Eryn liked him immediately and teased him unmercifully about being able to save his butt. After that, they were friends.

Four years after meeting, Paul finally asked Eryn out on their official date. He told her that he waited so long partly because of his deployments and partly because he knew she was mending a broken heart. Eryn told him about Chase and what happened; or at least what she suspected had happened. Being the kind man he was, he respected her need for time. It was one of the things Eryn admired the most about him.

Once they were a couple, he still held back and gave her the reins of their relationship. He never pressured her; he always told her he knew how he felt and that he would wait. Eryn remembered how she thought he was so different from the pilot persona and how he was exactly the opposite of all the other men in her life. That was the thing that made him especially attractive to Eryn.

Eryn waited almost a year to ask him to make love with her. Their kisses up until then were sweet and gentle but didn't take her breath away. Still, she knew it was time for them to take the next step.

Paul took her face into his hands and kissed her deeply. Instead of taking off her clothes he stood back, smiled, and asked her if she wanted to wait until after they were married.

Once Eryn realized he was proposing she smiled and nodded. Their engagement was short; in part because they wanted to make love and because Paul was due to ship out for another six months.

She called her parents and told them the news. She recalled how they seemed leery, which surprised her at the time. She assumed they would be happy for her and had met Paul so it didn't seem like a big deal. Paul's family was excited and wished them well.

The ceremony was short, with only a few friends at the base chapel. She wore a simple white dress and he wore his dress whites. It was touching and she cried. They stayed at the lodge on base for their wedding night since Paul's deployment was only days away.

Eryn blushed as she looked in the mirror of the hotel bathroom on her wedding night. She was nervous but finally mustered up enough courage to come out.

As he did with their relationship, Paul waited and let her set the pace for their lovemaking. It was tender and sweet. She was relieved that it wasn't as painful or embarrassing as friends told her. It was a rite of passage and Eryn felt like she finally grew up.

Their marriage consisted of more time apart than together but it seemed to suit them as individuals. Eryn enjoyed it when he was home but liked her independence as well. Paul always knew and accepted that about her. She did a lot of growing up during their marriage.

She became comfortable with lovemaking and even emboldened during their brief times together. Paul commented on more than one occasion that if he knew all of this earlier, he would've married her a lot sooner.

In Paul she found someone to love her and cherish her without needing to control her. It made her happy to know he was there for her.

After a few years, they started talking about children. They even tried during his infrequent trips home with no luck. They finally decided a vacation was in order so they could, as Paul put it, "hone their baby-making skills."

A Marine to Remember

Eryn picked the picture up off the nightstand and held it to her chest.

She was at work late one evening trying to finish up some paperwork. She was desperately trying to get everything squared away before she went on leave and met up with Paul in Australia. They never had a proper honeymoon so they decided a destination vacation was in order.

Sitting at her desk, Eryn looked up to see a Staff Sgt. standing in the doorway of her office. He was an MP (Military Policeman). He identified himself and entered her office. It was only then that Eryn noticed he was accompanied by a Chaplain and her squadron CO. Eryn grew up in the Marine Corps so she knew this meant bad news.

She was overcome with a numbness when they told her Paul was dead. She asked them to repeat it just to make sure she hadn't heard wrong. Afterwards, she asked the men to give her a moment in her office so she could call her family.

Calling her parents wasn't too hard. She gave them the news and listened as they told her they were on their way.

She walked out of her office and asked to be driven home. The Chaplain offered his company when they dropped her off but she declined.

After stepping into their house, Eryn felt confused. Her friend Emma, by coincidence, happened to be in Japan for a training conference so Eryn called her and asked her to come over.

By that time, Eryn knew she had to call Paul's parents and let them know. She didn't want someone else to tell them. She dialed the number and managed to get out the words before her control slipped.

Her voice started to hitch and the tears poured down her cheeks. The pain overwhelmed her when she heard Paul's mother shouting, "No!" on the phone. She had to hang up or she would crumble.

Emma showed up while she was on the phone with Paul's parents so she took the phone and finished the call. After that, she held Eryn in her arms like a baby and comforted her while she cried. Thank God Emma had been there.

The next days were filled with pain and confusion. Eryn's parents arrived from the States with Ben and Colleen. It took a few days for the Navy to transport Paul's body back to Japan.

Once he was there, they all went to the terminal to meet his body. Eryn stood next to her parents and watched, silently, as the casket was taken off the plane.

The next day everyone, including Emma, flew to Paul's home in Ohio so he could be buried.

She was in a fog while meeting his family for the first time. His mother held her so tight, she couldn't breathe. There were aunts, uncles, and cousins hugging her and reassuring her.

The group walked down to receive the casket from the plane and that's when the whole thing hit home. Paul was dead!

The funeral service was beautiful; Paul's parents made all of the arrangements. There was a Navy color guard there to show their support. She sat in a chair, her parents on one side and Paul's parents on the other side. She was handed a folded flag and realized that the service was over.

Afterward, everyone gathered at Paul's parents' house. She met more family members and was surprised at the sheer numbers in the Smith family. Everyone was so kind and Eryn started to feel like an imposter.

During their relationship they'd focused on Eryn so much that she didn't know very much about this whole other part of his life. Sure, he mentioned his family but was never descriptive; as if he knew their marriage was all about her. He didn't reveal a lot and Eryn was ashamed for it. She should have known these things about her husband.

The day after the funeral, Eryn sat down with Paul's mother. Amber Smith was as kind and patient as her son and she held Eryn's hand while she talked about her boy. She told stories about Paul's childhood and brought out photo albums.

Eryn greedily looked through all of the pictures. She smiled at the cute little boy, the gawky teenager, and the handsome man.

Amber told Eryn about how much Paul loved her. She said her only regret for her son was that he hadn't lived long enough to have children of his own. A fresh wave of guilt covered Eryn like a wet blanket.

She wondered if she really wanted children with Paul. She didn't know that much about him. He'd always been there for her but had she really been there for him? The question plagued her after that, stalking her conscience.

Eryn flew back to Okinawa to return to duty two weeks after Paul's death. She wasn't really there because the questions about herself and Paul haunted her. The guilt of not being a good wife kept her up at night. She was okay with being married to someone she rarely saw. Why was that?

Eating, sleeping, and functioning daily were becoming impossible. Her troops noticed and tried to pick up the slack but it was no use. She reached her breaking point when she didn't even notice what was going on during a training fire. It was pointless to go on the way she was.

The next morning she met with the base Chaplain. It was hard for Eryn to express her thoughts out loud and she was ashamed and embarrassed about her selfishness during their marriage. She eventually got out the whole story and waited for the Chaplain to tell her how awful she was.

Surprising Eryn, the Chaplain explained that each person makes their own decisions in life. He told her that Paul chose to accept what Eryn offered, even if it wasn't all it could be. Since Paul never expressed unhappiness or regret to anyone about their marriage, then he didn't view it as a shortcoming on Eryn's part. So, if Paul was okay with it, then Eryn needed to reconcile that within herself.

She took time off of work and met with the Chaplain on a regular basis. It was a painful process to work through but she did it. The hardest part was realizing that, although she loved Paul, it wasn't the kind of love that married people should have.

After weeks of counseling, she felt strong enough to go back to work. Everyone at Crash Crew welcomed her back. She dug into work and used that as an excuse for a while. Eventually she recognized that work wasn't a reason to live and worked on opening up her life again.

She worked with the Chaplain for several months, appreciating his objective opinion to help her deal with her heavy thoughts. She kept in touch with Paul's family, trying to help them through their grieving process as well.

Her confidence showed up one day and she figured out that she wasn't dead with Paul, so she needed to move on. He would always have a place in her heart. He saved her in life and in death.

Eryn put the picture back on the nightstand and wiped the tears from her eyes. She didn't want to go through the memories anymore today.

Why would this all come up again? Why now?

She sat up and took a deep breath. Because, she thought to herself, Chase opened up a wound that wasn't ever healed.

Going into the bathroom, Eryn took a shower and cleared her head. She needed all the strength she had to deal with Chase and this new situation.

Chapter 15

By late Saturday afternoon, Eryn was pacing her room like a caged animal.

Starting her new position on Monday would test everything she knew about herself. She would be the one to come out ahead this time around. No more letting her heart get trampled. With a new determination, she put on her running gear and went to the track to run off some of the pent up energy raging inside of her.

A few miles into her run, Eryn was deep in her rhythm when she felt the hairs on the back of her neck stand straight up.

She kept running but looked around for the cause. She should have known he would show up at some point. Even after ten years she had the most elemental reaction to him. How could that be? And where the hell was he?

She still couldn't see Chase but she felt him as if he was standing right in front of her. The feeling was monumentally unnerving so, after a few minutes, she got off the track to give her senses some relief. Distance would help.

Eryn was walking back toward her room when the feeling slammed into her again. Only this time it was a lot stronger. Her breath was so ragged that she stopped in her tracks. Turning around, she felt a jolt go right through her body. He was standing about fifty feet behind her and must have stopped when she did.

Staring at him, Eryn knew there was only one option for her to do and that was to run.

Chase watched Eryn take off and cursed. An hour ago he was at home and minding his own business. The next thing he knew, he was on his way to the base track.

He remembered she always ran when she was upset or had to work something out and, if she was as riled up as he was, she would be there. Sure enough, he saw her as soon as he parked his car. It was like he was the moth and she was the flame.

Watching her run, Chase studied her body. Her hair was still long, her ponytail bouncing as she ran. He loved it and wondered how it would feel on his fingers.

Still toned from all the running, he could see that her body was still exquisitely beautiful. That thought made his shorts tight. Her legs were solid muscle, her shoulders straight, and her face was set in concentration. He knew she was thinking about them.

When she started looking around, he wondered who she was looking for. It was only when she started to leave the track that he started walking in her direction.

He followed her like a lost, little puppy. That was pitiful but he couldn't help it. His whole body betrayed every bit of common sense where Eryn was concerned.

She stopped again and turned around. When her eyes met his, he was thrust into the craziest feelings. He couldn't say anything, only stand there and drink in the sight of her. He saw the same confusion in her eyes and was about to start moving when she took off.

Eryn's lungs were on fire. This was history repeating itself and she was panicking. He scared the hell out of her. But, then again, she let him. There were too many feelings running through her to figure this out so she had to get away from him and this tornado of emotions that threatened to consume her.

She could see the building where her room was when she felt his fingers wrap around her arm. In response, she jerked around quickly and lost the last bit of breath in her lungs. Bending over, Eryn gasped for breath. Unfortunately, Chase wouldn't leave her be and grabbed her arm again. He was dragging her away from the sidewalk toward a group of trees. Panic set in and Eryn started pulling away.

"What are you doing?" she yelled.

Chase didn't say anything, just kept pulling her behind him.

Eryn didn't know what to do, "Chase, please," she begged in between gasps for air.

Stopping at the sound of fear in Eryn's voice, Chase turned and looked at her. Just like years before, everything around them stopped. The breeze no longer made the palm leaves sway and the birds didn't chirp. There wasn't anyone around. It was like they were the only two people in the entire world.

Staring at Chase, Eryn knew he could see everything inside of her. His eyes burned into her soul and roused the pain and confusion of the young woman she was ten years earlier. Then, there was that overwhelming awareness that her body felt when he was anywhere near her.

He just wanted to stand there and look at her. That was all, he told himself.

Finally rational thought started to permeate his fuzzy mind and he realized what he did. He couldn't just drag a woman around, no matter what she did to him. His heart was pounding so loudly he could hear it, his breath was as ragged as hers, but for a different reason, and his emotions were spinning out of control. He wasn't able to resist his urge, and didn't want to, so he framed her face with his hands and brought his lips down to meet hers.

The kiss sent off fireworks throughout Eryn's entire body. The heat started in her toes and worked its way upward until it engulfed her completely. Her arms lifted and wrapped around his neck but she didn't know how.

This was heaven, pure and simple. It was like finding a part of yourself that was missing for far too long. His lips were firm but not possessive. He was giving her pleasure and letting her take what she wanted. There was power lying in wait and with the slightest encouragement, the kiss would become something much more. Eryn opened her mouth and touched her tongue to Chase's lips gently.

When Chase felt Eryn's tongue asking for entry, he growled and pulled her closer. He pushed his tongue into her mouth and swirled it deliciously around hers. The ride was crazy and sucked up all his energy. His hands moved up her arms.

Bodies were shifting to get closer in an effort to find relief of the torrential need pouring through them.

A car drove by and honked its horn, startling them. They broke apart and stared at one another.

Eryn was smoldering from the kiss and recognized what he wanted when he moved closer.

She shook her head and said, "No."

Knowing Eryn was serious but not wanting this to end, Chase said, "Eryn," in a pleading voice.

"No," Eryn repeated in a stronger voice.

Chase stood where he was and watched Eryn walk away. It was getting dark when he finally walked back to his car.

Monday morning, Eryn was still majorly conflicted about the situation but she decided she would deal with it the best way she could. She got in a quick run before getting ready, which helped clear her mind.

She was being formally introduced to the troops today so she wanted to be in top form. Having Chase there could compromise that and she was determined to do her best. She loved her job and the people she worked with. She just needed to get a handle on these residual feelings and she would be okay.

Grabbing her bag and taking a deep breath, Eryn left her room. She was walking up to her car when she noticed Chase standing a few feet away from it. Stopping momentarily, her heart skipped a beat at the sight of him. Taking a deep breath, she started walking and headed straight for her vehicle. She would not let him see how much he affected her.

A Marine to Remember

Chase watched Eryn walk out and was blown away by the shot of awareness that ran through him. He drove over here to clear the air with her before work. That was his plan anyway.

He felt like a complete louse after Saturday and was ashamed of his actions. That wasn't what he did and he wanted to reassure Eryn that it wouldn't happen again. She was his superior at work now. Watching her come toward him though, he couldn't reassure himself that he wouldn't keep his hands off of her.

"Good morning," Chase said as he pushed away from his vehicle and started toward her.

Eryn unlocked her door and turned to face him, "Hi."

They stood there silent and then both started talking at the same time.

Eryn chuckled, "I'm sorry about running away," she said while looking down at her hands.

The admission surprised them both.

Chase nodded, "And I'm sorry for grabbing you. It wasn't the time or place for that kind of behavior." He sighed, "It won't happen again."

Smiling, Eryn looked up into his blue eyes. She turned around, opened her car door, and said, "I'm sorry to hear that," and got in.

Chase stood there and watched her drive away. She was going to be the death of him. Smiling, he walked back to his own car to go to work.

The morning formation was conducted efficiently and professionally as far as Eryn could see. Everyone stood at attention when Chase introduced her. She made some announcements and asked GySgt. Rochelle and Master Sgt. Johnson to proceed. It was nice to stand back and observe the troops' interaction with both Abi and Chase. A good leader knew when to delegate.

After the formation was concluded, Eryn drove over to meet with the Squadron Commanding Officer.

Thoughts of feelings and Chase were put aside to focus on upcoming events. There was a review team coming from Washington D.C. in a couple of weeks. Rim Pac was gearing up so that meant service members from countries bordering the Pacific Ocean conducted war games and training. It also meant a lot more headaches for the airfield but Eryn was confident she and her crew would handle it well.

A Marine to Remember

When she got back to the Crash Barn, she knew it was protocol to meet with her NCOIC first. Since that happened to be Chase, she chickened out and met with Abi instead.

Abi sat across from Eryn smiling, "So, how has your morning been?"

Eryn responded with a smile; she liked that Abi was always down to business first. "It's been fine," she answered.

Nodding, Abi sat back in her chair.

"I see that you and Chase have a handle on things here," Eryn said as she straightened papers on her desk that didn't need to be straightened.

Wearing a mischievous look, Abi smiled, "So it's Chase now?" She asked and felt only a little bad for teasing when Eryn blushed. "Thank you," she added on a more serious note, "we think we've got a good crew. Have you met with him yet?"

Eryn sighed. Leave it to Abi to switch subjects on her so quickly.

"I'll take that as a no." Abi responded.

Watching Eryn closely, Abi could understand her reluctance. Anyone who knew them could see the electricity between them. Abi wasn't sure how either of them would end up handling it. Only time would tell.

Changing the subject back to work, Abi sat up straighter, "Well, we're on the clock so no talking about boys." She smiled and stood up, "I'll expect a full report tonight so how about dinner?"

"That sounds great," Eryn answered and looked at her watch. "I'll catch up with you at the end of the day."

Chase was in the hallway when Gunny Rochelle came out of Eryn's office. The thought that she wanted to meet with Abi first rubbed his ego raw. Even with the cluttered feelings between them, they were at work.

A few minutes later, he was called into meet with Eryn. As he entered the office, he noticed some changes she made. There was a box in the corner with frames in it. There were two pictures on her desk and he scanned them quickly. One was one of her family that he recognized from years ago in her barracks room and the other one was a picture of a Marine in front of an F-18.

Sitting down, Chase wondered who the guy was. He was jealous and pissed that he was. Eryn caught him looking at the picture again and turned it away from him. When he looked at her, he could see emotions skitter across her features.

Eryn cleared her throat, "Thanks for coming in," she said. "I know it's customary for me to meet with you first but I wanted to give us both some time."

Chase's eyebrows rose in surprise, "I appreciate your honesty, ma'am."

Trying not to fidget because of Chase's close proximity, Eryn struggled to keep her mind on work.

"I know you need to bring me up to speed," she stood and closed her office door. "And I'm sure you'll be glad to be relieved."

He waited for her to be seated again, "It wasn't too bad but I will be glad to get back to my own work." He smiled.

The awkwardness in the room was settling down. Maybe they needed the neutral ground of work to help them get on track.

Eryn and Chase spent the next hour going over Crash Crew business. Most of it was stuff already relayed to Eryn but Chase had an interesting take on some of the issues as they would relate specifically to Crash Crew operations.

Chase talked about some of the scheduled incoming squadrons that would be assigned to Kaneohe Bay for Rim Pac. He had a schedule roughed out for the visiting inspection team if they chose to tour Crash Crew.

It was nice to see him so confident with his position. Eryn surreptitiously studied him as he talked.

There weren't drastic changes in his appearance in the last ten years but he was still different. His hair was still dark and looked soft but now there was a little gray tucked in at the temples. It only made him look more distinguished. He was still lean and muscular from what she could tell through his flight suit. But now, the more she thought about him, the more she wasn't thinking about what he was saying.

Talking, Chase knew she wasn't paying attention. The look on her face was driving him nuts. It was a mix of awareness and curiosity. He wasn't sure if what he was saying was right because he was thinking so much about her. Finally he gave up and stood.

"Eryn," he said sharply, "what are you thinking about?" His voice sounded raspy and he didn't like it.

Landing with a thud back into reality, Eryn blushed. She didn't like his tone. "Master Sgt.," she said sharply back, "I'm listening to your update on what's going on around here."

Chase snorted and walked around his chair to put a little more distance between them. "You don't think I don't know what you're thinking about?" He walked up to her desk and put his hands down on either side of her. "You're thinking about the same damn thing I'm thinking about."

Looking up into his eyes, Eryn knew he was right. He pegged her. Trying to muster up some dignity, she cleared her throat.

"I don't think you need to use that tone with me, Master Sgt.," She stood as she said it, trying to add to her resolve.

Now he was pissed off. He stood up straight and wiped a hand over his face to try and compose himself.

Sitting back down, Chase started, "I have two years left here," he said quietly. "And I need to know right now if you think we can work together for that amount of time."

The hairs on the back of Eryn's neck stood up in indignation.

Chase saw her cheeks redden and knew he'd pushed a button.

Eryn walked around her desk and stood in front of him. "I can assure you, Master Sgt.," she pointed a finger at his chest, "that I will use the utmost professionalism when dealing with you." Her breathing was ragged from her pent up anger, "Do you think YOU can handle that?" she demanded.

Sitting there with Eryn looking down at him with murder in her eyes, Chase realized he was still in love with her. Dammit! She was infuriating and independent and vulnerable. She could hurt him so easily. She was also the most beautiful woman in the entire universe as far as he was concerned. And he couldn't tell her any of it.

Standing up, Chase nodded and said, "Yes, ma'am," and walked out of her office.

Eryn spent the rest of the day going over paperwork and getting her office in order. When she was done and sitting at her desk, she looked over at the picture of Paul. She berated herself for her own reaction to having Chase see it. For some bizarre reason, she felt like being married to Paul was cheating on Chase. It was absurd but she still felt that way.

Sitting back, she thought about Chase and sneered. He'd been the one to leave, without a word, and she moved on with her life. There was nothing to feel bad about or explain. A blanket of sadness covered her. She was still sitting there a while later when there was a knock at her door.

Abi stuck her head into Eryn's office doorway, "Hey."

A Marine to Remember

Embarrassed by being caught thinking about Chase, Eryn tried to look busy. "I'm sorry, I didn't hear you."

Not surprising, Abi thought, her friend was thinking about something. She'd let it go for now. "Dinner?" she asked.

Nodding, Eryn smiled, "That sounds great, let me clear this up and we'll go."

Chase was across the hall finishing up paperwork in his office when he heard Eryn leave with Gunny Rochelle. He nodded in acknowledgment when they passed his doorway and felt a twinge work its way up his back. What was wrong with him? He was actually jealous because Eryn chose to leave with Gunny Rochelle? Damn Right! Get a grip, Johnson, he told himself and finished up his work.

The next couple of weeks went smoothly at Crash Crew. Eryn and Chase only dealt with one another when absolutely necessary. They didn't go out of their way to avoid one another but they didn't leave their respective offices very often.

After three weeks, Eryn was able to finish going through the personnel files for her troops. If there was something that bothered her, she asked Chase or Abi but was glad that didn't happen often.

She met with the Section Leaders and the department heads in Training, Trucks, Admin, and Material. It was an easy going atmosphere where everybody did their job well.

There didn't seem to be any disciplinary problems either and Eryn was happy about that. She wasn't afraid to be a "hard ass" but didn't like to do that unless it was necessary.

One afternoon she was sitting with Gunny Fitzpatrick, going over the new training schedule, when she heard a dog barking outside. Needing a break anyway, she excused herself and went outside to investigate.

She was just rounding the corner of the building when a large mound of fur jumped up on her and almost knocked her down. There was a large tongue attached the fur that started licking her face. Once she got her balance back, she was able to look her attacker in the face.

"Ed?" Eryn whispered and was answered with a sloppy kiss. Hugging the dog, Eryn laughed, "Ed!"

Chase walked over and was mad at Ed for not listening. "Ed," he said in a low, stern voice, "down!"

Eryn had to hold back a laugh. Ed looked over at Chase like "whatever" and looked back at her.

Ed, figuring he better listen, gave Eryn another kiss and slid back down to all fours. He sat nicely next to Eryn and looked at Chase.

Breaking up the moment, Eryn looked at Chase, "He's still gorgeous." She reached down and scratched behind Ed's ears. When she stood back up and looked at Chase she could see how upset he was at Ed's apparent mutiny.

"Yeah," Chase said sarcastically, "he's a real gem."

Eryn giggled and petted Ed a little bit more.

Chase stood there watching with a scowl on his face. He wasn't upset that Ed was happy to see Eryn; he was jealous of the attentions she gave the dog. Why couldn't she be that happy to see him? Knowing that he was pretty pathetic at being jealous over a dog, he decided to take Ed home. He turned to go back to his jeep and whistled for Ed to follow.

Standing there, Eryn watched the exasperating man and his loyal sidekick get into the jeep and pull out. She smiled for the rest of the day.

By that Friday, Eryn figured her settling in period was really over. She liked her new command. No place was perfect but the pros definitely outweighed the cons. When she was finishing up paperwork she decided to go for a drive after work.

Her sightseeing was limited up to now and she really wanted to look around the island. She grabbed some clothes out of her bag and went into the bathroom to change.

Ten minutes later she emerged and didn't look the same. Her hair was just pulled back into a ponytail and she wore a pair of jean shorts, a tank top, and tennis shoes. She looked younger and smiled.

About halfway out to her car, Eryn heard a whistle from behind her. A woman could figure out pretty easily when a man was whistling at her.

When she turned around, she saw a group of Crash Crew guys walking toward the opposite end of the building. She wasn't sure who the whistler was but they all looked scared when she turned around and they realized it was her.

"Next time make sure you know who you're whistling at!" she shouted. "Thanks anyway," she said to herself as she got into her car.

Waving, she guessed the group was on its way to the Section Leaders office to explain what happened.

Chapter 16

Kailua Beach was a public beach about fifteen minutes from the base. A lot of people recommended she go there so that was her destination. She passed some beautiful homes that bordered the ocean and wondered what it must be like to have that view every day.

After finding a parking spot in the public parking area, Eryn got out of her car and removed her shoes. She was surprised at how busy it looked. Probably people like her, trying to get a jump on their weekend.

Leaving her blanket in the trunk, Eryn threw her shoes in with it and decided to walk the beach for a while.

There was a small rise between the beach and the parking lot so it took her a few minutes to see the view everyone told her about. But once she crested the little hill, she could why people recommended it. The water was crystal clear and blue.

She looked both ways and saw that there were less umbrellas and groups down the beach to her right so that's the direction she took.

Chase was very lucky to find a house for rent so close to the beach. The rent was high but totally worth it in his mind. Ed took him for a walk every day so they each got a good workout. Usually they would run or play catch but today they just walked along.

A few minutes after they hit the beach, Ed started acting up. Chase recognized the signs and nodded, "Go," he said and watched Ed go after whatever was so important.

Watching as Ed sprinted down the beach, he frowned when Ed bee-lined it toward a woman. Her hair was long and was blowing in the breeze. She was alone and didn't freak out when Ed caught up to her. She was bent down petting Ed when recognition hit Chase in the gut. Eryn!

Chase started walking toward them and wondered if there was some higher power at work here since they kept running into one another. This was driving him nuts. He could hear her laughter as he got closer and inwardly cringed when she saw the smile she was wearing for Ed fade.

It was almost painful for Chase to know that she wasn't happy about seeing him. It's not like he was thrilled to be around her all day either. It was like his body was on full alert all day long and only relaxed when he was away from Crash Crew.

Eryn watched Chase's approach with a mixture of apprehension and excitement. Her heart was beating so fast, it felt like it was going to beat right out of her chest. Thank goodness Ed was there so she could do something with her hands. All of this was so damn confusing.

When Eryn's eyesight focused again, he was standing right in front of her. He looked beautiful and made her body crave all sorts of things. For now, she had to fight it.

Chase lifted a hand in greeting when he was closer, "Hi," he said.

She couldn't answer. There was no voice, no signal form her brain to speak, nothing. All she could do was stand there and pet Ed.

Watching Eryn watch him made Chase feel aroused. He wanted to take her into his arms and kiss her senseless.

"What the hell," he murmured and walked up to her.

She didn't know what he meant to do at first so her eyes widened when she figured out he was going to kiss her. It was like they were moving in slow motion or something. He took her into his arms and brought his lips down to hers.

One minute she was laughing with Ed and the next she was kissing Chase. Going with it, Eryn lifted her arms and wrapped them around Chase's neck. A moment later, her tongue was dancing with his and creating a delicious friction.

It was like being protected, she was pressed up against hard muscle and held on tightly. Settling deeper into the kiss, Eryn sighed. It was like stepping into a hot bubble bath after a hard day or eating a freshly baked chocolate chip cookie. The kiss was a combination of comfort and guilty pleasure.

Her body wanted nothing more than to keep kissing Chase, but her mind was being irritated with the nagging voice of reason. Slowly, she started getting out of the mind-numbing pleasure of the kiss.

Chase knew the moment Eryn came to her senses. She stiffened and started stepping away from him. When he opened his eyes and looked down into hers, he could see the fear and confusion there. He was afraid she would run again, so he kept his arms around her.

Red-cheeked, Eryn looked up into his seductive blue eyes and sighed. She wanted to say something to him but had no idea what to say. Dropping her head to his shoulder, she stood there and just breathed him the smell of him. How could she say something or explain something when she had no clue what she felt?

Chase sensed her mood, "I know," he whispered.

They stood there on the beach and held each other for a while. Ed ran around playing and provided a distraction.

After a few minutes, Chase released her. She felt lost so she sat down. Being this confused drained her emotionally and physically. Once she was down on the soft, white sand, she pulled her knees up and wrapped her arms around them. She felt Chase sit down beside her in the sand.

They didn't say anything, just sat there and looked out over the soothing ocean. Ed played in the shallows chasing whatever appealed to him. People walked by and enjoyed the day but they just sat there.

Eryn didn't know how long they sat there because she was lost in thoughts about Chase. The first time she sees him in ten years, he doesn't say anything to her. The second time he sees her, he practically attacks her. Now he kisses her senseless. She learned to hate him over the years and now that whole plan was blowing up in her face.

Chase decided they were quiet long enough, "What are we going to do?" he asked without looking at her. He focused on Ed playing in the water.

What he was asking required her to use her brain to think and she didn't want to do that just yet. Her body was still humming from their heated kisses and she couldn't muster up the strength to answer.

"Eryn," he said when he looked at her.

She finally looked over and met his eyes. He was so beautiful and made her body want so much. But right now she needed to resist that.

"I'm sorry," she answered, "I was lost in my thoughts."

Nodding, Chase knew how she felt. "Well, can I bring you back to reality for a moment?" he asked.

Chuckling, Eryn responded, "Not if you keep kissing me that way."

She hadn't meant to blurt out the words; it was just a gut reaction. She saw his face transform from seriousness into relief. He started laughing. It was a deep, melodic laugh that made her nerve endings go crazy.

Chase stood and offered his hand to Eryn. When he pulled her up, she was less than a foot away from him, her palms gently touching his chest.

He looked around and saw the beach was deserted except for them. The sun was almost gone below the horizon and he could see the first dotting of stars in the sky above them. The tropical breeze blew softly and whisked loose wisps of hair around Eryn's face.

Eryn looked up and knew this was a moment she wouldn't forget anytime soon. It was almost magical but their circumstances hadn't changed. She made and effort to show strength and took a step away from him.

"Chase," She said on a breath. "I know that we're in trouble here."

When Chase tried to say something, Eryn put her hand up to his lips to silence him.

She looked into his eyes, "We are and we both know it." This was so much harder than she thought.

Eryn took his hand into hers and led him over to a lighted area. She wanted to see his face when they talked so she could tell whether he was listening. Once they were seated on a bench nearby, she turned to him.

"I want to get this out and then it's done." She recognized the finality in her own tone.

Chase looked at Eryn and got that bad feeling again. The one that told him he wasn't going to like what he was about to hear. Even after all this time, he knew when she had a point to make.

Eryn took a breath, "You hurt me," she started then shook her head. "No, that's wrong." She looked down at her lap then up to his eyes, "You shattered my heart, my self-esteem, and made me question my decision to love you." She was actually relieved to see the pain in his eyes that she carried for ten years.

He wanted to interrupt, to explain, but her look said she wasn't done yet.

"I think the worst part of the whole thing was now knowing what I did or didn't do that made you leave without one single word to me." Tears started down her cheeks and she let them go. "I don't think I want to know why now," she wrung her hands together, "the point is that I was able to move on and find someone else."

The words 'someone else' got his attention. He couldn't believe it. She couldn't kiss him like that and be involved with someone else! He looked around and it dawned on him. The picture of that pilot! And that led to another thought that threw his heart to the ground. She was married; that's why her name was different and that's why she didn't want him to look at the picture on her desk. That was him!

Chase finally looked back at Eryn, "I see," he said coolly.

Eryn looked back down at her lap and didn't see the look of anger cross his features.

Not being able to contain his emotions he reached over and grabbed Eryn's wrists, "Look at me!" he shouted at her. He didn't care that she was crying and looked devastated. "You're married?" he yelled.

A Marine to Remember

Eryn shook her head no but knew he didn't believe her. "You're lying!" A bitter laughed escaped. "I have my reasons for my actions and I don't excuse the pain I caused you but I wouldn't lie to you!"

Chase stood abruptly and let go of Eryn. She fell back against the back of the bench.

"I sure as hell wouldn't kiss you like that if I was with someone else!" He punctuated each word with sarcasm. The pain was like knives into his chest. "You haven't moved on, Eryn, so don't think I'm that stupid."

Eryn watched Chase pace in front of her and was scared. She wasn't afraid of him, she was afraid of herself. Afraid she would beg him to stay with her, beg him to let her explain. Of course, knowing that, she said nothing. It was easier to let him believe she was still married and had someone else. Maybe it would finally end things between them and make her life easier.

Chase called Ed then turned to her, "You may have found someone else but you're still hung up on what's between us!"

She sat there and looked at him, hoping the intense pain in her heart would go away. He turned and started walking down the beach with Ed trudging along after him.

Chase walked away feeling used up. He felt stupid for not realizing why her name was different and not asking about a husband. Anger built up inside him, making him stop. He wanted her to hurt as much as he did. He turned around and walked back to where she sat. When she looked up, the sheer vulnerability he saw almost made him stop. But now, there was not turning back.

"Eryn," he started, "why don't you ask your father why I left?" Spitting out the words hurt him more.

Chase was talking and saying exactly what she feared all those years ago. Her face contorted into a ball of torment. He walked away, leaving her....... again.

Eryn was in her car, driving back to the base when the full impact of what Chase said permeated her conscience. Her father.......what did he do? The memory of her suspicions and the conversation with Gunny Frinnel all those years ago replayed like a broken record in her mind.

The night was interminable for Eryn. By the time she got home it was too late to call her parents' home in South Carolina. So now, she was just alone with her thoughts. Not a good thing. The last time she felt this much of an upheaval was after Paul's death.

Why did all these crises in her life involve men? Was there something wrong with her? Well, she couldn't sit idly back anymore and let them control her life. She was stronger than that. There was going to be hell to pay and she was going to be the one handing out the checks!

Feeling a little guilty, Eryn had to admit, at least to herself, that not all the men in her life were controlling jackasses.

Paul and Uncle Ben were the ones who allowed her to be who she wanted to be. Although, since the fiasco with Chase, she hadn't been close with Uncle Ben. It was his signature she saw on the copy of Chase's orders that day in Gunny Frinnel's office. Now she realized he was covering for her father's manipulations. She should have known better.

Thinking back, she remembered that he was nice to Chase and wasn't as calculating as her father, General Fredricks. She was ashamed of her father's actions; especially since he knew about the falling out between her and Ben and still never owned up to his role in it.

Not only did she need to kick some ass, it looked like she needed to do some mending as well.

After a couple hours of fitful sleep, Eryn finally resigned to get up. She called Uncle Ben first. He and

Aunt Colleen were stationed in California now and should probably be up. She dialed the phone.

Ben picked up on the second ring, "Hello," he said brightly.

"Uncle Ben," Eryn said tentatively.

Ben cleared his throat, "Oh, Eryn, hold on I'll get Aunt Colleen." His voice tightened automatically.

"I, uh, actually called to talk to you," Eryn rushed. "I know we're three thousand miles apart and there's ten years of distance between us but I think I know what happened at Cherry Point." She stopped to take a breath, "I don't know if you know, but Chase Johnson is stationed here with me and he implied that dad was behind the whole thing." She stopped and waited for him to say something.

Ben closed his eyes. The girl was smart and it was only a matter of time before she figured out the crap Tom pulled.

Eryn started, "I should have known that was how it was back then but I didn't want to believe dad would stoop to that," she sniffled to keep the tears back.

Clearing his throat, Ben knew he had to spill, "Sweetheart," he began, "it's about damn time you realized what a jackass your father is when it comes to you."

She couldn't help it, Eryn laughed at his comment.

"Also," Ben said, "I didn't want you to hate your dad. I knew what he was up to and didn't stop him."

The rest of the conversation was spent clearing up all the misunderstanding the past ten years created between them. By the time she hung up with Uncle Ben, she felt relieved. Unfortunately, Ben filled in a few pieces that painted her father in a worse light. He would get his turn soon enough.

Feeling hungry, Eryn went and picked up some breakfast and went for a walk.

If history proved anything, it proved that about ten seconds after she hung up with Uncle Ben he would tell Aunt Colleen and about ten seconds after that, Eryn's mother would get a phone call. She only hoped that her mother wouldn't forewarn her father. Surprise was an advantage and she needed that.

Once she got back to her room, she picked up the phone to call her parents.

The phone barely rang when Beverly Fredricks picked it up, "Eryn?' She asked.

Smiling, Eryn replied, "Yes, Mom."

Danette Fogarty

Anticipating what her daughter would need, Beverly whispered, "He's here and I haven't said anything to him."

Eryn was thankful that her mother understood.

"Thanks, Mom," Eryn whispered to keep from crying.

A couple of seconds later, her father came on the line, "Eryn?" he asked excitedly. "How's Hawaii?"

She didn't answer the question, she said coolly, "Dad."

Tom knew his daughter's tones and this one was spoiling for a fight, "To what do I owe the honor?" he asked her in his most intimidating tone.

Eryn knew the game and knew that it wasn't going to work this time. "Well, I'm not sure if you know it, but Chase Johnson is stationed here." He didn't answer so she went on, "You remember Chase, right? He's actually my NCOIC now."

Her father didn't answer and that didn't surprise her. He wouldn't give up any ground in a fight.

"You know, the guy you decided had to be threatened into transferring so he was away from me?" She pushed on since she was on a role, "Or was it that you just didn't want me dating an enlisted man?" she asked with hurt obvious in her tone.

A Marine to Remember

The line was so quiet that Eryn wondered if he hung up.

Tom Fredricks was fuming, "What did he tell you?" he demanded.

Eryn mentally noted that he didn't deny it.

"It doesn't really matter what he told me, Dad," she started to cry, "it only matters that my own father didn't like who I fell in love with and decided that he would just take care of it by whatever force necessary."

Not accustomed to having anyone, especially his family, talk to him this way, Tom didn't know how to respond. He deserved her anger but he didn't know how to tell her that he realized years ago what a mistake he made. He didn't want to admit that to Eryn just yet.

Blowing out a breath, he started, "At the time," he paused, "I did what I thought was best for you and your career."

Eryn was so angry and hurt that no justification on his part could be believed. "Listen to me, Dad," she was trying not to start screaming at him. "You were wrong! And in the end, I got my heart broken." The tears were streaming again and she impatiently brushed them off of her cheeks, "I wasn't the wife I should have been to Paul and it's in a large part, because of your actions."

His daughter's words cut deeply. He deserved them but it still didn't lessen the blow. He looked helplessly at his wife.

"I know," Tom said sadly, "I'm not proud of what I did, Eryn." He took a breath. "But don't think it was just me." He wasn't going to take all the blame for this, "Your young man didn't object all that much and you yourself never really tried to figure out what happened at the time."

Each of his words, chipped at Eryn's heart. It was painful to think about how deeply all of them hurt.

She shook her head, he wasn't going to get off easy, "You're right," she wasn't above taking a fair share of blame, "but perhaps if my heart wasn't shattered into a million pieces from pain and rejection I might have had the strength to fight."

Tom held back tears of his own and couldn't even answer.

"Or maybe, if Chase wasn't as honorable as he was, then he would have told you to go to hell back then." She spat the words out.

Clearing his throat again, Tom nodded, "I agree." He wished this could all be different, "I feel badly about my actions now, Eryn." He could barely get the words out, "But you are my daughter and I love you."

Hearing pain in her father's voice, Eryn was surprised. He didn't exhibit that kind of emotion so hearing it tore at her wall of anger. "I know," she finally said. "I also know what's done is done and we can't go back."

"I'm sorry," Tom said softly.

Eryn nodded, "I know, and I don't think I would go back anyway because I had time with Paul." She sniffled, "We'll get through this, Dad."

Not able to talk anymore, Tom handed the phone to his wife and left the room. He desperately wanted space to think about mending fences with his daughter.

Beverly took the phone and watched her husband leave the room, his shoulders hunched. She hurt for him but knew he had to understand what he did. She put the phone to her ear.

"Are you okay, sweetie?" she asked her daughter with concern.

Eryn smiled through her tears, "Not yet, but I will be," she answered.

They talked a few minutes more; just long enough for her mother to be reassured that her baby was alright. After they hung up Eryn was so exhausted that she lay down and fell into a deep sleep. She dreamed of Chase.

Chapter 17

October rolled in and the work at Crash Crew started to get crazy.

Rim Pac was in full swing so there were new squadrons of aircraft coming in almost daily. The troops enjoyed the interaction between the different armed forces from other countries. The inspection team from Washington came and went without incident and the focus was now on keeping Crash Crew manned for the additional airfield hours.

With everything humming along, Eryn knew she should feel better. She was doing well here in Hawaii and the crews were operating without incident.

She talked to her father twice since her confrontation and that was a work in progress, but progress nonetheless. So why did she feel so unsettled and sad?

Because, her heart was broken......again. Even with mending the bridges between her and her father, she was unable to get anywhere with Chase. He avoided her unless absolutely necessary and it was weighing heavily on her heart.

It was ironic that, for a while, they kept running into one another and now she rarely had any contact with him at all. They each performed their respective duties and were professional around one another but it all seemed so cold. She couldn't explain about Paul since they were never alone. She needed to talk to someone but she was ashamed of what she did.

Sitting in her office, Eryn was lost in thoughts about this mess with Chase when the alarm went off.

It was ingrained into every Crash Crewman to respond quickly when the alarm sounded so Eryn jumped out of her chair and ran down the hall to the truck bay immediately. She jumped into the passenger side of the Command Vehicle as Chase jumped into the driver's side. Their gear was in the back of the truck in case they needed to get into it. Eryn got on the radio with the Control Tower as Chase pulled out of the Crash Barn.

The P-19's (fire trucks) they used were pulling out of the bay a few seconds after the Command Vehicle. There was a C-130 transport plane on approach to the airfield reporting an engine failure.

Eryn directed the two P-19's sitting hotspot at the end of the runway to be in place when the plane came to a stop. The Command Vehicle and two other P-19's were stopped halfway down the runway and were going to follow the plane in once it touched down on the runway.

Once they stopped, Chase picked up binoculars and got out of the truck. He watched the approaching aircraft and was telling Eryn everything he could see while Eryn was communicating the details to the other trucks and the Control Tower.

"I see flames on the right side!" he called to her.

Eryn passed on the info to the tower, who was relaying the info to the aircraft.

Eryn nodded and yelled to Chase, "The pilot reported smoke in the fuselage!"

They knew this would make landing the aircraft much more dangerous. Eryn directed the trucks to hold back until she gave the order to proceed.

As soon as the plane was on final approach, Chase jumped back into the vehicle to follow it down the runway.

When the wheels hit the tarmac, the Command Vehicle and two P-19's took off after it. Having the P-19's in such close proximity made it easier to douse the flames quickly and get the crew out that much faster.

Eryn directed the trucks as the aircraft came to a stop. As soon as the plane braked, the first P-19 was spraying it with foam. Chase and Eryn jumped out of the Command Vehicle and grabbed helmets.

Within two minutes, the fire in the engine was extinguished. Eryn signaled to the pilot that the fire was out and spoke to the tower over her portable radio. The crew opened the hatch and the rescue crew went in to get them out.

The whole incident only took about fifteen minutes but it felt like hours.

After the crew was taken off the aircraft, and there was no residual sign of fire, the men secured the area. The plane would be towed to a nearby hangar and inspected to figure out what happened to cause the malfunction.

The P-19's and the Command Vehicle returned to the Crash Barn and the crews were flying high on adrenaline. Eryn called a debriefing in the Rec Room that lasted for about an hour.

The entire emergency would be dissected to show any mistakes or areas where the crews needed to improve. Luckily, there wasn't much to correct since the crews responded appropriately and put out the fire quickly. Eryn was thankful for the new training schedule they implemented and was pleased with the crews' performance.

Eryn went back to her office smiling and sat down at her desk. Sighing, she pulled out some forms. After any incident on the airfield, the inevitable mountain of paperwork needed to be filled out. By the time Eryn got through the particulars and filled out the appropriate reports, it was after nine in the evening.

She would still need to meet with the squadron CO and wanted all of her documentation to be accurate. She left her office, absently rubbing her neck to get the kinks out of it.

Getting a bottled water, she decided it was time to go home. She left her office and walked out to the parking lot where she noticed Chase's car. That was strange since she didn't hear anyone inside. She thought that maybe someone gave him a ride home.

Just a few feet from her car, she could make out a figure, but with the lack of light in the parking lot, she couldn't make out who it was.

"Hello?" she asked into the darkness.

Chase stepped forward into the little amount of light provided by the building. "It's me," he answered.

He was out here waiting for her and had been for hours.

Eryn sighed in relief. The tension from work was replaced with a more primal tension caused by his closeness.

"What are you still doing here?" she asked in a shaky voice.

"I was waiting for you," he responded. The words sounded dumb but he wanted to talk to her. "I just wanted to say you did a great job today." It was impossible to keep his tone even with her only a few feet away.

Smiling, Eryn shifted from one foot to the other. His praise made her feel a little giddy.

She whispered, "Thank you."

They stood where they were for a few minutes but neither of them said anything.

Not knowing what else to do and feeling too on edge to stand there, Eryn got out her keys and turned so she could leave.

"Don't go," Chase said softly.

Turning around, Eryn felt conflicted.

"Why?" she asked him. There were a lot of underlying questions in that one word.

Chase didn't know what to do. Finally he growled, "Dammit," and grabbed her.

Within a millisecond, Chase's lips were on hers. There was the possibility that the adrenaline from work was behind his behavior and he would gladly grasp onto that excuse since it was easier than just admitting he was weak where Eryn was concerned.

He had one arm banded around her waist, holding her to him, and his hands were wrapped up in her hair.

Her head spinning in a haze of want, Eryn couldn't make heads or tails of what just happened, only that she didn't want it to stop. Her hair was being released from its bun by his quick fingers and she was drowning in the feel and taste of him.

It took a little bit for Chase to return to his senses but, once he did, it was like being blasted with a power washer. What the hell were they doing? They were making out in a parking lot at their work.

He let go of Eryn and stepped back.

When Chase let go of her, Eryn fell back against her car. She was off balance and trying to catch her breath. She could see, with some satisfaction, that Chase was having the same problem.

"Good night," Eryn said with more conviction than she felt.

There was nothing he could think of to say so he stood there while she got into her car and left. He was standing there in the parking lot, damning himself for being so weak, and damning her because she wasn't stopping him when she was with someone else. Now things just got worse to his way of thinking.

Eryn got back to her room and was thankful she lived close to work. After putting down her bag, she unzipped her flight suit and shrugged out of it. What was she going to do now? They had an attraction that, even after ten years, was so strong they couldn't seem to fight it.

She turned on the radio, hoping the music would soothe her frazzled nerves, and grabbed a glass of wine. She needed to relax in order to get herself under control.

Sipping her wine, Eryn recapped the day in her mind. They did a great job and that should be enough right? Nope! Because that mind-blowing, toe-curling kiss just reminded her that there was so much more to life than work. Just thinking about it made her senses go on full alert. How could she fathom getting through two years of working with him when she wasn't sure she could get through tomorrow?

Thinking back, Eryn could only blame herself for this. She let Chase think that she was still with Paul. At first, she wanted to use Paul as a buffer between them and that was the completely wrong thing to do. At that moment, self-preservation just kicked in and now, she was paying the price for her bad decision.

The next morning, Eryn met with the squadron CO and went over the whole emergency from the day before. As she thought, the consensus was that Crash Crew did a great job and Eryn received a verbal pat on the back for it.

Heading back to Crash Crew, Eryn's mood was light. She always noticed that crap moved down the chain of command but felt praise should as well. She told the crews that since they did such a great job during her first emergency here, she would put together a catered lunch on the next Saturday. The airfield was closed so they could have everyone and their families come down and have a good time.

At the end of the day on Friday, Eryn's phone rang. She was surprised since it was after quitting time and she was the only one left in the offices. "CWO Smith," She said into the phone.

"Well don't you sound tough," a gentle, male voice said.

It was Paul's father.

Eryn smiled, "Hey, George," she said brightly. It was good to hear from Paul's family.

George always liked talking to Eryn; it made him feel a little bit closer to his son. "I hope you don't mind me calling you at work?" he asked. "Your mom gave me the number."

Eryn wasn't surprised since her mother usually kept everyone in the loop. "Not at all, I was just finishing up here," she answered while straightening papers on her desk.

Paul's father started to fill her in on what was going on there in Ohio and asked her about her new position. After a few minutes, Eryn felt like he was working up to something since his tone sounded strange.

After the obligatory family chat, George cleared his throat, "Eryn," he started, "Amber and I have been going through Paul's things here." He felt the blanket of sadness settle in his chest.

Not sure what to say, Eryn sighed. This had to be done and his parents were the ones getting it done. She didn't envy them that.

George cleared his throat, "We're packing up most of it and donating it, but there were a few things we weren't sure you wanted." His voice sounded funny, even to himself.

A lump in her throat, Eryn tried to push it back and keep from crying. The sadness moved over her like a large thundercloud. She couldn't touch anything of Paul's after he died and asked her mother to pack it up and send it to his parents. She just wasn't able to deal with it at the time.

Knowing it was still tough for his daughter-in-law, George tried to be calm, "We know you're young and will probably remarry."

Eryn sucked in a breath and felt a ton of guilt fill her soul.

"Paul would want you to go on and be happy and we want that for you as well," George said softly. "Anyway, we have some of Paul's medals and the flag from his coffin and we weren't sure if you wanted them."

It took a minute for Eryn to compose herself enough to answer. Tears were flowing freely down her cheeks now.

Eryn choked out, "I know how much Paul loved his nieces and nephews and the medals should go to them," she took a breath, "as for the flag, you and Amber should keep that."

"You know," George smiled, "Amber said you'd say that." He chuckled, "I think that's part of the reason he married you." He loved Eryn and was saddened beyond words that she didn't get a chance to be with his son longer. "You reminded him of his mom, I think," He also teased her like he would his other children, "minus the good cooking part of course."

Eryn felt a weight shift off of her shoulders for the first time in a year. "I think you may be right about that," she said and couldn't help but laugh.

It was nice to be light and focus on the good things. They talked for a while longer, the tension surrounding the subject of Paul all but dissipated.

Before hanging up, Eryn said, "I miss you both." She didn't want to leave anything unsaid. "I love you," she said as she looked at Paul's picture.

Eryn heard Amber yell in the background, "We love you too."

Smiling, George felt better, "We know you do and we feel the same." He looked at his watch, "I'll let you go and we'll call you again."

Noticing that Paul's father didn't say 'soon,' Eryn felt like they were all tying up the loose ends as far as Paul was concerned. She was letting go little by little and she figured they were too.

During the call, Eryn's chair was looking out the window with her back to the door of her office. After hanging up, she spun around to find Chase standing in the doorway and wondered how much of her conversation he heard.

Chase looked at Eryn intensely, "I was just leaving and wondered if you needed anything for the lunch tomorrow?" He was pissed and couldn't keep the nasty tone out of his voice.

A Marine to Remember

It was obvious he heard at least a part of her conversation. Did he know that Paul was dead and she lied? Panic set in.

Noticing the change in Eryn's expression, Chase tensed up. "I did knock; you were just too busy talking to flyboy there." The sarcasm dripped off of the words as he said them.

That was it! Eryn screamed to herself. There was NO way he was going to speak about Paul that way!

Eryn stood, "Excuse me?" she asked in a raised voice. She was egging for a fight now. "How dare you say anything about who I speak to or what I say in MY office!"

She walked around her desk and stomped up to where he stood, "There is only so much, Master Sgt. that I'm going to let you get away with!" Poking a finger at his chest, she fumed, "you would never speak to a male OIC that way and I won't have it!"

Eryn didn't mean to lose her temper like that but he made her so frustrated and crazy that she couldn't help it.

Chase was seething under his skin. "Yes, ma'am," he replied and walked out of her office.

He was calling himself every kind of jackass on the way out to his car. She was right. He would never speak to any superior, male or female, like that. But his damn feelings got in the way time and time again where Eryn was concerned. There was no excuse that would be acceptable but that was the truth.

All he wanted to do was let her know he'd help out with anything for tomorrow. He knocked and entered, not realizing she was one the phone.

He heard her say, "I miss you," and, "I love you," and was looking at the picture of the pilot.

That was all it took for him to lose his mind. Jealousy swooped in and grabbed his heart. He was being a total idiot! What's worse is that it was because he was in love with her that he was acting like an idiot. How sad was that?

Saturday morning, Eryn woke up early. She had a terrible night tossing and turning for hours before finally falling into a fitful sleep. Her eyes were red and swollen and it felt like she had a cotton coating in her mouth.

The last time she woke up feeling like this was after the bender when she passed out at Chase's house in North Carolina. Getting up, she tried to push the thought out of her head. Now all the moments from their time together years ago were popping up and she didn't like it one bit.

A Marine to Remember

After she got going, she decided to go for a run and clear her head. She called Abi and arranged to meet at the track.

They met up a few minutes later and stretched. Being almost the same height, they had pretty similar strides so it made running easier.

On the second mile, Eryn was comparing running with Abi to the difficulty of running with Chase. His strides were longer and she had more trouble keeping up with him. There he was again! She ordered herself to stop thinking of him.

On mile three, Abi slowed to a walk, "Okay what's up," she asked Eryn. Her friend was running way too fast like she was running from something….or someone. "I can guess but I think that would be silly."

Eryn nodded and kept walking. Her pulse was settling from the running. "Why now?" she asked.

Abi smiled, "Well, if you want my honest opinion," she figured Eryn didn't have a choice but to hear it, "I don't think it *just happened*," she punctuated the words, "I think it was just high time you faced him and the pain from what happened back then."

Shaking her head in denial, Eryn started to get upset. Abi lightly touched her arm and that stopped her.

"Yes," Abi said vehemently, "You can't hide behind Paul's loss anymore. You're letting go of him and Chase is here."

Was the woman psychic? Eryn wondered how someone could be so wise. Her face reddened with shame.

Looking at Abi, Eryn started to tell her friend about what happened since she got here. She described the incident on the beach, the parking lot kiss, and then the altercation they had in her office the night before.

Abi waited patiently while Eryn talked. When her friend was done, she rolled her eyes.

"I'm pretty ticked off at you for not telling me all of this sooner but I'll kick your butt later for that," she muttered sarcastically.

They made another lap around the track before Abi spoke again, "I can see that misleading Chase about Paul isn't working out very well anyway, not to mention that keeping the truth from Chase is very wrong."

Embarrassment from her actions washed over Eryn, "You're right," she said quietly. "But I can't tell him now."

They walked over to the side of the track and sat down on a bench. "I won't go on letting him think I'm still with Paul," she took a deep breath, "but I'm also not going to just invite him back into my heart, Abi."

Abi nodded and they got up to walk back to their rooms. After a few minutes, they got to the parking lot outside of Eryn's barracks.

"This is my stop," she said to Abi.

Giving Eryn a fierce hug to show her support, Abi smiled and stepped back.

"You know it's too late right?" Abi asked.

Eryn cocked her head, confused.

"He never really left your heart, Eryn." Abi said and started walking toward her own barracks.

Eryn stood there for a bit and hated that her friend was right.

A few hours later, Eryn arrived at Crash Crew to make sure everything was set up for the lunch. She really wanted to have it off base but having it here ensured that the on-call crew was close and everyone could participate.

The food was delivered and set out as the guys put up a volleyball net in the grassy area beside the parking lot. The crewmen and their families started arriving soon after.

Several hours later, Eryn looked at her watch and frowned. Chase was the only one not accounted for and that disappointed her. Even if he was upset with her, he shouldn't have taken it out on the troops by not showing up. Several people asked about him and Eryn was mad because she didn't know what to say.

Sitting at a table, watching the volleyball game, Eryn jumped when Chase came up behind her a while later. She turned, looked at him, and knew something was up.

"Sorry," Chase mumbled, "family emergency."

Not saying anything, Eryn watched as he grabbed some food and a soda and went over to sit with some of the Gunnery Sgts. and their wives.

Knowing there was more to the story, but not wanting to have a confrontation in front of their crews, she went back to watching the game.

They were cleaning up a while later and Eryn was happy that everyone seemed happy about the get-together. By three-thirty, everyone was gone except the skeleton crew assigned to the Crash Barn, Abi, Chase, and Eryn.

Abi and Chase gave Eryn some money and asked her to put it towards the cost of the lunch. Abi also told her that they weren't splitting it evenly because Eryn made more money than they did.

The crew cleaned up and headed back into the Crash Barn to relax. Abi, Eryn, and Chase started walking to where their cars were parked.

Abi grabbed Eryn's arm and whispered, "Now would be a good time to clear the air with him."

"I don't," Eryn muttered in response.

Not giving Eryn time to get away, Abi called out, "Hey, Master Sgt.," and took off toward her own car.

Chase walked over to where Eryn stood, a weird look on his face. "Did you need something?" he asked her.

Hearing that his voice was off, Eryn's nerves were firing, "What's wrong?" she asked with concern in her voice.

"Nothing," Chase said curtly. He didn't want to stand here and make forced small talk, "If you don't need anything else, ma'am....." He turned to leave.

Eryn's hand shot out to his arm, stopping him. "Chase," she whispered his name and reveled in the feel of his name on her lips.

A current of longing moved from the point of contact between them up her arm. The overpowering feeling made Eryn acutely aware. She let go of his arm to try and get some composure.

"I know something's going on." She didn't know why but she had an incessant need to find out what was going on.

Chase shook his head, "I don't want to talk about it," he answered sharply.

Eryn watched him stand there. Although his words were saying one thing, his actions contradicted them.

In an attempt to make it easier on him, Eryn took the initiative, "Well, I don't feel like going back to my room. It's a beautiful day so I'm going to walk the beach." She smiled, "Would you like to join me?" she asked.

The impulsive decision was just asking for trouble and Eryn knew it. But, right now, she was worried about him. She wanted to say she was doing it out of friendship but that was a lie.

She and Chase were many things but friends wasn't quite one of them. Surprising her, he nodded. Without saying anything else, he got into his car and waited until she pulled out to follow.

Chapter 18

Eryn drove to Kailua Beach, where she saw him the last time. It wasn't that far from the base and she guessed it must be pretty close to where Chase lived since he walked there.

She got out of her car and waited for him to park and get out of his car. She was desperate to touch him again and was mad because she felt that way.

Therein lied the proverbial problem; she kept putting herself in situations where she could touch and kiss him and then wondered why she felt tortured.

Chase parked a few spaces down from Eryn. He got out and waited for her to meet up with him and walk down to the beach. He didn't say anything.

They were walking along the beach for a good twenty minutes when Eryn decided she needed to know what was wrong. She stopped and looked at him expectantly.

Finally, Chase spoke, "Ed is gone," he croaked.

Shocked, Eryn's brow creased, "What do you mean gone?" she asked with emotion lining her voice.

"We were out this morning and he was going a little slow but I just thought he was screwing around." He looked out to the water, "By the time we got back to the house, he was having trouble breathing." The words were shredding his heart, "I called the vet but it was too late."

Eryn's heart ached for him. He looked so lost. She probably looked the same when she was grieving.

Wanting to comfort, Eryn stepped closer and put her arms around him. He didn't push her away, but he didn't move to hold her back either.

She started to feel awkward so she started to pull away when his arms swept around her, pulling her back into him. The move was so fast, Eryn was startled. He turned more fully toward her and looked down with tears in his eyes. That was her undoing, she moved closer and started to cry.

They stood there, on the beach, holding one another and crying for a while afterward.

Chase felt so weak. He lost Ed, his best friend, and was alone. But here was Eryn, holding him and comforting his heart and soul. He felt peace and pain at the same time and was confused.

Eryn finally pulled back so she could look at him, but didn't stop holding him, "Let's sit," she said and guided him over to a vacant piece of the beach.

She sat first and once he was seated, she guided his head down onto her lap. They stayed that way for hours; Eryn finger-brushing his hair and aching for his loss. The breeze was gentle, the waves low, transfixing both of them.

Later, Eryn noticed the sky was getting darker, settling into a deep pink and orange color off on the horizon. Her legs were stiff from sitting so still. She looked down and saw Chase's eyes were closed. He looked so peaceful.

She brushed her fingers across his cheek and down his chin. He turned his face up and looked at her. The peacefulness she saw a moment before was gone as hurt permeated from him.

"I'm sorry," Eryn said as a tear slipped down her cheek.

Chase's lips formed a mere hint of a smile. He reached his hand up and wiped the tear from her cheek.

Blinking so he wouldn't cry, Chase said, "I knew it would happen." He sat up slowly, "It was his time."

Eryn watched him in fascination. He moved gracefully for a man. It was like she was looking at a beautiful and mysterious piece of art. Her thoughts must have been written on her face because his expression changed.

"I love you," Chase said.

Danette Fogarty

He wasn't expecting to say the words but they were the truth. Losing Ed made him realize that he had to say what he felt.

Eryn had a suspicion about his feelings, since hers were the same, but hearing it after all this time was difficult. She wanted to take things slow, she still needed to confess about Paul.

Becoming defensive, since it was all she had, she responded, "I know you're upset," she started to say.

Chase was confused. Didn't she hear him? He was admitting his feelings to her and she was blowing it off!

The realization dawned on him, "You don't believe me," he said flatly.

He was frustrated! Why couldn't they ever get this right? He dropped his head and shook it in exasperation.

Eryn wanted to explain, "I know that in the heat of a moment we may say things....." the words trailed off. She didn't want to dig into this right now. She stood and brushed the sand off of her legs, "I have to get back."

Torn up emotionally, Chase stood up, "Don't go, Eryn," he pleaded. "I'm not saying this because I'm upset about Ed. I just realize that I don't' want to wake up and see that I've lost you...... again."

A Marine to Remember

This was exquisite torture for Eryn. Chase was saying all of the things she wanted to hear but she couldn't handle it. A lot of that was because she misled him about Paul.

"I know," she said and looked crushed.

Eryn stated walking away and Chase followed her.

He asked, "Why are you running, Eryn?"

She knew he wanted and deserved answers. "I don't know what else to do!" she shouted out.

This is the time you should tell him the truth, she told herself. But seeing him like this, she couldn't do it.

"I'm so confused." she said instead, "I want so badly to throw all of the complications out the window and run to you." She was backing up as he was moving closer. "I want to make love with you so badly I ache." The pain in her chest made it hard to breathe, "But I can't."

Eryn started walking faster and got about ten feet away when Chase started yelling.

"There's no way you love him!" he shouted at her. "Not if you're here with me and feeling even a fraction of what I am!"

Standing there on the beach, Eryn looked at him and couldn't summon the strength to answer. When she turned away for the last time, he didn't stop her. She cried the whole way back to her car and even during the ride back to her room. She resigned herself to the fact that she would have a broken heart for the rest of her life.

Monday morning came quickly and Eryn dreaded it. Saturday and Sunday were filled with a deep restlessness that wouldn't give her any peace. She felt a longing for Chase she didn't think would ever be satisfied.

Her eyes were like sandpaper and she was sluggish. Their parting conversation played in her mind like a broken record. The opportunity to explain everything was right there and she blew it. Even though she was sure that she'd feel sadness forever, she couldn't show it at work.

She walked into the building and made quick work of the morning greetings. Then she holed herself up in her office, hoping no one would notice how miserable she felt.

At ten thirty her phone rang. It was the squadron CO's office. She and Master Sgt. Johnson were expected to attend a Marine Corps Ball planning meeting in the afternoon. Great, she thought, why didn't they just ask her to put bamboo shoots up under her fingernails? That would be less painful than this.

Just before she left for lunch, Eryn walked across the hall to Chase's office. She was not going to chicken out around him!

"Master Sgt.?" She asked in the doorway to his office.

Chase looked up, "Yes, Warrant Officer Smith," he acknowledged with a nod.

She didn't want to stand there looking like an idiot so she spoke up. "We have a ball meeting at the CO's hangar at thirteen thirty."

Not waiting for him to say anything, Eryn grabbed her stuff and left the office for lunch.

Abi caught up to Eryn outside and they decided to get some lunch together.

After ordering something to eat, Abi listened to what happened after the lunch on Saturday. She shook her head in sadness. These two just couldn't get it together, she thought to herself.

"What were you thinking?" Eryn demanded.

Abi looked at her friend innocently, "I'm the only one here who is thinking, Eryn!" She smiled reassuringly, "You seem to forget how long we've been friends, Eryn, and that I've been here working with Johnson for a while now." She paused to give Eryn a

Danette Fogarty

second to let that sink in. "I'm the only one who can see how you two really feel about each other."

Eryn looked down at the paper napkin in front of her and rearranged her silverware.

Abi looked at Eryn intently, "Why didn't you tell him about Paul?" she asked.

Guilt built up inside of Eryn. She looked up, "I don't know."

"Oh Eryn," shaking her head, Abi sighed.

Eryn nodded, "I know," she countered, "I just couldn't. I don't know why, dammit!" She lowered her voice when other customers looked over. "I just couldn't make myself open up and let him in. He broke my heart and Paul died and I'm just meant to be alone." She fought hard to keep the tears inside.

"Yeah, well," Abi leaned forward, "now your eyes should be wide open."

The waitress set down their food and moved away quietly.

Abi picked up the salt and looked back at Eryn, "You fell in love and somehow stayed in love with a guy you didn't even see for like ten years." Abi saw the drop in Eryn's face, "No," she stated sharply, "that doesn't mean that you didn't love Paul." It was hard to say what had to be said. "Eryn you would've stayed with Paul, we all know that, but he wasn't the man you were meant to be with."

Eryn's head shot around. The words were the truth but that didn't help ease all of the hurt and guilt she was feeling.

"I want you to do something," Abi said softly.

Abi never asked for anything so Eryn nodded.

Sighing, Abi grabbed her friend's hand, "I want you to just forget all of the obstacles and just search your feelings." She squeezed Eryn's hand. "Just see how you really feel about him and go with it."

Eryn nodded, hoping she could do what Abi asked her. They stopped talking and ate their lunches.

Arriving at the squadron hangar with only a few minutes to spare, Eryn got out of her car and hurried to where Chase stood. He brought over the Crash Crew truck and she would have driven with him except her lunch with Abi ran long. He only nodded at her and they walked inside.

The squadron CO, the planning committee, and other unit heads were all getting settled when they entered the conference room. The Marine Corps Ball was in celebration of the Corps' formation on November 10th. Each squadron had a little say as to when and where the ball would be held. It was a very formal affair complete with over two hundred years of pomp and circumstance.

Everyone settled down and took out paper to take notes. Eryn's mind started wandering as soon as the CO started talking. She didn't attend last year; she wasn't up to it after Paul's death. She wondered if Chase attended last year. Looking over discreetly, she studied him.

Chase could feel Eryn looking at him. It was that damn unspoken connection they had. She could be two feet or two hundred feet away and he would still feel her. This was not good considering they were in a meeting with a bunch of other Marines. He was getting hard and trying to clamp down on his reaction to her. Thank goodness the flight suits were a little loose.

The CO started the meeting by listing what was already handled.

Eryn half-listened. She was distracted by what Abi asked her to do. She tried to clear her head and listen but kept getting distracted by him.

The ball would be in Honolulu at the military hotel there. There were just a few details left to take care of.

"CWO Smith?" the CO asked.

Eryn sat up and answered quickly, "Yes, sir."

"Would you and Master Sgt. Johnson mind picking up the glasses we are having etched for the ball?" he asked her.

Eryn briefly glanced at Chase and answered, "Consider it done, sir."

It wasn't like they really had a choice in the matter.

The CO nodded, "Good," he put the paper on the bottom of his pile, "Lt. Anderson will give you the details on when and where."

That was the last thing Eryn remembered from the meeting. She only realized it was over when people started getting up and leaving. Her mind on autopilot, she stood, left the building, and drove back to the Crash Barn.

She was sitting in her office going over a training schedule when Chase knocked and entered.

Chase was ticked off, "Where did you go?" he asked in a clipped tone.

Eryn didn't know what he was talking about, "What do you mean?" she inquired.

He put a paper on her desk and stepped back, "Well, I stayed and got the info for the glasses from the Lt."

Sticking the paper into the mounting pile on her desk, Eryn looked up, "I'm sorry."

Chase turned and left her office. Walking over to his office, he didn't like being this worked up over her. Just after he sat down at his desk he heard a page saying he had a phone call.

"Master Sergeant Johnson," Chase said into the phone, all business.

Beverly Fredricks smiled, "Master Sgt., this is Beverly Fredricks, Eryn's mother," she said brightly.

Chase sat up straighter, "Yes, ma'am," he answered and wondered why Eryn's mother would call him.

Beverly laughed, "Please don't call me ma'am; it makes me feel old."

"Yes, um," He almost said ma'am again.

She liked this young man, "Chase," she said and interjected, "I hope it's alright if I call you, Chase."

Chase answered, "Of course."

Nodding, Beverly took a breath and began to explain. "I have some information for you that may shed some light on your current situation."

Leaning forward, Chase made sure that Eryn's door was closed. He listened very carefully to what Mrs. Fredricks was saying.

A Marine to Remember

Over the next couple of days, Eryn tried to talk to Chase alone but was unsuccessful. There just never seemed to be a good time. Even if she could gather up the courage to corner him and force the issue, she wasn't sure she would follow through and tell the truth.

She had to face the fact that she may have lost her shot with Chase and that was that.

The ball was a week off, she had her work to focus on and she didn't need the distraction of this non-relationship with Chase.

She was wallowing in self-pity later that night when her phone rang. She didn't really want to answer it but it could be work so she picked up.

"Hello," Eryn said flatly.

Beverly frowned, her daughter didn't sound happy, "Eryn," she said brightly, "it's Mom."

Smiling, Eryn wondered how her mom always knew when she needed a boost. "Hey, Mom," she said.

"I know it's a weekday," Beverly started, "but I was so excited when your father came home that I had to call you."

Eryn's curiosity was piqued, "What's up?" she asked.

Beverly bubbled with excitement, "Well, your father and I are coming to Hawaii next Monday."

Eryn's smile faded. She would normally love a visit but right now was not a good time. "What's going on?" she asked her mom.

It was easy to hear the hesitation in her daughter's voice, but that didn't dissuade Beverly from her mission.

She smiled, "Your father has some meetings planned and I wanted to tag along so I could visit with you." Sometimes it was easier to play the ignorant role.

"Well, Mom," Eryn sighed, "our squadron ball is next Friday and I'm trying to get stuff at work done."

Beverly laughed. Her husband and daughter were two peas in a pod. Both would hide behind work and neither could tell when she was manipulating them. Her husband came into the room so Beverly spoke up.

"Yes, I know," she nodded to her husband to sit down at the table, "you mentioned it and I thought your father and I could attend with you this year." She quickly added, "It would be like when you were younger."

Eryn remembered her and her sister being so excited when they were old enough to attend the ball.

Their mother would take them dress shopping and they would get all decked out.

Abi wanted to do that this year but Eryn's heart just wasn't in it. She shook her head and dropped her shoulders.

"Mom, I appreciate that but-" She started saying.

That was all Beverly would allow her daughter, she cut her off saying, "Eryn, we're coming." she used her stern "mom" tone. "Will you please be kind enough to get us tickets and plan on taking Tuesday off for shopping?"

Looking at the ceiling, Eryn felt blindsided. "Mom," she almost whined.

Beverly's patience was used up now, "Just do it, Eryn. I don't want excuses."

Hearing her mother's tone, Eryn was shocked.

She answered, "Okay," and waited while her mother gave her their flight information.

After hanging up the phone, Eryn sat there and wondered how things just got worse.

On Friday they got the schedule ironed out to accommodate for the ball. Eryn had to confirm who was going and who got their tickets and report to the

CO's office. It took a while to figure it out but they got it done.

Monday morning, Eryn made an appointment to see her CO. She had to tell him about her parents attending the ball with her. Given her father's rank, he needed to be announced before such a function.

She smiled at her CO's reaction since he didn't know who her father was. She always kept the information very hush-hush so that she would be judged on her own merit, not her father's rank. Of course, her CO was pretty excited that the General would be attending.

When she got back to her office, she sat in her chair and tried to stave off a headache. There was so much to figure out.

Her parents called Sunday to change their arrival date to Tuesday and she was secretly relieved. An extra day to put on her game face was greatly appreciated.

Tuesday she woke up early to go for a run. Her parents weren't due in until mid-morning so she took her time.

They managed to stop off in California for a quick visit with Uncle Ben and Aunt Colleen and Eryn wondered if her father and Ben would hash out what happened with her and Chase all those years ago.

A Marine to Remember

After she ran three miles, she went back and got ready to go and pick up her parents. She was still a little nervous about seeing her father but she did miss her them. They were flying space available on a military transport and renting a car so she offered to pick them up at the terminal and drive them over to the rental car office. She swapped cars with Abi the day before so she would have enough room to get everyone in and gave her parents her cell phone number in case there were any delays.

Getting ready after her shower, Eryn was worried about what she would wear. Her parents held certain expectations and, even as an adult, she didn't want to disappoint. She finally chose a soft pink skirt and a white silk blouse. Some pearl earrings and light make up completed the look. Grabbing a clutch, she left to pick them up.

Her parents' plane arrived on time and Eryn stood near the terminal waiting for them to deplane. After a few passengers got off, Eryn saw her father and waved. Her mother was right behind him and, not surprisingly, so were Ben and Colleen.

Feeling more anxious now, Eryn waited for the group to walk over.

Beverly Fredricks walked up and hugged her daughter tightly, "Look at you," she said into her daughter's ear.

"None of that," Tom Fredricks said from behind his wife trying to sound gruff but failing.

Colleen hugged Eryn next then stepped aside.

Eryn smiled when she looked up. "Uncle Ben," She whispered when she was engulfed by his arms. The relief that they didn't have the rift between them was wonderful.

Ben released her and stepped back, taking Colleen with him so Eryn and her father could have a private moment.

"Eryn," Tom Fredricks said quietly.

Eryn smiled and kissed her dad on the cheek, "Dad," she said in return.

Tom relaxed and grabbed his daughter to his chest. He was afraid she would turn him away because of his behavior.

She was happy that her father hugged her but she couldn't breathe so she pulled away a little bit.

"We'll talk later," Tom said into her ear before releasing her.

Eryn nodded and stepped away.

The group went inside the terminal to get the bags. Ben explained that after they met up in California, he and Colleen thought a little trip to Hawaii would be fun. His command wasn't holding their ball for another week so they thought it would be fun to attend one here.

Eryn shook he head and thought, rank really did have its privileges.

A few minutes later, they dropped her father and Uncle Ben off at the rental car place and drove into Honolulu to do some dress shopping.

They were able to go through three shops before stopping at a local café for lunch. The day was beautiful and Eryn was, surprisingly, very relaxed. She couldn't remember the last time she went shopping with her mother and Aunt Colleen.

Once they finished their lunch, they set off with a clear determination to find the perfect dresses. Her mother was able to find a beautiful gown in a pale blue. Eryn was surprised that the gown was so low cut in the front and teased her mom a little.

Beverly responded, "It's about time I made your father sit up and take notice again."

Eryn and Colleen laughed because they both knew that her father always took notice of her mother.

At the next shop, Colleen picked out a dress in gold with three quarter sleeves. It was form-fitting and showed off Colleen's trim figure perfectly.

Laughing as she looked in the mirror, Colleen remarked, "These guys won't know what hit them."

Eryn and her mother whistled and whooped while Colleen strutted around the dressing room in front of the mirrors.

Beverly turned to her daughter, "Now," she said in a firm voice, "it's your turn."

Eryn shrugged as if it was no big deal but now it kind of was. She wanted to feel beautiful like her mom and Aunt Colleen when she found her dress. Abi got her dress the weekend before and told Eryn how great it was. So now, it was important to find just the right one.

A couple of hours later, Eryn was getting pretty discouraged. They went to two more shops with no results. It was difficult not to get discouraged.

They were leaving yet another shop when Beverly suddenly stopped, "Eryn," she said while grabbing Eryn's arm, "look across the street."

Following her mother's gaze, Eryn looked across the street into a beautifully arranged window display. It was a pretty upscale place if the display was any indication. Her eyes finally settled on the gown featured in it and her breath hitched.

The three of them made their way across the street and stood in front of the window as if they were in a trance.

In the window was a gown done up in a deep, red satin material. The bodice was fitted and sleeveless with an overlay of red tulle crisscrossing the top of it and trailing down over the full skirt. Strategically placed crystals and sequins made it look like a red jewel glittering in the afternoon sunlight. Eryn stood there and admired the dress as if it were a treasure.

When Beverly saw her daughter's face, she looked over at Colleen, who noticed Eryn's look too.

"Oh," Beverly said to Eryn, "you have to go in and try it on."

Each of them grabbing one of Eryn's arms, they took her inside the shop.

A few minutes later, Eryn emerged from the dressing room. She was still stunned that the dress fit so perfectly. It slipped on over her body as if it were made for her. Her mother, Aunt Colleen, and the saleslady just stood there and gaped.

"What?" Eryn asked desperately.

Why wasn't anyone saying anything? She wondered if there was a tear or snag in the dress fabric.

Danette Fogarty

Beverly sighed, "Eryn," she almost started crying, "that dress was made for you. It's gorgeous!"

Her mother's compliment made her bubble with excitement.

Colleen stood up and gestured for Eryn to turn around. "Oh my," she said when Eryn was facing them again, "you're going to have every man in the room drooling."

They all started giggling. Eryn had to admit that it did look wonderful on her and made her feel stunning.

Eryn was putting the dress on the hangar in the dressing room when she noticed the price tag.

"Oh, geez," she said and frowned.

She could purchase it but it would put a pretty sizeable dent in her budget. Looking at the dress, she figured it was definitely worth it. She walked out with the dress and carried it over to the counter where her mother, Colleen, and the saleslady stood talking.

Pulling out her credit card, Eryn was about to pay when her mother stopped her.

"Let me do this for you," Beverly said to her daughter, the emotion building up in her chest.

Eryn shook her head, "No, Mom, I don't want you to do that."

Beverly was firm, "Yes."

The conversation was over and Eryn knew she'd never win. She stood their quietly and waited as the dress was put in a bag and handed back to her. They started talking about accessories and took a quick trip over to the mall.

They spent the rest of the afternoon getting everything necessary for their ball transformations.

After dropping off her mom and Aunt Colleen, Eryn went home to put all of her purchases away. As she hung up the dress and tucked the boxes with shoes and gloves and jewelry away, she daydreamed about how it would look.

Chapter 19

Wednesday flew by with issues to address after Eryn's day off, but nothing major.

The final work roster was posted for the day of the ball and, surprisingly, everybody seemed okay with it. A pizza party was promised to the skeleton crew assigned to the airfield. No one really wanted to work and there was more screwing around than work getting done.

Eryn was straightening up to go home when she heard a knock on her office doorframe.

"Enter," she said, then looked up to see Chase standing there.

Just the sight of him made her take pause. He was so damn handsome! They'd been avoiding each other so when she did see him, it was like she needed to drink in the sight of him.

Chase walked into Eryn's office and immediately noticed a change in her. She was much calmer and more relaxed than in the previous weeks. He knew her parents were here and he would've expected the opposite.

Of course, thinking about the conversation last week with Mrs. Fredricks, he figured she mended some of the problems with her father.

Things he was told made a big dent in clarifying some things for Chase. He wanted to talk to Eryn but the opportunity never did materialize so he was left with his conflicting thoughts and frustration.

"Uh," he said, pulling himself out of his thoughts, "I just wanted to remind you that we're picking up the glasses for the ball tomorrow afternoon and taking them over to the hotel."

Eryn rolled her eyes, how could she forget that? She wished she could get out of it but there was no way to now.

She blew out a breath, "Oh yeah," she answered, "What time do we need to leave here?" she asked him.

Chase looked at his watch, "About fifteen thirty."

Looking down, Eryn scribbled a reminder on her desk calendar. "Okay," she said when she finished and looked up at him.

He left and she felt lost, drifting on a raft of loneliness. It amazed her that they could be so potent when they were together but fought it so hard. She sat there at her desk and feared that they would never really be able to be honest with one another.

On Thursday morning Eryn called a meeting for all of her department heads. She wanted to make sure everyone knew the plan for the ball on Friday. She didn't like surprises and expected her staff to run things smoothly.

Everyone assured her that everything was taken care of. Before they adjourned, she reminded everyone that she and Master Sgt. Johnson were going to leave early to pick up the glasses for the ball.

After everyone cleared out, Abi got up and closed the door.

She sat down next to Eryn and whispered conspiratorially, "So you two……all alone…..for a few hours." She punctuated the comment by wiggling her eyebrows.

Eryn shook her head like she was surprised but the truth was, she spent all last night thinking the same thing.

Abi scooted forward and put her chin in the palm of her hand, "C'mon, I know you're thinking naughty thoughts."

Eryn crumpled up a piece of paper and threw it at her making both of them laugh.

"Well," Abi said and stood up, "I have to get back to work; my boss is a slave driver!" She sighed dramatically when she opened the door and left.

A Marine to Remember

Eryn waved goodbye and collected her own things. She smiled all the way down the hall into her own office.

At three-fifteen, Eryn got up to change. They were leaving the base and weren't allowed to wear their flight suits unless they were going to another military installation or home.

In the bathroom she slipped out of her flight suit and put on a pair of khaki shorts and a pale, turquoise top. She pulled on sandals and pulled her hair loose from the bun she wore it in. She refused to admit that she did that because Chase always said he liked her hair loose.

Once again, Eryn swapped cars with Abi so she would have enough room to haul the cases of glasses to the hotel. She picked up the keys and her purse from her office and headed out to the parking lot.

When she rounded the corner of the building, she saw Chase standing there looking at his watch. A tinge of anger sparked up at his impatience. He should know she wouldn't be late.

She looked him over as she approached the car. He had on jean shorts and a white t-shirt that was form-fitting enough to show off his lean torso and strong arms and shoulders. Flushing with embarrassment at her open gawking, she cleared her throat and put on a neutral face.

Danette Fogarty

"Would you like me to drive?" Chase asked her when she walked up.

Nodding, Eryn tossed him the keys and walked around the car.

They got in and were quiet while Chase drove off the base.

Ten minutes later, Eryn was staring at her sweaty palms and trying to work up the nerve to talk to him.

Finally she said, "Chase," she smiled when he glanced at her then back to the road, "I was wondering if I could talk to you."

Her voice was low and quivered from her nervousness.

"Is this professional or personal?" Chase asked her.

Without thinking, Eryn blurted out, "Oh definitely personal."

Chase checked his mirrors then pulled over to the side of the road.

Eryn was worried, "What are you doing?" she asked.

His actions took her off guard. She was counting on having him somewhat distracted from driving while she talked to him.

Pulling off the shoulder, Chase put the vehicle in park and looked over at Eryn.

"I'm pulling over because I want to see your face when you say whatever it is you need to say," he said in a soft voice.

Even though it made sense, Eryn wished he hadn't done that. The close proximity of them inside the car only increased the electricity that ran between them.

Chase put his arm up on the back of Eryn's seat and turned his body so he was somewhat facing her. She looked so scared and he couldn't figure out why. His eyes moved down and caught sight of her biting her lip as if she were nervous. In an effort to help her feel more comfortable, he reached over and brushed the back of his hand against her cheek

When Eryn felt Chase's hand on her cheek, she was a goner. She looked up and locked her gaze with his. She didn't move, even when he lowered his face to hers, she stayed right where she was.

Once their lips touched, the fireworks show started.

Eryn was trying to get closer but the arm rest in the car impeded her progress. Instead, she brought her hands up to cup his face and touched her tongue to his lips. As soon as her skin met his, a pulse of heat rushed to her core. The volatile feeling was intense and made her feel bold.

Tongues touched tentatively then dove for one another in the most exotic dance.

Eryn felt like she was being devoured. Her hands settled at the back of Chase's neck but didn't stay there for long. She wanted to feel him so she started moving her palms down his shoulders to the front of his shirt. Impulsively, she flicked his nipple with her fingernail. She was disappointed when he jerked away from her in surprise. She thought maybe she hurt him.

"I'm sorry," Eryn said quietly.

Chase smiled, "Whoa, don't be sorry." He cupped her chin and brought it up until they were eye to eye. "I didn't pull away because you hurt me," he kissed the tip of her nose quickly. "I was so turned on that I thought I'd embarrass myself right here."

Relief flooded through Eryn. "It's never been like this for me," she admitted, feeling a bit sheepish.

Feeling like a stud, Chase puffed up when she told him it never felt like that for her. What the hell kind of husband does she have that he didn't please her? All of a sudden, he remembered that she had a husband and he turned away. It was like a cold bucket of water poured onto his libido. What the hell were they doing? He did not fool around with another man's wife.

It wasn't difficult for Eryn to figure out what he was thinking. He was thinking of her husband. Now was the time to come clean.

"Chase, I haven't been completely honest with you," she began, "I'm afraid of everything between us since I got here so I tried to put up barriers between us."

Whipping his head back around, Chase watched her closely. A feeling of dread settled in his gut.

Eryn took a breath, "There isn't anyone else," she blurted out.

He didn't understand so he asked her, "What do you mean?"

Wringing her hands again, Eryn was too far now to turn back. She said, "The man in the picture, Paul, he was my husband." She could see he wanted to say something but she put her fingers to his lips before he could speak. "Please let me finish," She said in a rush. "He was killed in a training accident over a year ago."

Tears were streaming down Eryn's cheeks and she didn't care. He needed to see it all.

"When I found out you were here, I didn't know what to do." Her voice hitched, "Then when I realized I still had feelings for you, even after so many years, I felt guilty." She was tormented with the admission, "You saw the picture and just assumed and I didn't want to be hurt again so I let you believe I was still married."

Chase turned to face forward in his seat and started out the windshield. This definitely was not what he was expecting her to say.

Of course, now some things made sense, like her mother asking him to give her time, why the husband wasn't here with her, and, most importantly, why Eryn would kiss him and want him so badly. It was a relief to know that she wouldn't cheat on her husband. But more than that, he was pissed that she lied and let him believe the worst about her.

Once the information sank in, Chase turned back to face her. "It's okay, Eryn," he said softly and touched her cheek with his fingertips. "I understand."

Eryn thought he was going to kiss her again but he just pulled back onto the road and started driving like nothing happened between them.

The rest of the trip to Honolulu was quiet.

Eryn fully expected him to say something but he never did. She sat there and called herself ten kinds of fool. She was a fool ten years ago when she didn't fight for him and she was a fool to think that anyone else would be able to take his place in her heart.

Paul was a wonderful man and a great husband but he was gone and nothing would bring him back. She was given a second chance with Chase and didn't want to blow it, but she figured she pretty much had at this point.

Dusk was setting in when they got back to Crash Crew. Chase had to go back there so he could get his jeep. He hadn't spoken to Eryn since they were pulled over on the side of the road because he wasn't sure what to say to her. He was busy being torn between being pissed at her for lying and at himself for being such an ass.

They got out of the SUV and rounded the front so Eryn could get the keys from him.

She was supposed to return the vehicle to Abi's barracks then meet her parents for dinner. Now she wasn't sure she could get through it since she was so upset by the situation with Chase. She wondered if it wasn't a little easier when they were at odds than it was now.

When Eryn held out her hand to take the keys from Chase, she gasped in surprise when he grabbed her and pulled her to him.

Chase slid one arm around her and cupped the back of her head to his shoulder. Even if he couldn't say the words, he needed to let her know he was trying.

Being in Chase's arms was like being in heaven. It felt completely right and she hugged him back fiercely.

They couldn't stand there for long since they were at work and someone could come outside and see them.

Chase released her and waited for her to get into the SUV. He closed the door for her and stepped away so she could pull out.

Eryn watched him in the rear view mirror, standing there in the parking lot and watching her.

Even though they didn't talk, Eryn thought maybe they could come to some sort of understanding.

An hour later, Eryn was sitting with her parents for dinner and still confused. She went back to her room and changed and met up with her mom and dad at the Officer's Club. The club had a lovely dinner service with excellent food so she wanted to show it off to them.

She got through it, somehow, and even managed to keep up some form of conversation with them. Her mother looked at her a few times and Eryn was pretty sure her mom knew what was going on with her but Eryn appreciated not being asked about it.

Her father talked about the ball and regaled the ladies with some stories of the golf game he and Ben played earlier that day.

When her parents dropped her off at her room, she went in and sat down on her bed. She wondered what was going to happen now.

The day of the ball was absolutely beautiful. The weather was perfectly Hawaiian with a gorgeous blue sky and gentle breezes drifting inland off the ocean.

Eryn woke up feeling alive. A weight was lifted off of her and she said a quick prayer up thanking Paul for loving her.

Excitement started building up in her chest and she got up like a kid on Christmas morning.

She called Crash Crew to check in. The day workers had the day off to get ready for the ball tonight so she got to sleep in a little bit but wanted to make sure there was nothing going on there that she should know about. After hanging up with the Staff Sgt. on duty, she ran to the bathroom to get ready.

Danette Fogarty

Her mother scheduled a twelve-thirty spa appointment for all of them in Honolulu so they could get all dressed up for tonight's festivities.

Eryn was outside her room waiting at eleven-thirty when a limo pulled up in front of her.

Abi poked her head out of the car window and smiled.

"Want a ride?" she asked Eryn excitedly.

Laughing, Eryn gave her bags to the driver and climbed into the back seat. Abi was smiling slyly and handed her a glass of champagne.

"How's this for fun?" Abi asked loudly. "I decided I didn't want to drive and I wanted to make this ball fantastic!"

How could she possibly resist Abi's enthusiasm? "I love it," she said brightly.

The driver got in and they started heading out on their way to Honolulu.

Abi explained that they were going to check into the hotel and then would go over and meet her mother and Colleen at the spa. She watched Eryn as she talked and knew something was going on.

With narrowed eyes, Abi took Eryn's glass from her and placed it aside with her own.

She turned back and glared at Eryn, "Okay," she said, "what happened?"

Eryn blushed and looked out the window on her side of the car.

Abi demanded, "I want details," and refilled their glasses with champagne before turning around to face Eryn.

Eryn told her about the ride into Honolulu to pick up the glasses and then the hug they shared at Crash Crew once they got back.

Listening intently, Abi waited until Eryn was finished and smiled slowly. "Interesting," she said, hoping that her friends found the happiness they deserved.

Chase sat in his living room and stared at nothing.

The night before was one of the longest ones he could remember. After Eryn dropped him off at Crash Crew he drove out to the beach. He walked along the sand and thought about what she did and what she said.

She was willing to let him believe she was still married in an effort to keep from being hurt by him again. The magnitude of what he did ten years ago weighed heavy on his heart.

At the time, he thought he was the one sacrificing for her and he was the only one who suffered. Now, he could see that he was just scared; scared of loving another person so damn much that he allowed himself to be manipulated right out of it. He never gave them a chance and he was ashamed of himself for that.

And it was all for nothing because he still loved her. Time, distance, and even other people couldn't change It. Now he knew her husband was dead and she was free. Paul, he said to himself, trying out the name in his mind. Paul married her and loved her and yet she still loved Chase.

Walking along, he was humbled and mixed up with emotion. The only thing that bothered him was that Eryn never told him she loved him. She admitted feelings and wants but she never mentioned love.

He knew he would never answer everything so he went home to bed and dreamt of Eryn.

Now he was up and still walking around like a zombie trying to figure out what he should do. An idea came to him but he wasn't sure it would work so he called the one person he knew would help.

A Marine to Remember

Mitch Frinnel was sitting at his desk in Quantico, Virginia when his phone rang.

"Master Sgt. Frinnel," he answered when he picked up the receiver.

Chase started in right away, "Mitch, I'm in trouble here," he blurted out.

Mitch held back a laugh, "Geez, Chase," he chuckled, not being able to help it, "why don't you get right to the point."

Although he was teasing, Mitch couldn't remember Chase sounding this bad in years. The last time was when he was a Staff Sgt. here at Cherry Point. He stopped, a slow smile forming. No Way, he thought, it couldn't be happening again. If it was, there was a God.

"Oh, she's there isn't she?" Mitch asked smugly.

Chase rolled his eyes and huffed out a breath, "How did you know?" he asked his friend, pissed that Mitch was amused.

Mitch closed his office door and sat back down behind his desk, "It's simple, you never sounded like this other than when you were hung up on Eryn."

Knowing that Chase needed a friend to listen didn't disqualify him from getting a lecture. "I told you this would come back and bite you in the ass!" He remembered all too well calling Chase up and reaming him out for hurting Eryn so badly.

Chase didn't say anything because Mitch was right. He was right back then too but Chase was too proud and stubborn to fix it.

"Tell me everything," Mitch said as he pushed his paperwork aside.

Sighing, Chase started slowly, "Well, she's my OIC to begin with."

Chase barely got out the words before Mitch snorted into the phone and started laughing.

Shaking his head, Chase yelled, "Hey!" into the phone. He was getting mad and followed up with, "This isn't funny, Mitch!"

Hearing the emotion in Chase's voice sobered Mitch's. "I'm sorry, buddy." He sighed, "Okay, tell me what's gone on up til now and let's see what we can do."

Mitch listened to Chase's story about seeing Eryn for the first time, the kiss on the sidewalk, fighting in her office when he found out she was married, fighting his feelings for her, kissing her again, finding out she wasn't married anymore, and he explained that her mother called him and talked to him about giving Eryn time. The weird thing was how dramatic Chase was when he talked about the situation.

After he waited for Chase to finish, he said, "Listen," he wasn't exactly sure what he should say to his friend, "the only thing I can tell you is to keep telling her you love her."

Chase nodded but started to say something when Mitch interrupted him.

"Chase," Mitch said loudly, "Tell her you love her. You're over thinking this way too much."

It couldn't be that simple to Chase's way of thinking but he would do what Mitch said. "Okay," he said flatly.

Mitch smiled again, "You go get her!"

They hung up and Mitch hoped Chase wouldn't screw this up.

Chapter 20

The ballroom was decorated with the Marine Corps colors of red and gold. Each table had a red tablecloth with a gold overlay and the chairs had white covers giving them an elegant look. Every place setting was decorated with a glass etched with the Corps' emblem, the 237th birthday, and Marine Corps Base Hawaii on it. Programs were laid neatly on every plate explaining the ceremony and centerpieces on the tables were made up of various flowers over glass mirrors.

Chase walked into the ballroom and felt the festive atmosphere around him. People were still putting on the finishing touches when he arrived so he offered to help out. He was here early because he was so excited to see Eryn.

After hanging up with Mitch, Chase laid it out in his mind. Really, nothing else mattered as long as Eryn loved him. He wouldn't give up on her this time around. They would push aside anything that stood in their way, he was sure of it.

He walked around looking at decorations for a while then he went to the bar to get a drink. He got a hotel room here so he wouldn't have to worry about drinking and driving. He ordered his first drink, hoping it would give him the courage he needed.

A Marine to Remember

Eryn was standing in the hotel room she was sharing with Abi and looking at her reflection in the bathroom mirror.

Her mother treated them to the best spa adventure ever. They each got a massage, manicure, pedicure, makeup, and hair updos. It was hard not to feel gorgeous after all that pampering.

"Oh, Eryn," Abi said in a breath when she came out of the bedroom and saw her friend, "that dress is absolutely astonishing!"

Eryn smiled as she ran her hands over the full skirt. She couldn't have agreed with Abi more.

She said, "Thanks," as she looked over herself one last time.

The hairdresser swept up Eryn's long hair into an enormous pile of curls. She used clips with crystals on them to secure the hair. So every time Eryn moved, her hair literally sparkled. That, combined with the sequins and crystals on the dress, gave Eryn the appearance of shimmering with every movement.

Her makeup was done heavier than normal but gave her a polished, sexy look. The dress was complimented with matching gloves, purse, and silver shoes, studded with crystals as well. She topped off the outfit with a set of diamond teardrop earrings her parents gave her as a gift years earlier.

Danette Fogarty

Looking in the mirror, Eryn thought that this was how Cinderella must have felt before going to the ball. The question was, would her prince be waiting there for her?

"Well," Abi asked from behind Eryn.

Letting out a low whistle after she turned around, Eryn was stunned. "You are going to knock them dead," she said to Abi.

Abi's transformation was no less stunning than Eryn's. She was in a silver, form-fitting dress that accentuated every feminine curve and made her look like a Hollywood starlet on the red carpet. Eryn wondered if the changes were so much more pronounced because she and Abi wore such masculine clothes for work.

Grabbing her clutch, Abi peeked in the mirror to make sure her make-up was okay, "Thank you." She sighed. "I'm only trying to keep up with you."

They both laughed and hugged lightly so they wouldn't smudge make up or wrinkle dresses.

"Let's get this show on the road!" Abi yelled to Eryn when she went into the bedroom to make sure she had everything she needed in her small purse.

Eryn's parents had a room a few floors up from her and Abi so they agreed to meet up down at the lobby before going into the ballroom.

The elevator ride down was fun because there were some young gentlemen who didn't seem to know what to say to pretty ladies. She and Abi were giggling about them when they got off the elevator and walked into the lobby area.

Scanning the room, Eryn found her father first. He was tall and carried himself almost regally so she picked him out right away. She noticed he was standing in a group with her Commanding Officer and a few others. Eryn shook her head as she and Abi made their way toward him. Nobody wasted any time; hobnobbing was always in full swing at the balls.

Tom Fredricks was listening to a conversation between several other officers when he noticed his daughter enter the room with her friend, Abi. He excused himself immediately and started toward her. She was a sight. He couldn't take his eyes off of her until he was next to his wife.

"Our girl is here," Tom whispered into Beverly's ear, "and she's a vision."

Beverly looked up at her handsome husband and smiled. He had the oddest expression on his face so she looked over to where he gaze was focused. Once her eyes found Eryn, she gasped. Their daughter literally glowed. Smiling, Beverly wondered if it was from the dress or because she was in love.

Eryn's parents came up to her and her mother grabbed her hands.

"Oh," Beverly said with unshed tears in her eyes, "you are such a lovely sight."

Blushing, Eryn smiled her thanks.

Ben and Colleen came in a few minutes after Eryn and Abi. Once the initial greetings and compliments were done, the group started making their way toward the ballroom.

Eryn hung back and held her father's arm. She asked, "What were you talking to my CO about?"

Tom smiled and patted his daughter's arm. "It turns out," he answered, "that your dad is the oldest Marine attending the festivities."

It was tough not to laugh at her father's obvious disappointment at the news.

The Marine Corps had a tradition that the oldest Marine and youngest Marine attending the ball were served the first two pieces of birthday cake. It was done at the end of the ceremony so both of the persons with the honor had to be notified ahead of time.

Tom didn't want to do it, but he would for the Corps.

A Marine to Remember

Eryn walked in behind her parents and Uncle Ben and Aunt Colleen so she didn't notice the whispers right away. They made their way to their assigned table amidst murmurs about the beautiful woman in the red dress. It was like her arrival created a ripple effect through the room.

Chase was talking to one of the Section Leaders when he heard a group making noises beside them. You would have thought a famous person just entering with the way these guys were acting. He turned around to see what the fuss was all about.

The moment Eryn entered his line of sight, his jaw literally dropped open.

The Staff Sgt. next to Chase let out a whistle and asked, "Who is that gorgeous babe?" to Chase.

Looking over and giving the man a look that clearly said 'back off,' Chase said, "That's your OIC," through his gritted teeth.

Not waiting for any more comments, Chase moved from where he was and made his way to his assigned table for dinner.

The table Eryn and her parents were assigned to was close to the podium and dance floor; no doubt in thanks to her father's rank. She looked at the seating cards and noticed Chase wasn't assigned to their table. A niggle of disappointment ran through her. It was probably for the best since they didn't really resolve anything between them but it was still a letdown.

She wondered if maybe he wasn't coming but then she felt the all-too-familiar feeling of awareness skitter up her neck. He was watching her! She discreetly scanned the tables until her eyes found his. It was like coming home!

Neither of them moved, they only sat in their respective seats and stared at one another. It was like there was some invisible link joining them.

Eryn felt a jab as her side and looked over to see Abi frowning at her.

"Hey," Abi hissed in her ear, "your father is watching you make goo-goo eyes with your NCOIC."

Taking a breath, Eryn looked over at her father. He was looking at Chase then turned to look at her. She couldn't tell what he was thinking but, right now, it didn't matter to her.

Her eyes landing on her mother, Eryn thought she had an odd look on her face as well. When her mother winked at her and laid her hand on Eryn's father's arm to draw his attention away, Eryn breathed in relief.

Everyone turned their attention to the podium as the ceremony started. The color guard entered with the traditional Marine Corps Birthday cake. The squadron CO got up to say a few words and introduced the key note speaker.

The former Marine, who made a successful business on Wall Street, spoke about the influence the Corps had on his life.

During the speeches Eryn stole glances at Chase only to find him staring at her as well. Their eyes would lock and neither of them could look away.

Tumbling out of her haze, Eryn jolted when the applause started. Dinner service started and she was obligated to keep her eyes on her own table. She half listened to the conversation at her table and was glad no one asked her to participate.

After dinner was over, the cake was brought up front and Eryn smiled knowing what was going to happen.

Tom Fredricks was announced as the oldest Marine and a very young Private was called up as the youngest Marine present. They were served their cake and everyone applauded.

"He deserves it," Ben said slyly to the table.

Everyone chuckled and watched her father shake hands with the Private and have a few words with her CO.

She had to admit, he was very handsome in his dress uniform. It was impossible for her to think that he wasn't bigger than life itself and wouldn't be a Marine forever. She was thankful for the time they had to start repairing their relationship.

Tom sat back down at the table as the cake was served to the rest of the party goers. He took his ribbing with great aplomb.

The DJ announced the music would be starting and Eryn looked over to find Chase was gone from his seat. She sighed, disappointed that he was no longer there.

Her father stood as the music started and Eryn smiled, assuming he was going to ask her mother to dance. But he came around and held his hand out to her instead.

"Would you mind dancing with your old man?" Tom asked as he winked at his daughter.

Eryn looked at her mother first and, seeing her nod, smiled up at her father, "Of course," she answered.

She stood and held his hand as they walked out onto the dance floor.

Chase was making his way over to Eryn's table to ask her to dance when he saw her father taking her out to the dance floor. Damn! He said to himself. He'd been so wrapped up in Eryn that he forgot about her father. Who could blame him? She was the most beautiful woman in the world! He was captivated and literally could not stop looking at her.

When they were looking at one another during the ceremony, it was like they were right next to one another instead of tables apart. Her eyes sparkled and he was flushed with want. He stood there, watching her dance with her father and wondering what he was going to do.

His thoughts were interrupted by a hand on his shoulder. He turned his head and saw a lovely woman standing next to him.

"Chase?" Beverly Fredricks asked.

Eryn's mother, he thought. The resemblance was unmistakable.

Smiling, Chase simply said, "Mrs. Fredricks."

Beverly was surprised, "You know who I am?" She asked with a smile, "I wasn't sure you would."

Chase took her hand in his and commented, "Your daughter shares your beauty, Mrs. Fredricks."

Watching the man try to talk to her, while being so preoccupied with watching her daughter, touched Beverly's heart. Her suspicions were all confirmed.

She looked out to the dance floor where Eryn and Tom were dancing, "I can see now why my daughter is in love with you." The comment was said flippantly.

Chase turned his attention to Eryn's mother, his face shocked.

"Surely, Chase," Beverly nodded toward Eryn, "you can't doubt it."

Hearing the words Eryn's mother said and thinking about what Mitch told him gave Chase hope.

He turned to Mrs. Fredricks and gestured towards the dance floor, "Would you like to dance?" he asked her.

Beverly smiled and wound her arm through his as they made their way onto the floor.

Eryn was dancing with her father and trying to look for Chase as they moved around the dance floor. Even with her subtle approach, she should have known her father would catch on.

"Your young man is dancing with your mother," Tom whispered into his daughter's ear.

He almost laughed at the shocked look on her face.

Eryn flushed, "Dad, he's not my young man; he's my NCOIC."

Tom threw his head back and laughed outright.

"Eryn, I love you and I realize how wrong I was back then to interfere in your relationship with Chase." He cleared his throat and said, "I know I let my selfishness get in the way of your happiness and I don't intend to make the same mistake twice."

Her father kissed her cheek and released his hold on her. He walked over to where her mother and Chase were dancing and tapped Chase's shoulder.

"Excuse me," Tom said to Chase when their eyes met.

Coming face to face with Eryn's father, Chase instinctively stepped away from Mrs. Fredricks and stood at attention.

Without missing a beat, Tom smiled and took his wife into his arms. He looked at Chase and nodded to where Eryn stood.

"My daughter seems to be without a partner," Tom said to Chase and swept his wife away into the crowd of dancers.

Chase was no fool, he found Eryn with his eyes and walked toward her with determination.

Eryn was afraid of what her father would do and didn't want to witness it. She walked over to their table and just sat down when she heard a voice behind her.

"Warrant Officer Smith," Chase said.

Turning around in her seat, Eryn's eyes locked on Chase's immediately. He towered over her. She thought he looked like some knight coming to rescue her in some clichéd story about a princess.

His dress uniform was perfectly fitted; showing off his broad shoulders. The pants defined his lean waist and made his legs look long and powerful. The medals on his chest reflected the dim light in the room. He epitomized the saying "a man in uniform" in her opinion. She was pretty sure he was the reason women fell for Marines.

She couldn't speak, her thoughts were too scattered so she just placed her hand into his offered one and let him guide her out to the dance floor.

Once Chase had Eryn in his arms he had no plans to ever let her go. This was right! They were practically floating around to the music. No one else existed except for the two of them.

He looked into her eyes and got lost in the intensity of her gaze. He didn't want to speak, he only wanted to hold her close and feel her. Luckily, the music was slow for the first couple of songs so they were able to leisurely explore closeness in plain view of others.

The music picked up tempo and Eryn stopped. She had no intention of dancing to the fast paced music the DJ was starting up.

She was blushing as she made her way back to the table, wondering when Chase would be able to hold her in his arms again. Her blush deepened when she met her parents' stares. She looked away for a moment in embarrassment.

Chase could see Eryn needed a minute to recover from their closeness so he took the initiative. He nodded to Eryn's parents across the table and extended his hand out to Ben.

"Nice to see you again," Ben said to Chase with a smile and a wink.

Ben introduced Chase to Colleen who greeted Chase warmly.

Once Chase and Eryn were seated, Tom ordered a round of drinks for the table. The conversation started up and Eryn and Chase were brought into it quickly. It was like everyone there were old friends.

Before Eryn knew it, she looked at the clock and saw it was past midnight. Where did the time go?

Sometime during the evening, a handsome Gunnery Sgt. sat down next to Abi. It was pretty obvious there was an attraction between them and Eryn hoped Abi had a good time. If anyone deserved it, Abi did.

It was almost one in the morning when Eryn's parents, along with Ben and Colleen, excused themselves.

Tom announced that they were "old" and needed to turn in so he and Beverly stood. The younger men protested with good-natured ribbing and stood to shake hands.

Beverly rounded the table to kiss her daughter goodnight.

Whispering in Eryn's ear, Beverly said, "Have some fun tonight."

Eryn turned her head so she was looking at her mother. The knowing look in her mother's eyes was sweet. Not knowing what to say, Eryn only nodded and turned her attention back to Chase. He was involved in a conversation with Abi and her friend so she just watched him.

Chase felt Eryn's eyes on him so he turned toward her and smiled. She had a weird look on her face so he wondered if her mother said something to her.

After Eryn's parents left, Abi excused herself to the bathroom and nodded her head to silently tell Eryn to come with her. They were about to go into the bathroom when Abi pulled Eryn aside.

"Listen," Abi said intensely, "are you going back to our room tonight?" she asked Eryn.

Eryn wasn't sure what to say. She hoped Chase would ask her up to his room but he said nothing up to now. Probably because her parents were at the table.

Abi interrupted Eryn's thoughts, "Just tell him you want to go back up to his room with him."

It was so easy for Abi to suggest it but it was a whole other thing for Eryn to actually do it. It was natural for Abi to be direct and Eryn wished she possessed that particular trait.

Staring at Eryn expectantly, Abi asked, "Don't you want to?"

"Uh Yes!" Eryn answered loudly before she had time to think about it.

Abi smiled proudly, "Okay then," she was going to proceed into the restroom but stopped, "no chickening out now because our room will be occupied."

Wiggling her eyebrows, Abi looked like an imp.

They went into the ladies room and freshened up. They were at the mirror checking their makeup when Abi's eyes met Eryn's in their reflection.

She glared at Eryn and asked, "You're going to chicken out, aren't you?"

Eryn wanted to deny it but she couldn't with complete certainty.

"Ok," Abi grabbed Eryn's arm and pulled over to one of the stalls, "we've come to the moment when you are going to do something completely crazy." She opened the door to the stall and pointed, "Get into that stall and take off your panties."

Her mouth gaping, Eryn couldn't believe Abi even suggested such a thing. She looked around, hoping no one else heard their conversation.

Abi pointed again, "Go!" She waited for Eryn to go in and held the door closed. "This way you'll be so wound up you won't chicken out."

Not sure if she wanted to laugh or throw up, Eryn stood there. Seriously? She could see Abi's feet under the stall and dutifully removed her panties. When she came out, she nodded to Abi.

"Thank God!" Abi exclaimed. "Now you will go out there and have the night of your dreams."

A Marine to Remember

She could see the humor in the situation and laughed. "Okay," She hugged Abi quickly, "I'm going to hold you to that."

They went back to the table and giggled like school girls the whole way.

The DJ announced the last song right after they sat down.

Chase offered his hand to Eryn and led her back out for the last dance. A beautifully sad love song was playing and described how he felt.

As he did earlier, Chase held Eryn close to him. She wanted to focus on their movements but was wondering how to approach the "I want to go back to your room with you," subject. She only drank one glass of champagne and that wasn't enough for her to just blurt it out. She saw others getting up to leave and knew her window of opportunity was closing.

They got back to the table as Abi was standing up with her new friend. "I'll see you in the morning," she tossed over her should to Eryn as they walked away. "Goodnight, Chase," she said and turned to wink at him.

Confused, Chase looked at Eryn. He thought she and Abi were sharing a room but maybe he heard them wrong earlier. When her parents left he hoped they might have some time alone to talk but now he wasn't sure. Did he say goodnight or did he try to keep her with him as long as possible?

"Would you like to take a walk on the beach?" He asked Eryn before he lost his nerve.

Smiling, Eryn grabbed her purse, "Yes," she answered.

They slowly made their way out of the ballroom, stopping to say goodnight to acquaintances along the way. It was difficult because of the protocol their positions demanded they follow.

The beach was actually very quiet considering how bustling Honolulu was at night. The lights of the city could be seen down the curved coastline as they walked. There was a light breeze and the sky was full of bright stars.

Even with the mild temperatures, Eryn felt chilled. Chase was kind enough to remove his dress uniform jacket and placed it around her shoulders. She felt the warmth from his body in the fabric and reveled in it. There was a faint smell of his cologne that teased her senses.

Eryn removed her shoes so she could walk in the sand, carrying them in her hands as they walked.

A few minutes later, Eryn felt like she should say something, "It was a beautiful ball."

A Marine to Remember

Chase could hear the quiver in her voice and smiled, "Yes," he answered.

Was he unsure too? Eryn asked herself.

"Although," she stopped and looked up at him, "I don't remember much of the ceremony because there was this very handsome man stealing all my attention." The boldness of her words surprised her.

She started walking again.

Chase took a few steps then commented, "Well then, I don't remember much because this beautiful woman stepped into the room and stole my breath away."

He couldn't take the suspense and stopped, putting his hand on Eryn's arm to stop her too.

"What are we doing here, Eryn?" he asked in desperation.

Chase just needed to know what she wanted. He'd give it to her, whatever it was.

The city lights cast enough of a glow to illuminate Chase's features. She smiled and answered, "We're waiting for you to ask me back to your room."

Once she said the words, Eryn was relieved and excited.

Chase froze. He wasn't sure he heard what she said or just what he wanted to hear.

He took a deep breath and whispered, "I wasn't sure what you wanted."

She could feel the need shaking him because it was doing the same thing to her. She reached up and touched his cheek with her trembling fingers.

"I want you," she said in a low, husky voice.

Oh, he was gone! Chase placed his hands on either side of her face and brought his lips down to meet hers. The kiss flowed from tender to passionate and back again.

Eryn stepped away breathless. "We're wasting time here," she said quickly.

Chase swept her up into his arms and started running down the beach toward the hotel, her laughter floating away in the breeze.

Chapter 21

Chase and Eryn stepped apart the moment they entered the hotel.

There were still people from their command milling around the lobby and the last thing they needed was someone seeing them in a compromising way. It was most definitely against the Marine Corps rules to be involved with your commanding officer.

Eryn started to wonder if what they were doing was right and looked over at Chase.

As soon as Eryn's eyes met his, he knew what she was thinking. Now that they were back in reality it was time to make a decision. He knew what he wanted but he couldn't live with himself if he pressured her into a choice she regretted later on. The only thing he could do was give her the space to decide.

They got on the elevator and stepped to the back so other people could get on. Eryn looked over and winked at Chase, which he returned with a smile of his own.

Chase leaned over and whispered, "I'm on the sixth floor, room 612."

Nodding, Eryn smiled again but said nothing.

Danette Fogarty

The elevator stopped on the fifth floor and people got off. Eryn stepped off as well, which made Chase wonder if she had changed her mind. He gave her a perplexed look as the doors closed between them.

Eryn went down the hall to the stairwell. She climbed the steps up to the sixth floor as quietly as she could, hoping there wasn't anyone else using them. Once she got to the sixth floor, she peered through the little window leading to the hallway. She couldn't see anyone so she was about to open the door when it swung open on its own.

Chase laughed at Eryn's startled look when he opened the stairwell door. He poked his head through the door and smiled, "I figured this was what you were up to," he said in a whisper.

Giggling, Eryn nodded.

"My room is just around the corner," he spoke to her in hushed tones.

Eryn took his hand and they ran down the hall like children. It was fun to try to be sneaky. She waited as he used his key and quickly got them inside his room.

When she entered, Eryn thought Chase's room was just like hers. It had a small sitting area with two doors on one side and a balcony on the other side.

The room colors were in muted colors of tan and blue and reminded her of the ocean.

Chase locked the door and came up behind Eryn, gently putting his hands on her shoulders. She was trembling and he got a little worried.

"Are you cold?" he asked and bent down to kiss her shoulder.

Eryn shook her head no, "I'm just nervous I guess," she answered.

He was actually relieved because he figured he was the only one who was nervous. Waiting ten years to make love to someone was a little intimidating. He had Eryn back in his life again and he wasn't going to ruin it. They would go as slow as Eryn needed.

Looking out the window, Eryn's pulse beat loudly in her chest. She didn't want to wait one more second. She turned quickly and grabbed Chase's shirt, pulling him to her for a kiss.

Chase was so surprised by her movement that he had to take a step back to keep his balance. Of course, her lips on his helped him recover quickly. His arms wrapped around her and held her to him.

As they were kissing, Eryn was backing up and pulling him with her. She could hear the swish of her skirt as she moved combined with their ragged breathing while they were kissing deeply. It was turning her on and she wanted him......now!

When Eryn felt the sofa behind her, she pulled her head away. Chase's eyes were dark and stormy, like hers she supposed. She smiled wantonly and turned them so their bodies were reversed. He looked at her with a question in his eyes.

She was emboldened. His kisses and his looks made her feel that way. She pushed him back so he fell onto the sofa. The heat inside of her was like a roaring fire brought to life after years of being low embers.

All thoughts of complications and reasoning was shoved aside. There was a chance they may have regrets, but they would deal with that later.

Pulling up the skirt of her gown, Eryn straddled Chase on the sofa. His hands grasped her waist and held her still. Their kisses were all heat; steam permeating off of their joined bodies. Lips melded and tongues dueled in the most delicious ways.

Eryn's hands were wild; running over Chase's neck, head, and shoulders. He removed his dress jacket when they came into the room so she only had his shirt to contend with. She unbuttoned it quickly and brusquely yanked it out of his trousers.

Pulling back so he could look at her face, she made a show of throwing the shirt into the recesses of the room. His t-shirt was removed as well and she hummed when her fingers could feel the hard muscles of his chest.

"I love the feel of you," Eryn murmured against his lips.

Chase smiled and sucked in a deep breath when her nails found his nipples and flicked them like he did in the car a few days before. He threw his head back when the shock of want pulsed through him. Oh, she was driving him nuts!

Eryn was rubbing her hips against Chase's lap and loving the delicious pings of arousal the movement created.

His hands couldn't stay still, he had to feel her. The wanting to go slow thing was a distant memory. He moved his hands up under the skirt of her dress and cupped her bottom in his palms. When his hands encountered the naked flesh, he thought he would end it right there.

With roaming hands, he could feel her garter belt with the little straps that hooked onto the thigh high stockings and groaned.

Eryn had no idea this could be so mind-altering and earth-shattering. The need clawed at her insides so strongly that she thought she might burst open. It was exciting but scary too. She was on the brink of losing control and wasn't sure she wanted to do that.

Her lips were all over him. Desire drove her and she couldn't get a handle on it anymore. She tasted and explored him with her lips and tongue. He was wonderful and matched her touch with his own manipulations on her body. She could smell his cologne and his skin and wanted to be wild.

Chase could feel his control slipping and didn't want to disappoint Eryn. He tore his lips from Eryn's and set her away so he could look into her eyes.

"Are you sure?" Chase asked her, need making his voice shake.

He sure as hell didn't want to stop but he would if that's what she wanted to do.

Eryn looked at him, perplexed by his question. She was touched that he would be so close and still offer to stop if that's what she wanted. His consideration was almost as arousing as his kisses.

Smiling a womanly smile, Eryn nodded, "Oh yes." Tears were filling up her eyes, "thank you," she whispered.

He closed the space between them and caught her upper lip between his and suckled it. Scooting to the end of the couch, he cupped her bottom again and stood up. Her arms and legs instinctively wrapped around him.

"I'm not going to make love to you on a couch," he kissed her; "it's the bed or nothing."

Eryn smiled and held on while he carried her to the bedroom and kissed her as they went. She really had found her prince.

They almost fell twice on the way to the bedroom, hitting furniture and tripping over discarded clothes. Finally, Chase reached the bed and laid her gently down on top of the bedspread. He sat down next to her and pushed her hands down when they tried to pull him to her.

He stroked her cheek, "I want to feel your hair down and wrapped around us while we're making love."

She lay there and let him pull out the clips from her hair. He was so tender and stared into her eyes while he removed them. It was a potent thing, being the focus of someone's full attention.

There was just enough light in the room to make out his face and, after a few minutes, Eryn was becoming self-conscious.

"I'm scared," she admitted weakly.

Chase bent down and kissed the tip of her nose, "Oh, sweetheart," he murmured, "It's going to be so good for you, I promise."

She nodded but was no less scared, "I know, I'm just worried about controlling my feelings."

Looking down into her beautiful face, illuminated by the moon and soft light from a lamp, Chase thought she looked like an angel.

"Baby," he whispered, "don't. Just let go. Be with me. I want all of you." He said the words softly but he meant them with a fierceness he couldn't explain.

No more words, Eryn thought. They finally found each other and this moment was all they needed. She sighed when her hair was down and he pulled her up to unzip the back of her dress.

As he lowered the bodice of the dress, Chase could see her breasts. They were full, nipples hard, and begged him to touch and kiss them. He leaned into her and took first one, then the other, making love to them with his lips and tongue. He smiled when Eryn threw her head back in ecstasy.

Needing her more than ever, Chase stood up and looked down at her.

"I want you out of this dress or I'm going to rip it off," he said in a low growl.

A Marine to Remember

Eryn's eyes widened, "This dress was very expensive and you can't do that!" she exclaimed.

They gathered up the material and Chase gently pulled it up and over her head. Eryn gave him a mock look of anger when he tossed the garment onto the floor.

Once Chase turned his attention back to her, his lungs stopped working. She was kneeling on the bed with only a garter belt and stockings on. Her hair streamed down over her shoulders and covered her breasts. She was breathing fast and he could feel her heartbeat without even touching her.

Gently, Chase covered her shoulders with his hands and lay her back down on the bed. The rays of moonlight skirted across her skin as moved and gave her creamy skin a glow. He stood up and took off his pants, shoes, and socks quickly.

They were both naked and Eryn was on fire. He was more beautiful than she thought. He was all muscle and strength. His arousal drew her attention and, smiling, she reached over and lightly scraped her nails down the length of his erection. He closed his eyes and clenched his jaw which drove Eryn even crazier. She knew she had the power to evoke such strong physical reactions in him and that made her braver.

Chase didn't expect Eryn to touch him so openly so he was trying to hold on to his control as long as possible.

Eryn closed her eyes and wrapped her fingers around his pulsing arousal. The feel of him was her only focus. She licked her lips because they were parched and moaned in agony when he pulled away from her.

He reached into the nightstand and got out a condom. She watched him rip open the package and cover his hard shaft with the protection.

"Chase, I need you now," Eryn said while pulling him toward her.

It was impossible to resist her, "I know, baby," he replied, his voice husky.

He sat on the bed and unclipped her stockings from the garter. He had to avoid looking at the triangle of soft curls just above his fingers because if he focused on that, he would be inside her. Instead, he quickly rolled down the stockings and pulled them off of her feet. The garter was next.

Laying there on the bed completely naked made Eryn shy. She didn't want to be shy now, she wanted to feel Chase inside of her.

Eryn took his hand in hers and pulled him up to her. He straddled her upper thighs, making sure her legs were slightly spread. Moving his fingers down, he parted the folds of her and groaned when he could feel her moist heat. Parting her wet core, he placed his finger inside of her and explored the softness.

His touch was so intimate that Eryn thought she would jump off the bed. She felt the release build up and wash over her before she could do anything. She cried out and let the rampaging waves of pleasure sweep through her body and soul.

Chase whispered, "Yes, my love."

Now that Chase gave her the first orgasm, he felt like he couldn't hold out any longer.

Even after ten years, he wasn't prepared for the onslaught of feelings Eryn made him feel. He positioned himself over her and looked down into her eyes. His hands were tangled in her hair on either side of her head. The golden strands tickled the tips of his fingers, adding another layer of sensation to his system.

Chase lowered himself into her softness and sighed. She was tight and hot and slick. It was like coming home and he had to take a moment to gain his composure.

Eryn gasped when Chase slipped inside of her; she felt like she was finally complete. Still reeling from her orgasm, she wanted more and started to move her hips beneath him.

Once Eryn started moving, Chase followed her. He started out slowly, wanting to feel every millimeter of her and draw out her pleasure. But quickly, he started to move faster. He could see her looking at him with her eyes so dark, they looked like pools of night sky.

Arching up, Eryn yelled, "Yes, Chase!"

Chase groaned and felt his release building, "Yes, baby," he returned.

They both found the peak and tumbled over the side together.

Falling back to earth was almost as satisfying as the climb, at least Chase thought so. He moved to his side and tucked Eryn close to the front of him. He started running his hand down the side of her from her head to her thigh. He kept the touch feather light and meant to comfort her.

The sensations Chase's fingers left over her skin were amazing. It was so beautiful how he made her feel that she couldn't keep it contained. Tears started to come out and her shoulders shook with the emotional release.

Fear clawed at Chase when he realized Eryn was crying.

He sat up, "Baby," he choked out, "did I hurt you?" He'd rather die than hurt her.

Eryn turned so she could face him and smiled weakly, "No." She moved her hand up to cup his cheek, "I just never thought it would feel this way."

Relief washed over Chase and he squeezed her closer, "Neither did I," he was making a big effort to keep his emotions from taking over.

"Making love with you was beautiful," Eryn whispered into the darkness a few minutes later.

She was on her side and fit so perfectly against him. She could feel the whisper of his breathing against the top of her head. A deep sense of contentment filled up her heart and she fell asleep.

Later, in the deep darkness of night, they made love again.

This time was more physical. Eryn woke up with Chase's hand between her thighs, his fingers lightly massaging the skin inches below her wet core. Not even fully awake, she turned into his fingers to allow them full access to her womanhood. She felt him rouse and lean over to kiss her lips.

Passion flared up instantaneously. Eryn wanted control this time so she pushed him onto his back and straddled him. Her hair fell across her shoulders onto his chest, sending tantalizing sensations over their skin. With her hands pressed against his shoulders, she lifted herself onto his hardness. She was already wet with desire so she slid easily down his swollen shaft.

Immediately, pleasure erupted inside of her. She was surprised when his hands stilled her progress.

"What about protection?" Chase asked her. He would not compromise her.

Eryn felt wanted and cherished, "It's okay," she whispered.

She began moving over him in a delicious rhythm. Again, they reached the pinnacle together and crashed into the sensational bliss of release. Bodies sated, they fell asleep tangled up in one another's arms.

Eryn was having the best dream ever. She was snuggled into a bed with fluffy pillows all around her. She turned over and saw Chase was lying beside her and smiling. He kept telling her he loved her over and over. It was so wonderful that she didn't want to wake up.

Bright light! Eryn's mind was screaming at her to go back to sleep but the light brought her slowly to consciousness. Sighing, she stretched but didn't dare open her eyes yet. She slept so well and that dream.....that dream made her feel so safe.

She stretched her arms above her head and finally opened her eyes. It took a couple of seconds to figure out where she was.

In Chase's bed, she said to herself. They made love!

Eryn lay there smiling and blushing as she remembered what they did the night before. She turned her head to see Chase coming into the room, smiling at her.

Chase stopped at the end of the bed and looked at her.

"Good morning, gorgeous," he said.

Sitting up, Eryn pulled the sheets around her. How come she was so shy this morning? It didn't make a lot of sense when you were naked and made love the night before. She tried to finger comb her hair and gain some sense of balance. She was pretty sure she looked just awful.

She mumbled back, "Good morning," and cursed herself for sounding so weak.

Chase put down the bag he was holding and rounded the bed to sit beside her. He thought it was cute that she was so shy this morning. It was a constant surprise when he was around her.

He tilted his head and studied her, "What are you doing?" he asked, never losing the smile.

Eryn tried to burrow deeper beneath the covers but it was impossible with him sitting there. She could feel the red of embarrassment creep across her cheeks.

"I know I look like hell and I don't know how to do the morning after thing," she said in a tight voice.

Chase could understand her being unsure; he was too, but he didn't want her to push him away. "Well," he looked her up and down slowly, "you could start with giving me a kiss." He leaned in to kiss her lips but she turned her face at the last second so he got her cheek instead.

"No way," Eryn said as she scrambled to get off the other side of the bed, "I haven't even brushed my teeth yet."

Her confession made Chase laugh. She was delightful and didn't realize it. When he woke this morning with Eryn in his arms, he was floored by the collection of feelings rushing into him.

He walked over to the bathroom door and knocked, "Abi dropped off your bag for you," he called to her.

A Marine to Remember

Eryn opened the door, grabbed the bag, and closed it quickly.

"And she said to tell you, and I quote, 'to sleep in, have fun, and if you need a ride she's leaving about noon.' I'm sure your toothbrush is in the bag," he yelled when he heard the water come on.

Again, she opened the door, the toothbrush in her mouth, and nodded to him to let him know she heard him. She avoided his playful grabbing and closed the door again.

Turning around, Eryn cringed at her reflection in the bathroom mirror. It was worse than she thought.

Her hair looked like it was attacked by a couple of small animals and her face looked like a drunken clown took a shot at painting it. There were makeup smudges everywhere and she wondered if her hair would ever be completely detangled.

Sighing, she finished brushing her teeth and turned on the shower. It was all worth it, she thought as she stuck her hand in to wait for the shower water to warm. She felt different this morning.

Getting in the shower, Eryn felt decadent. There were four shower heads, at all different angles, so the water sluiced over her entire body. She compared it to feeling Chase's hands on her.

She could not remember ever being so thoroughly made love to. The thought stopped her hands from grabbing the washcloth. Paul, she thought.

Guilt, hot and quick, rushed into her chest. Did it mean that she wasn't a good lover to him? They had a good life right? Giving herself a mental shake, Eryn took a deep breath.

There was no use trying to change something and there was no reason to compare the two men. Tears started anyway and she was at a loss as to how to stop them.

Chase was pacing outside the bathroom. She'd been in there for about eight minutes now and he already missed her. The shower water turned on and images of the water sliding down her body made him hard.

That beautiful, sensuous, deliciously erotic body of hers. The images made him want and he couldn't resist going in.

He entered the room and could see the outline of Eryn in the shower. She was very still, which surprised him, but he walked over and opened the door slowly.

"Do you mind if I join you?" he asked.

Eryn stiffened. She hoped to have some time to figure this out before she had to face Chase.

A Marine to Remember

He was in the shower behind her and turned her around. All his yearnings fell away when he saw the tears in her face and the hurt look in her eyes. Alarm bells went off in his brain.

Chase pulled her to him, "Baby, what's wrong?" he asked as he held her.

Eryn felt stupid! Here she was, in love with Chase and she should be overjoyed. So why did she feel guilty? She didn't really know how to answer him.

"I guess," she pulled back so she could look into his beautiful blue eyes, "I'm just feeling overwhelmed."

Paul was still there, between them, but Eryn couldn't really talk to Chase about him just yet. Plus, she wasn't even sure where this thing with Chase was going. There was no need to add her insecurities to the pile of worries he carried.

Chase knew she wasn't telling him the whole truth but he didn't want to compromise the ground he won and strain the connection they found. Once things were more settled between them, she would tell him. Until then, he would just support her.

Squeezing her into a fierce hug, Chase stepped back and handed her the washcloth, "Could you wash my back then?" he asked, trying to lighten the mood.

Eryn stated to relax and was a little shy at first but recovered quickly. They finished showering together, each taking their time washing the other. It took another half hour to get out of the shower and they were both smiling when they took turns drying one another off.

A while later, they were dressed and packed. Chase smiled when Eryn went around the room picking up their discarded clothing from the night before. He helped her put her dress back on the hangar and kissed her when they finished.

After they made sure no items were left in the room, they carried their bags to the elevator to go downstairs.

"I'm starving," Chase said to her while they waited.

Looking at her watch, Eryn figured out why. It was half past eleven; she was hungry too.

She kissed him quickly, "Well, it's close enough to noon that maybe Abi is down there so we can get you some food."

Chapter 22

The elevator doors opened and Chase and Eryn stepped out into a bustling lobby. It was close to check out time so everyone was mulling around the reservation desk. Chase found the other couple and pointed to the far side of the room.

Eryn looked over and saw Abi, with her head bent, having a conversation with the Gunny she met the previous evening. Frowning because she couldn't remember his name, Eryn went over to speak with her friend.

Abi looked up to see Eryn coming toward her and smiled.

"Oh, Eryn," Abi said, her cheeks flushed.

Noticing that her friend looked a little out of sorts, Eryn responded, "Hey."

Nodding to her new friend, Abi stepped away with Eryn.

Eryn was worried about her friend and asked, "Are you okay?"

Waving her hand in dismissal, Abi smiled again. "I'm fine," She said and winked at her friend, "Bryan and I were just trying to figure out what to do today."

Eryn nodded in return. Bryan, she noted to herself. She looked up and waved Chase over. He shook hands with Bryan and they all stood together.

"Chase and I were going to get some lunch," she looked from Abi to Bryan, "and wanted to know if you wanted to join us."

Bryan answered first, "Sure if it's okay with, Abi."

Abi nodded, "Sure."

Standing there, Chase just stared at Eryn. Everything he saw, he loved; every time she moved, he wanted to be next to her. Now things were more complicated and he wanted to take her home with him and make love to her all day. Knowing that wasn't going to fly, at least not right now, he pasted on a smile and tried to follow the conversation.

"I'm getting a ride back with Bryan," Abi commented, "are you going back with Chase or your parents?" She asked Eryn.

Feeling silly for not knowing the answer, Eryn shrugged. "I don't know."

She looked over at Chase and waited for him to say something but he looked distracted.

Chase came out of his thoughts when he was poked in the ribs by Bryan.

"Yeah," he said loudly. He looked to see three pairs of eyes staring at him.

Abi spoke up first, "Master Sgt.," she looked like a teacher, "are you going to take our boss here back to the base or does she need to find alternate transportation?"

Now he felt like an ass! "Oh, I'll take her," he replied quickly.

The look on Eryn's face was unreadable but he had a sneaking suspicion he was in a little bit of trouble for being distracted.

Bryan smiled, glad Chase was in hot water with the ladies and not him. He waved and said, "We'll meet back her in fifteen then." He put his hand at the base of Abi's back and they headed to the parking area.

A few minutes later, Eryn and Chase were in the parking garage putting their bags in Chase's jeep. The tension was thick and Eryn couldn't figure out why. She couldn't function with it like this so she turned to him.

"What?" she demanded.

Chase closed the door on his side of the jeep and walked around the back to meet up with her.

Taking Eryn's hand, he looked into her eyes and whispered, "Nothing, Eryn."

She was looking up at him and his voice was so gentle but his eyes, they looked really wild. Something was going on.

"It doesn't seem like nothing," she said sarcastically and let go of his hand to walk back to the hotel.

After three steps, Chase grabbed her arm and spun her around into his arms. His lips found hers and his hands buried themselves in her hair.

The kiss took Eryn up into the upper atmosphere of her feelings and made her dizzy with awareness. His lips melded so perfectly with hers.

When Chase pulled away, he opened his eyes and looked down into her sea green eyes. "I needed that," he said.

They walked back to the lobby of the hotel and found Abi and Bryan waiting for them.

Eryn was glad the other couple seemed lost in one another too because she was still humming from the kiss Chase gave her. She was about to say something to Abi when she heard her mother behind them.

"Hello there, kids," Beverly Fredricks beamed. "Did everyone have a good time last night?" she asked, knowing the question would probably embarrass her daughter.

Looking at Abi, Eryn blushed. The guys nodded like little boys. They were joined by Eryn's father, Ben and Colleen so stood there for a few minutes longer talking about the ball.

Finally, Tom Fredricks piped up, "Okay, let's go into the restaurant for lunch," and took his wife's elbow to escort her.

Once the General issued an order, everyone just followed. Shrugging to Eryn, Chase smiled and followed the group. He didn't mind if it gave him some time to spend with Eryn in public.

They all made their way toward a beautiful garden restaurant just off the lobby area. Just before they entered, Eryn's mother pulled her aside.

Beverly felt a little nervous but wanted to speak to her daughter. "I know we don't really talk in detail about your love life," she held her daughter's hand, "but I can see in you all or the things I felt when your father and I started dating and fell in love."

Standing there, Eryn just stared at her mother. She was touched that her mom would make such a comparison given that her parents' marriage of thirty plus years was a strong one.

Eryn squeezed her mom's hand, "Thank you, Mom," she said and hugged her mom quickly in the hopes of catching up to the group.

Beverly held her daughter in place, "Your father and I just wanted you to know that we approve of your young man and we want you to be happy." She tried to keep from being too emotional.

A little embarrassed that her parents obviously discussed hers and Chase's relationship, Eryn answered, "He's not my young man, Mom, but thank you."

Eryn walked away before her mother could hold say anything else. This was too much to think about right now! She shook her head when she reached the table and was met with Chase's questioning look.

The next hour was spent listening to her father and Ben reminisce about "the old days." Both Chase and Bryan seemed fascinated and were asking questions. The ladies carried on much of their own conversations.

It kind of surprised Eryn that the group got on so well. She thought maybe last night was an in-the-moment kind of thing but today, they were all still involved.

Eryn spent the time observing Abi's little romance with Bryan and stealing her own glances at Chase.

A flush made its way up into her cheeks when she thought about the night before. She was relieved when the food came and she could focus on that. When she looked up, she caught a knowing look from her mother and even Aunt Colleen.

Lunch wound down so the couples meandered out into the lobby again. Her father paid for lunch and was in the midst of a good natured debate with the other gentlemen over that fact.

"We're going to stay here for some shopping and sight-seeing," Beverly said to her daughter as they walked out of the restaurant.

Nodding, Eryn smiled, "Okay," she responded, "I'll see you later then."

Beverly kissed her daughter's cheek, "Yes, you will. We love you."

Tom came over and kissed his daughter on the forehead and stood beside his wife.

No words were necessary right now; she loved her parents.

Everyone said good bye and parted ways.

Danette Fogarty

Back out in the parking garage, Chase helped Eryn into the jeep. "Did you want to stay in Honolulu?"

Lunch was fun but Chase noticed how quiet Eryn was. Was she regretting their night together? He was a little, no, a lot confused about what they would do now.

"No," Eryn said, "I'd like to go home."

Chase nodded and went around to get into the driver's side of the vehicle.

The drive back to the base was quiet; each of them lost in their own thoughts.

Everything was changed as far as Chase was concerned. He and Eryn needed to make some decisions. Her parents' acceptance of him went a long way in his mind of clearing things up. Maybe ten years ago, her father and he may have wanted different things for Eryn but Chase really felt like they were both on the same team now.

Eryn was glad the radio was on to break up the silence of the ride. She was in turmoil; thinking maybe he regretted their night together. Insecurities about what their actions did to their working relationship combined with guilt about Paul made her unsettled and confused. She would steal glances at Chase but couldn't stay anything.

A Marine to Remember

Pulling the jeep into the parking lot of the Officer's Quarters building, Chase knew he couldn't show any display of affection. He got out and pulled out Eryn's bags from the back. She met him there and took her bags from him.

"Thank you," she mumbled and turned to walk into the building.

Chase stood there and wondered what just happened.

Two hours later, Chase was still kicking himself. Why didn't he ask her to come back to his place? He should have told her he loved her! He should have been more open about his feelings. Loving Eryn shouldn't scare him but it did. It scared the hell out of him. They both knew what a relationship would mean.

He walked outside the house and sat on the lanai, wondering why he didn't get any answers from her.

Eryn felt sluggish for the rest of the day. She was glad she still had Sunday off before she had to go back to work. It would give her some extra time to get herself together.

How was she going to face everyone? How was she going to face Chase? The situation was getting more complicated by the minute.

Her mother called late in the afternoon to say thank you for allowing them to attend the ball with her. She laughed because she didn't have a choice in the matter. Her mother also asked some discreet questions about Chase and Eryn rolled her eyes. She couldn't speak to anyone about Chase until she figured it out.

By the evening, Eryn was almost in a tizzy. Why didn't Chase say anything to her when they got back to the base? He professed his love before but now that they slept together he says nothing? Just thinking it made Eryn sick. This whole thing would never work.

Deciding that a pity party was in order, Eryn did what any red-blooded American woman would do; she got chocolate, cheap wine, and romantic movies.

She called Abi but got the voicemail. At least her friend had someone to spend time with. Eryn sighed. Okay, that train of thought only made her feel worse. Abi could find someone in one night but Eryn couldn't get the man she wanted for a decade.

This sucked! She plopped down on the couch and put in the first movie. After the third glass of wine, she drifted off into a restless sleep. When she woke up, it was in the middle of the night so she left all of her stuff and went to bed.

Sunday afternoon Chase managed to get in touch with Mitch. They spent over an hour on the phone laying down the groundwork for Chase's plan. When they hung up, Chase felt better. It was nice to have someone to confide in and agree with what he decided to do.

All of this was pretty scary and he hoped that no one, especially Eryn, was hurt by it. Mitch reassured him that everything would work out and wished him luck.

Chase looked at his phone and knew he needed to make one more phone call and it would be either very good or very bad.

Eryn didn't hear from Chase for the rest of the weekend and, by Monday morning, she was a wreck. After everything they shared, physically and emotionally, she was sure he felt the same way she did. But, again, she was apparently wrong.

Sunday evening she had dinner with her parents and got them off on their return flight home. It was nice to see them but it was better that she have some time to herself. They asked about Chase at dinner but she didn't know what to say so she changed the subject. Thankful that they didn't pursue it and she pretended like Chase's name didn't even come up.

Danette Fogarty

After Eryn got home from dropping her parents off, she sat in her room and cried. She damned herself for still loving him. She damned him for making her believe he loved her too. Sleep was evasive so now she was tired and cranky.

Chase was in a great mood on his way to work Monday morning. He felt mellow and was excited to start the work week. His plan was in motion and he hoped it all went well. He was going to talk to Eryn about it as soon as he got in.

Walking into the building he was smiling, until he got to the doorway of Eryn's office and looked inside.

She looked like hell! There were slight bruises under her eyes and her face looked hollow. He was shocked that she looked so different than when he saw her day before yesterday.

"Warrant Officer Smith?" he asked from the doorway. He needed to use the formality of rank at work.

Eryn looked up from shuffling papers, "Yes, Master Sgt.," she said stiffly, "what did you need?"

Chase took a step inside her office and asked, "May I have a word?"

Eryn stood abruptly before he could finish the question, "I have a lot of things to do this morning so we'll have to put off any discussions right now, Master Sgt."

"Eryn?" he whispered softly.

Chase needed to know what the hell was wrong. She was pushing him away but why? After what they shared, he didn't understand.

Eryn looked at him directly when he wouldn't leave, "Master Sgt.," she said in a stern voice, "I would appreciate it if you would address me with my rank at work."

The comment floored Chase. She didn't even resemble the woman he held in his arms two days ago. She didn't seem to want to be anywhere near him. It hurt but he didn't have a choice since they were at work.

Nodding, Chase turned to leave, "Aye, ma'am," he said and left her office, closing the door behind him.

Once the door was closed, Eryn collapsed into her chair. She would not cry; at least not here. She would survive. She did it once before, she'd do it again. The trick was to keep telling herself that so she would eventually start to believe it.

Chase tried, repeatedly, to speak to Eryn during the day but everybody wanted a meeting with him today.

First, he went to an appointment with the squadron CO. He was lucky to get in the first business day after the long weekend so he wasn't complaining. After that, he went over to medical to make some appointments and then he went to the squadron Admin office to handle paperwork. All the while, he was wondering about Eryn. Seeing her look so upset hurt him.

Back at Crash Crew, Abi was the only soul brave enough to go into Eryn's office. She knocked and didn't wait for an answer.

Opening the door, Abi said, "Warrant Officer Smith."

Eryn motioned her to enter.

Once the door was firmly shut behind her, Abi turned around to face her boss and friend. She looked awful! Abi guessed that the reason for Eryn's mood was a certain Chase Johnson and frowned.

"Do you want to explain to me why nobody wants to come within fifty feet of your office for fear of losing a body part?" she asked dryly. No sense in beating around the bush.

Eryn made a hint of a smile. She could always rely on Abi not to pull punches. "I'm just trying to catch up and not doing a very good job of it," she answered and knew that Abi knew it was BS.

Abi snorted, "Yeah right," she said sarcastically. "Listen," Abi sat down across from Eryn and looked her in the eye, "I don't know what happened between you two but you both have to figure it out."

It was hard for Abi to see her friend look so upset.

Dropping her face in her hands, Eryn felt defeated. "You know," she mumbled into her palms, "I've been here before and you would think that I would've learned my lesson." The pain in her chest was excruciating, making her choke out the words.

Leaning forward, Abi asked, "What happened?"

Eryn stood and rounded the desk. She sat down next to Abi. "I don't know," she looked blankly at the wall and then at Abi, "we made love." Sighing, she smiled, "It was perfect!"

Abi smiled. She figured Eryn would say that.

"It was like what you see in the movies!" Eryn exclaimed. "Then," she threw up her hands, "Nothing!"

Frowning, Abi didn't understand. "What do you mean 'nothing'?" she asked.

Eryn stood and started pacing, "Nothing, no phone call, nothing. He just dropped me off at my room and that was that."

Now Abi really was confused. She saw the both of them on Saturday and it sure didn't look like nothing to her.

"Did you ask him about it?" she questioned Eryn.

Ashamed, Eryn dropped back down in the chair, "No, I couldn't." She looked up at the look in Abi's eyes, "I know, I should have but I was mortified." Slamming her fist down, Eryn said, "I realized he didn't feel the same way I did and I just have to get over it."

Abi blew out a breath. What was with these two, she wondered to herself. Pissed off that Chase would treat Eryn so callously and pissed that Eryn would give up so easily, she stood up.

"Well," she pointed at Eryn and spoke pointedly, "if you are just going to sit there and let him get away again then you deserve to be miserable."

Leaving Eryn's office, Abi went back to her own office to figure out whether she should slap Chase or Eryn or both.

The next few days were quiet around Crash Crew. Eryn was still in shock over her conversation with Abi and didn't know what to do. She knew Abi was right about a lot of it.

Eryn didn't say anything when he dropped her off and she could have. She didn't call him and ask if he wanted to join her and her parents for dinner on Sunday and she should have. In reality, she figured that Chase would make all the moves. Maybe he was just waiting for her to do something?

Since Monday he gave her a wide berth. Thinking about her actions, she couldn't blame him one bit for that.

It was time they grew up, they weren't kids anymore. It was time she stood up for what she wanted. They could resolve whatever complications came up as long as they did it together. Feeling better, Eryn left her office to look for Chase before she chickened out.

When she got out into the hallway, Eryn checked her watch and realized it was after hours and everyone was gone already. Damn! She was about to go back into her office when she heard a voice coming from Chase's office.

Smiling, she walked over to the door. It was half opened and she could see he was on the phone. He was turned away from her so she'd wait until he was done. Excitement simmered up inside her.

After a few seconds though, Eryn's excitement burst like a bubble. She was listening to his conversation and her hopes were falling.

"I love you too," Chase said into the phone. He smiled, "It has been a while but I promise we'll spend some time together."

Eryn wanted to die! How could he say he loved her and then speak to someone else like that? His voice was smooth and it made her sick listening to it. Every time she dared believe, she was just hurt more.

Chase turned around after he hung up the phone and was surprised to see Eryn standing there, "Eryn?" He smiled. "Did you want to see me?" he asked hoping she was feeling better.

How could he not see how much he was hurting her?

"No," Eryn croaked out and cleared her throat, "I was just on my way out and heard someone." She turned to leave.

Chase jumped up and came around his desk to follow her. He had a funny feeling again like something wasn't right. He just hung up the phone and saw her there, lost in her thoughts. She looked exhausted and he wanted nothing more than to gather her up in his arms and kiss all her worries away.

"Do you have a few minutes to talk?" Chase asked when he was coming behind her into her office.

There was no way Eryn would be able to sit and have a rational conversation with him now. He was the one who held her crushed heart in his hands.

She made a point of looking at her watch, "Actually," she said in a rushed voice, "I'm expected at the Officer's Club." The excuse was flimsy but it was the best she could do.

"Well," Chase stepped closer, "I'd like to sit down and talk when you have a chance." He watched her jerky movement with worry, "There are some things we need to discuss. It's important."

Grabbing her bag, Eryn moved around the opposite side of her desk to avoid touching him, "I'll let you know," she stammered and left her office with Chase standing there.

Chase walked out of her office and looked out the window in the hallway as she practically ran to her car. This was not going at all like he planned.

Chapter 23

Friday was a welcome relief for Eryn. She managed to out maneuver Chase, making up excuses to avoid him for the rest of the week.

After her talk with Abi, she pretty much avoided her as well. Eryn wasn't mad at Abi exactly; she was just frustrated that Abi kept telling her to fight. And when Eryn did fight, she got her teeth kicked in every single time. There was only so much a person could take and Eryn reached her limit.

Everyone was out of the office for lunch when the phone rang in Chase's office. Since Eryn was right outside the door, she stepped in and picked up the phone.

"Warrant Officer Smith," Eryn said into the phone.

The female caller hesitated, "Um yes, ma'am," she said, "this is Sgt. Collins over at S-1 Admin Office and I was just calling to let Master Sgt. Johnson know that his orders were approved and he could pick them up at any time."

Eryn was dumbfounded! What?

She finally composed herself enough to say, "I'll pass on the message," and hung up the phone.

A Marine to Remember

Standing in Chase's office, Eryn felt her world tilting off its axis.

"You have got to be kidding me!" she yelled into the air. "He is not going to pull this crap on me again!"

Stomping back to her office, Eryn slammed the door behind her.

Chase got back to his office later than he planned of Friday. His meeting with the Section Leaders ran long and there was a repair problem with one of the trucks that he needed to deal with. It was after three in the afternoon when he was able to sit down at his desk and look through his messages.

The second one had him jumping to his feet. It was in Eryn's writing and said, 'Your orders are ready.'

Crap! He said to himself. Well, the jig was up and it was time he made his move.

Eryn left work early on Friday. She was just too tired to deal with everything and she wanted some rest. She got back to her room, unplugged her phone, put her cell phone on vibrate, and fell onto her bed.

She managed to fall into a restless sleep and dreamed about Chase. When she woke up, the sun was setting. She threw off the covers and got up. There was no use sitting her and sulking for the rest of her life. Space....she needed space.

Danette Fogarty

Changing clothes quickly, she grabbed her keys and purse and left her room.

After she drove around for a while, Eryn decided to go to the beach. After all, she did all of her heart breaking years ago on the beach, why not now as well?

She pulled into the parking lot, slipped off her shoes, and got out.

The breeze was picking up a little and blowing her hair around wildly. She didn't care because that's how she felt on the inside.

Walking along, she noticed the beach was almost deserted and was thankful for it. She wanted to be alone. After walking for a while, she sat down in the sand and cried.

Chase found Eryn there, sitting and crying on the beach.

He talked to Abi after he found out Eryn left work early. It was tough to talk to her because she was majorly pissed at him. She yelled at him and told him about the conversation she and Eryn had on Monday afternoon. He apologized and told Abi about his plans. By the time he left her office, he was pretty sure he wasn't going to get his ass kicked……yet.

A Marine to Remember

Now seeing Eryn, he ached. She sat there, in obvious emotional pain, and yet she looked so beautiful. The breeze was blowing her hair gently as if to comfort her. He walked up to her quietly.

"Eryn," Chase said slowly.

Eryn stiffened but didn't say anything. She couldn't even look at him right now.

Not giving up, Chase sat down next to her but was careful not to touch her. He didn't know where to start so he waited.

Finally, realizing she wasn't going to start, he did. "I got your message. I'm sorry I didn't tell you sooner."

Eryn finally looked at him, her eyes wild with anger, "I'll just bet you're sorry," she spat out the words.

She stood up quickly and looked down at him.

"You couldn't just skip out this time unnoticed, could you?" she demanded, anger streaming like venom through her body.

Chase stood up. What was she talking about? What did she mean skipping out?

He asked, "Excuse me?" feeling his temper rise up.

Without thinking, Eryn let her anger out. She punched him in the stomach as hard as she could. He doubled over, clearly not expecting it, and his obvious pain gave Eryn a sick sense of satisfaction.

All the air whooshed out of Chase's lungs and it took him a minute to catch his breath.

"What was that for?" he asked weakly.

Eryn sneered at him. "I don't know," she pushed him in the chest, making him take a step back. "Maybe because you pulled this crap ten years ago and I was stupid enough to let you go."

She stomped a few steps away and spun around.

Pointing at him, she yelled, "I'm not young and naïve anymore, Chase. Dammit! You can't just take what you want and walk away!"

Hearing Eryn almost scream at him shook Chase to the core. There was a lot of missing pieces she didn't have and that was his fault but he wouldn't stand here and let her rage at him.

"Eryn, stop!" he yelled, his voice loud and angry.

Chase's tone stopped Eryn abruptly. She stared at him, anger pulsing through her body.

Chase walked over and took her hand to get her to sit. She didn't push him away so that was a good sign.

"Let's sit down and talk about this," he said soothingly.

Not completely giving into her pain, Eryn finally sat down. Something in his eyes told her he was hurting too. She sank down to the sand feeling defeated.

Chase fell to his knees in front of her. "I'm not going anywhere," he said and stared into her eyes.

Eryn watched him in the dim light. She could still see his features and they did look as tortured as hers were. Her heart was pounding and she wasn't sure whether to believe him or not.

Cupping Eryn's chin in his hand, Chase took a deep breath. "Now," he began, "I know that I should have come to you first with the orders but I wanted to make sure everything was pushed through." He looked up at the deep blue sky praying for the right words. "I am so in love with you that it's driving me crazy!"

Eryn was both excited and scared at the intensity of his words. She opened her mouth to say something but he gently silenced her with a finger to her lips.

"Please," he pleaded, "let me finish." His tone was just above a whisper from emotion, "I didn't know

Danette Fogarty

what to say to you after the ball; that night was more than I could have possibly dreamed."

Even in the semi-darkness, Eryn blushed. "It was for me too," she admitted.

Chase breathed a sigh of relief. He sat down next to her and pulled her onto his lap. Their faces were only inches apart. "There are some things we have to discuss, Eryn," he said.

She couldn't move, couldn't talk. What did he mean?

"I know that you feel guilty after our night of making love because you felt like you cheated on Paul. Am I right?" he asked softly.

There was no point denying anything anymore, "Yes and no," she answered.

Her answer surprised Chase, "Explain it to me," he said.

Taking a deep breath, Eryn slid off his lap and stood. She needed to move while she spoke.

"I didn't feel guilty about making love with you, Chase. I just thought that it was never like that with Paul so I must've cheated him out of something." She said the words slowly, the pain of them sneaking into her voice.

A Marine to Remember

Chase nodded, "I can see how you might think that," he responded and stood up. "But, if Paul was half the man I think he was for having married you, then I truly think he had what he felt was everything."

Knowing that Chase tried to understand made Eryn's heart break open. Relief rushed out. "I hope so," she cried.

Taking Eryn into his arms, he said, "I know so."

Chase pulled her back down so she was once again on his lap. "I know we need to work through your feelings about Paul but I'm here for you."

Hearing the words, made Eryn's heart swell. She reached up and kissed Chase deeply, letting all of her feelings go, and finally, feeling peace.

The kiss was tender and soothing to her soul. She welcomed Chase's touch as he held her tightly to him.

Pulling his lips from hers slowly, Chase set her back, "Now," he said seriously, "Our current situation......."

Eryn was afraid of what he was going to say. She still feared he was going to leave.

"I can't go on working with you," he started, "not with the way I feel about you and hopefully how you feel about me." He smiled, "So I've decided to retire from the Marine Corps."

Her eyes flew open in shock, "What!" Eryn yelled, "You can't do that!"

Chase wanted to laugh at the expression on her face but he tamped it down. "Yes," he said pointedly, "I can."

Scooting off his lap, Eryn jumped up and walked around in a circle. "What will you do?" she asked, "Where will you go?"

Watching Eryn's mind work was amazing. He stood back up and knew she'd never give him a dull moment. Thank God!

"First," Chase walked up to her, "I'm going to marry you," he tapped his finger on her chin, "then I'm going to work for the Department of Defense."

Pacing again, Eryn was flabbergasted. "What?" she asked incredulously.

"I said," he smiled, "I'm going to marry you then I'm going to get another job."

Eryn's heart wanted to beat right out of her chest.

"Oh, Chase!" she screamed and jumped into his arms. Her hands touched his shoulders and wound up in his hair as she kissed him again and again.

Pulling away from the kiss Eryn said, "Wait," she frowned. "Who was the woman you were talking on the phone to and telling you loved her?"

Chase chuckled, "That, my love, was my cousin Bethany." He kissed her again, "She's coming for a visit and I asked her to wait until we had a wedding date set."

"Oh," Eryn muttered, feeling chagrined. She was going to kiss him again and stopped just before their lips met. "Wait," she said, "I didn't answer you and shouldn't I be the one giving orders here since I outrank you?"

Seeing as she was teasing him, Chase tilted his head in mock consideration.

He looked into her eyes, serious. "I know you'll marry me because you love me as much as I love you."

She tried to push him away but he held her tightly.

"Besides, technically I didn't ask you." He kissed her quickly, "But I asked your mom and dad for their blessing and they gave it so I think I'm good."

Eryn smiled, tears filling her eyes.

Chase touched her cheek with his palm, "And, you don't outrank me in matters of the heart, love. We're equals."

Releasing her, Chase knelt down in the sand and pulled a black box out of his pocket. With a flourish, he opened it up and pulled out the ring. He looked up to see tears of joy running down Eryn's cheeks.

Eryn let him slip the ring onto her trembling finger, the diamond sparkling with the last rays of light from the day.

Chase swept Eryn up into his arms and started to walk back to his house. There were still some big issues they needed to iron out but he wasn't worried. They would figure it all out later; right now there were more pressing matters to attend to.

I hope you enjoyed reading Eryn and Chase's story and look forward to the continuing the

Semper Fi in Love

book series......

The Lady & The Marine
(August, 2013)

Moonlight & A Marine
(October, 2013)

A Marine & Her Sensibilities
(March, 2014)